once we MET

ANNABELLE McCORMACK

Published by Annabelle McCormack

Editor by Marion Archer

Cover by Kari March Designs (ebook, paperback, hardcover)

Patrick Knowles (special edition paperback)

www.annabellemccormack.com

once
we
MET

CHAPTER ONE

Now

Avery Moretti didn't really believe in curses, except for the one that had condemned every woman in her family: that she'd be engaged at least twice before she found her spouse. Which was exactly why Avery was sure she might actually die on this godforsaken airplane. Bryan was only her first fiancé, and they got along great. They were deeply in love and had been for a year.

With the wedding only a few weeks away, it would take something like an accident to end their relationship.

Not to mention that Avery could visualize the newspaper headline: *"Bride-to-be and Maid of Honor Die in Fiery Mountain Plane Crash."*

The plane touched down in the small airport near the mountains of Western Maryland, and her left hand curled into a fist, the diamond of her engagement ring digging into her palm as she prayed for good luck. The pilot had predicted this would be a bumpy landing, and her stomach was already prepared to drop from not enough food. She mashed down on the chewing gum, giving Erika a sidelong glance. Her best friend wasn't afraid of flying and had her head still buried in her e-reader.

Weren't electronics supposed to be off during landing?

The whole plane shook, then took a deep bounce, and they were on the tarmac. Not exactly smooth.

As Avery exhaled, tension released from her shoulders. Erika raised a brow at her. "See? I told you we wouldn't die."

Avery leaned back in her seat, still trembling. "Bryan was right. I shouldn't have gotten on this contraption. I can't believe my father thought this would be easier than flying in from Pittsburgh. This was terrifying. Did you know if a plane catches on fire, you have, like, ninety seconds to exit before it burns up?" *Great, now I sound like Bryan, repeating frightening statistics about flying.*

Erika grinned, then pulled her carry-on out from under the seat. "Yeah, it must be such a burden having your dad get you on a private, chartered flight. Since when are you so afraid of flying?" She fished a box of mints from her purse. "Want one? It's no chamomile, but it'll settle your stomach. You're looking green."

Avery unlatched her seat belt. The nice thing about this chartered flight was that there wasn't a flight attendant to scold her for unbuckling too soon.

Her knee bounced. She didn't have a fear of flying. The flight from San Diego had been fine. But when she'd met up with Erika in the airport in West Virginia and seen the tiny plane, all of Bryan's warnings flooded back. Erika, still half-asleep because of her early flight from Miami, hadn't cared about the plane's size. "I can't help it. I'm just nervous."

Erika chewed on her lower lip, then frowned. She pulled a pot of her homemade lip balm from her bag and smoothed it on her lips. "It's going to be fine. I'm sure of it. You just need to get your heels on the ground. It's the fun part now. Just a half-dozen appointments, and we can relax."

"I should have listened to my gut and hired a day-of coordinator from Brandywood." Bryan had strongly objected to the extra expense, though, and she hadn't wanted yet another wedding-related argument. The arguments had started from the moment her parents had offered to pay for the wedding, which Bryan didn't want. He claimed it would give them too much control.

Avery tucked a loose strand of hair behind the neat bun she'd made that morning before she left her apartment. It wasn't the summery look that she imagined went with the lake house trip of her dreams, but it had tamed her thick, wavy auburn locks well when she'd left at four in the morning.

Erika slipped her e-reader into her bag as the plane finished taxiing to a stop. "As Halmeoni always says, 'Even a monkey sometimes falls from the tree.' Mistakes happen. We still have plenty of time to sort everything out."

Avery gave a taut nod. Usually, Erika quoting her Korean grandmother's proverbs made her smile, but now it didn't.

She had two weeks. That was it. Planning a wedding from across the country had been harder than she'd expected it to be, even in a town that she'd been visiting every summer since she was born. Since she'd started doing work for a major publisher a year earlier, she could hardly keep up with designing book covers, let alone plan a wedding. Not that she wanted to scale back on the work. She was finally doing her dream job.

But the wedding planning probably should have gotten a smidge more attention. Everything would be fine at the venue, at least. She'd reserved every room in Serendipity Lake Lodge nine months ago, when Bryan had proposed. And she'd spoken to the ancient owner, Mr. Harrison, about holding her wedding on the grounds there, and he'd assured her it wouldn't be a problem. He'd even let her make payments, and she'd dutifully been putting them in the mail all year.

The problem was that Mr. Harrison told her everything for the wedding had to be brought in from off-site—florals, a tent, chairs, catering, a band, *everything*—because the Serendipity wasn't a wedding venue. But all that trouble seemed worth it, because Avery's parents and grandparents had both had their weddings at Serendipity.

Of course, when their weddings had been there, weddings weren't what they were now. Avery had more than one hundred guests coming in from all over the country. Besides the ten rooms she'd booked at Serendipity, her guests had booked short-term rentals and cabins throughout the town. Brandy-wood wasn't exactly swimming in hotels, and since the whole town had come into the national spotlight recently, those rentals and rooms were scarce.

A local day-of coordinator would have saved Avery's sanity, but Bryan had thought it was excessive. "We are both highly educated professionals, Avery," Bryan had said. "I think we can coordinate our own wedding. That's another made-up job created by the wedding industry to add to the ridiculous cost of weddings in America."

Well, it's too late now. She was here, and her work email had an out-of-office auto response message. She'd fix whatever she could at this point and let go of the rest . . . or at least *try* to let go.

Avery pulled her phone out and turned it back on. She checked her watch. "Okay. We're early. We can probably go straight to Serendipity, drop our bags off, then head to the bakery. After that, we can get some lunch."

"Aye, Captain." Erika grinned. "Relax already. You're at your vacation paradise, aren't you?" She leaned past Avery to see out the window and grimaced. "Though I have to admit, my idea of paradise is more palm trees, more blue sparkling ocean waves, and a lot more drinks in my hand. Are we in the middle of a field?"

The pilot opened the door to the cockpit and nodded toward them. "Welcome to Accident, ladies."

"Accident?" Erika gave him an odd look.

"That's where the airport is located." He said it with a straight face and not a hint of irony.

Avery's jaw dropped. Of all the terrible names for a town with an airport. *Thank God I didn't know that before I landed.*

The pilot helped them grab their suitcases from the plane, and they made their way out to the tarmac, carry-ons in hand. Standing on the nearly empty airport landing strip, Avery gave a disheartening glance around.

They really were in the middle of nowhere. Beyond a neatly mown field, trees lined the short airstrip. A few buildings and hangars made up the rest of the "airport." As they parted from the pilot, she checked her phone for service. One dismal bar.

Hopefully, she could call an Uber. They stopped near one building off the tarmac as Avery unsuccessfully logged into the app. "Crap."

Erika pulled out her sunglasses, fanning her face. "Aren't the mountains supposed to be cooler than this?"

"Even the mountains can get warm in August." Erika's comment struck Avery. The whole reason her Floridian family had come to Brandywood was to get away to a cooler lakeside summer retreat each year. At least, according to her grandmother. Her grandfather's friend from his younger days in the army had been from there, too, and it was a good chance for them to catch up until they'd both passed away.

But with the beach at her disposal every weekend in Miami, a trip to the lake had always felt special. Brandywood was where her family felt the most at home . . . and where she'd first fallen in love at eighteen. She'd even given that first love one of the most precious items she owned—her grandfather's St. Christopher medal. She was still mad at herself for giving it to Dan Klein.

Her jaw set. She didn't have time to reminisce about lazy summer days splashing in the lake *or* bruised hearts right now. "I can't get the Uber app to pull up."

Erika sneezed and scrunched her nose, her dark eyes scanning the barren parking lot. "Is anyone even here?"

No one was in sight. Where had the pilot gone? He appeared to have hightailed it out of there. Avery's gaze zeroed in on a security guard near the entrance, who appeared to be asleep in his metal folding chair. She marched toward him, heels wobbling. "Excuse me?"

He lifted his head from his chin. "Yes, ma'am?"

"I'm trying to get a ride into Brandywood from here and can't get cell service. Do you know if there's a taxi service or a bus?"

His gray brows pushed together quizzically. "Bus?"

"Into Brandywood." She did her best to keep a calm, polite tone. Her question hadn't been that complicated.

"No, ma'am."

"Well, do you have a taxi service around here?"

"Taxi service?"

Not this again.

Erika sneezed beside her. "I feel like my throat is getting itchy. Do you have a tissue, Ave?"

"Probably ragweed. You're not from around here, are you?"

The old man gave Erika a sympathetic look and pulled a handkerchief from his pocket. "You can use this. It's clean."

Erika stared at the handkerchief as though he'd offered her a dead bird. "I-I . . ."

Avery retrieved a fresh package of travel tissues from her purse and thrust it into Erika's hands. "We're fine, thanks. So about that taxi service . . ."

The security guard shrugged. "Nothing like that around here. You should try one of those handy app services my grandson is always talking about."

Avery forced a patient smile on her face. "I would, but I don't have cell service. So it doesn't work."

"I don't have a fancy phone. I'd give you a ride, but my shift isn't over. You want me to call my grandson? I'm sure he could help."

Erika wiped her nose. "That'd be gre—"

"Uh, Erika, why don't we talk?" Avery tugged her several feet away. She eyed the security guard. "I don't think so. We have no way of telling anyone where we're going or who we're going with. Bryan wouldn't like me getting in a car with a perfect stranger."

Erika rolled her eyes. "Didn't you hitchhike across California once? And then end up hooking up with some random magician?"

"Yeah, I'd like to think I've gotten slightly smarter and more mature since that incident. And please never tell Bryan about the magician. He already questioned my judgment enough when I told him about the hitchhiking."

"You'd get into a car with a stranger if it were an Uber."

She couldn't argue with her logic. But that didn't mean Bryan would agree. "But it's not Uber. And at least there, the app could track us. I could send Bryan a license plate. Something. We can walk. It's safer, and we're both reasonably fit women. We'll be fine. I'll just change my shoes."

"Take a picture of the license plate of whoever takes us, then. You can still send it." Sneezing again, Erika turned toward the security guard. "How far is it to the lake from here?"

"'Bout eleven miles."

Erika gave Avery a sharp look. "I'm not walking eleven miles. Whatever is triggering my allergies has me ready to claw my eyes out already. I need to find my way to a pharmacy. Stat."

"But—"

"If it makes you feel better, tell Bryan I made you do it. Or better yet, don't tell him at all. I don't see what the big deal is." Erika started back toward the security guard.

Avery released a slow stream of air between her lips. She didn't want to resort to lying. She'd worked so hard not to be that person anymore. But maybe this was nothing to worry about.

Flying into a town named Accident. Not having service or access to an Uber. Those weren't signs of bad omens. Because curses weren't real. And she'd laid Avery, the superstitious, impulsive, irresponsible girl, to rest. She needed to stop worrying. She'd survived the flight. *Nothing is going to happen.*

Avery raised her chin and gave Erika her most promising smile. "Sure. We'd appreciate the offer of a ride." She just needed to relax and get through the next couple of weeks. After that, she'd never have to worry about any sort of curse again. Erika gave her a grateful look, then sneezed.

"Where're you two girls heading?" The security guard stood and limped toward a nearby phone on the wall.

"Serendipity Lake Lodge. It's on the lake."

The security guard squinted at her. "You sure about that?"

She didn't like the sound of that. Her hands grew strangely

damp and achy. "Positive." Avery's voice sounded overly bright. "I've been going there on summer vacation for almost thirty years. It's right on the lake."

The old man scrunched his face, giving a slow shake to his head as he scratched it. "No, no. I don't mean that. I mean, you sure that's where you're going? The owner of the lodge, Ken Harrison, was a good friend of mine. But he died in January. The place has been shut down for the past few months. His daughter just sold it."

Avery's knees wobbled, the air whooshing past her ears as her brain struggled to process his words.

The Serendipity . . .

The one place she hadn't worried about at all.

Because Mr. Harrison knew her by name. He'd faithfully held on to her family's reservations for over fifty years. She'd mailed in her payments, rented the whole place out—what had there been to call about?

How could she have overlooked this?

The Serendipity was the site of her wedding. She should have confirmed the reservation, even if she'd never had to worry about it before.

A silent scream formed inside her, but no sound came from her parted lips as her eyes locked with Erika's.

So much for nothing going wrong.

CHAPTER TWO

THE RENOVATION WAS GOING BETTER than Dan Klein had expected it would.

His sisters had the hold on all the creative genes. His brother was good with numbers. And then there were his brothers-in-law. One was internationally known in business and a multi-millionaire, another was so busy with his home improvement and house-flipping work that he had to turn customers away, and the third was so good at helping his wife run their family rental cabins that they'd tripled the number of cabins on their property in the past two years.

And then there's me.

Dan set the sledgehammer down and stripped his sweat-soaked shirt from his back.

He didn't really know a damn thing about renovating a house, let alone one this old, with this many rooms. When he'd shown his dad around the property, his expression indicated he thought Dan had bitten off more than he could chew.

"You can always go back to being a cop if it doesn't work out," was the polite way Dad had put it.

As though that was supposed to be reassuring.

Dan reached for the bottle of water in the cooler and popped the top open. Taking a swig, he let his eyes wander the space. He'd taken the past few days to demo this room, carefully. He didn't want to do more than one major room at a time. The more he did, the bigger chance he'd get overwhelmed and quit.

He was good at quitting. *Succeeding, though . . .*

He sighed. He had to succeed with this. The lodge was like an institution to Brandywood summers to so many people. The Serendipity had served as a second home to him for several summers when he was a teenager.

Mr. Harrison had given Dan his first job, right in this room, which served as the main sitting room for the guests. It had large French doors with picture windows on either side that led out to the verandah in the back. The view was unmatched in the summer evenings, with the sun setting over the lake, just steps beyond the wide, flat lawn.

The problem with buying a massive 120-year-old farmhouse that had been converted into an inn, though, was that it came with its share of problems. Like everything else in the lodge, the ten bedrooms required some changes, but they were mostly in good shape.

The sitting room and some of the common areas on the first floor required skills well beyond his limited ones. But Dan was determined to do as much as he could on his own. For once, he wanted to build something he could be proud of. And if it took him longer than it would take others, so be it.

He had some help. Dan had hired a kid just out of college to have another set of hands. Peyton had spent most of his time outdoors, digging into the massive upkeep the grounds and gardens required, but he'd barely made a dent. Brenda

Harrison had let this place get too overgrown between the time Dan had put his offer in and closing.

Tossing the closed bottle back into the cooler, he rubbed his shoulder. The muscles in his shoulders and arms ached down to the bones. He couldn't remember the last time he'd been this sore, even when he'd gone to the police academy. Or played basketball in high school—the only thing he'd been naturally good at.

But he was a hard worker. And this was his chance to turn his luck around and bring the Serendipity into the twenty-first century. And it was his new home. Unless he wanted to move back in with his parents, he'd need to live here until he got it operating as a bed-and-breakfast. It'd make it easier to run the place anyway.

Even if this sitting room was going to give him a challenge. He'd torn the drywall down to reveal a massive mold problem, which had forced him to shut down the renovation to get that issue addressed first. Three plumbers, a septic tank replacement, and a mold mitigation team later, and he'd already spent thousands of dollars more than expected.

Who knew the entire thing would drain more than half his budget for this whole renovation?

How the hell was he going to do so much with so little left?

"Officer Klein?" Peyton MacLuckie knocked on the door frame. Dan jerked his gaze toward him, still unaccustomed to the kid milling about. He paid him well enough, but Peyton worked slower than he'd expected. He'd taken two days to repaint the front door before Dan had moved him to work on weeding the front garden bed.

Dan smirked at him. "I told you before, you don't have to call me that. Just Dan. I'm not a cop anymore."

Peyton nodded. "Yeah, sorry. Uh, there's someone here. On the front porch."

Dan furrowed his brow. *Delivery, maybe?* He reached for his shirt, then paused. *Never mind.* Nothing more gross than putting on a damp shirt. He made his way out of the room toward the long, open foyer that led to the front. Since he'd stopped being a cop a few months ago, he'd let himself grow a wild, tawny beard—a single act of rebellion now that he could do whatever he wanted with his facial hair—and he scratched at his jaw as he approached the open screen door, not bothering to remove the eye protection goggles from his face.

A petite auburn-haired woman who appeared to be dressed for a business meeting in a gray skirt that hugged her hips and a pristine cream-toned blouse stood on the wide front porch. Her high heels clicked against the wooden floorboards as she paced. Her back was turned to him, and she didn't see him approach.

Dan's gaze flicked farther down the driveway, where Ben Pearson's pickup truck idled. A black-haired young woman stood beside him, chatting. What did Ben have to do with all this? Ben was helping unload what looked like several months' worth of luggage from the bed of his truck.

The slats in front of the doorway creaked as Dan stepped onto the porch. "How can I help you?"

The woman whirled around, then froze. Her blue-gray eyes blinked rapidly at him.

Man, she's pretty.

And . . . familiar.

He studied her, a feeling of recognition flickering at the back of his mind, of warm summer nights, fireflies over the waters of the lake, and stolen kisses on the dock.

But she couldn't be. The girl he'd known had been wild and beautiful, willing to jump out of her window and shimmy her way down the tall oak beside a third-floor window of the lodge. This woman looked like she didn't know the meaning of the word *fun.*

The look on her face wasn't one of recognition but molten fury. She stepped forward, her eyes narrowed. "You're the new owner of the Serendipity?"

Dan nodded, feeling the urge to step back from her, the hair on his arms standing on end. "Yup, and you are?"

She straightened to her full height, which must have been a full foot short of him. "Avery Moretti."

Holy shit. He kept an even expression, but his heart rate ticked up a notch.

It was her.

The muscles in his shoulders felt taut, his spine stiff.

Nothing in her eyes indicated she recognized him. Should he remind her they'd met before? It'd been . . . twelve years.

Did she remember that week from when they were eighteen?

Dan hadn't been able to forget it.

But then again, this wasn't the way he'd wanted to come face-to-face with Avery Moretti again. *Do I even want to face her at all?*

She didn't exactly look thrilled to be here—or looking for a cheerful reunion.

He nodded at her curtly, then closed the door. "We're closed right now."

He ripped the goggles from his eyes and walked away. The door flew open again, bouncing off the drywall behind it with a thud. A spray of drywall from a new dent courtesy of the door knob crumbled onto the floor.

"Oh, I'm so sorry. Excuse me." The clack of heels followed as she rushed toward him. "Wait one second, please." She tripped over an extension cord and stumbled forward.

Dan's hand shot out, catching her before she could fall. He steadied her, and their eyes met. His throat went tight, and he swallowed hard as her eyes widened.

"Oh my God, it's . . . you."

A flush crept into her cheeks as he released her. He stepped back, bumping into the wall behind him, then ran a hand through his hair, which was probably sticking up in thousands of directions like Wolverine. He didn't want to look as nervous as he felt right now, but it took him longer than normal to get his wits together.

Then he offered a wry grin. "You mean you didn't come here to see me? I'd say I'm hurt, but I guess that's twelve years too late and a dollar short."

"Dan? Um, is that really you?" Steadying herself on the wall, she said, "I barely recognized you with that survivalist beard you have going on."

"Well, right back at you. Except in your case, I think it was more the death glare. Not saying you have a beard." He caught the trace of a smile curling in her lips at his awkwardness before she coaxed it into a frown.

He grimaced, then gave her a one-eyed squint. "Though maybe I should have recognized that expression. Pretty sure that's the last look you ever gave me before you stomped on my teenage heart and left. But if that's what you're here about, I would really rather not reminisce."

Avery rolled her eyes. "Yeah, I didn't even know that you'd be here, but thanks for the welcome. As pleasant as this catch-up has been, I'm actually here because I made a reservation nine months ago."

Dan shook his head. *Right.* As though he wouldn't have noticed her name in the reservation book. "No, you didn't. And even if you did once upon a time, you can't stay here now."

The door opened once again, and Peyton popped his dark, shaggy head in. "Everything okay?"

"Yup."

"No!" Dan and Avery answered in unison. Peyton

exchanged a glance at them both. "This lady's leaving, Peyton. Maybe you can walk her out?"

"I'm not leaving!" Avery stamped her foot. "I have a reservation."

There was that temper he remembered.

"Oh." Peyton's smile was bright and conciliatory, as though he'd solved the problem. "Mr. Klein's got plenty of room. There's even a sign on the window." Peyton pointed at a rough sign Dan had scribbled on the top flap of a pizza box with the words "MOSTLY VACANT" when Peyton had asked why he didn't have one of those vacancy signs up.

The sign was supposed to poke fun at the fact that the lodge was vacant of its furniture. Guess the joke was lost on the kid.

Avery marched to the window and snatched up the sign. Her nose wrinkled as though she could still smell the cheese grease from it, and then she turned it toward Dan, cocking her chin. "You're right, it does say that. Thank you so much for pointing that out."

"Yes, thank you *so* much, Peyton." Dan scowled at him. "I think we're good. Maybe you can go back to pulling weeds?"

Peyton nodded and headed out again, the screen door banging as he left.

A deep, irritated silence filled the air between them as Avery and Dan squared off. "I have a reservation." Avery's voice was flat.

"There aren't any. At least not according to Mr. Harrison's reservation book. And we're closed, so I can't accommodate your request, unfortunately." Dan glanced back down the hall, wishing he could levitate his shirt back over to him.

"Listen, Dan. I'm here because I had reserved the Serendipity—the whole lodge—for next week. My reservation was for this week so I could get a jumpstart on finalizing plans. My wedding is supposed to be here in two weeks."

Dan stared at her, his heart slowing again, and the giant diamond glistening from her left hand somehow seemed more prominent. *She's engaged. Not here to talk to you. Obviously.* His brain failed to process the rest of what she'd said with as much clarity. Then he blinked hard and focused. *What the hell?*

There had been no bookings on the schedule for August. At least not when Brenda Harrison had sold him the place. He *had* promised to honor existing reservations, but Brenda had told him she'd called all the numbers in the logbook and canceled the reservations when her father died, which was why the Serendipity had been left unattended all year. If Avery hadn't gotten one of those calls, then it was even more evidence that her so-called reservation had never existed.

A mosquito pricked his forehead, and he slapped it away, then rubbed the itch it left behind. "Your wedding is supposed to be here?" He sounded like an idiot.

"Yes, here. In two weeks." She peeked around him, and a horrified expression crossed her face. "Are you doing *construction?*" She edged past him, then marched into the place like she owned it.

Dan followed Avery into the lodge, barely able to keep up. She headed straight back, toward the sitting room where he'd been working, her hands covering her mouth. The room was stripped down to the studs, even on the ceiling. All that faintly resembled the former grandeur of the lodge's most iconic room were the large picture windows, which looked out toward the serene lake.

"Oh my God. This can't be happening." Avery's eyes took on a glassy look, her lips still parted in shock.

Dan reached for his shirt and pulled it on, the thin, damp

white fabric bearing a beer logo somehow feeling like protection. He swallowed hard. How could he have missed a reservation of this magnitude? He'd gone through the logbook, and there had been nothing—he was sure of it.

Swinging away from her, he took the few steps from the sitting room to the small cupboard of a room Ken had used as an office. Dust motes filtered through the air as the light switched on, revealing the space exactly as Ken had left it. The one place where Brenda hadn't taken everything out to put in long-term storage. The logbook lay open on a pine desk Ken must have built to fit the space.

Dan flipped to August as the sound of Avery's steps shuffled in behind him.

Nothing.

Well, that's a relief.

Still, he flipped the book forward, toward the end of the book. Had he missed something? Ken's insistence on using pen and paper instead of changing to a computer system had made finding existing reservations a challenge. Whatever his system had been, it must have made sense to him, but it had done nothing to move the lodge into modern technology.

Sure enough, at the end of the book in neatly printed script, he found "Roberts Wedding" written in pencil, with some August dates noted beside them. Ken had written it someplace easily missed, but that didn't make Dan less culpable. He had missed it, after all. The back of his neck broke out into an aching sweat.

Do I really have to admit I've found something?

"Is this it?" Dan stepped to the side to let her look.

Avery stared at the ledger. She lifted tearful eyes toward him, then glanced away. "Yeah, that's my fiancé's last name."

"I didn't know Ken put this here." Dan swallowed hard and shifted his weight onto his back foot. "But I don't have any rooms available, because all the furniture is in storage while I remodel."

"What am I supposed to do?" Avery covered her mouth again, looking sick. "I've been sending checks to Mr. Harrison. Didn't you get them? Someone should have seen them."

Uh oh. Dan grimaced. "Did you send them directly to Ken?"

She nodded.

"Anything that was addressed to him would have gone to his daughter. I'm still sorting out his mail and send it down to her about once a month. But I don't think she's been the best at opening it up. He gets a ton of junk." Dan peered at her and hesitated. He didn't want to ask the obvious, but how could this have gotten so mixed up? "Didn't you notice your checks weren't cashed?"

She reddened. "I'm not used to writing checks or balancing a checkbook. Ken was the only vendor who requested paper checks."

Dan held back a retort. She'd also been a spoiled rich girl when they'd first met. *Probably still is one.* Otherwise, how could she not notice sizable sums of money not getting pulled?

"Okay, but why didn't you call to check on things?"

"I didn't think I needed to. I rented the whole place, and Mr. Harrison has always kept our reservation. What was I supposed to ask? 'Hey, Mr. Harrison, you're still planning on renting the whole lodge to me? You're not dead, right?'"

He nearly guffawed. *Well, it wouldn't have hurt.*

She stepped falteringly toward the rickety chair in the room and sat. "I have one hundred sixteen people arriving in Brandywood next week. Some who are expecting to stay here, including me and my family. I told those people I had the whole place, that I took care of their accommodations. Where am I supposed to hold my wedding? I have a tent and caterer and flowers and everything." She sounded close to hyperventilating and fanned her reddening face. "They're all coming here. Everything . . ."

Their personal history aside, Dan couldn't help feeling a twinge of guilt. She looked crushed. And those tear-filled eyes had manipulated him long ago.

He was also the least gifted person possible to handle this. His gaze moved toward the door, and he briefly considered making a run for it, as he did every time women teared up around him. But one he had some sort of prior relationship with? Nothing could make him more awkward.

A knot of tension rose in his chest. "Um. I'm not set up right now to handle guests." How many ways did he have to say it?

Avery's eyes snapped up toward him. "Please, Dan? Isn't there something you can do? I have everything ordered and ready to go—a-and the Serendipity means so much to me. I've been dreaming of getting married here since I was five years old."

Her chest heaved, then fat tears rolled down her cheeks. "It has to be here. Is this the only room where you're doing construction?"

Dan avoided squirming. "Yeah, but there's no furniture. I'd have to move everything back in. I'm living here, and I can tell you—it's rough. The whole place needs repairs." *Which is why I'm remodeling.* He'd thought he could take a dose of the great outdoors until he'd moved into the Serendipity. But after he'd discovered a nest of snakes in the bedroom he'd picked to sleep in, it turned out he didn't enjoy being as close to nature as he thought.

Was there any way he could compromise?

"You could use the grounds for a ceremony and reception, but I'm supposed to have a crew coming to tear down the dock and rebuild it next week. The landscaping crew won't be out before a month, though. Things have sort of gotten overgrown while the place was empty."

Because I wasn't supposed to have any guests. And Brenda didn't take care of the place.

Avery dashed the tears from her eyes with a swipe of her fingertips. "I can pull weeds and help you move furniture, if that's what it takes." A glimmer of hope came to her face. "If you're willing to let me hold the ceremony, it might give us a starting point. Maybe we can fix some of this. Please."

Dan nodded slowly, unconvinced that the lodge could host a wedding in any capacity. But his words had stopped her tears, and anything was better than having a crying woman in his office.

The lodge host a wedding . . .

Who was he kidding? There was no "lodge." No staff, unless you counted Peyton MacLuckie, who was only here doing odds and ends. So really, no one. Just him. He was the lodge. The construction crew.

But as she looked up at him, he remembered a younger version of himself. One that couldn't say no. Who had spent every dollar he'd saved that summer on little trinkets and a date to the county fair.

Nice guys always finish last.

And Avery could be difficult when she was mad.

He didn't even know how he'd start, or whether he'd be able to fix this place in time for her wedding. He'd need to get the furniture from storage, move it all in, get the sitting room insulated and dry-walled and painted, do some painting and power-washing outside, and get the landscaping looking like . . . less of a wild jungle. And that didn't include all the things he'd need to do to make the place run like a bed-and-breakfast should.

But he didn't want to tell her no. She didn't have to know he hadn't amounted to much. He wanted to be a competent, successful business owner. One who would solve problems for his customers, even pain-in-the-ass ones like Avery.

She whipped out her phone. "This is what Mr. Harrison told me the cost would be of renting the place for all next week, plus hosting the event, plus my room stay this week. This is what I'm prepared to pay, even with the lodge in this condition. Maybe this will help sway you?" She showed him the screen.

He let out a low whistle, feeling his chest lurch.

Almost eighteen thousand dollars.

Money to help get him on the right path again.

And a reasonable incentive to help her.

The words should have stayed deeply buried, not have passed his lips. But they came out anyway, a deep, throaty gurgle that he regretted as he said, "Yeah, I think I can do that. We'll make the lodge work for your wedding. Somehow. But I don't have all the mechanics of the lodge together yet—no staff or guest services or things like that. And it's going to take time for me to get the furniture out, so I don't have anywhere for you to stay tonight."

Avery's features relaxed.

"Yeah, well, there's nowhere to stay in this whole town. My guests have been telling me what a hard time they're having booking lodging around here. There aren't reservations in any of the towns within forty minutes."

"There's been a boon in the tourist industry lately—and a movie is being filmed in town this summer. Lots of tourists."

"Yeah, there's no place to stay. I'll keep looking, but in the meantime, I just flew across the country with my best friend, and we need to sleep somewhere."

Dan stared at her in stony silence, feeling as though his arm was being twisted behind his back. Like Warren used to do when they were kids. His brother always had the advantage of being bigger. *Do I really want to go out of my way for Avery Moretti?*

And weirdly, he wanted to impress her. Show her she no longer affected him.

Yeah, you've done a good job with that already, hothead.

If he could find the damn key to the storage unit—Brenda hadn't exactly been organized about transferring things to his care—maybe he could get some furniture for them in the next couple of days.

"Fine," he gritted through his teeth. "I have an air mattress you can borrow."

His air mattress. From his room. He'd figure out where to sleep later.

Relief filled Avery's face. "Thank you." She gave a conciliatory nod. "I appreciate you being so willing to work with me. It really means a lot to me."

Anger curled in his stomach. Whatever excuse he had for deciding to ignore reason, he didn't want Avery to mistake his intentions. The past was in the past, and he was determined to leave it that way—especially with the girl who'd hurt him so much as a teenager.

"It's not for you. I'd do the same for anyone else in your position. Understood?" Then he walked back toward the front door, hoping she'd follow. "I'll help get your bags."

CHAPTER THREE

Avery

12 Years Ago

THE TOAD in the boathouse with Avery either hadn't seen her or was cheerfully oblivious. Either way, the croak sounded off the wood slats that made the walls. Avery shifted her weight, tucking her bare feet in a little closer as Mom's voice drew near. "Avery! Come on, sweetheart. We're going to be late for dinner."

Would Mom think to look in the boathouse? She hugged her legs to her chest, ducking beside the kayaks.

"She probably went for a walk, Maria. It's fine. Let her cool off." Dad's voice wasn't too far away.

"Avery!"

God, she's relentless.

The side door to the boathouse creaked open, and Avery held her breath. She wanted to slip into the water and disappear under the dock. She'd tread water there until Mom went away. But it was too late for that now.

Except it wasn't Mom or Dad who came into the boathouse. It was a guy, about her age, the tall one who'd helped carry their luggage up to their room when they'd arrived the day before.

She'd recognized him from the year before. He worked at the Sports Shack, helping guests at the lodge get sporting equipment for the outdoor activities around the lake. Avery had noticed him because he'd been one of the few other teenagers around the Serendipity.

And because he's really cute.

He blinked in the dark, but despite that, his eyes found hers.

His hand rested on the door, and she raised a finger to her lips, begging him not to give her away.

"You! Excuse me. Over here."

Oh God, is Mom actually snapping to get his attention?

"Have you seen our daughter? She's about your age. About five-three. Auburn hair." Mom couldn't be more than a few feet from him.

Avery's heart pounded in her chest, and she gave the guy a pleading look, which she was sure he didn't see because he was still staring at her mom.

The guy shook his head. "Nope. Haven't seen anyone. But I'll keep an eye out."

"What about in there? She loves to take those boats out." Mom's voice came closer.

The door to the boathouse shut as the guy stepped back out. "No, ma'am. All the boats are there. I'm locking up the door for the night."

"If you could let me—"

"Come on, Maria. Give the kid a break. He already said he

was locking up. Avery knows the grounds around here better than we do. We'll grab her some takeout and bring it back. If she's not back by then, you can send out the FBI."

"Not funny, George. You know, this is exactly why she wants to go with you. You let her get away with everything." Mom and Dad's voices faded as they left the vicinity of the boathouse, taking their arguments with them.

Avery released a relieved breath, her heart still pounding. She palmed her cell phone, turning it off before her mom got the idea to locate her device. As the blue light from the screen faded, the door to the boathouse opened again, and she startled. The guy stepped in.

He closed the door behind him. "You okay?" He came a few steps closer, then squatted in front of her.

Avery moistened her lips, searching his blue eyes. His pupils were large in the dim light, but he had a gentle look.

A few fat tears slipped onto her cheeks. She wiped them away with the back of her hand. "Not really."

"I think they're gone now. They said something about going to dinner. Your parents?"

Avery sniffled, stretching her feet out in front of her. "Yeah. My parents." Her fingers tightened around the case of her cell phone. "They told me an hour ago that they're getting a divorce. And I'm moving. My mom wants to live in Tampa, so I have to go with her instead of staying in Miami, where I've lived my whole life. I'm supposed to start my senior year in two weeks. With all my friends. Not go to some new stupid school in stupid Tampa with a bunch of stupid people I've never met before and—" A sob shook her chest as the crushing reality of it came hurtling back to her.

The words had poured out of her easily enough. Accepting them was an entirely different proposition.

The guy said nothing, watching her silently.

She wiped her cheeks. "God, you probably think I'm so dumb. I mean, who doesn't figure out her parents are on the verge of divorce? Sure, they fight, but all parents fight. And maybe things aren't perfect all the time, but they work together. They do everything together. Why in the heck would they get a divorce?"

"I don't think you're dumb." He shifted. "But it could be anything. Parents have a way of hiding their problems sometimes."

"Not *my* parents. We tell each other everything. They've never hidden anything from me. We've always been really close." She chewed on her lip. "Or at least until a couple years and Mom started worrying I was going to be a rebel."

"So you never hide things from your parents?" Surprise registered on his face.

She barely heard him. "Ugh . . . this sucks. Divorce is the stupidest thing on the planet. Why get married at all if it means you still have to worry about someone breaking up with you? Doesn't that make it sort of pointless? Isn't the whole reason you do the marriage thing is so that you have someone to love you forever?"

"I don't know," the guy answered after a beat. Then he gave her a wry smile. "But my parents are divorced, too."

"Really?" She searched his gaze. "Is it awful? Do you have to go from house to house? Ugh, this is horrible. We're never going to be all three of us together for Christmas again." Her voice sounded nasally and whiny, even to her, but the reality of it was overwhelming.

The guy sat next to her, then dangled his legs off the side of the dock. "I don't go from house to house. My dad left my mom before I was born. Had a family with someone else and pretended my brother and I didn't exist. Then he got arrested for trafficking narcotics, and now he's in prison." He leaned back on his hands, looking out toward the water. "And you might be the first person I've ever told that to."

"Oh." Avery studied his profile. *Wow.*

Now she felt like a jerk. Bitching and complaining about how terrible she had it.

At least her parents got along well enough to do one last family vacation at the cabin for "old time's sake." Even if they were sleeping in separate bedrooms.

She scooted over next to him and wiped her nose with her sleeve. "I'm sorry."

The guy shrugged. "Divorce sucks. You're right. Luckily, my mom married my stepdad, and he's my real dad now."

They sat together in silence, staring at the water, where the occasional dive of an insect caused a ripple. The sound of the toad filled the space again—it must have thought it was safe to sing when they weren't talking.

"I'm Avery, by the way."

The guy looked over his shoulder at her, a smile hinting at his mouth. "I figured. You know, with your mom hollering your name like she was." Then he added, "I'm Dan."

She considered telling him she'd noticed him the year before but had been too shy to introduce herself. She sighed, releasing a long breath.

"I don't know how I'm going to face them this week. I really don't want to walk around pretending everything is great and I'm happy when I'm miserable."

"So don't pretend." Dan rubbed his neck. "I mean, screw that. What's the point of it? Don't pretend."

She raised a brow. "So just mope around?"

"Or you could have the best week of your life. Just to spite them."

Have fun to spite her parents? It didn't exactly sound like a good way of getting back at them. They *wanted* her to have fun. "And how do you suggest I do that?"

Dan checked his watch. "I'm just getting off my shift. Feel like taking a boat across the lake to go get snowballs?"

She blinked at him. Was he asking her out?

Then her heart did a funny thing in her chest, growing tight and fluttery all at once, reminding her of her crush on him the year before and that her parents had a strict rule about "no dating in high school."

But as he'd said, screw that.

This could be the last time she ever came to Serendipity, so she'd never see him again anyway.

She stood, dusting off her shorts. "Sure. Let's go."

CHAPTER FOUR

Avery
14 Months Ago

AVERY ADJUSTED HER HEEL, nearly tripping as she tried to buckle the strap in midair. She checked the time on her cell phone, her ankle twisting. "Oomph." She tumbled to the floor of her apartment, almost landing on a pizza box. She caught herself at the last minute against the trash can.

Or maybe she'd tripped on the pizza box. Damn things never fit in the trash can and then took up most of a new can if you put them in a fresh bag. Most of the time, they stayed on top of the lid until she took the trash to the chute.

The doorbell rang, and she hobbled over toward it, then checked through the peephole. The guy on the other side of the door matched the profile picture from the dating site. "Dammit."

Why is he here so early? Punctual people were bad enough,

but twenty minutes early? *Ugh. Thank God I've at least finished putting my makeup on.* Clearly, he knew nothing about "Latina time," what Erika teasingly called Avery's sense of punctuality. Though she'd grown up in Miami around other Latinos, Avery never had noticed what Erika was talking about until college.

Her hand hesitated on the door knob, then she glanced around. She hadn't even had time to tidy up the apartment. *Not the best first impression.*

"One second," she called, then tripped her way back to the kitchen. She threw the pizza box in the pantry, tossed the dishes from the sink and counter into a pile in the dishwasher, then made her way past the couch, straightening the pillows as she walked. She stuffed a few articles of clothing under the couch, then went back to the door.

As she opened the door, she smiled. "Hey, sorry about that."

He's even cuter in person.

The slightest dimple showed in his cheek as he held out a hand, his dark brown eyes twinkling. "I'm Bryan."

She clasped his hand. "Avery." He had a nice, firm grip, something she liked in a man. "Come on in for a second. I'm just going to grab my purse."

As she reached for her purse from the coffee table, it occurred to her she had broken the cardinal rule of Internet dating without a second thought. She'd invited a random stranger to her apartment instead of asking him to meet her at the restaurant.

Erika's going to be so mad at me when I tell her.

Hopefully, Bryan's credentials would help her here. She tried to look confident as she slung her shoulder strap over her shoulder. "Did you have any trouble getting in? I thought I might have to ring you up."

"No, someone was coming out when I got here and let me in." Bryan nodded toward the sunset outside her window. "Sorry I'm so early. It's such a pleasant night out, I figured we could walk. I hope you don't mind, but I made us reservations at my favorite spot around here. Thought it might be smarter than having to face a long wait time."

Walk? She wouldn't have worn stilettos if she was planning on walking. Still, it was a sweet idea—and spur of the moment, too, which she loved. "Sounds fantastic."

They left the apartment, and Avery let him lead the way, noting how he held open the door. Mom would smile at that one. Not to mention the fact that he was a doctor. *Check and check.*

Bryan wasn't the type of guy she normally swiped right on. But then, she had been making the worst choices with men for a while now. So when she'd promised Erika to give someone "different" a shot, Bryan had seemed to be a good fit.

"I was thinking," Avery said as they headed out into the balmy night in the Gaslamp District. "There's this cool new nightclub right around the corner from here. It might be fun to check it out after we eat." He'd had something about dancing in his profile, right? She couldn't keep all the profiles straight these days.

Bryan flinched as a cyclist whizzed past them, his hand darting out in front of Avery to hold her back from getting hit. Avery stopped just in time, but the gentle pressure of his open palm against her midsection caused her to glance at him in surprise. And then a small flush of pleasure replaced any fright she might have had from the contact or cyclist.

He's protective. And has good reflexes, too.

"Asshole," Bryan breathed in a low voice, his eyes narrowing at the cyclist. "Don't know what the hell he's doing on the sidewalk." Then his gaze snapped back to Avery and the darkness to his features faded. He grinned. "Sorry about that." He dropped his hand and held his palm up, gesturing them forward. "Dancing, if you don't mind my two left feet, sounds great."

Avery bit her lip, hiding her smile. The self-deprecation was sort of sweet.

By the end of the night, Bryan had not only proven to be sweet and protective, but extremely interesting, too. He was a good listener, attentive, and Avery wondered if she might have found the man of her dreams.

CHAPTER FIVE

Now

THE DOOR to the balcony creaked open, and Avery looked up from the cup of coffee she'd grabbed in town. The guy who had driven them over from the airport, Ben, had done them the favor of taking them into town to get Erika to a pharmacy and then driven them back. By the time they returned, Dan had swept out a room and set them up temporarily with an air mattress and clean sheets.

That was all the furniture there was in the room. Dan had also given them two metal folding chairs on the balcony and two bath towels, one of which Erika had claimed to take a shower.

Erika stepped out to the porch, her eyes still looking red but better.

Avery gestured toward the chair beside her. "You look better."

"Eh. I feel like I could start sneezing immediately. I haven't had something trigger my allergies this way for ages."

"But Erika, I thought Asians didn't *get* allergies?" Avery teased. An eighth grade math teacher had made that claim once when Erika told him she didn't have a cold, just allergies. It had been a running joke between them since. They'd bonded as kids over their shared "half-Cuban" status in Miami, which meant that frequently people pegged them for the stereotypes of their "other side"—though in Avery's case it was Italian, and in Erika's it was Korean.

Erika laughed. "We don't. We stare at all you allergy-prone white people from our dry cleaners and nail salons, listening to our perfect children playing the violin and quoting calculus equations while thinking to ourselves how much it must suck to be you."

"Damn you Asians. You get all the good stereotypes. I tell people I'm Cuban and Italian, and they'll say, 'Oh, so you have a temper.'" Avery rolled her eyes.

"Well, in fairness, you *do* have a temper. And at least they think you can cook. I say I'm bringing something to a potluck, and they think I'm going to show up with Chinese food."

Avery sipped her coffee, keeping a straight face. "Korean, Chinese—what's the difference?" She winked, having had a lifetime of people expecting her to love Mexican food and knowing her friend's gripe.

"None. It's the same damn country. All of Asia. Just one country. Sort of like all you Mexican people." Erika sat in one of the folding chairs, and it creaked under her weight. Erika settled back, her eyes drifting to the back yard, which needed a good mow. "I'm sure it's pretty when it doesn't look like this."

Avery sank back in her chair. She hated that this was the way Erika had to experience the Serendipity for the first time. "I know you think I'm crazy for still wanting to do it here."

"Honey, it's not that I think you're crazy for wanting to do it here. That's completely natural. It's just that it's probably impossible for that to happen. Admit that. How are we supposed to stay here? There's got to be some other place near here."

"I spent a while going through all the apps and hotel sites on my phone while I was in town, and I couldn't find anything. Even called some places. Everything is booked. It's a good thing I had the wedding guests book their rooms so early—but now I have no idea what I'm going to do about the people who are supposed to stay here. It's mostly family, but I don't think my grandmother or Bryan's parents are going to want to sleep on an air mattress."

Avery covered her face with her hands. Little things that she may not have paid attention to in the past now screamed for attention. But it didn't look so bad from the outside. In need of repair and some love, but fixable.

But that's not even the biggest problem, is it?

A lump formed in the back of her throat, and she swallowed hard.

"Erika?" She peeked between two fingers toward her friend, then drew a deep breath. "There's something else. The new owner of the Serendipity . . . he's not just any guy. He's Dan."

Erika's dark brows drew together in confusion. "What?" Then her eyes widened. "Oh no, you don't mean *your Dan*?"

Avery nodded slowly. "Yeah, that's the one. And I'm pretty sure he still hates me."

The soft sounds of the Maryland summer filled the stunned air between them. Crickets sang an unending hymn, joined in a chorus by tree frogs and cicadas. The sharp punctuations of mockingbirds trilled from the tall, swaying treetops.

Avery closed her eyes, remembering that hazy summer. So long ago. So many heartbreaks later.

But that had been the first one.

The first heartbreak is always the hardest.

"You think he hates you?" Erika's voice brought her to the present.

Avery smoothed her hands on her lap and sighed. "Yes."

"I don't know about that. He's letting you do the wedding here, isn't he?" Erika pulled a tissue from her pocket.

"Yeah, but that's because I offered him a lot of money." Avery sighed, surprised at her regret. "I think somehow it was easier to think about him when I didn't have to see how much he doesn't like me anymore. Like, 'Oh, remember that guy I fell so hard for when I was eighteen and how I've always wondered what happened to him?' He's always been my what-if. Now I know. He's still here in Brandywood, and he hates me."

"You remember you're here to get married?" Erika tilted her head to the side as she gave Avery a wary look.

"I know, but what if this is one more thing that's supposed to throw me off? Make me doubt?" If it were anyone other than Erika, she wouldn't say such thoughts out loud. But Erika was the one person she could actually say this to.

"Don't tell me you're convinced this is all that family curse stuff. You don't still have feelings for this guy, Avery. It's been twelve years. And time has a way of romanticizing past relationships. You barely knew each other."

Avery's fingers curled into her palms. Even though Erika had been the only person she'd ever spoken to about Dan, Avery had brushed the whole thing off, acting like it had meant a lot less than it had. What choice had she had, anyway? Mom had deleted Dan's contact information from her phone and forbidden her to use social media for her entire senior year.

Mom had always been strict, but things went haywire after

that. Avery's curfew had gone from ten to eight. On the weekends. No parties or school dances.

Not after she'd screwed up so badly with Dan Klein.

She chewed on her lower lip. Something about the air here normally brought her a sense of calm she didn't find anywhere else, but she didn't feel it right now. Bryan had teased her about her love for Brandywood until he'd come with her last summer. She was glad she'd brought him. He had complained the whole time, of course, but when she'd suggested the Serendipity for the wedding, he'd agreed to it with only minor wrangling.

She sighed. She'd been so sure that if she skipped right to the place where love had found a way in her family, everything would go smoothly—curse or not. "It's not that I really think Bryan and I won't get married." Avery swirled the lukewarm coffee in her cup. A gnat tried to dive toward the sweet liquid, and she swatted it away. "But even you have to admit there have been a lot of crazy things happen, just in the past few hours."

"Not *that* crazy. So a guy you once slept with bought and is remodeling your wedding venue, and there's nowhere for you or your family to stay for the wedding, and your wedding probably shouldn't happen here." Erika frowned, then winced. "Okay. I take it back. You're cursed."

"Don't forget the part where my best friend who came all the way from Miami to help me with wedding plans is ridiculously allergic to ragweed." Seeing the gnat had succeeded in drowning itself in her coffee, Avery wrinkled her nose and set the cup down on the floorboards.

"But look. Even if all that stuff really was real, you and Bryan love each other, right? This is what you want? To be here and to get married here. That won't change because your wedding venue changes."

Avery shook her head slowly. "Unless the fact that I'm

trying to do it here and I can't is exactly why my wedding won't happen at all. It honestly feels like *something* is trying to stop everything. Like I thought I was so smart by trying to outsmart fate by holding the wedding here, and now that's the one decision that will blow it all up."

"So don't do your wedding here. It's that simple, Ave. Maybe it's not a bad thing. You and Bryan have had this super-intense thing. You only dated for four months before getting engaged and moving in together. Maybe this is fate stepping in, giving you a chance to take a breath before marrying so fast."

Her words cut in a way Avery didn't quite know how to explain. They'd even gotten into an argument when Avery had called to tell Erika about her engagement. Erika hadn't shown the enthusiasm Avery had hoped for, and the thought of it still stung.

What was worse, when she'd vented about it to Bryan, he'd been so furious, she thought he'd hold it against Erika. She'd learned a lesson that day: never vent to Bryan about Erika.

"I know you think us getting engaged was just another impulsive move on my part—"

"It was impulsive. But I didn't blame you, did I? Bryan's the one who proposed. I was just . . . surprised. You've come a long way in becoming more cautious, which I appreciate. Maybe a smidge too cautious considering how anxious you were about that Uber thing earlier."

"Bryan brings out a more cautious side of me. He's everything I needed to get back to my more responsible side. My delivery schedule for clients has never been more timely, I've gotten organized, and I'm making healthier choices. He encourages me in those things." Despite her best effort, Avery couldn't help keeping the defensive tone out of her voice.

"And that's great. Really. You were sort of floating along, being carried by the wind for a while."

Ouch. Not that Avery could argue. She'd gone through a rough patch the first few years after college, and then moving to San Diego.

Erika reached up and rubbed a knot out of her shoulder, as though the conversation had her tense. "I'm not trying to question your relationship. It all seemed a little fast. But we're here now, and we've got a bigger problem to deal with—and I don't mean your 'curse.' Maybe we should come up with a list of alternatives?"

"Unless . . . the fact that I'm now worried about doing it here is meant to discourage me so that I don't do it here, which will keep the curse going. Which means I have to do it here." Avery grimaced as the words came out of her own mouth.

Erika blinked at her. "Do you even hear yourself? This isn't Disney World. Curses aren't real. You're making my head spin with all this."

If she was honest, Avery would admit she was making her own head spin. Did she really put that much weight in "the curse?"

Her mom had been engaged twice before Dad, as had her grandmother before Abuelo.

Although, her parents' marriage had ended in divorce, so perhaps that shouldn't be an example to live by.

Her great-grandmother had been engaged a whopping four times.

But even if the curse wasn't true, she'd been dreaming of having her wedding here since she was a girl. She'd visualized saying her vows in front of the shimmering waters of the lake, dancing under the golden glow of sunset, while the scent of sweet mulled apple cider drifted from the buffet set up with the Smith Island cake she'd fallen in love with as a toddler and a display of Italian cookies, cannoli, tres leches, and mini flans.

Was she ready to let all that go?

Not yet.

She'd always had an inexplicable tug to the Serendipity. *My first proposal happened here, after all.* She smiled at the memory. Gosh, she hadn't thought about that for years. What had that little boy's name been that she'd played with that summer? Johnny?

"We could be married. Then you'd never have to leave."

Avery rubbed the glossy surface of her manicured thumbnail. "I've always wanted my wedding here, Erika. The curse stuff—it's just extra motivation."

Erika reached over and set a hand on Avery's knee, which had been bouncing nervously without Avery even noticing it. "Okay." Erika's voice was gentle but firm.

"Okay?" Avery raised an eyebrow.

Erika grinned. "If this is where you have your heart set on, then I'll do whatever it takes to help you have the wedding of your dreams there." She sniffled. "Even if your chosen wedding site is actively trying to kill me."

Avery's heart lurched. *Thank God for Erika.*

CHAPTER SIX

D AN DUMPED the contents of the box on the linoleum floor of the kitchen in front of where Peyton was sitting. A random spool of pink thread tumbled from the pile of junk and rolled across the floor, leaving a trail of string until it bounced against the old black refrigerator and spun to a stop.

"Great," Dan muttered. He exchanged a look with Peyton, who gave the pile a skeptical look. By now, Peyton had been with him long enough that they'd figured out that both Ken Harrison and his daughter had practiced a similar level of organization and disposition for cutting corners. In fact, they'd run into so many half-assed repair attempts, they'd made the family's last name into a verb and started saying things around the house were "Harrisoned."

Brenda had handed Dan a box at closing and told him some important things were in it, including the keys to the storage unit where she'd stored all the furnishings, which she'd also sold to him. He hadn't needed the keys yet, because he wasn't ready to furnish the place again—or so he thought.

"I'm looking for a key?" Peyton inspected the tangled pile of junk skeptically.

"Yeah. There should be a tag on it that has the storage unit information. I think." Dan plucked a few soy sauce packets from the top of the pile. "And if you see anything like this, just toss it." He stood, steadying himself on the counter.

Peyton pushed a dark lock of hair from his eyes. "You're not really trying to move all the furniture back, are you?"

"Right now, I'll settle for getting those women beds. I gave them the air mattress I had up in my room, but it won't be comfortable. I didn't want to promise them beds tonight, but if I can swing it, I'd like to make it happen."

Peyton gestured at the pile of junk. "You sure that key is even in here?"

It had better be. Brenda Harrison was in Georgia. If she hadn't given him the key, that meant even more delays to getting into the unit. "I'm not sure of anything. But that's where she said it would be."

"Hello?" Avery's voice rang out in the hall, and Dan left Peyton there, searching through the junk.

His heart slammed into his chest as he rounded the corner. She'd changed into khaki pants and a more casual sleeveless blouse and loosened her hair from the uptight bun into a pony-tail. She still didn't look like she was here for anything other than a business meeting, but *damn—that ass.* He checked himself, stopping his gaze from traversing her figure.

She's engaged, idiot.

And it's Avery.

Dan gave her the easiest smile he could, sure he looked awkward. "How can I help you?" Trying to be cordial to this woman just might kill him.

"I was thinking of going into town to grab a sleeping bag.

Any place you can recommend? The closest Target is an hour away."

"Uh, yeah. Floyd's. They have all that stuff. Tents, kayaks, hiking boots."

A divot formed between her eyebrows, the corners of her luscious lips turning up. *Nope. Stop thinking about her lips that way.*

"If you're telling me we all need tents, I may go cry."

"You, cry? Never." Dan chuckled sarcastically. The first time he'd met her, she'd been crying. Hell, he was pretty sure she'd cried in some form or another every day he'd spent with her.

"Hey! Cheap shot." She glared, giving him a look of mock outrage. "Not all of us can be stoics, you know."

"Yeah, I know. There's only so much room for perfection in this world." He winked. Being able to say whatever he wanted to her now was fun and oddly freeing. No pretense. No anxiety about wanting to make her like him. Hell, even with the average woman he met, he tried to be polite. But he didn't have to do that with Avery. "Anyway, you should be good without a tent. I'm doing my best to get some furniture for the place."

"Thank you, I really appreciate it." Avery clasped her hands in front of her tensely. If she had something else on her mind to say, she was struggling to do it.

He cleared his throat. If someone ought to pay for the sleeping bag, it shouldn't be her. Hell, he probably had a sleeping bag at his parents' house, where he'd stored the few belongings he'd been able to recover from his place with Melissa before she'd changed the locks. His ex-girlfriend had been brutal in the division of possessions when he'd broken up with her—but Dan had been the idiot for getting rid of most of his things when they'd moved in together. And money for basics like a new mattress had felt low on the scale of priorities.

Regardless of all that, he hadn't thought twice about it when he was thinking of himself. But with Avery and her friend here, he couldn't be so practical.

As much as Avery had created a disaster for him to deal with, this situation wasn't her fault either. That she'd never called to check on her own reservations seemed ludicrous, though. But he supposed that with her family coming here for so long, they had a certain way of doing things and feeling like plans would be taken care of.

He sighed, cutting the awkward silence short. "You know, I think I have a sleeping bag. It's not here, but I can take you with me to get it and then drive you into town for anything else you need, if it's helpful."

Avery hesitated, looking over her shoulder for a split second. Then she nodded. "Yeah, that works. Let me just go tell my friend. She took so much Benadryl that I think she'll be down for the count tonight. I may need to go buy some groceries next week, too. My fiancé is picky. Is it all right if we store them in your fridge?"

"No problem." Dan fidgeted as Avery slipped away again. He had little in the fridge anyway. A six-pack of beer he'd bought in anticipation of someone stopping by. All six remained. And a half-filled carton of milk, which he had with cereal every morning and with his peanut butter and jelly sandwich at lunch. Add that milk and some butter to a box of mac and cheese at night, and that rounded out his culinary skills.

Come to think of it, he wasn't sure he wanted Avery to know those details about his life. Back when he'd been on the force, they'd occasionally get calls to check on the shut-ins or elderly. Their fridges sometimes looked like his. Of all the tasks Dan disliked, that was the one that haunted him the most. People didn't know just how many lonely people there were within the boundaries of their town.

Avery returned with a purse slung over her shoulder. "Ready."

Seeing her dressed more comfortably reminded him of times long since passed. He said little as he led her outside and started toward his truck. What could he say? For so long, he'd had a snarky remark on his tongue in case he ever saw her again. He'd even claimed he hated her.

For a full year after she'd gone home, he'd wondered how she'd fooled him so much. She saw him as outdoorsy and fun, and maybe that was why she'd been that way with him. Given the radical change in her appearance and clothing, she was probably engaged to someone inflexible and uptight.

Unless she'd become just like her mother.

He hoped that wasn't true, but there was a reason people claimed the apple didn't fall far from the tree. *Even when you spent a lifetime trying to prove you were nothing like the man who fathered you.*

He helped her into the passenger seat and then got in behind the wheel. Avery was sitting stiffly beside him, her eyes transfixed on the St. Christopher medal hanging from his rearview mirror.

Shiiiiit.

He held his breath, turning his body toward her as her eyes locked with his. "You kept that?" she said, astonishment in her eyes.

Damn medal. He had thought little about her seeing it, because he hadn't thought Avery would ever be in his truck again. But he could picture the wide-eyed innocent look of happiness she'd had when she'd pressed the cool medal in his hands years ago.

"I have something for you."

"Oh, yeah? What is it?"

"St. Christopher. It belonged to my grandfather. To keep you safe. When we go on all those adventures we've talked about."

Dan tore his gaze from the medal, and he glanced back at her, trying to figure out how to answer. If he'd learned anything in the past few years, it was that honesty was a good starting point out of a sticky situation. He swallowed hard, then nodded. Reaching over, he pulled it free of the rearview mirror.

She probably had the wrong impression of why he'd put it up there.

Dropping it in her lap, he said, "I never had the chance to give it back to you. And I didn't think it belonged in the trash can. When I became a cop, I figured I needed as much good luck with me as possible, so I put it on the dash and just got used to it being there."

That's true enough, right?

Avery pressed her lips together, as though trying to figure out how to respond as he started the engine. Her hand enclosed around it, and she pressed it to her heart. "Thank you. For not throwing it out. I assumed you had."

He shifted into drive. "Family heirlooms don't belong in a landfill. And I would have tried to find an address, but your mom made it very clear I wasn't ever to contact you again."

Her eyes darted out the window as he pulled out of the driveway, as though she was looking for an escape. "I didn't know she did that. But it doesn't surprise me either. I spent my entire senior year grounded after . . . you." She shifted, setting her purse on her lap and clasping it tightly. "Seeing you here is . . . it's . . . wow. It's hard to believe. I never expected you to be the owner of the Serendipity."

A strange, defensive feeling curled in his chest. His palm shifted over the steering wheel, his eyes locking on the dappled light of the late-afternoon sun filtering in through the thick foliage on the tree-lined road. "Well, we met there. Just because you were the guest while I was the disposable help, doesn't mean I didn't like the place."

He cringed inwardly. He hadn't meant to sound so butthurt about it, but it'd come out that way.

Avery smiled sadly. "You weren't disposable, Dan. At least not to me. My mom was awful to you, I know. And I've always regretted the way things ended between us. I wondered what happened to you, but after a while I figured it was better to leave the past in the past. Plus, I just figured you might have left Brandywood after high school. Gone off to be a photojournalist, like you wanted."

Dan sucked a breath in through his teeth. *That old dream.* But the way things had ended between him and Avery had set him on the trajectory to becoming a cop . . . proving he was nothing like his asshole of a birth father. "Actually, I was a cop until recently. I got out of that when I bought the Serendipity."

"Law enforcement, really?" She gave him an odd look. "What happened to traveling?"

"People change, right?" He didn't want to talk about it, especially not with her. She'd obviously changed, too, so she should be able to accept that as an explanation. "What keeps you busy these days? Other than wedding planning."

"Graphic design." Her face brightened. "Mostly, I work with publishers, doing book covers. But I have my own business, so I can set my schedule and be choosy about the projects I take on."

"Do you still draw?" When they'd been younger, she'd shown him some of her sketches, and it had blown him away how good she was. She'd even drawn a picture of him.

"Only with my Apple Pencil." She shrugged sheepishly. "Not in journals these days."

That differed from before, too. She'd railed about technology when they were younger, going on about how people didn't draw like they used to. How art was getting lost to computers.

Dan turned onto the street that would lead into Main Street, and the familiar sights of his hometown made him frown. After he'd joined the police force, a new love for Brandywood had taken root in him. But that old itch to pick up and start somewhere new had been nagging him again. Not that it was going to happen now that he'd bought the Serendipity. He pulled into a spot in the main lot at the top of Main Street near Bunny's Café, then parked.

"This place never really changes, does it?" Avery asked, looking at the sign for the café. "I swear I have memories of going there with my dad when I was a toddler to get cookies. Does the owner still have some epic rivalry with the guy who runs Yardley's?"

"Yeah, that hasn't changed. Neither have all the theories about why they hate each other. But really, under the surface, a lot *has* changed. Mr. Yardley has expanded his business, and Bunny's nearly as famous—she's got a baking column in a magazine, a new cookbook, and a line of cookware coming out for a big box store. And not everyone in town is happy about it either."

The changes had worked out well for his family, but he could picture the snarl on Melissa's face during their last big fight. *"Yeah, I wouldn't want to say anything against the beloved Klein clan, would I? News flash, Dan—not everyone is in love with your 'perfect' family or the way you all and your friends have ruined our town."*

That and a few choice words about his mom and sister had been when Dan's delusions about Melissa had worn away completely. One of the only regrets Dan had was that he had stayed with Melissa long enough for her to ruin Jen and Jason's wedding for him. *And losing his dog Milo, of course.*

"Wouldn't that be fabulous for tourism?" Avery's voice interrupted the darker thoughts, and he looked at her, strangely relieved that it was her and not Melissa in the truck with him. Guess it just went to show that even Avery Moretti, who also crushed his heart, was preferable to the company of Melissa Rosner.

"That's the problem, actually. So many tourists that some locals are frustrated at the lines in their favorite spots, the crowds at events, and the lack of parking on Main Street. It's definitely the minority, but they're loud."

Dan set his hand on the latch to open the door when Avery said, "Hey, listen—"

He paused, glancing back at her.

Before she could speak, her phone rang, and she checked to see who was calling. She held up a finger, turning her body away from him. "Hey, babe."

Must be her fiancé. Funny how that word made his gut clench. Dan's fingers curled against the latch. Should he step out and let her have her privacy?

She spoke again. "Yeah, I'm here. I tried to call you when we landed, but there was no service at the airport. Did you get my texts? You should be able to use *Find My* now again if you want to see where I am. Service is spotty in some places around town, though."

Find My? To track her?

"Yeah, it's perfect. Just how I said it would be." Avery lowered her voice, glancing out the window. "Nothing to worry about at all. I can't wait to see you next week."

Dan's brow furrowed. *That's weird.* Why would she lie to her fiancé about the state of things?

"No, babe. The flight was great. No problems at all. But I still think you flying into Pittsburgh is a better idea. That way you can rent a car." A few beats. Avery looked down at her lap.

"Oh. I'm sorry. I'll update you better. Yeah, no, go ahead. Love you!"

As she lowered the phone from her ear, she stared at it, her body radiating with tension.

Dan raised a brow at her. "Your fiancé?"

Avery nodded. "Bryan." She locked the screen. "Sorry. I missed one of his earlier calls, and then I didn't have service, and he thought something might have happened." She lifted her chin. "He has really serious anxiety." Then she cleared her throat and added, "That's why I didn't tell him about the way I found things at the Serendipity. I don't need him freaking out right now."

Even though there was a definite case to be made that Dan wasn't the most cool-headed person on the planet, her words worried him. And while he might not always handle his feelings about people correctly, he still had good instincts. He'd made a damn good cop. And working in law enforcement had only sharpened his intuition.

"But what happens when he comes next week and sees that things aren't so perfect?"

"Well, we have a week, don't we? We'll see how far we can get. If worse comes to worst, if people have a place to sleep and the outside is looking okay, we can just tape off the sitting room." She sounded much calmer and more confident than a few hours earlier. "I was planning on doing cocktail hour there, but if the weather is good, then we can just do the whole wedding and reception outside."

Dan nodded, his neck feeling stiff. *If* he could find the key to the storage unit. He could not afford to furnish the whole place right now. He gave her a sidelong glance, curious to know more about her fiancé without sounding too inquisitive. "So what does Bryan do?"

"He's a doctor. Cardiologist." Avery twisted her engagement ring around her finger. "He works a lot, so he couldn't take any time to come beforehand like me." She didn't sound thrilled to be out here by herself.

A rich and successful doctor. Dan's jaw tensed. If he remembered correctly, Avery's dad was a doctor, too. It made sense that was the type of guy she'd gone for in the long run.

Dan normally wouldn't have commented on any part of her private conversation, but she'd been the one to open up the topic. "What's the deal with *Find My?*"

"Oh, it's just something we started when we moved in together, so he could track my cell phone location to figure out when I would be home from work and all." Avery's smile was taut.

That sounded reasonable enough. *Yet it doesn't.*

Avery double-checked her phone again, as though to make sure she hadn't left it on, and then said, "Anyway, I just wanted to say, I know we have a weird history and all, and if we're going to spend so much time around each other for the next few weeks, I'd prefer we try to put the past behind us. So if there's anything you feel like we should talk about—"

"Ancient history." Dan pushed the door open but didn't climb out. What difference did it make now? It wasn't like she'd come back even looking for him. No reason to dredge up those old wounds. "I'm fine. And you seem like you're fine too, right? Better than fine. Happily engaged and all that."

Did he detect a flicker of disappointment in her eyes? *Probably not.* But maybe she—like him—had thought them running into each other would detonate more fireworks. Good or bad.

Guess things should have ended when they did.

Anyway, he was in no danger of letting Avery Moretti affect him ever again. Because he hadn't forgotten what she'd done to him that summer.

CHAPTER SEVEN

Dan

12 Years Ago

DAN HAD JUST FINISHED PACKING the bait fridge with the bloodworms he'd brought in from town. He bent to stack the bait buckets, when cool fingers slid in front of his eyes from behind. "Guess who?" Avery's voice was in his ear.

He smiled, his heart giving a thump, and set his hands on her biceps to draw her arms around his neck as he stood.

She cried out with surprise, laughing, as he reached for her waist, then swung her around his body so she was facing him. She was light. Or she made him feel strong. Either way, he couldn't believe they'd known each other for less than a day. They'd talked long after sunset, then kissed, then spent the entire night texting. He'd come into work early that morning just so he could try to see her.

His whole body buzzed as he set her on her feet. It was still early, the pink light of dawn on the horizon making the waters of the lake look magical. The outdoor Sports Shack—little more than a shed with shelves organized with outdoor sporting equipment and counter where Dan could handle the rentals for the kayaks and fishing equipment—was still dark.

Avery didn't release his neck, and before he knew it, their lips had come together as though they were drawn magnetically.

She'd obviously been thinking about him just as much.

Dan groaned, hardening immediately as he pushed her back against the wall. He hoisted her up, and her legs wrapped around his waist, settling tightly against him. Her lips were soft, warm, her tongue brushing against his without an ounce of timidity or girlish hesitation.

"God, you're such a good kisser," she whispered as they pulled apart for a breathless moment. His lips roved toward her neck, trailing down from her jaw toward that soft spot below her earlobe. "I kept dreaming about kissing you all last night."

"Me, too," he managed, feeling as if he could hardly get the words out.

He pulled away and then checked his watch. "Hang on— come with me for a second."

"Now?" Her eyes were wide.

"It's worth it."

He took her hand and led her out the side door. Within a few seconds of walking through the dew on the early morning grass, his flip-flops were soaked, so he left them by the first wooden planks of the dock.

The sunrise was just creeping over the horizon behind them, since they were facing west. A foggy haze hung over the water, which would grow thicker the closer they got to autumn. He tugged her to the end of the dock, and they stood there, hand in hand, watching as the sky filled with streaks of pink and orange and violet.

She gave him a sidelong glance. "Is this . . .?"

"Shhh." He winked, then pointed at a rowboat that came through the fog, slowly gliding across the water. The old man rowing it was trailed by at least thirty ducks and geese, who followed him like a mother duck leading her ducklings.

Avery broke out into a wide smile. "Oh my gosh, why are they doing that?"

He shrugged. "They know him by now. His name is Mr. Jenson. He and his wife lived in the house closest to the lodge, but she died a few years ago. She used to feed the ducks, and when she died, he took over. He comes out here and feeds them every morning. To be close to her, Mr. Jenson says."

Avery's eyes sparkled in the soft hues of the morning light as she watched Mr. Jenson. She raised her hand over her heart. "That's so sweet."

"Yeah, but"—he squeezed her hand—"last night when we were talking, you said you didn't know if love like the movies was just a big lie. And I don't know, maybe it is. But old Mr. Jenson seems like he found whatever those movies are talking about." He gave her a crooked grin. "Both with his wife and the ducks."

Avery swallowed hard. "Now I'm going to cry." She pulled her hand from his and held her hands over her cheeks. Then she sat on the dock, hanging her legs over the side, watching the ducks and Mr. Jenson with a reverent look.

He sat beside her, and they watched until Mr. Jenson was out of sight and the sun was brightening the water, the faint ripples of fish and insects some of the only sounds of the quiet morning. She leaned her head against his shoulder. "I'm glad you found me in the boathouse."

"I'm glad I did, too." He glanced back over his shoulder. "I was hoping I would get the chance to talk to you when I brought your bags up."

"I remember you from last year, actually. There was this one time I watched you wrangling these canoes for this lady and her husband who kept changing their minds about which ones they wanted to take out. And you were so nice to them, kept taking the new one out, dragging it into the water. I would have probably lost my temper and told them to make up their frickin' minds already."

Dan laughed lightly. He remembered that couple *and* how annoyed he'd been by them, even if he hadn't said anything. "You saw that? Why didn't you come up and say something?"

"Well, to begin with, you clearly didn't notice me." She gave him a pointed look. "Not that I blame you. I spent most of last year's vacation with my head buried in a series of books I was reading because I caught mono—not from kissing, but from sharing a drink with my friend—and I had no energy to do anything. And also, I was way too shy. I'm not the best at making friends with people."

"You're shy?" He raised a brow. She didn't seem shy. And he should know. He was well known for his introversion. "You sure about that?"

"Yes, I'm sure. Don't give me that look." She swatted at his forearm playfully.

"Yeah, real shy, this one. So, Miss Shy, why is it you aren't good at being friends with people? Because somehow, I doubt it's because you're shy." At least, she hadn't been with him.

She set her hands on either side of her thighs, against the wooden planks, then crossed her ankles. After another moment of silence, she said, "I don't know. I guess it never seemed worth trying to get close to most people when my mom was just going to tell me I couldn't be friends with them. Or—even worse—tell *them* I couldn't be friends with them. Which is probably the most embarrassing thing ever when you're a senior in high school."

Ouch. Dan couldn't imagine that. Sure, his parents were strict when they needed to be—but mostly when he came home with a bad grade or a detention or didn't do things to "his full potential." Fortunately, his doctor had finally put him on an ADHD medicine this spring that actually worked. For the first time, he'd brought home good grades, and his parents were happy.

"Your mom's pretty tough on you, then?" Dan asked.

"Understatement. Everything is academics and discipline with her. And even with that, I still don't know that I make her proud of me."

"If you can't make her proud no matter what you do, then it sounds like standing up for yourself should be easier." The ding of the counter bell on the Sports Shack caught his attention. Dan checked the time on his watch. He didn't want to go back to work and wished he could spend the day with her instead. But someone was already waiting at the Sports Shack. "I should get going."

Avery looked toward the Sports Shack, then whirled her face back toward the water, stiffening. "Oh my God, it's my dad. Do you think he saw me here? My mom will kill me."

"He'd probably say something if he did, right?" Dan stood. "Just sit tight for a second. I'll go find out what he needs, and while he's distracted, you can sneak past and go back inside."

Dan hurried off the dock, then slipped on his flip-flops. Rather than drawing attention to the dock, he made a beeline for the back door to the shack and slipped in and over to the counter. "How can I help you?" Dan asked.

"Yes, I'd like to rent a couple of fishing rods and a canoe," Mr. Moretti said, setting his hands on the counter. "I want to surprise my daughter with an early morning fishing trip. Do you have any bait that isn't alive and squirming?"

"Sure. Do you want a fifteen or eighteen-foot canoe?" Dan fought the urge to hold his breath as he noticed Avery slipping up the dock, out of the corner of his eye. She was walking backward, as though that would attract less attention. *Turn around, Avery, you're heading sideways.*

"What's the difference?"

"Uh—" *Oh, God . . .* He almost lurched forward as a muffled cry sounded, followed by a splash. Walking backward had led Avery straight off the far side. Mr. Moretti turned to look, but fortunately, any view of Avery was blocked by the dock.

"Someone swimming this early?" Mr. Moretti asked, his eyebrows raised.

Stay in the water, Avery.

Dan felt his face turning red. "Yeah, there's all sorts of people who swim this early." Which was ridiculous. because the lake temperature was freezing.

What the hell had Avery's dad asked him before? He did his best not to look for Avery, but as her dad turned back, there she was, peeking around the dock, dripping with water. He pressed his lips together tightly, trying to keep the laughter in. She clearly had no experience with sneaking around.

Think.

Canoes. Mr. Moretti asked about canoes.

"Um . . ." he managed at last. "I don't really know." That couldn't be further from the truth, but he couldn't form the right words. As Avery crawled forward, Dan ripped a poster from the wall beside him, then tossed it onto the counter to draw Mr. Moretti's attention back. "Here, this chart should help."

Avery stood now and ran toward the lodge, and Dan forced

himself to look away from her, barely stifling the need to laugh. He clenched his jaw hard, trying to keep a straight face.

"I guess a fifteen-foot one, then. It's just the two of us."

Dan was dimly aware that he was staring at Mr. Moretti blankly, unable to move.

"Okay, then." Mr. Moretti gave him an odd look. "How much is that?"

"Uh . . . on the house." Dan sucked in a deep breath. There was no way he was going to make it through this without laughing. "Actually, why don't you meet me at the boathouse? I'll grab some rods and tackle."

Mr. Moretti stepped back. "Okay. I might go wake up my daughter in the meantime." He walked away.

When he was gone, a peal of laughter broke out of Dan's throat, his shoulders shaking as he gripped the plywood counter.

He'd never met a girl like Avery before.

After they'd gone for snowballs that first night, they'd spent a long time talking on the dock on the other side of the lake. She'd shared all her dreams of going to Paris and studying art and how her parents refused to pay for an art degree. She loved ballet, but her mom wouldn't let her dance anymore because it took too much time away from schoolwork. She was a straight-A student on the honor roll, the top of her class, but she wasn't allowed to go to parties.

He wondered where she'd learned to kiss. Or if she was a virgin, like he was.

And somehow, despite all that, she was into him.

That never happened. He wasn't the guy who got the girl. Or popular like his brother, Warren, even though he was a pretty good basketball player and partied with all the jocks.

He didn't really fit in with them, though. He wasn't funny, wasn't the one the girls all wanted to hook up with.

Which left him to be the surly jerk, according to some of his classmates.

But he was okay with it. It was easy. He didn't have to try too hard, and few people had high expectations of him. He didn't disappoint anyone that way. Thanks to his new meds, his mom had spent all summer talking about how much better he was going to do senior year. He couldn't help worrying that he was going to mess up, though.

He fell into the familiar routine of getting fishing gear together, then grabbed the keys to the boathouse. After gathering all the supplies, he left the Sports Shack. He didn't see Mr. Moretti, so he set the supplies down and started toward the boathouse, smiling at the thought of how he'd met Avery in there.

"Listen, sweetheart, I know. I miss you, too. And it's only a week." Mr. Moretti's voice came in low, hushed tones. Then Dan saw him, standing on the dock, but not too far out.

Dan slipped the key to the boathouse into the palm of his hand, trying not to listen in on Mr. Moretti's conversation.

"I know. But we're not together again. Maria knows we're finished. And we just broke the news to Avery yesterday."

As Dan opened the door to the boathouse, the hinge squeaked, and Mr. Moretti spotted him. "I should get going, but I'll call you every chance I get . . . I love you, too. Can't wait to see you again, babe."

Dan went into the boathouse, blinking in the cool dark, and a feeling of dread rose in the pit of his stomach. Now he understood why Avery's parents were getting divorced out of the blue.

Avery's father was having an affair.

CHAPTER EIGHT

Avery

12 Months Ago

"I don't know, Er . . ." Avery wrinkled her nose at the smell of the stargazer lilies in the flower arrangement beside her desk. She hated the scent. They reminded her of funerals, which she doubted was what Bryan's goal had been. He'd been sending flowers weekly, which had started out cute but was starting to drive her crazy. What was she supposed to do with all these vases?

Leaning back into her chair, she laid down her tablet and digital pen and glanced more directly at the camera. With her best friend living on the opposite coast, weekly online "wine nights" was the best way they'd found to keep in touch. Avery was deluged with work right now, though, and she'd spent most of their chat fiddling with a design and ignoring the glass of Pinot Grigio in front of her. She remedied that now and took a sip before continuing, "The guy is nice. Even though he gets me the most banal flower arrangements on the planet."

She flicked one lily and pollen dusted her desktop. "But there's something . . . just missing."

Erika rolled her eyes, settling back into her couch. "So he doesn't know what type of flowers you like. You sound like a brat complaining, for what it's worth. He bought you flowers— that's supposed to be a nice thing. Why don't you just tell him you prefer sunflowers, and then he can get it right next time?"

Avery cringed. She didn't want to sound so ungrateful, and it was easy to pin her uncertainty on him on his mediocre taste in flowers. "Is it bad that I'm not sure I want there to be a next time? We've had seven dates. And they were fine. Two months of fine dates. Sweet, even. He's a sweet, nice guy. But I'm just—"

"You're just determined to put the guy to the side and go for one of your oh-so-exciting assholes again?" Erika rolled her eyes. "You know you can't complain about all the good guys being taken if you hold every nice guy you date to some impossible standard. Didn't you say he's taken you on unique and thoughtful dates?"

She nodded. He had. They'd gone to a drive-in movie. A picnic on the beach. Hiking in the state park. Rock climbing at Santee Boulders. "Yeah, I have fun with him."

"That's got to count for something. What is it you're looking for, exactly?" Then she made a face. "Is he just not great in bed?"

"No!" Avery covered her face, then peeked between her fingers. "I haven't slept with him." Just saying it made her self-conscious.

Erika's eyes widened. "Really?"

"Look, I'm honestly trying to listen to your advice. I figured after Tyler that the next guy I would date, I would wait until three months or ten dates, whatever comes first."

"Ten dates? Holy shit. No wonder you're overthinking this. You don't have to make hard and fast rules like that, you know." Erika poured herself more wine. "The chances of you hooking up again with a guy with two other girlfriends is probably slim. Just maybe don't sleep with a guy after knowing him for under an hour."

Avery's new rule *had* been torturous, but somehow it made her feel like when she did sleep with Bryan, it would be more special. "Yeah, well, if Bryan can't wait that long, maybe it's a bad sign." Avery stretched her shoulders back, then rolled her wrist. The carpal tunnel was reminder enough that she'd spent too much of her life wasting her time on losers and dead-end relationships. This time, she wanted to be in a relationship moving toward *forever*.

"And while I completely respect that, don't you think it's better to base when you go to bed with someone on the connection you feel with them?" Erika yawned, then checked her watch. "Speaking of bed, I know you're still living the joys of yesterday, but over on this side of the world, we've moved on to tomorrow. Catch you next week?"

Avery blew her a kiss as they disconnected, then stared at the black void left on the screen.

An apt metaphor for my life.

She swirled the wine in her glass, then took another sip. Maybe she was being too picky. Erika was usually the voice of reason in her life, after all. Bryan was nice. A little bland, but he'd been so thoughtful. He sent her texts every morning just to say hello and every night before he went to sleep.

Feeling the warm flush of wine, she pulled out her phone. Then before she could overthink it, she called Bryan.

"Hey, beautiful." He sounded sleepy.

"Hey, yourself." She should have looked at the time before she called. It was already after nine. "Did I wake you up?"

"No—no." Bryan cleared his throat. "It's fine. I'm happy to hear from you. What's up?"

Avery smiled, twisting back in her chair lazily. "I was thinking, want to come over?"

CHAPTER NINE

Now

AVERY TURNED ONTO HER BACK, her shoulder aching. As the groggy fog of sleep wore off, she blinked and peeled the eye mask from her face. She was on the floor in a sleeping bag in the Serendipity. Erika was asleep on the nearby air mattress, but she wasn't sure how. The damned thing had deflated during the night, forcing Avery to abandon her attempts to sleep on it and move to the floor.

Avery unzipped the sleeping bag and crawled out stiffly, trying to be as quiet as possible. Erika had snored throughout the night, probably a result of still being stuffy from her allergies. Avery padded over in bare feet toward her suitcase, hearing Bryan's voice in her head about how disgusting the floors of hotels were. He always wore socks. Even in bed. Now that they'd been together a little while, he sometimes wore them during sex, too.

How was that for sexy?

She bent and reached into the bag of clothes she'd picked up in town the night before. If she was going to get her hands dirty and pull weeds, the nice clothes she'd brought wouldn't suffice.

Tiptoeing out of the room, she hugged her clothes to her chest. This wasn't the first time she'd tiptoed out of the rooms in the Serendipity, and ironically, when she'd done it before, it had been to meet Dan.

Gosh, that feels like such a long time ago.

She left the room and changed in the hall, then made her way down to the first floor. When Mr. Harrison owned the place, the sitting room would have been set up with a buffet breakfast by now—one of her favorite things about the Serendipity. She was used to the routine of grabbing a hot cup of tea and going outside to watch the world wake up at dawn. Then she'd go back inside and scarf down the best biscuits and sausage gravy she'd ever tasted.

Would Dan hire the same chef someday? She'd have to recommend to him that he try to.

She didn't want anything about the old place to change. But it wasn't hers to say. It was Dan's now.

Instead of the aroma of enticing coffee or bacon, the sitting room was dusty and cold, stripped down to the studs. Whatever motivation Dan had for destroying the room, she hoped his vision could do justice to what had previously been there. But her heart broke at the thought that she'd never see it again the way it was before.

As she rounded the corner, she ran headlong into Dan, who was exiting the powder room with a toothbrush in his mouth. He wore nothing but boxers, and his hair stuck straight up in thirty directions, the grizzly beard looking wild.

He startled when he saw her.

Time had been kind to Dan. The lean muscles of his legs and torso of his youth had turned into well-built and chiseled ones. He had a fine sheen of curly hair on his chest. His shoulders were broader, too.

And I really shouldn't be thinking about his body.

The self-chastisement only made her cheeks flame, and she turned away. "Good morning," she managed.

Dan took a few steps away to the office and shut the door. She stared at it, surprised at the coolness of his response. Awkwardly, she turned and glanced back at the stairs. Maybe she should have waited for Erika to wake up.

Avery definitely wouldn't get through the day without a few cups of coffee.

She hurried out of the main hall and found her way onto the front porch. It shouldn't bother her that Dan had been rude. Their brief trip into Main Street had been pleasant enough, all things considered. But being near him made her miss the camaraderie she'd once shared with him.

Dan obviously didn't feel the same way.

She checked her phone, surprised with herself that she'd held out until now.

She had missed eighteen calls and several texts from Bryan. Cringing, she scrolled through them.

BRYAN: *Finally off work. How are things going? Don't forget to make sure the caterer has gluten-free for my mom.*

Bryan: You still having trouble with service?

Bryan: Hello?

Bryan: . . .

Bryan: I tried calling, and it went to voicemail. I'm guessing you don't have service.

Bryan: *I'm really getting worried. Please call me when you get this. It's nearly midnight your time.*

Bryan: *I tried calling Erika, but she's not picking up either.*

Bryan: HELLO?

Bryan: *I* REALLY *don't like not being able to get in touch with you.*

AVERY LET OUT a guttural grumble and then moaned. Why hadn't she gotten the notification on any of these? Bryan hated it when she didn't pick up. She typed up a quick message.

Avery: *Hey . . . I am so, so sorry. I had no idea you were trying to get in touch with me. Is now a good time to call?*

She was about to hit Send but then paused.

He might be sleeping. He'd sent the last message at three in the morning, her time. If Bryan hated one thing more than being unable to talk to her when he called, it was being woken up from sleep. He didn't sleep nearly enough with his long shifts at the hospital. And since it was just three o'clock Pacific time, he still had an hour to go before he got up for work.

The door on the front porch opened, and she jerked up her head. Dan stepped out, dressed in shorts and a T-shirt, a pair of flip-flops on his feet. He gave her an apologetic look. "Sorry about that. I ended up sleeping in the office last night and had to use the hall bathroom since there isn't one right next to it."

He'd slept in the office?

She bit her lip. Poor guy.

"No worries." She gave him a conciliatory smile. "Actually, I was hoping to catch you before everyone was up." She gulped a breath. "I was thinking of heading to Main Street to get some breakfast for Erika and me. Is that new bakery on Main any good?"

A soft, proud look lit Dan's eyes. "Yeah, it's great. My kid sister owns it." Then he chuckled. "Not so much of a kid anymore, but you get what I mean." He glanced at his truck. "You want me to drive you?"

"Oh, I didn't . . ." She trailed off. Having him take her would be better than trying to catch an Uber. "I mean, unless you still have bikes at the Sports Shack."

"Actually, that's the one place Brenda Harrison didn't touch. Everything is still in there. So if you really feel like riding a bike into Brandywood, you're in luck."

She grimaced. "To be honest, I haven't ridden a bike in about ten years. At least, not one that wasn't stationary."

"Well, you know what they say about riding a bike." Dan shrugged. "It's pretty much used as the prime example of hopping back on and doing something again."

Her lips pursed in a smile. "Is this your way of getting out of taking me into town?"

He crossed his arms. "Hell, no. I'll go with you. Any breakfast my sister makes is going to be better than the cereal I have sitting in the cupboard. Besides, I want to see if she can cater some breakfasts here next week when your guests arrive, since I'm technically supposed to be a B&B. But I have dibs on the bike with the basket in the front."

She cocked her head to the side. Was he being serious?

Within minutes, Avery found herself whizzing down the streets of Brandywood, heading away from the lake and toward the town. Dan had been right: getting on the bike had been easy. At first, she'd worried she wouldn't know how to get on and off—or even balance—again. But it came back to her quickly.

With the cool air of morning breezing against her face, Avery fought the urge to close her eyes as she coasted down a hill. Her gaze focused on Dan, who rode in front of her, and she threw her head back with a laugh. He really had taken the bike with the basket, and each time she saw it bobbing in front of him, she couldn't help wondering if he'd done it just to make her smile.

The Dan she'd known had a surprisingly playful and gentle side—something that didn't seem to fit with his height and mountain man beard. He had to be at least six-two or three. He heard her laughter and turned back with a wry grin, then honked twice on the old-fashioned bike horn.

She pedaled harder to catch up to him. "You're quite the vision on that bike. You look like you belong in an old musical— like *Oklahoma* or something."

"Ohhhhhhhhhhhhhhhklahoma, where the wind blows . . ." Dan gave a deep, throaty laugh. "I forgot my bonnet at home."

She guffawed. He knew the music. Of course he did. And he had a good singing voice. "You're into musicals?"

"Good God, no. I could lose my reputation with gossip like that." Dan wrinkled his nose. "But I grew up watching all of them with my sister, especially when my mom wanted me to help with her."

Mom.

Crap. She'd forgotten to call her own mom last night.

Maybe it was better. She had no idea how to tell Mom about the mess at the Serendipity. But she'd have to think of something sooner rather than later. Mom was coming up from Tampa in a handful of days—before Bryan. She wouldn't be happy to find out about the Serendipity. Or to see Dan again.

She'd worked so hard to get back to a good relationship with Mom. Dan being in the picture in any way was a threat to that. For the first time since she had been in her early teens, Mom had moved away from being overbearing and untrusting to actually being someone Avery could talk to. Of course, she couldn't go to Mom with problems about men or tell her about some of the more irresponsible things she'd done, but that's what Erika was for anyway.

But Mom liked Bryan. Or at least, she liked who Avery was as a result of dating Bryan. For so long, Avery had dreamt of having that sort of relationship with Mom—something more akin to a friendship. One where Avery finally had approval.

Tires crunched near them, and she glanced over her shoulder as a truck took a wide berth as it zoomed around. One thing she'd always loved about Brandywood was how polite people were here. She couldn't imagine riding a bike in some of the places she'd lived, where people actively resented cyclists—Bryan among them.

They turned their bikes onto Main Street, and Avery's heart lightened. She loved this town so much. From the old historic-looking stone buildings on Main to iconic buildings like Yardley's Pub and Bunny's Café, which had been there since before she was born.

For a couple of summers, her parents had been forced to come early, and she'd gotten to see the way Brandywood did Fourth of July, which was amazing. From parades to fireworks over the lake to hot-dog and apple-pie-eating contests, the whole thing just smacked of small-town Americana. And she loved every bit.

Brandywood had always been the one thing everyone in her family could agree on. Even after her parents had divorced, they each had continued coming here. It meant two weeks in Brandywood for Avery for a few years. Once Dad and Tina had gotten married and they'd had the twins, Avery couldn't help feeling like the odd member out of Dad's new family. And she didn't exactly fit in with twins twenty years younger than her. She'd started skipping lake week with her dad about seven years ago, and she wasn't sure he even noticed.

The worst part of it was that it was one of the few times of the year she ever got to be around her sisters. *Did they miss seeing their big sister, or had they forgotten about her, too?*

She gripped the handlebars tighter, the scent of baking bread and freshly cut grass filling the air. Dan led her to the main parking lot at the far end of Main Street, and they jimmied the bikes onto the bike rack.

As they started off, Avery hesitated. "Shouldn't we lock them up?"

Dan gave her a shrug. "It's Brandywood. You can leave a bike there for a month, and no one will take it."

He's not wrong.

She could visualize the way Bryan's eye would twitch at Dan's blasé attitude toward it, though, and she held back a smile.

Dan ran his hand through his hair, which had flattened from the bike helmet. "By the way, I have some bad news."

Her gaze traced the lit purple sign on a small local tarot place. "What's that?" She wasn't sure she wanted to hear it.

"I haven't found the key to the storage unit yet. The kid I have working for me was looking for it for about three hours and . . . nothing."

"You were a cop. Is there a way you can pick the lock?"

Dan's lips curled in a smile. "A cop, not a robber." He shrugged. "Yeah, I can probably hire a locksmith. Or see if I can cut the lock off. I just don't want to damage the door, or the storage facility won't be happy."

"Maybe we can all go up there after breakfast. Erika and I could help you move some things." She smiled as they slowed in front of the bakery, emblazoned with the sign *Sweet Escapes*. "I don't think they had opened this place when I came last summer. Although, we had to cut the trip short. We only made it to town twice. Bryan got called back to take part in an important surgery."

That and the fact that most places they went, Bryan ended up looking for a grocery store with a good selection of organic foods and just did his own thing. On their first date, she'd thought he was so thoughtful to pick the restaurant and make a reservation, but it turned out to be one of the few restaurants in San Diego where he'd actually eat anything.

"Your folks still come here for vacation, then?" Dan held the door open for her, and the sweet scent of cinnamon and chocolate floated out of the bakery.

Before Avery could answer, a blond little boy called out, "Uncle Danny!" and came racing toward the door, his arms outstretched.

Dan caught his nephew in a bear hug and swung him around, a wide grin on his face. "Colby. I didn't expect to see you here this morning." He set the boy down, then ruffled his hair.

"He's been waking up at four all week," an equally blonde woman said, popping up from behind the counter. She wore a cream-colored apron with the bakery's logo embroidered on the front, her hair tied up in a messy bun. "Jason has Blake this week, so I've been bringing Colby so he doesn't wake his brother at the ass crack of dawn and Jason can get some sleep."

This must be Dan's sister. Even though she didn't look exactly like her brother, the repartee was there, just like Dan had with his brother the day before. Dan's sister went back to adjusting a tray of cinnamon rolls behind the glass display case, and Dan squatted in front of Colby. "Why have you been getting up so early?"

Colby shrugged. "I don't know. I just wake up." He tugged at Dan's shirt. "Can you take me to the playground?"

"Aw, I wish I could, bud. But I have to help this nice lady with a big project at Uncle Danny's new place." Dan squeezed Colby's shoulder. "How about you guys come by this weekend?

We can take the boat out on the lake. Maybe even do some tubing."

"Yeah! Can we, Mommy? Please?" Colby gave his mother a bright, hopeful look.

Dan's sister straightened again, then set both hands on the counter. She quirked a brow at Dan. "Maybe. I have to talk to Daddy. How about you go back to sorting those sugar packets you dumped out earlier? It's going to get busy here soon, Colbs."

As Colby raced away once again, Dan's sister came out from behind the counter, wiping her hands on her apron. "Next time, ask me before you put the idea in his head," she hissed. She still wore a smile, though. "Now he'll be asking me about it a hundred times." She stopped near them, then held out her hand to Avery. "Hi, I'm Jen."

Avery couldn't help liking Jen instantly. She seemed warm and welcoming but also down-to-earth. She shook Jen's hand. "Avery Moretti. You have a beautiful place. It's so cozy."

"Avery . . ." Jen ducked her chin, giving Dan a quick look. "Thanks, I think so, too. I'm lucky, really. And it's nice to meet you."

Had Dan mentioned her to his sister years ago? Her reaction indicated that he had. But if that was the case, it was likely Jen wouldn't end up being so welcoming after all.

Dan cleared his throat. "Avery is getting married at the Serendipity in a couple of weeks. It turns out there was a mix-up and Ken Harrison didn't put it on the books. She and her friend are staying there, but we don't have a chef yet."

"Oh, you're staying there?" Jen drew her head back, her eyes shocked. "Isn't it completely empty?"

"I slept in a sleeping bag last night," Avery answered with a grimace, rubbing her shoulder.

"Sounds miserable." Jen moved back toward the counter.

"As soon as Dan is operational, I'm planning on helping him with breakfasts and baked goods, but I didn't think it would be this soon."

Dan followed his sister, leaving Avery to catch up to them slowly, feeling like the odd person out. "Yeah, I was actually going to ask you about that. I didn't know if maybe you could try to cover breakfast for the rest of this week and next—until Avery's reservation ends."

Jen hesitated. "Delivered?"

"I could come pick it up."

Jen pulled a pad out from beside the register. "I could. What are you looking for—breads and pastries and fruit?"

Dan glanced at Avery. "What do you think? What type of breakfast foods do you want for your guests?" He tugged a catering menu out from behind the counter as though he was familiar enough with the bakery to do so.

"Yeah, that would be great," Avery managed, flipping open the menu. "There's so much to choose from."

"Would you want coffee and juice, too?" Jen asked, scribbling on her pad.

As they continued talking, Avery looked from Dan back to Jen, and a strange apprehensive feeling rose in her chest. *Wow, he's being nice.*

She didn't want to take that the wrong way. Dan had always been nice to her, really. But they'd never been very good at being just friends. From the get-go, their relationship had been a deep dive into emotions she'd never experienced. And it had been physical.

Don't think about that.

He's not being a friend to you right now. He's being a business owner who's in a tight spot.

She twisted her engagement ring, pushing the diamond around her finger with her thumb. Was she being naïve to think she and Dan could have a friendly relationship? Sure, they'd hurt each other, but she felt strangely comfortable around him, even after all these years.

But it had been so long ago. *You're not imagining the lightness you feel around him, though, are you?*

"Avery?" Dan's voice cut into her thoughts.

She jerked her chin up. "Sorry. I was lost in thought. What was that?"

"What're you having today?" Dan asked.

She scanned the chalkboard menu behind Jen. "Are you open for customers yet?" There wasn't anyone else there yet.

"Absolutely." Jen smiled again, putting away the notepad. "Normally I open at seven, but I'm handling the breakfast catering for the film crew in town, so I've pushed my hours back so that I open at eight. But that doesn't include family." She winked at Dan.

Their relationship gave Avery a jealous stab in her gut. She'd always longed for siblings when she was growing up. Then when she'd finally gotten them, she was already in college. And as much as she tried to lavish Madeline and Vivienne with attention, they were more like nieces than sisters. She couldn't hang out with them in an adult capacity.

As Avery ordered a few oatmeals, fruit cups, and black coffees to go, her phone rang.

Bryan.

She'd never sent the text message she'd typed up, for fear of waking him. It had only been thirty minutes since then, which meant it was *very* early in San Diego. Had he slept at all?

"Hey, babe."

"Avery, what the hell? Where have you been?" Bryan's voice was loud in her ear. She pressed the button several times to lower the volume, giving Dan a quick glance. He appeared to be studying the catering menu his sister had given him. Had he heard Bryan?

"I'm so sorry. I got your messages this morning, and I was going to text you back, but then I wasn't sure if you were up, and I didn't want to wake you." She took out some money to cover her bill and put it on the counter, then slipped out the door.

"I was one hundred percent awake. How in the hell did you expect me to sleep with you not answering the phone? And the main line to the Serendipity is out of service, by the way. I tried to call them."

"Yeah, I have no idea why I didn't get any notifications until this morning. Service is randomly spotty. It's the mountains. You remember how it was last year."

"I don't remember any problems with cell service last year. And that's one thing I always pay attention to."

Avery rolled her eyes. She clearly remembered Bryan complaining the entire time that he could barely get a signal, even when she had full bars of service. But he was annoyed with her right now, and it wasn't the time to argue. They'd both been under so much stress lately with the wedding planning and his job that she'd been trying to practice letting things like this go.

"I'm sorry you couldn't get any sleep. I promise you if I die, you'll be the first person to know."

"Not funny." Bryan let out a displeased grunt. "I'm worried about you because I love you, you know. I'm allowed to get concerned when my fiancée goes missing in action. You're important to me. What do you have on the books for today?"

"Meeting with the caterer around lunch. And then, um, just going through the grounds with the owner of the Serendipity. And hopefully looking for some of the wedding furnishings."

She felt bad stretching the truth. But Bryan didn't need to stress about this yet. And if anything, she'd learned early in their relationship that sometimes the best way to handle him was with those little white lies of omission. God knew she'd had years of practice with that.

"Sounds exciting." Bryan sounded like he was stretching. "I have to get going and get some climbing in before work."

"Okay, have fun. Love you." She could practically see him chalking his hands. He'd set up a climbing wall in their basement to get his "daily dose" of climbing in. His ritual included an hour before work and an hour after work to unwind. When they'd first moved in together, Avery hadn't loved his routine, but now she sometimes joined him if he was okay with company. Climbing the same routes on an eight-foot-high wall was less than challenging, and she didn't know why he enjoyed it, but at least they got to spend that time together.

"Love you, too. And don't forget to check in. Oh, by the way. Did you get the message about my mom? She was really concerned about the menu I sent her to look over. Make sure the caterer is giving you some decent gluten-free options."

Caterer. Avery scrunched her nose. Something she didn't feel like dealing with. "I will."

They said their goodbyes, and Avery clicked off the phone call, feeling more jittery than she had before. Bryan's stress levels were getting to her. He'd wanted a small elopement at the courthouse months ago, and she was the one who had insisted they do something big there at the lodge. Would he want to cancel everything when he found out just how badly plans were going?

The bells rang on the bakery door behind her, and she turned to see Dan carrying a few paper bags and to-go coffee dispenser in his other hand. "Ready?"

"Wow, that fast?" How could Jen have made everything to order so quickly? Bryan's voice rang in her ear: *microwave.*

"Yeah, Jen had extras from the catering order for the film crew, so she set us up with some good stuff."

Oh. Avery instantly felt bad for her snap judgment. Jen had been nothing but nice. Why did her brain go to such negative thoughts so quickly these days? "One second. Let me go thank her," Avery said, then pushed past him to go back into the bakery.

Jen looked up from behind the counter, then smiled. "Forget something?"

"No, no. I just wanted to say thanks. And it was nice to meet you."

"Can I ask you a question?" Jen set her hands on the counter, leaning forward on her elbows.

Somehow, it felt as if the space between Avery's heart and ribs constricted painfully. *Would Jen tell her to stay away from Dan?* "Sure."

"Why Brandywood? I mean, when I got married, my husband took me on this incredible honeymoon—and there's so much out there. I'm just curious why this would be where you'd have your wedding, especially with the place like it is."

A cool sense of relief spread through Avery's lungs, and she smiled. She glanced out the window, spotting Dan waiting just beyond the doorway with the bags. "I don't know. Something about it just feels like home."

Jen scanned her gaze for a flash, then grinned. "That's a good reason."

Avery rejoined Dan outside, feeling as though she'd passed some sort of test. Or maybe she was making it all up.

Avery fell in step with Dan, which was hard to do with his stride being so much longer than hers. Every person who Dan passed greeted him by name. By the time they reached the bikes, Avery studied him with curiosity. "Do you know *everyone* in this town?"

He shrugged. "I know a fair amount of people. Kind of the nature of being a cop for a while." Dan set the bags into the basket. "Plus, Brandywood isn't that big." Rather than climb on his bike, Dan pulled it out of the bike rack and started walking through the parking lot with it. Avery followed suit, walking beside him.

"That's one thing I've always loved about this place. How homey it feels. Every town I've ever lived in has been so metropolitan, and I've moved so many times by now that this is the only place that feels like home. The Serendipity has been the one constant in my life."

Avery felt a wave of nostalgia coming over her and pushed the feeling down and away. She was probably thinking about it thanks to Jen's question, but she didn't want to tell Dan and make him worry that Jen had asked anything out of line. "Your sister is nice."

"She's great. Speaking of people in Brandywood knowing someone in my family—literally everyone knows her. And most love her. And then there are my other sisters, Laura and Sam. Laura owns and operates the Redding Cabins, which are these amazing family rentals. And Sam's an internationally known photographer."

Avery raised her brows, but her heart warmed at the pride in his face. "Wow, your sisters sound intimidating." Then she peered at him. "The cabins sound familiar. I think some of my guests are staying there for the wedding. Do you think your sister has any cabins available for rent this week that aren't showing up online? It might be smart for us to stay somewhere else until you get some furniture."

"I sent her a text last night. Just in case. She said they're full, unfortunately."

A hiss caught their attention, and Dan's head rose sharply. They were in front of a Victorian house with a white picket fence, and Dan slowed. "Shit. Get on your bike."

"What?" Avery's heart slammed into her ribs. "What is it?"

"I'm serious. Get on, now!"

But Avery froze, scanning the vicinity for trouble. A flash of black and white fur shot out from between the fence slats, a large raccoon heading right for them, teeth bared.

Dan shoved Avery toward her bike, and she wobbled, climbing on as Dan tried to divert the attention to himself. The raccoon pawed at him, hissing as Dan shooed at it. As Avery pulled away from the curb on her bike, the raccoon took a flying leap toward Dan, missing him by inches.

Dan yelped and grabbed a stick to keep it off him, trying to shake it off his tail as he went. Horrified, Avery hopped off her bike and clattered onto the street and against the curb. She rushed toward Dan's bike, reached into the breakfast bag, and grabbed something wrapped in paper. "Here!" She waved the packet at Dan, chasing after him.

Without stopping, Dan took a flying leap over the fence and sprinted toward the house.

Avery tried to follow, but climbing the fence proved to be a bigger challenge than she'd expected, and her pants leg caught on the top of a post. The sound of fabric ripping followed as she fell, catching herself on the garden bed below. "Oomph!" Her cheek hit the dirt as thorns from a rosebush scratched her arms.

She steadied herself, stems snapping as she raced toward Dan. The packet had opened to reveal a breakfast sandwich, which smelled amazing but was limply hanging out of the paper wrapping. Dan pounded on the front door of the house. "Mrs. Washington, open up! I need help with your cat!"

He turned his back to the door, his eyes wide as the raccoon tried to pounce again, then ducked behind a hanging swing on the porch. "Get out of here!"

Avery was on the porch now. "Here—" *How the hell do you get a raccoon's attention?* "You miserable bastard. How about a sandwich?"

The raccoon turned, teeth still bared, watching her intently with its dark, beady eyes, nose twitching.

"You know you want this sandwich, you stupid raccoon. Come on," Avery said in the softest singsong tone she could manage.

She lowered the package to the floorboards of the porch, when a spray of water jetted at her from behind. It was icy cold, and the shock of it made Avery stiffen into an upright position, then jump. "Oh, my God!"

"You kids get off my front porch!" an elderly lady hollered, spraying the hose at both Avery and Dan.

Ten minutes, two hundred dollars in cash to cover the damaged rose bushes, and multiple apologies later, Avery and Dan got on their bikes once again. "You were saying how wonderful Brandywood is?" Dan muttered, pedaling.

Avery let out a peal of laughter. She sucked on a scratch on the back of her knuckle, then started off beside him. "I'm still not sure what the hell just happened. Why on earth were you telling that lady to get her cat?"

Dan glanced back at her and then slowed to be at her side. "Mrs. Washington took it upon herself to feed a local raccoon whom she named Jasper. She also thinks he's a cat. Animal Control tried to take him, and she sued the city. And somehow won. Raccoons can't be pets, but Jasper lives outside and is mostly pretty domesticated. But the critter hates me, so if he notices me around, things don't go so well. This isn't our first run-in."

Avery guffawed, unable to wipe the smile from her face.

Her clothes were soaked through, her hair sticking to her cheek and neck, causing goose bumps on her arms as she rode through the warm summer breeze with the early morning sun on her face.

Dan's wet T-shirt clung to his skin, and Avery couldn't help noticing the outline of muscles underneath. For years, she'd told Erika that her "type" was tall and lean, and she couldn't help wondering if she'd just decided that after that summer with Dan—because that was how she remembered him. She might have to add muscular to that list.

And that's about enough thinking about Dan's body. She demurred her gaze, but the grumpy expression on his face before she looked away made the corners of her mouth curl up.

The entire experience had been equally terrifying and strangely ridiculous.

And she hadn't felt so free in ages.

CHAPTER TEN

THE DOOR to the storage unit wobbled as Dan stopped the Dremel tool, making one last cut. He handed the Dremel to Peyton, then pulled the broken lock free.

Sweat poured down his temple, and he wiped his face with his shirt, too frustrated at the damned lock to feel like celebrating. The lock had been a disc lock, impossible to cut with bolt cutters. He hadn't wanted to, but he'd had to resort to a Dremel and YouTube instructions and hope for the best.

It had taken him an hour.

"Goddamn, that took forever," Peyton said, sipping a frozen slushie he'd gotten at the local convenience store. "Too bad we didn't bring the angle grinder you have back at the lodge. That would have been so much faster. Takes just a couple of minutes with that."

Dan gave him a questioning look. "Angle grinder?" *And why didn't you say something sooner?* He resisted the urge to throttle the kid.

"Yeah, I saw one in your tool shed the other day when you wanted me to get the paint scraper. I only know because my buddy used to buy storage sheds at auction. Never made any money with it, but he did once get this whole unit of nothing but blow-up dolls." Peyton snickered.

Dan gave a dry, half-hearted chuckle to humor him, still stuck on the fact that he had failed to mention he had any experience with cutting disc locks.

Well, that was fantastic. To be fair, he hadn't asked Peyton's opinion of anything when he'd started doing this. And neither did he know what an angle grinder even was. He'd bought all the tools in the tool shed off Brenda Harrison, but unlike Ken, he didn't know what most of them were. Maybe he'd have to ask Garrett to give him a quick lesson.

Dan was thankful he hadn't brought Avery and her friend to witness his embarrassing lack of skill. He'd left them at the lodge, pulling weeds.

He held a smile back, thinking of the way Avery had looked after Mrs. Washington's damned raccoon had chased them. He'd actively tried not to think of her all morning, especially how her wet shirt had been nearly transparent after the incident.

The fact was, even after everything and so much time had passed, he was still physically attracted to her. There was no use denying that. But he certainly wouldn't be acting on it. Avery would soon be married to another man—*and then I'll never have to wonder "what if" I had seen Avery again.* That was a good thing, for both of them.

He tossed the ruined lock on the pavement and then grabbed the handle to the door. Pushing the door up and open, he blinked into the dark space, and a sea of blue tarps caught his eye.

Followed by a tidal wave of mildew.

Peyton covered his nose. "What died in there?"

Dan flipped a light switch and then yanked back a tarp

from what looked like a couch. Colorful mold stained it all the way up to the top of the back cushions. He swore under his breath, feeling sick, both from the sight and the smell of the place. "My hopes and dreams?"

He stepped back, loosening his jaw as he cupped his hands over his mouth. Was it just the couch? Or the other furniture as well?

One by one, they peeled back the tarps to reveal ruined furniture. Without the tarps, the smell was substantially worse. And from the looks of it, not much had survived. Wood and other organic materials weren't any match for this amount of mold. One thing was clear: the storage unit must have flooded. And in all likelihood, it had happened several months ago.

Checking out the full extent of the damage would require pulling out enough furniture to make a path through the stacks of mattresses and bed frames, chairs, nightstands, and dressers —a task Dan hadn't mentally prepared for. Or brought the manpower for. The ancient couches from the living room that Dan had thought to reupholster might be salvageable. Maybe. But they'd have to be re-stuffed at minimum.

He dropped back to a squat, sitting on his heels as he pulled down one more tarp, revealing a water-stained mirror.

What the hell, Brenda?

Had she known the unit had flooded? Selling it to him in this condition would be beyond her, wouldn't it? Even though Ken Harrison hadn't ended up being the best boss in the world, he'd been an honest man. One that was well-liked in town. Brenda wouldn't be such a shit-bag, would she?

Dan pulled the collar of his shirt over his nose, sighing. Peyton waited just outside the storage unit door, catching his breath. "What's the plan?" Peyton asked. "I vote for a bonfire."

"That'd be my preference, too, but only if you can do it here and not get caught." He gritted his teeth as another realization struck him. Insurance wouldn't cover this. They didn't cover losses because of outside water.

Maybe burning it is a good idea.

Great, a few months out of the force, and he was thinking about arson.

Dan's fingers curled into fists. He grabbed a chair close to him and threw it into a pile of ruined mattresses. It bounced off and then landed on its side against some lamps, which fell over with a crash, ceramic bases shattering. Peyton flinched.

Fantastic. The one thing that might have been salvageable.

And this was why he needed to control his anger better.

In twenty-four hours, his life had been completely upended. He hadn't expected the transition into the hospitality industry to go without a hitch, but everything all at once?

His frustration simmered at the surface of his skin, making his muscles ache. He'd been suckered into trying to help Avery as much by his resolution to be a better person as his hope to not have his business fail right out of the gate.

But what had being a better person gotten him?

A relationship with a woman like Melissa, who'd held his nuts in such a tight vise that he'd almost choked.

At least when everyone in town just called him an asshole out loud, he didn't have to pretend to be better. But he'd hurt his family, especially Jen and Colby, that way, and he was determined not to backslide.

Still, he couldn't help imagining taking a flamethrower to this whole storage unit. *Or kicking things around like Chevy Chase when he finally loses it in that Christmas movie.*

He took a few deep breaths, the way they'd trained him to do in that class he'd been forced to take when he'd gotten in trouble for stalking Garrett Doyle a few years ago. Oxygen did help, and the more he forced those deep breaths, the calmer he felt.

Sighing, he turned back to Peyton and stalked out of the unit. "Let's close it up."

The door rattled as Peyton pulled it down. "Shouldn't we put a lock back on it?"

"Why? There's nothing worth saving in there anyway."

The two men headed back to Dan's truck, and Dan climbed in and slammed the door. He sank against the back of his seat, tapping his thumbs on the bottom of the steering wheel.

"What are you going to do?" Peyton asked, grimacing. "Maybe you can clean some of it off with that power washer you got?"

Is he serious? Dan squinted at him, unsure if Peyton could really be that dimwitted or was just trying and failing to be helpful. "I'm not sure more water will help the problem." This wasn't a simple issue of some mold anyway, even if he could take a risk of putting guests on mattresses that had been covered in mold spores—which he couldn't. Everything was wrecked.

He needed furniture—and fast. Outside of buying it, he didn't have a ton of options. Except the best option involved going to visit one of the only people in this town who might hear about Avery and call Dan crazy for helping her: his former best friend, Corbin White.

Dan put the car in Drive and pushed down on the gas pedal.

What other choice is there?

THE EXTERIOR of the warehouse was nicer than Dan had expected—Corbin must have been doing well. Floor-to-ceiling display windows had been added to the front, along with a new electric sign that read "White's Furniture Depot." A separate door had been added for the retail area of the store, but the two large doors still led to the rental area, which was the bulk of the business that Corbin handled.

Dan glanced over his shoulder at Peyton as they made their way inside. "Don't touch anything," Dan warned. The guy had an uncanny ability to break things.

Peyton rolled his eyes. "Yes, Mom."

The sound of approaching footsteps made them look up. Corbin wore a suit that looked tailored—at least, Dan never could find a suit that fit him that well. When they'd been friends in high school, they occasionally showed up to school twinning. There was only so much to select from in the big and tall section of the local stores for teenage boys.

Corbin faltered in his step just briefly, then smiled. "Well, look who it is. Dan Klein."

"Good to see you, Corbin." Dan shoved his hands in the pockets of his jeans, feeling the awkwardness of being in the company of someone he'd once felt he shared the bond of brotherhood with.

Then again, there were plenty of people he'd feel awkward around these days.

Corbin nodded, then held a hand back toward the display floor. "Why don't we walk on back to my office?"

They started toward the back of the warehouse. "It looks like things are going really well for you here," Dan said. *Why is it always so hard to string two words together with Corbin nearby?*

"Yeah, this summer has gone particularly well, thanks to Eli Parker. His production company has rented and bought a ton of stuff from me." Corbin said it casually, but Dan caught the undercurrent. Corbin knew how much Dan had bickered with Eli and Garrett in school. But he had to know Dan and Garrett had buried the proverbial hatchet—didn't he? Maybe he didn't care enough to keep up with that sort of thing either.

"Well, I'm happy for you. You deserve it."

"There's a loaded word if I ever heard one. No one really gets what they deserve, do they?" Corbin's dark face was shadowed, and Dan stopped short.

If Corbin found out who I'm trying to help, he'd only hate me more, wouldn't he?

A crash sounded behind him. Dan whirled back to see Peyton straightening himself from the end table he'd tripped on. A decorative stack of antique books lay on the floor.

Dan went over to Peyton and picked up the books, then placed them back on the table. He gave Peyton a nod toward the door. "Why don't you wait for me in the truck?"

He turned back to Corbin's amused look. "Your protégé?"

"More like my sole employee. And I was never that clumsy. Kid trips on his own feet."

"You were never that graceful either." Corbin crossed his arms, looking every bit the polished businessman. Hell, he even smelled good, and Dan grew more conscious of the pit stains on his ratty T-shirt.

"So I have a situation where I need to outfit the Serendipity Lodge for just a couple of weeks. There's a wedding happening there the Saturday after next, and the bride needs her guests to have a place to sleep."

"Yeah, I heard you bought that old place." Corbin's eyes glittered. "Heard you're remodeling it, too. Never knew you to swing a hammer. Unless it was into your own damn fingers."

"It's a work in progress." Dan hooked his thumbs into his belt loops. When they'd been in school together, Corbin had frequently laughed at Dan's attempts in shop class. Dan had almost broken a finger with a hammer once. Not that reminiscing about those things felt easy and lighthearted now.

Nothing had ever been the same with Corbin since that party twelve summers ago.

The party that had blown up his life.

"Do you think you could help outfit me? I need the whole place furnished. You have that much in stock for rent?"

Corbin nodded. "Probably. But we require a deposit. Half upfront. Minimum rental period is for a month. And for a place as big as the Serendipity—it's got, what? Five or six rooms?"

"Ten."

"Yeah, that's going to be a bundle. I'll check the inventory, get you a list of what we have, and what we can do for you."

This was going to stretch his budget for furniture much sooner than he'd expected. He nodded, feeling the gnawing worry in his stomach. "Sounds good. Do you rent with the option to buy?" If he was going to drop so much money on this, he may as well have something to show for it at the end.

"Yeah, we can. I'll get you a quote. Oh, and one more thing —we probably can't get a delivery this size together until Saturday. That work for you?"

Saturday. That left four nights of trying to figure out what to do about Avery and her friend. But Dan nodded anyway. "Yeah, that works."

CHAPTER ELEVEN

Dan

12 Years Ago

DAN SANK the basketball through the net off the backboard and fist-pumped as he trotted backward. He threw a grin at Corbin. "Best two out of three?"

Corbin didn't look nearly as pleased with the outcome of their one-on-one. As the two best basketball players on the team, neither of them enjoyed getting beat by the other one. "Someone's in a good mood this morning." He scowled, but his dark brown eyes hinted of humor. "What has you all bouncy?"

"I'm not bouncy." Dan was already sweating and flushed from their game, but heat crept into his cheeks as he swigged from his water bottle. A few drops of water trickled down from the corner of his mouth and sluiced across his neck.

Corbin was watching him warily when he lowered the water bottle. "Spill."

They'd been best friends since the start of high school, when genetics and the school basketball coach had dictated that since Dan and Corbin were tall, they should be on the JV team. Stereotyping had paid off for Coach Hawkes well in that regard.

Dan was so good, he already had visits from college recruiters with the Big Four universities. Which was great, considering he'd never have gotten a scholarship for his academic record.

Dan jogged over to his gym bag and grabbed a towel from it. He wiped the sweat from his face, which was already attracting gnats at this early hour of the morning. They had little time to practice this summer with Dan's work schedule, but Corbin got up early so they could play before Dan went to work. This early in the day, the high school basketball courts were empty anyway. The only people around were a couple playing racquetball on the tennis court and a woman walking her dog around the high school grounds.

He tucked the towel away as Corbin approached. "I may have met a girl."

Corbin grinned, his eyes twinkling. "You're in love." The sarcasm in his voice dripped.

"Har. Har." But Dan couldn't stop thinking about her.

Corbin's jaw dropped, and he pointed at Dan. "Look at that goofy expression on your face." He clapped his hands together once and bent over laughing. "Smitten like a kitten."

Dan rolled his eyes. "Whatever. I just met her a couple of days ago."

Shrugging, Corbin stored the basketball in his gym bag. "What difference does time make? Some people just fall hard and fast. Nothing wrong with that."

"Yeah, that's your excuse for having a new girlfriend every few months."

"No, my excuse for that is boredom." Corbin shrugged and zipped his bag shut.

"Because you keep looking in all the wrong places. You want someone on the chemistry team, not the cheerleading squad."

"Then the chemistry girls need to start showing up at parties. What am I supposed to do, go knocking on doors in town and asking, 'Hey, are you cute and into chemistry?'" They headed out of the basketball court toward Dan's house. Mom had been making them breakfasts on the mornings they practiced together, which Dan suspected was half the reason Corbin wanted to practice. His mom had died when he was still a toddler, and he'd been raised by his grandfather.

"At least when you go to medical school, a bunch of science dorks'll surround you."

Corbin chuckled. "Don't think I haven't noticed that you've changed the subject from your new girlfriend to me. But check out this perfect segue. You should bring her to Adam's party tonight. You still planning on going?"

Dan nearly tripped. He'd forgotten about the summer bonfire party the captain of the basketball team threw every summer. With Avery taking up his time and his desire to see her and be around her, he'd pushed to the side thoughts of doing anything else. It worked out that Mom had been on the night shift two nights ago and Dad was on a work trip this week—his coming in past curfew had gone unnoticed.

Mom didn't love him going to Adam's parties, but it might be a good excuse to stay out late with Avery once again. If he could get her to go with him. "Yeah, maybe."

"You should. I want to meet whoever has you all distracted. Whoever she is, she's given you *confidence*, man. Dan Klein has a beating heart after all."

Dan shot him a fake warning look. "Don't let the word get

out. I don't need my reputation getting blown up. Speaking of you being smart, I have a question for you."

"We weren't speaking of me being smart, but go on." Corbin quirked a brow. "And that, by the way, is an example of a bad segue."

"Yeah, I don't know what the hell the word 'segue' means. Other than those scooter things the cops used to use to patrol the park."

A garbage truck rumbled past them, then stopped. They went around, stepping past the fuming streams of exhaust. Corbin's older brother, Curtis, had taken a job for the sanitation department this summer. But he didn't appear to be working on this truck, which was probably better. Proud as Corbin was of his brother trying to get his life back together, he didn't love the fact that other guys in the basketball team used bits of information like that to make fun of him. He acted embarrassed about it, even in front of Dan.

"Anyway." Dan cleared his throat, wrinkling his nose at the smell of rotting trash. "The girl—her name's Avery. She's from Florida. And she and her family are at the lodge this week on vacation."

Corbin winced. "Ouch. So she's not going to be around for long."

"Right." Dan didn't want to think about that part. "She's upset because her parents just told her they're getting a divorce and doesn't understand why. She says it came out of left field. But I overheard her father talking to his girlfriend on the phone —who Avery probably doesn't know about."

"Whom."

"Whatever." Dan shook his head, some of his long sandy hair falling in his eyes. "Should I tell her?"

Corbin studied Dan's profile, a skeptical look on his face. "Are you crazy?"

"I just—I feel like she'll be mad if I don't tell her."

"How's she going to know that you know? That's her parents' business. My advice? Stay out of it. That sounds like a lot of drama."

Could he be right? "I know, but—"

"But nothing. You just met this girl. She's leaving in a few days. If you really like her, then just have fun right now. I guarantee you she's not looking for more drama."

Dan drew his lips to a line. He wanted to believe Corbin was right. But as they walked into his house, he couldn't help feeling like Avery would want to know.

You'd want to know, Dan. Tell her.

But what if he ruined everything with her?

CHAPTER TWELVE

Now

"You ᴋɴᴏᴡ. You and Royce might be the only people I'm willing to do this for," Erika said, sitting back on her heels. She wiped the sweat from her brow with her forearm, then peeled a pair of garden gloves from her hand. "And fortunately for me, Royce hates gardening as much as I do."

Avery smirked. Erika's boyfriend would be shocked to see her sitting on the grass, face streaked with dirt. "Yeah, well, I never understood just how serious you were about nature wanting to kill you before we got here."

"Most people think I'm kidding, but I'm not. I told you how things were when Royce and I went to Hawaii. Coconut everything does not make for a happy vacation when you're deathly allergic to it."

Avery wrapped her fingers around a weed and tugged, but the damned thing didn't budge. "Hand me that digger thingy."

Dan had given them a bunch of tools before he'd left, but neither she nor Erika knew the names for most of them. They'd been describing most of them by shape or color and laughing at their incompetence along the way. At thirty, their lack of knowledge about this stuff was embarrassing.

"Hey, did you put sunscreen on before starting out here today?" Erika frowned at her.

"No . . ."

"Yeah, well, you're definitely sunburned. Forehead, nose, and cheeks."

Oh, crap. She hadn't even thought about the possibility that she might burn—she lived in California, for goodness sake. *Oh gosh, please let the sunburn go away before my wedding.*

Avery groaned and then rubbed her forehead. She felt nothing yet, but the movement caused some dirt to drop into her eyes. She blinked, feeling the contact lens in her right eye fold over. "Oh, shit. I think I just messed up my contact."

She sat back in the garden bed where she'd been working, ignoring the tangle of weeds beneath her. Once she'd pulled off her glove, she pushed her eyelid open, trying to remove the folded contact. Slipping it onto her finger, she blinked hard, her eye burning and watering.

"Avery, you should probably get up. Fast." Dan's voice came from a few feet away, and both women looked up at him. Peyton was a few feet behind him, his eyes wide.

Avery stiffened and froze. "Is there a snake near me?" She closed her burning eye, squinting at him with the other.

"No, but you're sitting in a patch of poison ivy."

"Oh, shit." Avery scrambled forward, dropping her contact in the rush. She stopped and turned back. "Shit, where did it go?" She'd completely forgotten to pack extras.

"Where did what go?" Dan asked, coming closer. He pulled her back from the dirt.

She got to her hands and knees. "My contact lens. I forgot to bring extra lenses. Even if I order some today, my eye doctor takes forever to approve the prescription for the online place—if they even have it in stock. I need to find this one."

Erika watched the poison ivy patch warily. "If it's in poison ivy, I'd call it gone. Isn't it some chemical from the planet that makes you itchy? You're not going to want to stick that back in your eye. It's not like you can wash a disposable lens with soap."

"Yeah, your friend is right. It's got urushiol in it—an oily resin. Not good to get that in your eye," Peyton piped up from behind Dan.

Three sets of eyes swung in his direction. "Wow, you know a lot about plants," Erika said.

Peyton shrugged, tossing the hair from his eyes. "I took a few plant biology classes. I want to run a landscaping company someday."

Dan turned and gave Peyton a surprised look. "You want to own a landscaping company?"

"Yeah." Peyton stuffed his hands in his pockets. "Speaking of which, don't you think we should probably hire someone to do this? This is a big project."

"Oh my God, yes," Avery spoke up, rubbing her arms and stumbling away from the garden bed. The last thing she needed was to get poison ivy and have one more thing ruin her wedding. "I will pay for it myself. I have a card for my business that Bryan doesn't—" She grimaced. They didn't need to know she kept a secret credit card from Bryan. Or that he'd been grumbling about wedding expenses.

Dan caught her wrists firmly in his hands and held her arms still. "Don't rub. If you've got poison ivy on your skin, rubbing it is only going to make it worse."

This close to Dan, Avery couldn't help feeling the tug in

her core, like a light tickle of hummingbird wings in her nerves. She met his gaze, her eyes locking with his, her breath caught in her throat.

She could appreciate how caring he was—that wasn't wrong. Still, she tugged her wrists away and stepped back, her skin tingling where he'd held her wrists. *Or maybe it's the poison ivy.* "And you don't have to pay for anything," Dan went on. "I have landscaping budgeted for. You have enough you're probably paying for, with things like wedding bands and food and all."

His words made Avery gasp. *The caterer.*

"Oh, my God—I totally skipped my meeting with my caterer." She checked her watch, looking frantically at Erika. "Shit, shit, they were going to have this huge tasting for me. I bet she called. I just have no cell service—ugh." She scrambled away, digging her cell phone out of her pocket as she made her way around the lodge toward the front of the house.

Erika and Dan were only steps behind her when the notification bells came in. Avery wrinkled her nose. A few missed calls and texts. *Ugh.* Avery dialed the number, lifting the phone to her ear.

"Rosner's Catering, can I help you?" The voice of the woman on the line was cool.

"Hi, this is Avery Moretti. I am so sorry, I had an appointment with you at noon, and I completely lost track of time, and I haven't been getting service, actually. First, I apologize, it's been a crazy trip. And second, I didn't know if I could still come in and—"

The woman cleared her throat. "Yes, I know who you are. Ms. Moretti, your appointment was four hours ago. All the food I had prepared for you is cold. I tried to get in touch with you several times."

Avery felt heat creep into her cheeks, and she turned,

seeking comfort in Erika's gaze. Erika looked just as anxious as Avery felt. She glanced at Dan, and his brows rose expectantly. "I know, and I am so, so sorry. I just—it really doesn't matter if things aren't warm. I would just like to taste them, and I'm certain I know what I want. I can be over to you in,"—she looked down at the state of her clothes—"twenty minutes?"

Terse silence followed. At last, the woman sighed. "All right, but be here in twenty minutes. I close at five."

Before Avery could thank her, the line went dead.

Well, the lady could have been nicer.

Avery stared at the phone in her hand, her heart pounding.

"What'd she say?" Erika asked.

"She said she'll let me do the tasting if I get there in twenty minutes. I'm going to go shower and change in two minutes, and then we can call an Uber—"

"I'll take you," Dan said. He raised his palms up to cut off any protest she might make. "It'll get you there sooner. Rideshare isn't always the fastest around here."

Avery didn't have time to question it—she was already on her way into the lodge.

Erika followed her. "Do you want me to come?" she asked, falling into step beside her. "I won't even shower. I'll just get dressed real quick."

"That would be amazing, thank you. I'm a little scared of this caterer. She wasn't exactly thrilled about me missing the appointment."

Within ten minutes, Avery had showered and dressed and was climbing into Dan's truck with Erika.

"Where we heading?" Dan asked, backing out of the driveway.

"Main Street. I'll just put the GPS on, and maybe you can pull in front of the place? I think she said there's two street parking spaces reserved there. You're welcome to come in with us, if you want. It might help to have a local person to smooth things over."

"What's the name? I know every place on Main." Dan steered onto the main road, and Avery sneaked a glance at him from the passenger seat, thankful he was driving. He was calm and composed and somehow had even showered and changed, too. She sort of missed being able to see his face better, though. Behind that wild beard, his serious nature came out more than she remembered.

"Rosner's Catering. Do you know it?" Avery asked. She felt a little sheepish. He'd known the roads in Brandywood by the time they'd met at eighteen. After spending years as a cop, she imagined he'd only gotten more familiar with them. She doubted he ever needed a GPS around here—or would get lost. And there was something incredibly *reliable* about that.

Dan gave a stiff nod. "I know it." His gaze stayed fixed on the road. "It would probably be better if I wait out in the truck, though." He glanced back at Erika. "You doing okay in the back there? Lots of people who aren't from around here complain about car sickness on these back roads."

Erika rubbed her eyes. "I can see why. I'll be fine, though, thanks for asking. Turns out I should have packed my whole pharmacy to come to your wedding, Ave. Between the Dramamine and Benadryl I'll need to survive this town, I may not be awake for the actual ceremony."

That Dan had taken the time to ask Erika about how she was feeling was oddly endearing. She'd forgotten how good he was at noticing details.

Avery gave Erika a sheepish, apologetic look. "I'm so sorry. I promised you two weeks of fun and wedding adventure before you go back to teaching middle schoolers, and instead I'm giving you misery and putting you to hard labor."

"Well, maybe Mr. Local Guide can take us somewhere fun

after this appointment," Erika said, leaning forward and resting her hands on the center console between them. "Because I, for one, have had enough gardening for the day. The beds of my fingernails hurt, which I didn't even know was possible."

Avery glanced down at her own nails. Her manicure was ruined from the yard work, though she'd booked an appointment for a few days before the wedding. "At this rate, I'm going to make quite the bride." She wrinkled her nose, digging through her purse. "I can only see with one eye until Bryan brings my spare lenses. I have a sunburn and scratches from falling in the rosebush. Speaking of which, I should probably put some makeup on for this appointment."

She pulled down the mirror and grabbed a compact from her bag. Erika was right—Avery's face was getting even redder from the sun. "And don't worry, Dan, you don't have to take us anywhere. We've already completely blown up your plans for the next couple of weeks."

Dan gave a light chuckle. "Ah, it's good. All I would be doing right now is swinging a sledgehammer and eating pizza or mac and cheese. I can take you all out. If you're interested."

Am I interested? She felt that knot of tension around her heart again and studied her own face in the mirror as she continued applying makeup. She was intrigued by how much easier it was to be around Dan than she'd imagined it would. If she'd known they'd still get along so well, she would have looked him up years ago. And now it was too late for—

Stop, just stop. She could control any attraction she had to him, after all. And what he was offering was friendship, nothing more. She'd never been very good at navigating friendships with guys. They either turned into something more, or the friendship just ended because she didn't want it to turn into something more.

Tad had been a comfortable friendship, precisely because

that wasn't an issue—but even his friendship had turned out too complex for her to handle, because of Bryan.

Realizing she'd let too much time pass without answering, Avery said, "Oh—um. Yeah, that would be good."

Erika laughed, slugging her softly on the shoulder. "You're such a freaking space cadet. The only person I know that can totally stop paying attention and then randomly realize someone asked her a question—and answer it—five minutes after everyone in the conversation has moved on."

Avery finished applying lip gloss and blew her a kiss. "What can I say? My brain works at a delay."

They turned onto Main Street a few minutes later, and Dan pulled into a parking spot in front of a cute shop among three-story stone row houses. As he stopped, his gaze transfixed on the front steps of the storefront, where a leggy blonde stood in front of the door. "Ah, fuck," he muttered in a low voice.

Avery felt her stomach drop as she unbuckled her seat belt. "What's wrong?"

"My ex-girlfriend. Melissa Rosner." The muscles in Dan's forearms were taut as he gripped the steering wheel. "She owns the catering company. I didn't want to say anything—figured I'd just slip away and let you handle things. But she's obviously seen me now."

The blonde had stiffened at the sight of the truck, and she set her hands on her hips, glaring at them. *Ex-girlfriend?* Avery felt the urge to flee, but she took a breath, trying to talk sense into her own flight instinct. Just because this woman had a history with Dan, didn't mean she'd take it out on Avery. After all, Avery was just an unconnected stranger.

Dan didn't look all right, though, and that concerned her. She gave him the most reassuring look she could. "Don't worry, it'll be fine. You don't have to talk to her. We won't be long. Thanks so much for bringing us."

But as Avery closed the door to the truck, Erika behind her, she could practically feel the frosty chill Melissa directed their way. Avery held her breath, wishing she'd had more time to blow-dry her hair rather than throw it in a wet bun. "Hi, Ms. Rosner? Avery Moretti." Avery approached with her hand outstretched.

Melissa stared at Avery's hand but didn't shake it. Her eyes narrowed further. "Oh, my God." Melissa covered her mouth. "I get it now. You're *that* Avery. The bitch that ruined him."

CHAPTER THIRTEEN

Dan didn't have to hear Melissa's comments to know it wasn't going well. For one, Avery and Erika hadn't made any further progress into the catering shop. And then there was that look on Melissa's face, which he knew well. Much as he didn't want to face Melissa right here, he gritted his teeth and unbuckled his seat belt. Swinging open the door to his truck, he stepped out. "Everything okay?"

Melissa's gaze snapped to him. "You get back in your truck."

Avery's lips had parted, a stunned expression on her face as she looked back and forth from Melissa to Dan. "Just checking to make sure you're not displacing your feelings about me on someone who has nothing to do with what happened to us," Dan said smoothly to Melissa, setting his hand on the door.

"Nothing to do with us? Are you kidding me?" Melissa gawked at him. "She's Avery. *The* Avery? If it hadn't been for her, you wouldn't have such horrible trust issues with women. No matter what I did, I lived in the shadow of that selfish little bitch."

"I think we should go." Avery stepped back, closer to Erika. "I am so sorry for missing our appointment, but clearly this isn't the best time."

Melissa now directed all the anger in her posture toward Avery. "Yeah, you should be sorry. Because it turns out I won't be able to cater your wedding now. Without the tasting, you're technically in breach of contract, so tough."

Feeling his anger roiling, Dan slammed the door and stepped onto the sidewalk beside Avery. "She's got nothing to do with us, Melissa. Don't take your anger with me out on her."

"She's got everything to do with it." Melissa crossed her arms. "And you stay right there, Dan. I don't want to get another restraining order."

"Well, considering the judge didn't grant you one last time, I wouldn't call it *another* one." Dan glared, and he felt Avery shift uncomfortably beside him. He really shouldn't take her bait, but he couldn't help himself, wanting to offer a defense for himself before Avery and her friend got the wrong impression. "Considering that I let you get away with stealing my dog just to be rid of you, you're lucky I didn't take you to court. And speaking of the law, you can't legally cancel Avery's wedding. You told her it was okay to show up late for the tasting."

Melissa dipped her chin. "Prove it." She took another step up, opening the door to the shop. "And you know what, it's fine. Because I'll just refund her deposit, less an administrative fee for the tasting. If I had known who she was, I never would have booked her wedding. Now fuck off." Melissa turned and walked inside, and the bolt clicked shut.

Stunned silence hung between Dan and the women. Erika stepped shoulder-to-shoulder with Dan. "Wow, she's a piece of work."

"That's an understatement." Dan snuck a glance at Avery,

trying to gauge her reaction. She was still staring at the door, blinking. "Avery, I'm so sorry—"

"You told her about me?" Avery turned toward him, confusion in her eyes. "Just what did you say?"

Surprised that Avery seemed more concerned about that than just having lost her wedding caterer, Dan rubbed the back of his neck. "I-I didn't say *that* much. She was always trying to play an armchair psychologist. Figure out what was wrong with me." He'd told Melissa about that brief summer romance as a teenager and what it had led to because she'd demanded to know about his dating history, but she'd always made a bigger deal of it than he'd imagined she would, blaming it as the start of his "inability to be in a mature relationship."

"You've had so much toxicity in your life, baby. That's why you can't commit. Why you're so attached to whatever family you feel you can cling to—even though they treat you like you're the one to shit on. I get it, I really do. What your dad did to you all—dumping your mom and leaving her while she was pregnant with you—that leaves a permanent mark. Because deep down inside, you know you're not a Klein, no matter what. And we need to talk about that, get to the root of all of this shit so we can forge forward together."

Dan hadn't seen at the time how much damage Melissa was doing to his relationship with his family. Whatever reason she had to feel threatened by them and by past relationships like Avery, that was on her. And even though his family had his back when he'd finally found his way out of Melissa's life, he'd lost the other family he'd built in the police force.

His thoughts were broken by Erika, who watched both him and Avery with a curious expression. "Well, as the only person here who apparently isn't grappling with something that is clearly a lot deeper than cold canapes, can I suggest we reconvene somewhere else? Literally anywhere other than in front of this psycho's shop. Preferably somewhere with alcohol?"

"Maybe just some carry-out?" Avery sounded strangely tired. "We can stop by a liquor store, too. I'm just feeling a little spent." She didn't wait for Dan and Erika and hurried back to Dan's truck.

Dan exchanged a look with Erika. "What'd I do?"

"I don't think you did anything." Erika shrugged. "I mean, other than be someone she once had feelings for. And yes, she told me about you two—we've been best friends since kindergarten—so I'm not sure why she's making a deal about you telling your ex about her. She's probably just upset about the catering thing." Erika tossed her jet black hair over her shoulder. "What's good for carry-out?"

"Bunny's." He got her signal loud and clear—she didn't want to talk about Avery with him. *That's fair.* And it was a relief, too, knowing Avery had someone like Erika in her life. The few interactions he'd witnessed between Avery and her fiancé on the phone had planted a strange worry in the back of his mind. The guy had been yelling at her this morning when he'd called, and it had been clear Avery tried to turn the phone volume down so Dan wouldn't hear. He'd watched her whole body shrink when talking to the douche, something Dan had seen on occasion over the years on the force.

He wasn't in any position to meddle or question Avery about it, but Erika would. And she seemed like she had a good head on her shoulders.

Dan climbed back into the truck and glanced at Avery, who was staring at her cell phone. "You okay?" She had to be feeling like she was going to crumble under the strain of the last few days. Nothing she'd planned seemed to be working out.

"I haven't figured that out yet." Avery was strangely quiet

as they left. In the cab of Dan's truck once again, she asked, "What happened to your dog?"

The last thing Dan wanted to discuss was Milo, but he didn't want to tell her that either.

"Um, when Melissa and I broke up, I came over to get him, and she'd changed the locks." And then Melissa had recorded him on her doorbell camera when he'd gotten angry and pounded on the door and kicked over a planter.

As though stealing Milo hadn't been enough.

"That's horrible." Avery had paled. "Isn't that illegal? Can't you petition the court or something?"

"Unfortunately, she bought him for me when we moved in together. I was the one who took care of him and spent time with him, but that's a lot harder to prove in court." Dan stared at his hands, surprised to see them steady. Losing Milo had been the hardest part of all he'd gone through in the spring, and talking about it—to anyone—hadn't been easy. That he could say anything at all to Avery was strangely comforting.

"So awful. What type of dog is he?" Erika asked from behind them.

"Boxer. Fawn-colored with a black face." Thinking about Milo with Melissa made him want to punch something, and his fingers curled into a fist. "Sweetest damn dog. He was the best thing about that relationship." Milo had made life better whenever he came home from a hard day of work. Especially with the line of work Dan had been in. Dogs had a way of balancing the scales when humanity got especially ugly.

"I have a little Maltipoo at home. Cutest little fluff ball. Her name is Pixie," Erika said, then pulled out her phone to pull up a picture. A smile spread through her face. "I would be devastated if I lost her. But it sounds like you need to do something legally, Dan. Melissa's clearly a bully, and she shouldn't be allowed to get away with stealing your dog."

Dan grimaced. "Unfortunately, not everyone else sees that side of her. In fact, *that* Melissa you met back there? I don't know that I've ever seen her act that way in front of anyone, except me. So, really, I'm probably to blame for that. There are plenty of people in this community who love her." *And I'm the one who has the reputation as a bully.*

"Given that she clearly has a dark side, I think we should all breathe a gigantic sigh of relief that she won't be catering the wedding." Erika sat back and crossed her arms. "She seems like the type of person who wouldn't think twice about spitting in your food."

"Not sure about that, but I *can* tell you she does a fair amount of microwaving."

Avery rubbed her eyes. "Don't even remind me. I have no place for my guests to sleep, no wedding venue, and now no food. Remind me how any of this is going to be okay?"

"Do you think your sister could help?" Erika asked Dan.

Dan shook his head. "She has the skill set, but she's pretty slammed right now. And she only does breakfasts because she's more of a bakery than anything else. She didn't want to set up too much competition with Bunny, who was her mentor. She might bake you a cake or do desserts if you need, though. I can ask. I'm sure she'll be willing to make something like that work."

"Or you could rent a bunch of tents for people to sleep in and then do a sunrise ceremony and serve breakfast foods?" Erika said.

Avery let out something that sounded like a mixture of a choked laugh and a sniffle. "I have to admit that's sounding like a more appealing option by the minute." She covered her face with her hands.

Four hours later, they were on the back patio of the Serendipity, watching the sunset, a few empty wine and beer bottles scattered among the trash of the carry-out containers they'd brought back from Bunny's. Dan couldn't help feeling like they'd accomplished little as he looked out at the lawn and the half-dug garden beds and too-long grass, but Erika was right. Alcohol had helped.

He felt practically cheerful.

Avery had let her hair down, and it cascaded over her shoulders as she stretched bare feet out in front of her into the grass, her red cheeks looking brighter with the ruby tone of the sky. Dan had brought out a speaker to play a local country radio station, and Avery swayed, closing her eyes, looking relaxed for once.

She looks beautiful.

"Ugh, I'm going to wake up tomorrow with the worst headache in the history of headaches," Erika said, upending the bottle in front of her. Only a couple of drops dripped out, and she wrinkled her nose. "Remind me again why we drank straight from the bottle?"

"Because we didn't have cups," Avery said cheerily, her eyes still closed.

Beer had been a much better choice. Dan still couldn't stomach red wine too well, and a couple of glasses had the tendency to make him fall asleep. He'd never been much of a drinker, even when he was younger. He didn't like the loss of control that came with getting drunk.

Erika stood. "Three cheers for not missing wine night." She gave Dan a slight bow. "And congratulations to you, Dan, for being the first non-member of our club to attend one of our wine nights. I may have to keep this one from Royce when we talk. He's still mad that I won't let him join me. Even though you technically drank the wrong type of fermented plant, so it might not count." She winked at them both. "Goodnight. I'm going to call Royce, then go snuggle up with an air mattress.

Don't stay up too late, bride-to-be. We have lots of destroying of your wedding to do tomorrow."

Avery cackled, wiping tears of laughter from the corners of her eyes as Erika slipped inside. "I shouldn't be laughing at that, because it really wouldn't be funny if I weren't tipsy, but it's sort of true, isn't it?"

Dan sipped his beer and sat on the edge of the patio beside her. He'd have to get patio furniture out here, stat. That he hadn't enjoyed many nights like this since owning the place was a damned crime, really. "I'm glad you're able to laugh about it at all."

She gestured with her palms up, shrugging. "What else am I going to do about it? Clearly, something is trying to intervene to ruin my wedding." Her expression grew more serious. "Maybe even stop me from getting married at all."

The cautious part of his brain threw up a few flares, and he set his beer bottle beside him. "You think so?"

"I don't know." She sighed, then took another pull from her wine bottle. "Do you ever wonder if stuff like fate and destiny and all—if it's real? What if there's some larger cosmic force at play here, systematically dismantling everything I planned until there's nothing left?"

He was the last person who should offer advice on this, but he cleared his throat. "If, at the end of this, even if there is no lodge and there are no guests and there's no food, or flowers, or music, as long as there's a man who loves you and wants to marry you standing there, waiting to spend the rest of his life with you, what difference does it make?"

Avery turned toward him, and her eyes met his. If they hadn't been this close, he might not have noticed the almost imperceptible widening of her eyes, the way her gaze lingered. Dan felt his breath catch in the back of his throat, and his heart gave a giant *thump* in his chest, painful and strong.

You still have feelings for this woman.
You dumb lug.

He'd thought he could get this close, listen to her like he'd done years before, yet stay impartial and unaffected. "Do you have worries about getting married?" he asked in the most neutral tone he could muster. Their gazes were still locked, making him feel uncomfortably exposed, as if she had read his thoughts just moments ago.

Her shoulders bunched. "I don't know. It just . . . it all happened so fast, you know? We got engaged after dating four months, and everyone keeps asking me what the rush is, and it's not . . . it's not that there's a rush. Bryan is . . . he's just intense sometimes. And when we started dating, that was one thing that drew me to him—his passion for things. Ironically, he has a way of tempering my impulsiveness. I finally feel like I'm in an adult relationship with someone who has all his ducks in a row. And anyway, if you find the person you're meant to be with, then why not get married? When you know, you know."

Yet somehow, it sounds like she doesn't know.

He couldn't let the foolish notion of hope take root here. What was he going to do? Make a play for a woman who was engaged? He'd never be able to live with himself. No, their time had passed. The time had long since passed for unresolved feelings. Entertaining them would only end badly, especially if Avery had completely moved on. Which she probably had. But if Avery had concerns she wasn't vocalizing, she might need a friend or a listening ear.

Then he remembered the way Avery's fiancé had yelled at her on the phone and the multiple apologies she'd offered him. "Do you feel respected?"

Avery's fingers tightened around the neck of the wine bottle. "Yeah." Her voice was quiet.

"That's good."

And if she were being questioned at the precinct, he wouldn't have believed her.

He wasn't an expert at relationships, but his parents had a pretty good marriage. He'd never even seen them argue—not that they didn't, of course—but Mom and Dad decided a long time ago they wouldn't ever do it in front of their kids. Which Mom had once later admitted weirdly led to most of their disagreements being resolved by the time they cooled off and talked about it later.

But that was the thing about his Dad. He'd always treated Mom with respect.

"That's what led me to break up with Melissa. I gave myself a hard look in the mirror one day and asked, does this person respect me? And it wasn't easy. Because the disrespect had come in degrees. Isolating me from my friends and my hobbies by telling me she wanted me to spend that time with her. Disrespecting my family by criticizing the way they did holidays and celebrations. I spent most of my sister's wedding hearing Melissa complain she hadn't gotten to spend enough time with me because I was busy with groomsman duties. So, I finally broke up with her."

Avery gulped down another swig of wine, then stood abruptly. She raked her fingers through her hair, staring at the waterline in the distance. "I miss the Adirondack chairs that used to be there."

He blinked at her, confused by her reaction. As though he'd stirred up some memory. Then Avery turned to face him again and she brushed a tear from her cheek. "I'm sorry about your dog, Dan. I didn't say it before, but I'm really sorry. It sounds like things ended badly in that relationship."

"They did." Dan stretched his arms out on the patio behind him and settled his weight on his palms, getting more comfortable. "She got stupid about things, vengeful. I got mad and kicked over a planter on her porch, pounding on the door so she'd let me get Milo back. She took that video to the local news and my chief at the station, then filed for a temporary restraining order, saying she felt threatened. It's not the first time I've lost my temper in a big way before and had a reputation, so most people believed her. And . . . I resigned. But I never, ever did anything ever to threaten her. Not once."

"That's a shame. You seem like you would have been a good cop." She furrowed her brow. "What do you mean you had a reputation?"

Admitting it wasn't his favorite thing, but there was no use trying to hide it. "My sister—she's always been pretty. Had boys chasing her from the time she was in middle school. Warren and I took it upon ourselves to tell them to get lost, so I got a reputation for being a bully."

Not so terrible to confess until he brought up what had happened with Garrett. He dipped his chin, the familiar humiliation burning like acid in his throat. "But then I got into a fistfight with a guy I'd hated my whole life who I thought was interested in Jen. He was a drunk who'd left his fiancée at the altar years before, so I felt justified in keeping him away from her. Especially because she'd just been abandoned to be a single mom by her drug-abusing boyfriend a few years earlier. But it turns out I was wrong about the guy I picked a fight with, and he actually got sober and ended up marrying my other half-sister."

Avery stared at him, her gaze thoughtful. She sat on the grass unsteadily, wrinkling her nose as she realized it was already damp with dew. "I'm sure it was worse living through that, but as an outsider, it doesn't sound like you were so terrible. It sounds like you were trying to protect your sister. That's admirable, even if maybe you took it a little too far."

"Oh, I deserved the reprimand I got for what happened

with my brother-in-law. But I did nothing to threaten Melissa. And that's what bothers me so much about what happened with her. I screwed myself, and I know that. But that people might believe her? I've never laid a hand on a woman. And I know she didn't accuse me of that, but . . ." Dan shook his head, feeling sick.

"Yet you took the risk of driving me to her place today when I needed to get there." Avery tilted her head to the side. "You should have told me. Honestly, I'm glad I don't have to work with her now, even if I don't have a caterer. But you don't have to self-sacrifice like that. I wouldn't want you to."

Her words were strangely ironic, given what had happened between them years before.

Yet he didn't want to go there. Rehashing what had gone wrong between them was too much like peeling back the scab on a cut that hadn't healed quite right.

Avery scooted closer to him, then pulled out a blade of grass. She twirled it between her thumb and forefinger. "Do you ever wonder what would have happened if we'd talked after—"

"Always." *Well, that came out fast.* He was at an unfair advantage here. She'd had a bottle of wine to drink. And neither of them needed to say something they'd regret. "But we were kids, really. What the hell did we know about anything? And we're both different people now. The Avery I knew was scared as hell but still finding her wings. You've flown the nest now, Ave."

She kept twirling the grass, her gaze focused on it. "I don't know. I miss the Avery I found that summer." Lying back on the grass, she said, "That Avery wore colorful clothes and didn't care about getting dirt under her fingernails or jumping into a lake from a rope swing in the dark. That was the summer I felt like I came alive. Maybe I took it a little far afterward . . . I needed someone like Bryan to come along and keep me from being too crazy." She propped herself up on her elbows suddenly. "Is that old rope swing still there?"

The way she's saying it sounds like she wants to go jump from it again.

Dan cracked a smile. "Nah, they pulled it down years ago."

"Damn." She flopped back down again.

Dan felt the muscles in his shoulders getting tight, and he stood and held out a hand to her. "Well, whatever Avery you want to be, I'm sure you can be. Even one who gets tipsy on a random Monday before sunset and then wants to go jump in a cold lake at night. But consider getting some sleep before you make any other decisions, in case morning Avery doesn't agree so much with nighttime drunk Avery."

"I'm not drunk." She took his hand, and he helped her stand. She wobbled, balancing on his arm. "Okay, maybe a bit."

Dan chuckled. Slightly drunk Avery was cute. He missed that spirited and self-confident side she'd shown when they were younger. What had convinced her she'd had it so wrong?

He helped her make her way to the French doors. "You know, as the owner of this fine establishment, I may have to charge you extra for all this five-star service you're getting. No minibar here—nope, you get full bottles of wine. And assistance back to your accommodations."

Avery chortled. "Hilarious."

"Thanks. I'm here all week." Dan smiled to himself. The truth was, Avery made him feel funnier than he often was—she could bring out that side of him that was normally reserved for only the very closest members of his family, like Warren.

But the realization was a double-edged sword, one that cut deeply as he felt the warmth of her touch on his forearm. He'd let her get too close once before.

He'd be a fool to let it happen again.

CHAPTER FOURTEEN

Avery

12 Years Ago

"You and I need to talk about your attitude, young lady." Mom's voice came through the open door of the attached bedroom as Avery finished swiping some mascara on her eyelashes and straightened.

Avery's eyes narrowed at Mom through the mirror. "What attitude?"

"Don't get smart with me. You think I haven't noticed the way you've been skipping out on family time and going off by yourself?"

"Maybe I need some alone time, Mom." Avery shrugged, then put her mascara wand away. She turned to face her mom as she drew closer. Her mom, an older-looking version of her, was already dressed for dinner tonight.

"Well, it's going to stop. We didn't bring you here so you

could spend the vacation avoiding us. Your behavior is incredibly disappointing." Mom set her hands on her hips as she stopped in front of Avery. "And I thought I told you not to bring that blouse? It's too low-cut. I don't know how you convinced your father to let you buy it. And those shorts—for dinner? Seriously? Honestly, Avery, don't you listen to anything?"

Anger flared in Avery's gut. "You know what, Mom, I'm pretty disappointed in you and Dad deciding to blow up my life in the middle of lake week, so maybe you can cut me some slack and lay off my clothes for once."

Mom's eyes widened. Then she raised her hand and slapped Avery across the cheek.

Avery reeled back, holding her stinging cheek. "You hit me!"

"That's enough sass out of you! Now go change. And wipe that gunk off your eyes—you look ridiculous." Mom stepped closer still. "You think your teenage life is so hard? Ask Abuela what it was like to flee Cuba at fourteen with nothing but the clothes on her back. To come to a country with nothing and build the life you enjoy now from the ground up. You're completely ungrateful, kiddo. And you don't know how good you've got it. I'll be downstairs waiting."

Whirling around, Mom stormed out of the room, her high heels clicking down the hallway.

Avery turned to look at her cheek, her eyes brimming with tears. *I hate her.*

She sniffled, then reached for a hoodie, despite the heat. Yanking it down over her head, she left her room and went down the hallway to the room her father had moved into after their "big announcement."

She tapped on the door. "Daddy?"

The floorboards squeaked, and her dad opened the door

moments later. "Avery." His brow furrowed with concern. "What's wrong?"

"Mom slapped me." She swallowed back tears. "And if it's okay with you, I really don't feel like going to dinner again tonight."

Dad hesitated and looked down the hall toward Mom's room. "Were you talking back?"

She gave a meek nod. "But she still shouldn't have slapped me."

"No, I know, sweetheart. I just was wondering what brought it about." Dad frowned and sighed. "Of course you can sit it out. I'll try to smooth things over with her. But you and Mom need to figure out how to work through this stuff. I know it doesn't seem like it, but Mom's having a hard time now, too. This isn't easy on any of us. Maybe you can try to remember that, Ave."

"And when you're not around to smooth things over? Do you have any idea what life is going to be like for me when it's just Mom and me?" The idea freaked Avery out more than she could even process.

"Mom loves you, Avery. She just wants the best for you."

Avery nodded, then left her father's room, not really wanting to talk to him about it anymore. *"This isn't easy on any of us."* Forget that. They were the ones who had made this all difficult. *Why am I the last to hear about their divorce? How did I not see this coming?*

She drew the hood over her head and then made her way down the back stairwell. She didn't want Mom to see her on the way out.

Bursting out the back door, she broke out into a run toward the Sports Shack. She liked Dan, but more than that seemed to push her toward him right now. She needed someone to look her in the eye and tell her she wasn't crazy and it would be all right. Somehow, the world felt easier to face when she was talking to him.

When Dan didn't appear to be at the Sports Shack, the wave of disappointment that followed was tinged with fear. What if he didn't want to see her? For all she knew, he kissed other girls who came around the Serendipity, or even worked there. And it wasn't like she even knew *how* to kiss. She'd kissed exactly one other guy, and it had been the most chaste peck in the history of kisses.

But with the way she'd been all over him, now he probably thought she was really experienced, and maybe even easy.

Then she spotted him. He had a kayak hoisted over one shoulder and was carrying it up from the lake, a trail of water dripping down behind him.

God, he's so cute.

His eyes locked with hers, and he set the kayak down near the boathouse. Wiping the sweat from his brow with the back of his hand, he sauntered toward her. "It's, like, a zillion degrees out. What are you doing in that sweatshirt?"

"Hiding from my mom. Again." She forced a tense smile, then stiffened as she saw his eyes zero in on her cheek.

He pushed the hood back on that side, his fingertips grazing her skin. "What happened?"

I will not cry. "My mom slapped me." She shrugged it off like it didn't matter. "Latina moms. They have tempers. She loves hard, too, though." *Why did she feel the need to defend her mom right now?*

"Not all of them, I'm sure. That's not okay, Avery." He set a hand on her shoulder. "What can I do?"

"Nothing, it's fine." She stuffed her hands in her pockets.

"Is it really, though? I know you said you're close to your mom, but you all seem to not really get along. She shouldn't be hitting you."

"I . . ." *If only it could be simple again.* There had once been a time when everything she did made Mom so happy. So proud. But nowadays, no matter what Avery did, no matter how she tried to do her best, Mom always found a flaw with her. She never just smiled and said she was proud of Avery, the way she used to. She cleared her throat. "Anyway, I'm not going to dinner with them tonight. Want to hang out?"

Dan's blue eyes were unreadable, and his lips twitched as though he was restraining himself from talking. Finally, he nodded. "Yeah, I got off ten minutes ago. And I've been wanting to hang out since you left me on that dock yesterday morning."

She resisted squirming, then stared at the lake. "I just wanted to say . . . about when I kissed you yesterday. I-I didn't mean to give you the wrong impression." She moistened her lips, then tried to find the right words. "I like you, Dan. But I'm not really the type of girl who fools around."

He laughed. "I didn't think you were."

Relief crested in his words. "Okay. Because I've never slept with anyone. And I'm not sure that I'm ready for that. I'm leaving at the end of the week, and then what? We can't date when you're here, and I'm living in Tampa." She halted. "And also, how old are you? Because I'm a senior, but I just had a birthday, and since I was born in August, my parents held me back from starting kindergarten until I was six. I'm actually already eighteen, and I know that could be illegal—"

"I'm eighteen, too." Dan's smile widened. "You talk faster than I can keep up with sometimes, you know that?"

She couldn't help giggling. "I know. My dad always says my brain works faster than my mouth, and my mouth can't keep up." Then she met his gaze. "So you're eighteen? But you're a senior, too?"

He nodded slowly. "Yeah, I got held back because I was a problem child in kindergarten."

She held her hand up. "High-five for being legal adults in senior year."

His hand met hers, but instead of a quick high-five, his fingertips interlaced with hers. The touch of his hand was dizzying, her skin tingling where their hands met.

"Listen, we don't have to do anything you're not ready to do." Dan squeezed her hand. "We can just be friends, if that's what you want."

She nodded. It was probably for the best, but she would miss kissing him. Being around this guy made her want to do things she had never done before. She'd watched one too many of her friends get their hearts broken over guys. As the studious type, she'd never had to worry about that until now. "Friends is good. So where are we off to?"

"Want to go for a hike? There's a really cool trail along the lake that leads to a rope swing over the water. This time of day, I doubt anyone else would be there. And the water is pretty warm. For the lake, anyway."

"That sounds perfect."

She was now glad she'd worn her flip-flops with her outfit. That would make it easy to keep up with Dan.

SOMEWHERE ALONG THE trail to the rope swing, Avery came up for air as Dan's lips pulled away from hers. Her lips felt bruised. They'd been making out for so long, the sun had gone down. The sweatshirt had actually been a blessing in disguise—it gave them a place to lay their heads on the leaves as they tumbled on the ground.

So much for being "just friends."

She tried to catch her breath, panting as Dan's eyes searched hers. "You okay?" he asked.

"Better than okay." She pulled his lips down to hers once again, wanting so badly to tell him she wanted to be with him. But it was crazy. Sleep with a guy she didn't know?

People always talked about "wild and crazy teenage hormones," and she'd laughed at that concept. No guy she'd ever met made her lose her head.

But with Dan's hands cupping her breasts, and his lips and tongue colliding with hers, she wanted to know what it felt like. To be with a guy like that.

She wanted to have sex.

Except, when his hand smoothed down the flat of her belly and brushed against the wetness of her panties, she stiffened. She couldn't lose her head. She couldn't do this yet.

"I'm not—"

Dan pulled his hand away immediately and pulled his mouth back again. "It's fine, Avery." He breathed hard as he sat up. "You never have to worry about me forcing you to do anything you don't want to do."

She grinned, his words making her happier than she'd felt in a long time. "Now take me to that damn rope swing you promised me."

Setting both hands on the log, Dan stayed sitting. "Just give me a second." After a few moments, he stood.

He clasped his hand with hers, then led her through the woods without a word. The moon was full, making the forest seem lit up now that her eyes had adjusted to the dark. "Are you sure you can only stay in Brandywood for a week?" Dan finally asked.

"Five days, actually. I've already been here three." The thought was suddenly depressing. "I don't want to think about that, though. And I want to spend every second you're not working with you, so you better not make plans for anything else."

His fingers tightened. "Don't worry, I won't."

They stopped at last beside the lake. A large oak hung out over the water, a rope swing on a low branch.

The water glistened in the moonlight, rippling in the breeze. She'd never been swimming at nighttime before, even though she'd always wanted to. Her mom had been strict about bedtime for most of her life, but now that she was eighteen, she could stay up later.

And Mom wasn't here right now. For once, Mom didn't get a say.

Avery stood shoulder-to-shoulder with Dan, then he slipped his arm around her shoulder. She leaned against him, sagging her weight into him.

"Thanks for not making a thing about my mom slapping me earlier," she whispered in a soft voice.

"Whenever you want to talk about it, I'm here."

"I want to make her proud. But I'm not sure I'm growing up to be a person she likes very much. And that's really hard."

"She should be worthy of that approval you're seeking, Avery. You're amazing."

Amazing? Avery stood there for a moment longer, and Dan pressed a kiss to her temple. Her heart fluttered. It was hard to be sad when she was standing beside him.

A wild, adventurous feeling rose in her. She pulled away, then tugged her shirt off. *How's that for a low-cut top, Mom?*

Wiggling out of her shorts, she threw a laughing grin at Dan as she stood in her bra and underwear. "See you in the water!" Then she grabbed the rope swing, took a flying leap, and plunged in.

CHAPTER FIFTEEN

Avery

10 Months Ago

AVERY LEANED across the seat and held out a pack of gum. "Here, take one. Please." Bryan still looked sick, his features drawn and serious. The plane was getting ready to descend, and the air pressure change was likely to affect him.

Bryan shook his head. "I should have just taken that decongestant." He gripped the sides of his armrests, his knuckles white. "Did you know that eighty percent of plane crashes take place in the last eight minutes of a flight?"

Before Avery could respond, Bryan realized what he'd done and released the armrests. He ignored the gum and reached into his pocket for hand wipes. "You have no idea how many people catch viruses on these things."

Avery rolled her eyes. He'd told her, like, twenty times.

"We'll be fine, Bry. You come into contact with viruses every day, don't you?"

"Yeah, but you don't. You should use this." Bryan held the hand wipes out to her.

She shook her head. "I'm fine. I hate the way they dry out my hands. And I just want to relax. I finally have a week off work for the first time in ages, and I'm with the cutest guy I know."

He grinned. "Well, thank you. But I still think you should have finished up that big project you have due next week. You're going to have a hard time actually relaxing with it hanging over your head."

This time, she *did* roll her eyes. "It's fine. I'm not stressed about it. I only have, like, another day or so of work to put into it, and I'll be finished. I'll take care of it first thing next week." *He seriously needs to learn how to procrastinate happily.*

Once they'd landed, Avery's focus shifted to her own nerves, which she'd ignored while Bryan's fears had dominated the conversation. Her mom was going to meet them by the baggage claim. Avery still couldn't believe Mom had been cool with Bryan coming to lake week, and her request that Bryan stay in a separate room was an easy compromise, considering how little Mom had protested.

She released a slow puff of air from her cheeks and glanced at Bryan as they made their way down the escalator. "Feeling any better?"

"Just happy to be back on land." Bryan blinked hard, like he was trying to wake up.

"Nervous about meeting my mother?" Avery reached for his hand to steady herself.

Bryan drew his hand back. "We should probably stop in a bathroom so you can wash your hands after being in that plane." He gave a smile, then nodded toward a fluorescent restroom sign they approached. "But no, I'm not nervous. Why should I be?" He shrugged. "I'm sure she's great."

Yeah, because I haven't told you the horror stories. Avery headed toward the bathroom, glad Bryan had suggested the stop. It would give her a moment to collect herself, make sure her hair was perfectly in place, her teeth brushed. Mom had a way of zeroing in on those details.

Not that she'd shared the more complicated aspect of her relationship with her mom with Bryan. And she wouldn't either. Loyalty didn't work that way. Throughout the years, she learned even if things got complex with Mom, she'd always be there for Avery, through thick and thin. Her mom might be disappointed in Avery, but she'd still be there. *Unlike Dad.*

Speaking disparagingly about Mom to a guy she'd barely been dating for four months would only make him hate Mom. And Avery really, really wanted him to get along well with Mom, as things were going better with Bryan than she'd expected them to.

Avery washed her hands, then looked in the mirror. "Definitely need a touch-up," she said to herself. Bryan had told her he liked a more natural look, which had the bonus of helping her reduce her makeup routine. It was sweet, too, that he thought she was naturally beautiful like that.

She pulled out her phone to check the messages from her mom and then froze at the email notification on the lock screen. "URGENT: Update required." From the client she had a project due to next week.

Shrinking back against the wall beside a hand dryer, she clicked on the message. The art director for one of the publishing companies she worked with was asking for an update . . . and why the final book cover hadn't been delivered yet.

A cold sweat broke out on Avery's neck, nausea roiling her stomach. *What the hell?*

She checked her calendar. The project was definitely due next week, wasn't it? She wasn't the best at organizing herself, but she always put delivery dates in her calendar the moment she was given a firm deadline.

The calendar said next week.

Combing through the email threads with the art director, she looked for the email with the delivery date. She pulled it up and then gripped the object nearest to her, which turned out to be the hand dryer. It started with a roar, and Avery dropped the phone on the tile floor with a clatter.

Shit. Shit.

She'd written the wrong date.

How in the hell had she written the wrong date?

Grabbing the phone from the floor, Avery hurried out of the bathroom, head spinning. Bryan might even be wondering what the hell had happened to her by now.

Bryan stood just outside the door, staring at his cell phone. He glanced up and met her eyes, a cute grin on his lips. Then his brow furrowed and he straightened. "What's wrong?"

"I . . ." Avery tried to keep herself from panicking, feeling as though she was failing miserably. No wonder he'd sensed her distress immediately. In as calm a voice as she could, she explained the situation to him, then said, "I-I'm so screwed. Even if I go back to the lodge and work for the rest of the day, this is still going to be late and I'm going to lose my contract with this publisher and . . ."

She couldn't even finish, with all the horrible possibilities of what might happen as a result of this spiraling in her brain. In the back of her mind, all she could think of was how Bryan had been right. She should have just gotten this project finished before vacation.

And why didn't I, really?

There had been time. She'd just spent it on other things. Gone to lunch with friends and on dates with Bryan.

Bryan set his hands on her shoulders. "Relax. Take a breath. Have you called the art director yet?"

She shook her head, fighting back tears.

Bryan stroked her shoulders with his thumbs. "Okay. This is what we're going to do. Call her. Tell her you had a family emergency and you're going to get it to her tonight—can you get it done by tonight?"

Avery nodded and sniffled. It was a stretch, but if she went straight to her room and didn't take any breaks, she could do it.

"Then do it. And then, when we get back from vacation, we're going to go through your upcoming deadlines, make sure you have everything written down correctly. Would you be willing to give that software I mentioned a try? The one that has all your client information organized and sends invoices and tracks your projects?"

Avery gulped down a breath and nodded again.

Bryan leaned forward and kissed her gently. "And if the art director gives you problems, put her on the phone with me." He winked. "I *am* a cardiologist, by the way. I might be able to help buy you a little excuse."

By the time they met Mom by the baggage claim, Avery had managed to calm herself down—and talked to the art director. With Bryan's skillful help at defusing situations, Avery bought herself the extra time, even if she still felt sick to her stomach about messing up. A surge of pride welled in Avery as she glanced at Bryan. Thank God things could be different with a guy like him, *different from Mom and Dad's relationship.* He could help her be a better version of herself.

Strangely, Mom was on her best behavior. She embraced Avery *and* Bryan, and by the time they'd rented a car to leave the airport at Pittsburgh, Bryan and Mom were talking as if they'd known each other for years. Mom especially seemed touched by the box of saltwater taffy Bryan had given her.

For the first time, Mom looked at a boyfriend of Avery's with approval in her eyes—something Avery had always dreamed about.

CHAPTER SIXTEEN

Now

THE DOORBELL WOKE Dan before his alarm went off, and he blinked groggily, feeling around the floorboards for his cell phone. The floor was a lot closer than it'd been when he'd gone to sleep and he sat up. The air mattress he'd filled the night before lifted on the floor on the opposite side.

You need to get a bed.

He threw some clothes on—he wasn't about to be caught running around in his boxers again—and hurried to the door.

His brother-in-law, Jason, stood there, holding Jen's food delivery. "Morning, sunshine," Jason said, breezing through the open door. He came in, then frowned. "Where the hell do you want me to put this?"

Dan rubbed the back of his neck. "I don't know. Kitchen counter?"

"Lead the way." Jason gestured with a lift of his chin. "You know you have someone sleeping on your front porch swing?"

"Yeah, Peyton. He gets here early and then chills out there until we're ready to start. But I'll probably call him in for breakfast in a few."

"Okay. That's weird." Jason followed him into the kitchen, then set the plastic tray and paper bags on the old butcher block. He stepped back, wiping his hands on his jeans. "How's the place coming along?"

"Slowly. And now I'm on a time crunch to make it at least usable."

"Yeah, Jen told me about the wedding." Jason crossed his arms, and his crystal blue eyes clouded over. "You really have people staying here right now?"

"The bride and her best friend. Apparently, there's nowhere else available in a thirty-mile radius. Brandywood can't take this sort of traffic for too much longer."

"Well, it'll be good for you when you're done with the reno." Jason set his hand down on the counter, then swiped with his fingertips, noticing the thick layer of dust. "But you're going to need all hands on deck to get this place in shape for a wedding so soon. Did you call Garrett yet?"

"He's booked for the next couple of months." And calling in favors wasn't Dan's preference, particularly with Garrett. They got along well enough now, but after a lifetime of butting heads, Dan didn't feel comfortable enough just texting him to ask for anything.

Speaking of favors . . .

"Hey, so." Dan felt heat crawling up the back of his neck. "I may need a few days to get the money together for this month's loan interest payment. I had to make a large purchase for furniture yesterday." With all his expenses recently, he needed to wait until the end of next week, when the check Avery gave him for the wedding cleared. "I can get it, but it'll take a couple of weeks."

Dan squirmed under the weight of Jason's sharp gaze. Jason was a businessman, and a good one, and borrowing money from Jason had been Jen's idea. Jason had been investing in a lot of properties around town, to the point that now even he and Garrett were working together to flip homes and buildings, with Jason as the primary investor.

"I don't mind you paying me back a few days late, Dan, but I have to ask—why are you doing all this? Making business decisions driven by emotion is rarely a good idea."

Dammit, Jen. Trust his baby sister to have told Jason about Avery. She'd given him a gentle warning herself, but knowing her, she was probably worried.

"It's not that." He chuckled awkwardly. The last thing he needed was a dressing-down by his brother-in-law.

"I'm not accusing you of anything, by the way—God knows I'm not in any position to judge. But Jen was worried. She wanted me to talk to you."

At least Jason was honest.

"I appreciate it, Jason, but you know Jen. She gets a little overly worried about everything. I'm doing this because I should have found that reservation in Mr. Harrison's logbook. It was scribbled in the back, but it was there. And knowing the bride means I know how much this place means to her. Look around—anyone still determined to hold an event here has to be dead-set on it."

Jason nodded, then stepped back. "All right. Listen, this week is crammed for me, but I can come help on the weekend. What do you need? And don't say no. In fact, make it a point to ask Garrett, Warren, Mark, your dad—anyone you can think of. I'd say ask the women, too, but with the number of kids in the family, it'd only slow things down. Unless your mom can watch all of them. You have the benefit of having a family who will jump at the opportunity to help you, Dan. That's not something to be squandered."

Dan shifted, wishing he'd had a cup of coffee before this conversation. His brain felt foggy. But Jason wasn't one to take something like family lightly. After years of facing things mostly alone, he'd finally found family when he'd come here to Brandywood—including Dan, who viewed him as a close friend. Dan was grateful for Jason, and one thing he'd always liked about Jason was the fact that he was down-to-earth and easy to talk to. They'd had a strange bond because they were both older brothers, and it made him approachable. And he was right—his family would help him, if he just asked.

"That's not a bad idea. Maybe Saturday. I'm supposed to have that furniture moved in here, and it might not be a bad thing to spend the morning and early afternoon getting as much done around here as possible before next week. But I invited Colby to come over that day. So maybe we can grill and take the boat out afterward, too."

"I'll skip the boat, but it sounds good to me." Jason took a step toward the door, then paused. "Do we need to bring a grill?"

Dan gave him a wry smile, then poured himself a cup of coffee from the dispenser Jason had brought over. "Nah, there are those in-ground types over by the picnic tables next to the lake."

"This really is an impressive property, Dan. In case anyone else hasn't told you, it's a good idea you've got here. And I'm always happy to help in any way I can."

Dan appreciated Jason's praise. Interestingly, Jason had been the one person in his family who hadn't been shocked when he'd bought the lodge. Dan didn't really love people all that much—his family aside—and operating a lodge meant a lot of interaction with outsiders. He really wouldn't know if he'd make it work until a year passed, but with Jason's endorsement, he felt more confident in his decision.

Dan walked Jason back out to the front door and then popped his head out once he'd gone. Peyton was propped up on the front porch swing, a sweatshirt under his head. He jerked up when Dan gave a low whistle.

"You sleeping there a while, Peyton?" Dan asked. He sipped his coffee. Damn, Jen did everything amazingly. Even her coffee was a thousand times better than anything he could brew himself.

Peyton sat up and rubbed his eyes. "Not long. I just wanted to get an early start."

Dan stared at him over the rim of the paper cup and then walked over to him. The coming early, staying late, asking to shower before he left for the day. The nagging in the back of Dan's mind had been telling him to pay attention.

As he sat, the porch swing gave a tremulous groan, and Dan winced. "We may have to work on this next." Not that either he or Peyton probably knew anything about fixing this swing.

Peyton grunted, folding his sweatshirt into his backpack.

"How long you been homeless, Peyton?"

Peyton blinked at Dan, surprise in his expression. "I'm not—"

"I'm a cop, Peyton." Dan cleared his throat. "Was a cop. I know a thing or two about the habits of people who don't have a place to go at night. So what's the deal?"

Peyton clasped his hands together, bowing his head. "About a year."

That Peyton had told him the truth now was a good start. But it probably meant he'd been fibbing about some other things. "Parents?"

"They kicked me out. Said they'd fulfilled their part of the bargain, kept me until I was an adult. It's not that they're bad parents, but they live paycheck to paycheck."

Still sounded like lousy parents to Dan, but he wouldn't pass judgment either. His parents had been more than willing to let Dan move in after things had gone south with Melissa, but a few months to get back on his feet was the most Dan had been willing to consider. Then again, his parents weren't struggling.

Dan took another sip of his coffee. "And college?" He already knew the answer. It was written on Peyton's face.

"Didn't finish." Peyton stood, picking up his backpack. "I appreciate you giving me a chance, Officer Klein. I really do. I'll get going now." He got about halfway to his bicycle before Dan got up from the swing and walked up to the rail.

"You're quitting?" He raised his brows.

Peyton turned and gave him a confused look. "No, I just figured you wanted me to go. You know, for squatting."

"I'm not asking you to quit." Dan set his free hand on the rail, leaning against it. "It's not easy getting a job when you've got things against you, Peyton. I know that. And you're, what— twenty-two?"

Peyton nodded.

"I'm not that much older than you, but enough to tell you you're way too young to not be able to find your way back from hard times. But just be upfront if you can, Peyton. It's easier to get the help you need that way. Get inside, get some breakfast, and then we'll talk about you staying here from now on."

Peyton took one step toward the house, then the front porch rail gave way with a loud crack.

Dan went tumbling forward into the boxwood bushes below. They didn't quite break his fall, but twigs and branches dug into his arms, legs, and torso. "Fuck!" Dan managed, hot coffee searing his skin.

When he stopped, he blinked, pulling himself up from the bushes. *What in the hell?*

"How the heck did that even happen?" Peyton stared at him in shock. "You okay?"

"I have no clue. But I'm fine." The front porch rail hadn't even seemed loose. But luck had turned on him the last few days—and not in a good way. He dusted himself off, then waded through the broken bushes.

Looking back, he fought the temptation to cover his face with his hands. The broken front rail made the place look like a haunted mansion more than the upscale bed-and-breakfast he was going for. The bushes looked like someone had attacked them with a hacksaw.

"One step forward, three steps back," he muttered.

"Do you think maybe this place is cursed or something?" Peyton asked, with a laugh.

"Feels like it." Dan fished the broken rail pieces out from the bushes and set them on the grass.

Or maybe he was just still paying the consequences for mistakes he'd made years before.

He sighed and rescued the crushed coffee cup from the bush. Jason was right—this project was getting to be too much for him. He needed outside help. He wouldn't prove his competency by failing spectacularly at this lodge-owner thing with his "first" booking.

Dan trudged up the front steps, Peyton trailing behind him.

Maybe he just needed to move on from thinking he could rebuild his life so easily—*and* get a new dog.

CHAPTER SEVENTEEN

Erika was already showered and dressed for the day by the time Avery convinced herself to get up in the morning. Avery groaned and sat on the sleeping bag, unknotting her hair with her fingertips. "Wine was such a bad idea."

"Wine is never a bad idea. It's the quantity that gets you." Erika squatted in front of her suitcase, brushing out her wet hair.

"How is it possible that you had the same amount as me and are completely chipper?" Avery felt around the sleeping bag for her cell phone to check the time. She'd probably missed some calls and emails, but there was no way of knowing until she got to the front of the lodge. Thank goodness she'd set up an out-of-office auto-response for her email and social media messenger apps. That bought her time to respond.

"You stayed up later than me reminiscing about old times with your former flame." Erika gave her a sly wink. "What's going to happen when Bryan gets here and realizes how into each other you two still are?"

Avery turned, the hair on the back of her neck standing, her mouth already feeling dry from the alcohol. "It's not funny, Erika. Seriously. Maybe while it's just you and me, it's not such a big deal, but it really isn't a joke. And once Bryan gets here, if he even has the slightest suspicion Dan and I were ever involved, he'll pull the plug on the wedding being here."

Erika laughed. "He would not"—she sobered—"would he?" The worry in her eyes bothered Avery more than it should have.

"He absolutely would. You know how jealous he is. Don't you remember that editor who kept emailing me at all hours with requests? Bryan got so upset about it, he made me turn down the last pitch I got from him."

Erika's eyes narrowed. "Are you serious?" She set her hands on her hips. "Why the hell was Bryan reading your emails?"

Avery steadied her breath, her stomach twisting. "He didn't just go reading my emails, I was just telling him about it. And he got worried, so he looked. I mean, the guy was inappropriate. I would get notifications on my phone at two and three in the morning." Except it wasn't entirely true, because Bryan read her emails occasionally when he picked up her phone. But she could do the same with his if she wanted. They knew each other's passcodes.

Except you never pick up his phone. Because why would you need to?

Erika zipped her case shut, her movements a little too forceful to be natural. "For what it's worth, I've never read any of Royce's emails. Ever. And I don't think I would."

Great. She really didn't need this from Erika right now. "You're forgetting the part where I said it was fine. If I don't care about it, why should you?"

"Okay, then, if you all are so open and honest with everything, why not tell him about Dan? Because you clearly haven't. You wouldn't have been so upset yesterday when that caterer knew who you were if you had—like Dan somehow violated some secrecy agreement. It makes way more sense to tell the person you're dating about your former relationships than it does for them to read your email."

"Dan didn't 'violate some secrecy agreement.' I just was surprised he'd mentioned me by name enough that she could figure it out." It still made Avery uncomfortable to think about what Dan might have said, especially to someone so nasty. "But you're right. I haven't told Bryan about Dan, and there's really no point. It was twelve years ago. Water under the bridge."

"Is it, though?" Erika asked sharply, her eyes drilling into Avery's. "I don't have as many exes as you do, but I think if one of them showed up in my life and was treating me as nicely as he is you, it'd make me wonder if something might still be there. Because he seems like a really decent person. The way you talked about things ending between you all, I assumed he'd sort of be a jerk to you."

"As many exes as I do? What's that supposed to mean?" Avery tried to ignore the point of Erika's question—it wasn't something she *wanted* to think about. *Why is Erika even bringing it up?*

Erika rolled her eyes and stood. "You want to pretend you didn't flit from one douchebag to the next for ten years? Fine. But I was seriously getting worried for you for a while, Ave."

Not that many guys.

Just . . . okay, so maybe it was a handful or two of guys. Florida and California both had their share of jackasses.

But Erika seemed to take Avery's silence as an invitation to keep going. "I'm still not sure I shouldn't be worried. I mean, I don't even know Bryan that well—I've met him twice. Now I'm finding out he reads your emails and you hide stuff from him. And let's not even mention the newfound fear of flying and all your new personality traits I've never seen before."

Avery clenched her jaw. She didn't want to fight with Erika. They were like sisters, and that was why Erika worried for her. Erika just didn't know Bryan. One of the hardest things about having a best friend who lived on the other side of the country was that they rarely saw each other.

She breathed out slowly. "Bryan has his quirks, Erika, but he's a good person. He just loves me so much, he wants to make sure I'm not getting harassed, that's all."

"Yeah, but what about what *you* want? Do you want to be married this fast? I know you're fun and spontaneous—or can be—but this is marriage we're talking about. I just want you to be one hundred percent sure. I want you to know deep inside your heart that Bryan is the best thing for you, not that you think he *feels* like the best thing. Where's Avery in all this?"

"I'm right here. Trying to get married." Avery felt her throat thickening, on the verge of tears. "Would I be here if this wasn't what I wanted? And I don't think I'm being that spontaneous." She wiped a tear from her cheek. "You know, Bryan once said he could just steal me to Vegas, make the wedding happen rather than waiting for August. I'm the one who put the brakes on things. But he's sweet and romantic like that."

"Is it sweet and romantic, though?" Erika's eyes narrowed. "It doesn't sound . . . pushy, to you?"

Avery bit her lip, staring at her hands. She couldn't tell Erika about the nonstop arguments about the wedding and how it was causing so much stress between her and Bryan. Or that once or twice, when he'd been yelling, she'd actually worried he might try to force her into an elopement to prove her love for him.

And then it hadn't felt romantic at all.

"I love Bryan." Avery rubbed her teary eyes.

Erika looked at Avery with concern, then sighed as though she felt she had pushed too hard and too far. A smile graced her face, and she said, "Well, I wouldn't get to wear my bridesmaid dress if you'd gone to Vegas, so I'm glad you didn't."

Avery laughed, thankful Erika knew how to lighten her fear. *And I wouldn't have the wedding of my dreams either.*

Erika left to go down for breakfast, giving Avery a chance to collect herself. She breathed out and dug through her bag, looking for something to wear for the day. The outfit she'd worn the previous day was filthy, and she didn't have many options in the clothes she'd packed. As she shifted through the gray and black and cream-colored outfits, looking for her new bag of clothes, Avery sat on the floor.

She hated the clothes she'd brought from home.

There wasn't a single thing she'd packed that was comfortable. Everything was perfect for meetings with florists or caterers or sitting at business meetings or her rehearsal dinner. But not for vacation. Then again, all her clothes in her closet at home looked like this.

In colors Bryan likes.

When had she stopped wearing clothes she actually liked? Or going out with her friends? Felicity or Tad weren't even invited to the wedding. For the first year she'd been in San Diego, they'd been her life raft to navigating life in California.

Why did I give it all up so easily? Bryan liked things a certain way, yes, but Avery was happy with those changes. And then Erika's words came back to her. *"Where's Avery in all this?"*

I used to love wearing bright colors.

She'd worn a red dress to one of Bryan's friend's weddings a while ago, and she remembered vividly the scolding she'd received later that night for trying to upstage the bride. She'd cried and given the dress away to Goodwill the next day. That may have even been the last time she'd worn red. Then again, when she wore her new clothes, Bryan didn't seem to stop complimenting her.

She found the bag of new clothes, zipped up the suitcase, and dragged it over to the closet. As she opened the door, she caught sight of her wedding gown in its garment case, hung carefully to keep it safe. Somehow the sight of it made her feel calm, as though it was a tether to her purpose there.

She didn't need to freak out about Erika's comments. She had a couple of other new outfits to wear, and if she needed more, she'd go to the store. Simple enough.

Erika had unnerved Avery, but considering the ugly accusations, she felt disloyal to Bryan. Not only was Bryan not there to defend himself, it also wasn't fair. And while his anxiety might be a burden, she could handle the weight of it. They worked well together.

They had everything in common. They were goal-oriented and motivated with friends in the professional world at top firms and hospitals in San Diego. At night, they sat and read in bed, and dinner conversations were a breeze. And he made her smile. He was considerate and encouraged her to be her best.

He was respected and brilliant. And his work mattered. Mom *was* thrilled to be getting a doctor for a son-in-law and had raved to all her friends about him. Bryan was the type of guy she could brag about to Mom. Avery couldn't ask for a better fiancé, really.

Yet there'd been a moment last night when she'd looked into Dan's eyes and her heart had yearned to know what could happen with him if she let her guard down again. He was so easy to talk to. So easy to let in.

A memory flashed into her mind of swimming in the lake under the starlight, clinging to each other in the water, her lips aching from making out for so long.

She'd convinced herself through the years that what they'd

felt for each other was nothing more than hormonal-fueled adolescent lust.

Because what else could it have been? They'd barely spent a week together, yet they'd crammed in a lot of activities . . . *and made really amazing memories.*

And there was something in Dan's eyes, something that made her chest tickle like she'd swallowed champagne too fast. *He was looking at me with fondness. Kindness.* And strangely, she'd felt a wistfulness—a yearning to be someone more unfettered—in a way she hadn't felt in a long time.

That was just the magic of Brandywood, right?

Yet the aftershocks from that one week she'd spent with Dan had impacted her life for years. Every now and then, she still felt a shift of the earth related to that summer.

She'd grown up in more ways than one during those few, short days.

Her life as she'd known it had ended during that week. Everything she'd known—security, happiness, having her dad in her life daily—was just gone. And then she'd found out about Tina, and her life became exponentially worse. *I still miss my dad.* He'd once been her most ardent defender.

At the bottom of the main staircase, she was greeted once more by notifications from her cell phone—more calls from Bryan. Mom, too, who would be easier to get in touch with.

The call went right to voicemail. Mom had become a little less rigid about calling Avery every day after Avery had gotten engaged, but it didn't keep the tone of resentment out of her voice when Avery went more than a few days without calling. For years, Avery had hoped Mom would find a boyfriend so she could focus her attention on someone else. She was lonely, and Avery hated that fact, but she also hated that her mom had put her into the role of husband after the divorce.

Moving to the other side of the country had helped Avery

feel less suffocated, but the guilt was hard to deal with. Mom let her know at every opportunity how abandoned she felt. Culturally, she knew her Latina mother did some things without even thinking about how much pressure it put on Avery—her grandmother also used guilt as a leverage, and so did a lot of the mothers of her Latina friends from Miami.

But it was one thing to joke about how funny it was to have a mom who told you how beautiful you were one second, and then in the next breath how you should brush *"the rats nest"* out from your hair. Avery had struggled for years trying to reconcile the insecurities Mom had planted in her in the name of "cultural" behaviors.

Footsteps made her look up. Dan was coming down the hallway, and he'd changed—and shaved. She blinked, and a dizzying feeling crested in the top of her head. He looked younger without the beard, more like the guy she'd known as a teenager, but grown up.

And one freaking handsome and mature man.

Turned out that beard had been hiding just how sexy Dan was now, which wasn't at all good for Avery's pulse. She'd have to control her reactions to him. She came across good looking men frequently enough without imagining crossing any lines with them, so why should it be any different with Dan?

"Hey," she greeted. "You shaved."

He grinned. "Yeah. I got covered in coffee this morning after falling through the front porch—long story—and when I was pulling twigs and boxwood leaves from my beard, I decided it was time."

"You fell through the front porch?" Avery's jaw dropped, and she stared at him, her mouth open, blinking. Before he could answer, she made a beeline for the front door.

Avery's heart slowed as she opened the door. When she'd

gone to bed the night before, the front of the lodge had been unkempt but fixable.

Now it was in shambles.

It looked as if Dan had ripped apart the front porch with his bare hands. Peyton stood where the front porch had once been, leaning on a sledgehammer. The front porch swing was on the front lawn, on its side. Her eyes widened. "What the hell happened?"

"He fell through the porch rail this morning," Peyton said as helpfully as possible. "The board was rotten at the base. A bunch of the deck boards were. The whole porch has to be dismantled. Rebuilt from the bottom up." Peyton tossed a board into the pile.

"Are you kidding me? Right now?" Avery felt sick. How in the hell were they going to get this done on time?

"What's going on?" Erika's voice came from inside the lodge, and Avery turned to see her approaching with a cup of coffee.

"Just look." Avery stepped to the side so Erika could look out. Erika's lips parted with shock, then she cringed, giving Avery a cautious look. She put her drink down so she could step out, moving closer to where Peyton stood.

"Dan fell through this section right here, right into these bushes." Peyton gestured toward a sizable gap in the boxwoods.

Avery peered at Dan. She'd missed the scratches on his cheek and arms before. "Are you okay?"

"Fine." But any warmth that had been in his eyes just moments ago had disappeared.

"Wow, this looks pretty bad." Erika pushed her thumb through some of the soft wood on a board. "You're lucky no one else fell through. How in the hell did this house pass inspections when you bought it?"

Dan grimaced and stood at Avery's side. "It didn't."

"It didn't pass inspections?" Avery gave him a hard stare.

"It didn't get inspected." He straightened, rolling his shoulders back. "The competition to buy it was fierce, so I added an 'as is' clause to my offer."

Wow, he must have really wanted it.

"That was stupid." Peyton guffawed, his lips vibrating as he let out a breath.

"Thank you, Captain Obvious." Dan gave Peyton a mock salute.

Avery gave a sardonic laugh of disbelief. "I didn't think it was possible for this to get any worse. But somehow, I just keep being wrong about that."

"It's going to be fine." Now Dan sounded irritated. "I'm going into town tonight to talk to my brother-in-law, who's a contractor. Hopefully, he can help us out."

The crunch of gravel as a car turned onto the driveway caught their attention. A white Prius came up the drive slowly. "You expecting someone else?" Peyton asked Dan.

Dan shook his head and then hopped down from the front door onto the ground to climb over to the front walk. "I need to rope off these damned steps before the mailman falls through."

The car stopped, and the door opened. Then a woman stepped out and pushed back her sunglasses onto her shoulder-length black hair.

Avery gripped the door frame.

Mom.

CHAPTER EIGHTEEN

Avery
12 Years Ago

Avery pushed a roasted Brussels sprout around on her plate, listening to the quiet din of the conversation in The Dutchman, the most upscale restaurant in Brandywood. She preferred it when her parents wanted to go into town to Yardley's Pub or Bunny's Café, or even the China Red Dragon—they had the dumplings Erika had helped her fall in love with. But her parents, being her parents, made it a point to visit The Dutchman at least a couple of times during their vacation.

They loved fine dining and could go on for a while about how much better the foie gras was at one place or how much they had enjoyed the truffles, the Kobe beef, or whatever other random thing their fancy food magazines told them they should like.

Her parents had weird things like that in common.

They both spoke a second language fluently—her father, Italian, and her mother, Spanish. And dancing. Mom and Dad had taken salsa and merengue lessons together. They'd even participated in some ballroom dancing competitions. They went everywhere together, did everything together.

And now it was just over?

"How's the crab cake?" Dad asked her, breaking the silence at the table.

"Great." Avery gave a halfhearted smile, looking at his blue eyes through the glint of light on his glasses. Dad was at least trying to be friendly. Mom, in the meantime, had been acting like she was auditioning for a job at a butcher shop with the way she was hacking away at her steak.

Dad sipped his red wine. "I'm glad you were finally feeling well enough to join us for dinner tonight. I was thinking maybe tomorrow we could ride bikes over to the rail station. Take a trip on that old steam engine through the mountains? For old times' sake."

Avery set her fork down and placed her hands on her lap. "So does that mean this is the last time I'm ever coming back to Brandywood?"

"No, no—"

"Yes." Her mother's expression was terse. "At least as a family—now that your father is leaving us. *We* can still come, you and I."

"You know she can come with me, too." Dad wiped the corners of his mouth with his napkin and then set it back on his lap.

"Well, I'd imagine she's going to want to spend summers with me. I'm the one who always organized this trip. My father is the one who started coming here." Mom set her knife across the top of her plate and buttered a piece of a roll.

Dad was staring at Avery with a questioning look.

And then it occurred to Avery.

She was eighteen. There wouldn't be a custody battle. The court wouldn't have to order her to spend a month here and a month there.

She was a legal adult. She could go wherever she wanted.

Which meant she'd have to choose between her parents.

And it means you don't have to go to Tampa if you don't want to.

Avery lifted her chin, then looked Mom squarely in the eye. "I think I'll live with Dad for the school year. I can come to Brandywood for the summer vacation with you, Mom, but I want to go to school with my friends."

Her mother flinched, then stopped buttering her roll. "Avery, we had this discussion. That's not an option. You're coming with me to Tampa."

"But that's the point, right? You were just implying *I* need to choose what I want to do, who I spend summers with. Because legally, you can't make me do anything."

"Oh, for fuck's sake—"

"Maria!" Her dad's jaw dropped open.

"After everything I've done for her, she wants to choose to go be with you! As if you'll have room for *her*. And why? Because you spoil her, that's why!"

Avery stiffened. *Mom must be furious.* She never cursed like that in public. But it also meant Avery had hit a nerve. And she was right. The freedom her age brought her was something she'd never really stopped to consider before. She was old enough to make a lot of choices for herself. *And old enough to decide I don't want to be slapped for having an opinion other than my mom's.*

For a moment, she imagined herself standing up and saying, *"You know, Mom, I'm a good kid. I get straight As. I'm at the top of my class. I'm going to get a full scholarship for college and for grad school, just like you always wanted. Even though nothing I do ever impresses you or makes you proud of me. But right now, I'm going to go be a teenager. Because a guy I like invited me to a party tonight."*

Then she would march out of the door of The Dutchman dramatically, like in the movies.

But she said nothing. She stared at her mom's eyes, which brimmed with tears, and reached over to take her hand. "I'm sorry, Mom. I love you. I'm not saying I prefer Dad. Can't you just stay in—"

Mom pulled her hand back and wiped her eyes. "I know this is a difficult time for all of us, Avery, but I only want what's best for you. The school in Tampa I want to send you to is a Blue Ribbon school. Think about how it'll look on your record."

Avery swallowed hard. She'd already decided, so she didn't have to think about it. But there was no point in ruining their vacation. As soon as she got back home, she'd make it clear she was staying in Miami with her dad. No one could force her to move if she didn't want to. And if Mom wanted Avery to stay with her so much, she wouldn't move away.

Excusing herself from the table, Avery slipped her purse onto her shoulder and hurried to the bathroom. She stepped into the stall and slid the lock shut, then leaned back against the door.

This sucks.

If this was going to be her last summer in Brandywood, she didn't want it to be like this. She loved this place more than anywhere else in the world. She wanted to have fun and have everything feel like normal. *Happy.*

She slipped her phone out of her purse and pulled up her text message app. She typed quickly.

Avery: *Still want me to go to that party?*

Her phone dinged a response as if Dan had been holding his when her message went through.

Dan: *Abso-frikkin-lutely.*

Avery smiled, her heart rate ticking up a notch.

Avery: *Cool. Meet me by the oak tree near where all the Adirondack chairs are later tonight.*

She closed her eyes and leaned her head back against the door, holding her phone to her pounding heart. And if she got caught, she just needed to remind her parents she was old enough to do whatever she wanted.

THE CLIMB down the tree was a lot more intimidating than Avery had imagined, but she also hadn't climbed a tree since she was five. She scraped her hand on the rough bark of the branch she was reaching for, groping blindly in the dark. She probably should have found another route out of her room and outside, but this had seemed preferable to tiptoeing down the hallway.

A twig snapped below her flip-flop, and then she heard a voice whisper below her, "Avery?"

She laughed lightly. "Up here."

"Holy shit, what the hell are you doing up there?"

She wished she could see the expression on Dan's face.

"Keep it down. You don't want me to get caught, do you?" She shimmied down a few more branches, then lowered herself until she was hanging. "Can you catch me?"

Dan's arms were on her thighs, and the touch of his hands shot electric sparks up to her belly. "I got you."

She released the branch, then slid down until his arms locked firmly around her butt. He lowered her, and her arms wrapped around his neck. She smiled at him, then her lips found their way to his.

His lips were soft, and he tasted like spearmint chewing gum, which wasn't her favorite but somehow tasted amazing on his mouth. The tip of his tongue ran along her lips, and her mouth parted for his. Then the kiss deepened, and their tongues collided with an intense pace as Dan crushed her against him.

When he released her, she grinned, biting her lower lip as he set her feet on the ground. He interlaced his fingers with hers. "I missed you, too."

He tugged her through the lawn and around the side of the lodge, and she practically giggled. "And you wanted me not to wake anyone?" Dan squeezed her hand. "I'm glad you're coming with me."

"Did I make you late for the party? It's almost ten. It's got to be over."

"It's not a cocktail party. They'll be going all night." Dan stopped at his truck. He'd parked it down the street like she'd asked him to. He held the door open for her, and she slipped into the passenger seat, buzzing with energy. Dan shut the door and then came around to the driver's side.

No sooner had he sat did she lean across the console in the middle and kiss his neck, just below the earlobe. He groaned. "You're making me not want to go anywhere."

Her hand slid down to his thigh, and he turned his face toward hers. She kissed his lips, gently, then sank back into the passenger seat. "I don't want to tease you." Sitting back down was impossibly harder than she thought it would be, though. She wanted to be on his lap, kissing him.

But she'd also never been to a party before, and she was too excited to miss it.

Dan pulled forward and turned on some music, then reached across and held her hand. "How was dinner?"

"Awful. Except. I have good news." She smiled, squeezing his hand. "I'm not going to Tampa. I'm staying in Miami."

Dan looked over his shoulder at her. "Really? That's awesome." He sounded genuinely happy for her, and she slid her fingers against his, relishing the way he made her skin tingle.

"Yeah. I'm going to stay with my dad. My mom still wants me to go with her, but I realized at dinner she doesn't get to choose. I'm eighteen. No judge is going to order me to go stay with her. So I'm going to do what I want."

Dan's thumb brushed the inside of her palm. "Won't that make your mom mad?"

"Yeah, but she doesn't get to make this decision. Why should I go with her instead of with my dad? I love them both equally. She's the one choosing to move."

The movement of Dan's thumb against her palm stopped. Then he cleared his throat. "Do you think maybe there's another reason she wants to move?"

"Other than to torture me? What reason could she possibly have?" Avery rolled her eyes and leaned back, squinting in the lights of passing cars.

Dan turned down the volume on the music. "I don't know. To make a fresh start? My mom had to live in the same damn town as my birth dad, watching as he took his new family out everywhere. It was humiliating for her."

"Yeah, and I get that, but that's entirely different, Dan." Avery felt a knot of tension rise in her shoulders. She didn't want him to argue it would be better for her to stay with her mom. She wanted him on her side. "You have no idea what my mom is like. She doesn't let me do anything. One time when I was in freshman year, she found out this boy in my class wanted to ask me to homecoming, and she hung around the parking lot after school, asking other kids in my class who he was. Then when she found him, she told him he was never to even consider dating her daughter. You can guess how many times I got asked to homecoming after that. Not once in three years."

The humiliation of it burned her esophagus, and she swallowed back the acid that had risen in her throat.

Dan's thumb stroked her palm once more, lulling her to calm. "She sounds really overprotective."

"When I auditioned for a play one time, she found the theater teacher and told him I wasn't allowed to participate. She refused to take me to volleyball team tryouts. And now she wants to cut me off from the only friends I've been allowed to have." Avery shook her head. "*Overprotective* isn't strong enough. She wants to live my life for me. And I've never done anything really bad, like drugs or something. And maybe I should. If she's going to think I'm such a rebel, I may as well be one."

The light of bonfires up ahead came into view as Dan pulled off the main road and into a parking lot by a lake house. He turned the truck off but didn't make a move to get out. Something seemed to trouble him. "Avery . . ."

She raised a brow. "Yes?"

Leaning across the console, he kissed her. "Just try to have fun tonight, okay?"

She melted into his kiss, the tension of their conversation dissipating with the sound of drum beats from loud music outside. "I think I can manage that."

CHAPTER NINETEEN

Avery
10 Months Ago

THE SERVER POURED a glass of wine for Avery, then turned toward Bryan with the bottle.

"Only a little," Bryan said, with a wave of his hand. "I have to be up early tomorrow morning, and alcohol makes me sleep horribly."

"I think you can make an exception for celebrating our engagement," Avery said and reflexively looked at the sparkling diamond on her left hand.

"We've been celebrating for the last week," Bryan said with a laugh. He motioned to the server to stop the wine pour after the glass was only an inch full.

The engagement had taken Avery by surprise. They'd just come back from their lake week two weeks ago but hadn't seen each other much, since Avery had been bogged down with work and trying to reorganize herself. Catching a reprieve from what could have been a disaster for her job had given her a new energy to tackle so many of the bad habits she'd let herself get into since moving out on her own.

Mom had been right about more things than Avery realized when she'd left home. The artistic, "free-spirited" guys Avery had dated for years had never encouraged her to excel at her work. If anything, they pulled her away from it. And Mom had been right about Avery's tendency toward disorder on her own, too. But with Bryan's help, Avery felt like she had someone by her side who wanted her to be responsible.

On their first date after the trip, they'd gone out for dinner, then a walk on the beach near the Hotel del Coronado. Near sunset, Bryan had dropped to one knee and proposed. "I asked for your mom's blessing last week. Be my wife, Avery Moretti?"

Of all the guys she'd dated, she never would have imagined Bryan would spring a proposal on her. But as she stared at his earnest, soulful expression, she thought of all the ways he'd made her life better the last few months. She wanted that for the rest of her life.

Afterward, they'd spent the night at the hotel, where Bryan had booked them a suite.

Romantic, lavish, and wonderful. Yes, it was a fast engagement, *but who cares?* Lots of women in her family had a habit of getting engaged to men they'd only been dating a few months. Mom and Dad had only known each other for three weeks, and she'd been engaged to someone else. Mom had broken up with the other guy, and a week later Dad had proposed.

A fiery love affair, even if it had turned so sour at the end.

Avery sighed contentedly. "Speaking of celebrating, I was talking to my friend Felicity today, and she wants to throw us an engagement party here with all my friends."

Bryan buttered a roll. "Which friends?"

"I don't know. Everyone you met at the nightclub a month ago? And a few more." She regretted that more people hadn't met Bryan yet—Erika especially was appalled that Avery had a fiancé she hadn't even had a chance to say hello to—but hopefully, the engagement party here and in Miami could remedy that.

Chewing on his roll, Bryan gave her a thoughtful look, then swallowed. "Is that guy Tad fellow one of those people?"

"Yeah, he's one of my closest friends from my old job."

Bryan shook his head and grimaced. "I'm not comfortable with him coming. I didn't like the way he looked at you."

What? Avery's jaw dropped. "Bryan, Tad is gay. He didn't look at me in any way that should concern you."

"He was rubbing up all over you, Avery. The man kept touching you. I know what I'm talking about." Bryan swallowed some wine, then sat back.

"Well, in this case, you don't. He's not even remotely interested in me." She shook her head in confusion. "I-I don't even know where this is coming from. You couldn't tell he was gay?"

Bryan sighed heavily. "How could I tell? That nightclub was so loud, I could barely hear anyone."

"I thought you liked that place. You said you liked dancing." Tension rose in the back of Avery's neck. *Why is he being this way?* "And Tad is honestly one of the most fun guys I know. All the people at my old job get along great with him. He's always the life of the party."

"First of all, I enjoy dancing with *you*. I'm not into it otherwise." Bryan shrugged. "And I didn't get that impression from Tad. He seemed really fake to me." Then he met Avery's eyes. "But maybe I'm wrong and overreacting."

She appreciated he was willing to concede he may be wrong, but his comment about the dancing had also left her unsettled. Still, he wasn't being nasty about it, just assertive. She nodded, then reached across the table. "You *are* overreacting. Because Tad is not interested. Not in the slightest. And once you get to know him better, you'll see."

"Just because we're getting married, doesn't mean I'm going to like all of your friends, Avery. It's okay if I don't like some of them."

Avery squeezed her jaw shut as she stared down at him. How had they gone from a party offer to this? She'd been so excited to show him off to the friends he hadn't met yet—what if he didn't like them? But she'd also never been in a more serious, mature relationship like this. Bryan was levelheaded. He may have a point about them not having to like each other's friends.

Bryan seemed to sense he'd upset her, and his expression softened. "Avery, you know I only have your best interest at heart. I tend to have good instincts about things like this. I wouldn't even say anything if I didn't think it was something you might want to think about."

Before she could say anything else, her purse vibrated from her ringing phone. Normally, she wouldn't have even looked at it during dinner with him, but she welcomed the break in tension. Mom was calling.

"Hey, Mom." Avery gave Bryan an apologetic look as she lifted the phone to her ear. "I'm at dinner with Bryan. What's up?"

"Avery, *mi amor*, sorry to interrupt." Mom sounded like she was breathless. "I just spoke to your abuela, and we're anxious to get started with planning, especially if we're all going to be traveling. Have you started talking about that?"

"We're tossing a few dates in the air." She grinned at Bryan, her heart lightening at the thought of wedding plans. She'd gone to the bookstore earlier to pick up wedding magazines. "It's all been a surprise, so I haven't gotten too far in planning."

"Avery, you know I don't like surprises, but in this case, this engagement is a good one." Mom had been doing nothing but gushing since Avery had told her the news.

Avery reached across the table for Bryan's hand, and he clasped her fingers. *This is a good surprise.* She pushed the nagging worries about their disagreement to the side. She had a handsome and successful new fiancé—what more could she want?

CHAPTER TWENTY

Now

NOT A LOT of things made Dan want to take off running, but the look in Maria Moretti's eyes as she stared at the front of the Serendipity sure did.

This is . . . how would an angry Latina mother put it? No bueno?

Ten-thirty-three, emergency. In need of immediate assistance.

Even if he had his police radio, who could fix this?

Avery's mother slammed the car door and strode across the lawn toward the front porch. Dan ducked behind the boxwood bushes, trying to gather his thoughts. He wasn't sure if she'd seen him yet since he was on the ground—or if she would recognize him—but he imagined that wouldn't put her in a better mood.

Then again, he wasn't eighteen anymore. There had been a

time in his life when he'd kicked himself for not standing his ground against Avery's mother. But he wasn't used to standing up to adults at that age. He no longer needed to cower. He'd faced far worse than Avery's mother in his life.

He straightened, taking a calming breath as he stepped out from behind the bush. Avery was busy crawling down from the front porch and then wove around the steps, intercepting her mother as she drew closer.

"Mom! What are you doing here?"

Avery's mother's gaze surveyed the space for just a moment before her eyes landed on Dan's face. She studied him distrustfully, then looked back at Avery. "I'm here because I've spent the last two days trying to get in touch with you. I got worried, so I hopped on the first plane I could catch from Tampa." Then she placed the tip of her finger on Avery's cheek. "Oh my God, what did you do to your face?"

Avery put a hand to her forehead as though she'd forgotten about the sunburn, then adjusted her glasses. She looked good in glasses, but from the way she fidgeted with them, Dan got the impression she didn't wear them often.

And once again, he heard her words from the night before. *"I miss the Avery I found that summer."* It hadn't been self-pity, just a simple statement of fact, as if something—or someone— was still holding her back. During the handful of days they'd spent together before, it had been clear her mother was that someone. And now?

"Sunburn." Avery's smile was tense as she gave her mother a tepid hug and kiss on the cheek. "I'm so surprised to see you here. I'm so sorry about not returning your phone calls. I've just had spotty reception at the lodge, and there's no Wi-Fi."

"You shouldn't be getting sunburns like that when your wedding is around the corner. Wear a hat next time, sweetheart." Her mother reached into her purse and pulled out a tube of cream. "Put some of this on it. It's a moisturizer with tea tree oil. It'll make it better right away." She clasped her purse in front of her. "Now, what is going on here? Why is the lodge in shambles? Where's Ken? What happened to the Wi-Fi?"

If Avery's mother was any other client, Dan would have introduced himself by now. Hanging back and expecting Avery to handle everything as a personal matter wouldn't be fair to her. Maybe she wouldn't remember his name? He took a few steps toward her and held out his hand. "Dan Klein. I'm the new owner of the Serendipity. Unfortunately, Mr. Harrison passed away in January."

Mrs. Moretti stared at Dan's proffered hand, then her gaze scanned his. "Dan . . . *Klein?* Oh, my God." She didn't shake his hand, her gaze becoming accusatory. She scowled at Avery. "Is this why you haven't been calling me? Pensé que estabas muerte or something!"

Avery groaned. "For the last time, Mom, when I don't call you back for a day or so, it's not because I'm dead."

A fast stream of Spanish followed from Avery's mom, one Dan could never hope to keep up with, especially considering his knowledge of the language was rudimentary. From her tone, though, she was scolding Avery.

"Mom, you remember Dan, don't you?" Avery finally choked out, as though her mother wasn't making it obvious that she did. "Yeah, it was a shock, but it turns out Dan bought the Serendipity and—"

"You didn't think to tell me that?" Avery's mother was pale. She placed a hand over her heart and took a shaky breath. "He may not have been family, but I've known Ken Harrison my whole life, Avery. And then *este cabrón* is here instead? Where the hell are you going to have your wedding? Does Bryan know that—"

"Mrs. Moretti, you've just had a long trip, haven't you?

Why don't we head on inside and talk?" Dan's voice remained smooth and calm.

"Right here is fine," Avery said, giving Dan a hard look.

Her mother looked at her quizzically. "Is there something you don't want me to see inside?"

Dan groaned inwardly. Avery probably didn't want her mother to see the place without furniture or the sitting room in its current state. But the woman was perceptive. Of course, if Avery's mother was here, she'd want to see things or stay here, so there wasn't really a way to hide it all now.

Erika, who had been conspicuously absent during Mrs. Moretti's arrival, made an appearance then, coming around from the far side of the boxwood bushes. Peyton appeared to have vanished, too—maybe to the back of the house—something Dan couldn't help wondering if it was Erika's doing. She'd probably caught on by now the kid had a way of saying the wrong thing to exactly the wrong person and wanted him a mile away from Avery's mother.

"Hey there, you are . . ." Erika paused as she got closer. "Mrs. M! Wow, I can't believe you're here. It's so good to see you." She gave Avery's mother a hug and big smile before turning to Dan. "I see you've met our gracious host. He's been wonderful. Really stepped it up with helping hands on for all the things we need to get done for the wedding."

Remarkably, Erika's presence somehow defused the tension, as though Erika had been around Avery's mother for long enough to know how to handle her. Mrs. Moretti's scowl softened, and she composed herself.

Avery sucked in a breath, standing straighter. "Mom, my wedding reservation wasn't officially on the books like I thought, and Dan didn't know to expect our wedding guests. So he started to renovate the Serendipity, which is in need of repairs. But he's done me the courtesy of agreeing to honor the reservation and do what he can to accommodate our guests and fix things in time for the wedding. That's the sum of it."

Her mother gave Dan a hard stare. "*Qué cagada.*" Then she turned to Avery and spoke in low tones, once again in Spanish.

"What'd she say?" Dan muttered to Erika.

"Roughly translates to 'what a shit show.' Or just shit. Either way, she's not thrilled," Erika breathed back, then she stepped closer to her friend. "Mrs. Moretti, I'm so, so glad you're here. Avery and Dan are heading into town to talk to some contractors, and I'm going to go to a few local restaurants to see about getting a new caterer. But now that you're here, would you be willing to drive me? I could use your expertise. I'll be happy to explain the catering situation along the way."

Once again, Erika's ability to handle Avery's mother impressed Dan. As Avery's mother was startled into silence, Dan said, "Mrs. Moretti, I'm doing everything I can to get the lodge in shape for Avery's wedding. We'll have it ready."

Clearly appearing disarmed, her mother frowned. Then Dan added with a nod, "Anyhow, this sounds like you all have family business to discuss. I'm happy to answer questions about the lodge later, but I'll leave you ladies to figure out what you want to do without my intrusion."

As Dan walked away, he heard Avery saying, "Mom. I know it looks rough, but if we can get the outside in shape for the ceremony and reception, I think it will be fine. The rooms need furnishing, but Dan is going to have it all brought back from storage . . ."

Stepping into the house, Dan released a sigh. Would Avery's mother be flexible? He didn't remember her being reasonable, and he was glad for Erika's handling of the situation. Erika must have spent years helping Avery survive her mother's rigidity. And she obviously wanted to spare Avery from facing the brunt of her mother's immediate reaction, or she wouldn't have made up the story about Dan taking Avery into town.

Of course, the problem with Erika's plan was that now he had to figure out how to kill a few hours with Avery, rather than getting the work done they were already running out of time for.

But spending more time with Avery wasn't unwelcome at all—and that fact was worrying him.

"SO YOUR MOTHER actually went with Erika," Dan said as they sped down the back roads. Ten in the morning, and the day was shot to hell, but at least Peyton was still working on the landscaping. Not that Maria Moretti had been completely easygoing about it all. She'd insisted on a tour of the Serendipity and the grounds, to assess the task ahead of them.

"Well, she wasn't happy about me going anywhere with you. But I told her we've both moved on from teenage puppy love and she has nothing to worry about."

Teenage puppy love. Ouch.

And why tell him that? To make sure he understood where the boundaries were?

Avery continued. "My mom loves Erika. Otherwise, she wouldn't have let me be friends with her." Avery shrugged. "Even when she was less than thrilled with Erika during 'her rebellious teenage years,' Erika always had the upper-hand because she was a straight-A student who never, ever got in trouble."

"You're lucky to have someone like that in your life." Dan glanced at her. Avery had been withdrawn and quiet since they'd left the lodge. "It sounds like she helped you survive a lot of things."

"She did." Avery cleared her throat, then looked out the passenger side window.

He'd said something wrong but wasn't entirely sure what. Unwilling to continue a topic that clearly made Avery miserable, he settled for silence, which he preferred anyway. Whenever he was quiet, Melissa had insisted on knowing what he was thinking, which he'd told her at least fifty times was frequently nothing at all. That only irritated her, though, because she didn't believe it could be true.

She'd been equally mad when he'd gone out with his friends and then said they "hadn't talked about much." *Men don't need to speak as many words. Fact.*

He smirked, the steering wheel gliding smoothly under his palms as he took a turn. After a few more minutes of silence, he finally asked, "You okay?"

Avery's blue-gray eyes were troubled as she shot him a look. "What do you think?"

"I think you came to Brandywood to dot some is and cross some ts and instead are overwhelmed, sunburned, probably sore from gardening, and short on some contact lenses." He pulled up into a parking spot.

They were near Main Street on one of the side roads. Avery's blank look as she took in their surroundings confirmed that her family had probably only stuck to the iconic spots on Main—she wouldn't know about the hidden gems tucked away in the alleys that sprawled on either side of Main Street. "The last thing I can help with, though. One of my buddies in the force has a wife who's an eye doctor. This is her office right here. I'm pretty sure she could set you up with a free sample lens if you have your prescription information."

Avery blinked at him, a slow smile curving her lips. "Really?"

Small victories. Her smile had a way of making his heart

squeeze. "Yup. I figure since Erika is going to have your mom over on the more popular side of town, we could do a tour of the spots only locals know about. You need a break from stress anyway."

She still wasn't talking much, but he was certain he saw gratefulness in her eyes as they got out of the truck.

Dan rubbed his jaw, which felt naked since he'd shaved—odd, considering he'd never worn a beard until recently. Even if he hadn't admitted it to himself, the beard had partially been a way to feel anonymous.

He hadn't wanted to show his face around here.

Buying the Serendipity had felt like buying a place to hide. He could be one of the townspeople on the fringe. But Avery's wedding had been a hiccup in that plan, and in two days he'd spent more time in the heart of town than he had in months.

Somehow, being with her didn't make it as bad as he'd feared. But he still needed to face going to Yardley's later tonight to ask Garrett for his help with the Serendipity.

And using Avery like a Band-Aid for a gunshot wound is going to end badly for you, idiot. But no matter how many times he tried to tell himself letting her close was a dumb idea, he just couldn't seem to find it in him to take his own advice to heart.

Maybe that was why he had ended up crushed the first time after that handful of days they'd spent together, while she shrugged it off as "puppy love." Maybe Avery Moretti had always meant a lot more to him than the other way around.

CHAPTER TWENTY-ONE

Avery studied the silver ring in the booth at the antique mall, drawn in by the intricate design on the band. The elderly man behind the booth smiled pleasantly at her, taking a few steps closer.

"It's a puzzle ring. Not as fancy as that sparkly diamond on your left hand, but look," he said, reaching for it. A tremor in his hands made it harder to see the design, but he took the ring from the box, then slipped it apart into three distinct bands. "A band for the past, one for the present, and one for the future. Sometimes it takes some work to get the right pieces to line up, but when they do"—he slid the pieces back together into one band—"everything falls right into place."

An apt metaphor for life sometimes, too.

"How much is it?" Avery asked, scanning the empty box. It didn't have a price tag.

"Eighty-two." The man winked at her. "But I bet that handsome fiancé of yours will get it for you if you ask. And I'll give him a twenty percent discount for being in law enforcement."

He nodded to Dan, who was still over by the display of framed regional maps.

"Oh, he's—"

"Not in law enforcement anymore." Dan glanced up sharply, then came over toward them.

"Don't matter to me. I know how well you served our town. Congratulations on the beautiful new fiancée, by the way. If I were a couple of years younger, I'd fight ya for her." The man winked. Then looked back at Avery. "Should I wrap it up?"

Tempted as she was to take advantage of the discount he was offering Dan, Avery shook her head. She did like the ring, but that wouldn't be right. Besides, she'd never actually wear it these days. Before she and Bryan had dated, she often wore a different ring on half her fingers. Bryan had told her a few horror stories about rings—and fingers—having to be cut off in the emergency department, and that had been the end of that.

Twenty minutes later, Avery was heading out of the antique mall, examining the puzzle ring on her finger, which she'd ended up paying forty dollars for. "You know, you didn't have to haggle. He was already offering you twenty percent."

"Highway robbery. Never let old Mr. Peters take you for a ride. Everyone around here knows you can always talk him down in price. He's the only one in that mall who doesn't put a price tag on things, because he likes to keep his pricing flexible." Dan nodded toward the shop across the street. "Feel like ice cream?"

Avery's stomach growled in response. She'd never had time to eat the breakfast Dan's sister had delivered that morning. Thoughts of the morning threatened to dim her spirits once again.

She checked up and down the alleyway. They were relatively alone in the shadowed, cool light between the brick buildings. Cobblestones ran the length of the alleyway, as though someone hadn't had the heart to cover them over with asphalt. It gave the alley some charm.

"First, tell me why you didn't correct that sweet old man," Avery hissed, playfully swatting Dan in the arm. Dan letting Mr. Peters think they were engaged was odd but had also produced a fair share of flutters in her stomach, which she'd been actively trying to ignore.

Dan chuckled lightly. "It's Brandywood. You pick the rumors you want according to who's feeding the mill. In the case of Mr. Peters, I could have him tell people he saw Dan Klein's beautiful new fiancée. While intriguing, that can be easily corrected and isn't interesting enough to spread far. On the other hand, he could tell someone he saw Dan running around in the shadowed corners of Paradise Street with a gorgeous—but engaged-to-someone-else—mystery woman . . ."

Avery's jaw dropped, the implication clear. "And you're saying the rumor mill would spread that?"

Dan quirked a brow. "Of course they would. Negative gossip always spreads ten times faster than positive. Welcome to small-town life and one of its biggest drawbacks."

That Mr. Peters, or anyone, would say something like that had never occurred to Avery. Disappointment rankled her. "And here I thought he was a sweet old man."

"He is sweet. Fairly harmless." Dan shrugged. "But he runs a shop, so it's second nature for him to say, 'Oh, you know who I saw in the store the other day?'" They stopped in front of the wooden door of a nondescript place that had a small white sign that read "Baltimore Deli."

His explanation about Mr. Peters was reasonable enough, but Avery couldn't help feeling unsettled. She'd always pictured life in Brandywood as perfect and wonderful because people were more likely to know one another. She guessed gossip was just as alive and well here as anywhere else. *Or you were purposely being naïve.* She looked at the shop sign. "What's this?"

"Best damn spot in town for overstuffed sandwiches and ice cream. Mr. and Mrs. Wong run it—don't put a ton of money into advertising or décor, and everything is to go—but everyone who's anyone in town knows about it. We're here early for the lunchtime rush, but come back in about a half-hour, and the line will be down the alley."

He held the door for her. The sandwiches looked too good to pass up, and within minutes they were back in the alley, strolling with their ice creams in one hand and a paper bag of sandwiches in the other. Avery followed him out of the alley and onto a grassy area that led down to a narrow river that ran behind the shops. "I didn't know there was anything like this in Brandywood," Avery said with wide eyes as they stopped at a park bench near the water.

"Some locals are trying to keep it that way. Tourist-free. They want to put up a fence." Dan set his sandwich bag down on the bench and sat, taking a bite out of his mint chocolate chip ice cream.

"Really?" Avery sat beside him, feeling strangely carefree. She never ate dessert before any meal. "I guess I could see that. Have some place that's not spoiled by outsiders. Although, maybe that means I shouldn't be here."

Dan rolled his eyes. "I'm not one of those people. Brandywood isn't perfect, by any means. But I've seen this community rally together and offer both forgiveness and support to many people. Like earlier this summer, when one librarian had a little girl who came down with leukemia—the whole town did a fundraiser to cover all her medical costs completely. That's the sort of place I want Brandywood to be."

Avery studied his profile and licked the raspberry ice cream that was dripping down the side of her cone. "If that's the case, then why did you quit being a cop? You didn't think people would offer you forgiveness and support?"

"It's not quite the same thing." Dan shifted, looking away. His jaw set, as though she'd struck a nerve.

Maybe he doesn't think he deserved forgiveness and support.

She looked away from him. He'd told her a lot about himself the previous night—personal information she had no right to pry into further. And she wasn't being fair. She'd been guarding her own heart, not telling him much about her own fears and troubles. Because it was Dan she was talking to, and the last time she'd let her guard down around him, she'd gotten really hurt.

Yet he'd respected her silence, hadn't pried in the truck when she wasn't feeling like talking about her mom's sudden arrival and what a disaster the last couple of days had been.

And when he'd cautiously asked about Bryan, he hadn't asked to know what his deal was—just wanted to make sure *she* was feeling all right and respected. But Dan had been that way when he was a teenager. Not much had changed, it seemed.

Maybe that was why she had been so certain she'd loved him when they were teenagers. When she was around him, he'd had a way of making her feel seen, her feelings valid. He made her feel as though she wasn't crazy to think about things a certain way, even when all he did was listen to her vent.

That unconditional support must have been what she'd missed so much about him. And it was an unusual trait in a guy, too. She'd never met another guy who did that—not even Bryan. "Your ex was crazy to let you go," she said in a soft voice that surprised even her. She'd wanted to say something to make him feel better, but that had been a bit much. Her cheeks grew warm with embarrassment. "Um, I mean . . ."

Dan gave her an odd look that made her want to hide her face behind her ice cream cone. "My ex was crazy. That's about it." He smiled and finished his ice cream, wiping his mouth with the thin napkin they'd wrapped around the cone. "But speaking of significant others, when does your fiancé get into town? We should probably come up with a rough timeline of everything we need to get done and when. That way, when your mother asks questions later, we seem more confident."

Bryan . . . She grimaced. She'd neglected to call him this morning, which meant he'd be unhappy when they talked later. *He'd be furious if he knew about me being here with Dan.* Should she even be spending time around Dan if she knew how much her fiancé would hate it?

Well, it wasn't like she was doing anything wrong.

"He comes next Wednesday. I wanted him to take off the week of the wedding, but he wanted to leave that time for the honeymoon."

"Where you heading for that?"

"Red Rock, Nevada." She smiled tautly. "Bryan wanted to plan the honeymoon destination since I planned the wedding destination, so I gave him free rein."

Dan gave her a quizzical look. "What's in Red Rock?"

Her throat prickled, then she answered with as bright a smile as possible. "Rock climbing."

Digging into his sandwich bag, Dan pulled out a cheesesteak that smelled so heavenly, it made Avery want to abandon her ice cream. "I didn't realize you were so into rock climbing. You trade the pencil skirts and stilettos by day for climbing gear and ropes by night, eh?" He gave her a wink.

She hadn't expected tears, but they came anyway, burning the rims of her eyes. "Actually, I hate climbing." She drew a shaky breath, then got up and crossed over to a trash can. Dumping the rest of her ice cream, she wiped her eyes and turned back.

Dan had set his sandwich down and stared at her, a frown

etching his features. He stood, slowly. "Does Bryan know you hate climbing?"

She sniffed and shook her head. "I've never told him." She choked back a cry. "I've never told anyone, actually. I just . . . didn't want him to know I hated his favorite hobby. So I went along with it and pretended I liked it. And now I'm stuck climbing on my honeymoon."

Dan came closer, then drew her into a hug.

Avery sank against him, trying to avoid thinking about the way her nerves flared in response to his touch, her heart speeding. His arms offered more than warmth and comfort, though maybe that was all he intended. Leaning against him, she felt his strength bolstering her, keeping her steady.

For one moment, she closed her eyes, remembering how easy it had been to fall in love with Dan Klein as a teenager. She'd convinced herself for years it had just been hormones and sexual attraction, but had it?

No, it was him. We had something special.

She shut those thoughts down and pulled away, needing to sever the contact. Wiping her cheeks, she sniffed again. "It's stupid, I know. Poor little me, crying about the honeymoon my thoughtful fiancé has planned for me."

Something dark and unreadable glittered in Dan's eyes. "I don't know about that, Avery. A honeymoon should be about you both. Bryan may not know you hate climbing, but I'm not sure he thought that much about what *you* wanted when he planned it."

That's how I felt when Bryan told me about the plans.

She hadn't really wanted to think about it then, though. Because Bryan hadn't planned something cheap for their honeymoon—there were plenty of luxuries involved. But the nagging feeling that he planned something more for himself than for her had bothered her.

A sudden movement caught Avery's attention. A Canadian goose had stealthily come up from the waterline to the bench and was curiously bending its long black neck toward Dan's sandwich.

"Oh no, you don't." Avery darted around Dan to stop it and chase it away. The goose immediately reared its head and neck, flapping its wings and honking.

Dan whirled around, then dashed between Avery and the goose, putting an arm out to keep her back. "Just leave it."

"But your sandwich." Avery held out a hand, and the goose charged at them, wings still flapping.

"I can get another sandwich. These geese are dicks." He turned to scurry her away, then yelped.

When Avery turned, Dan had grabbed a handful of mulch from the base of a nearby tree. He threw it at the goose. "Get going!" he yelled, stomping at it.

The bird backed away, still honking, and Avery came up behind Dan. "You okay?"

"Damn fucker bit me in the ass. It just feels like someone pinched me, but still." Dan rubbed his backside with a wince. Then he cocked his head at Avery. "You sure nature doesn't have some sort of curse on you?"

Avery laughed half-heartedly.

She didn't really believe in that damn curse . . . did she?

CHAPTER TWENTY-TWO

DAN SCANNED the bar area of Yardley's Pub and hesitated. He almost hadn't come here this afternoon after dropping off Avery back at the lodge. Spending the day with her already had his stomach and brain in turmoil. Not to mention that damn bruise he had on his ass cheek from the goose that had stolen his sandwich.

The guys from the precinct liked to come here, and he'd been doing his best to avoid familiar faces since he'd retired from the force. Not that they weren't friends. But it wasn't like old times. No shooting the shit over a beer and darts.

They were in. He was out.

No matter how much they all tried to pretend everything was the same, it just wasn't. He'd sensed it the few times he'd gotten together with them.

On the other hand, his brother-in-law, Garrett Doyle, was here with a few of his friends during happy hour. Since Garrett had gotten sober and married, his poker night had become trivia happy hour, to include wives and girlfriends. But now that Sam was home with the baby and Garrett's friends were newly single, it was back to an all-male outing.

Dan spotted Garrett by a table on the far side of the bar, close to where the trivia emcee was set up. His gaze flicked to the glass of Coke in front of Garrett. They'd come a long way—to where Dan nearly considered Garrett a friend now—but Dan couldn't help worrying for Sam whenever Garrett came here without her.

Still, Peter Yardley had assured Dan he'd never serve Garrett an alcoholic drink, and Brandywood was the sort of place where that wouldn't happen without *someone* saying something. Garrett was open enough about his sobriety for his friends to drink comfortably around him. For that, Dan had to admire him. Garrett had learned to control his vices.

If only I could forgive the wrong I caused Garrett. Maybe I never will.

Dan pushed the thought down deep and shuffled into the bar, avoiding looking at the high-tops where his friends from the force were gathered. Before he could reach Garrett, though, he was intercepted by Peter Yardley, the owner of the bar.

The old man greeted him with twinkling blue eyes. "How's my favorite cop?" He greeted Dan with a clap on the back. "I've missed seeing you in here, kid."

"*Former* cop."

"Eh, once a cop, always a cop." Peter winked at him.

Dan laughed. "It's not the priesthood, Yardley."

"Yeah, but you never lose those instincts." Peter reached into his pocket and pulled out a business card. "Speaking of which, if you ever decide you want to do something more like that again, call me. I could use a good bodyguard these days. Much as I love the show, it's gotten bigger than I ever planned. And now that people have found out I still bartend here some-times, things get crazy."

Dan didn't have the heart to tell the old man no outright, and he nodded, then said goodbye, continuing toward Garrett.

Garrett saw him and raised his chin, giving Dan a concerned, questioning look. He stood as Dan reached the table.

"Everything okay?"

Dan set his hands on the back of a chair. "Yeah, yeah, everything's fine. How are Sam and Reese?"

Garrett beamed. "Great. Sam follows her around with a camera all day, documenting her every movement."

"First kid thing, right? I think Warren said he has two thousand pictures of Cameron, and three of Sarah." Dan nodded toward Ben, who'd stayed seated at the table. "Good to see you again, Pearson."

"You, too. Joining us for trivia?" Ben asked, shifting his drink so Dan could take the empty seat beside him.

"No, just stopped in to see about getting some work done with the lodge." Dan sat, despite the stab of awkwardness that lingered. He shot a pleading look at Garrett. "You wouldn't have any openings in your schedule for the next couple of weeks? Ken Harrison had apparently booked a wedding for the lodge for a week and a half from now, and the bride showed up earlier this week to get things ready. I told her I'd do what I could to make the place work for her, but I've torn apart my sitting room, and I fell through the front porch this morning. Boards rotted through in several places."

Garrett, who was sipping his Coke, nearly choked on it. He coughed into his hand, his eyes widening. "You fell through it?" He coughed again and set his glass on the coaster.

Before Dan could answer, Ben leaned forward. "Is that one of the women I drove over to your place the other day? Shit, man, I didn't know that. No wonder that one woman was so upset when she saw the place."

"Yeah, that was the bride. Avery. She and her family have been coming to the Serendipity since she was a kid—I met her when we were teens. She told me even back then she wanted to do her wedding there."

"Wow." Ben blew out a low whistle, shaking his head. "Well, good luck to you, man. I don't know how the hell you're going to get all that fixed in time."

He inspired little hope in Dan. Ben had seen the state of the Serendipity when he'd helped Erika and Avery bring in their things.

Garrett, recovered from coughing, cleared his throat. "How much work are we talking?"

Another figure arrived at the table—his brother, Warren. Warren gave Dan a surprised look as he sat. "You here for trivia?"

Since when had Warren started hanging out with Garrett? It shouldn't surprise Dan. They were all family now. And now that Garrett and Sam had a baby, it was likely Warren had even more in common with Garrett than with Dan.

Warren was almost as tall as Dan and Garrett, who were nearly matched in height, and for years Warren had called himself Dan's "shorter, better-looking older brother."

Ben answered for Dan. He grinned. "Nah, he apparently stopped in to get Garrett to do some contracting work for him. Some woman named Avery is making him move heaven and earth for her to have her wedding at the Serendipity in two weeks and suckered him into saying he'd fix up that money pit on time."

The weight of Warren's hard stare transfixed on Dan.

The emcee for the trivia night started talking, and Dan was grateful for the chance to avoid looking at Warren. He hadn't expected this. He'd even gotten Jen to swear not to say anything to Warren about Avery.

As one of Garrett's other friends, Luis, arrived at the table, Dan stood, hoping to take advantage of Luis's arrival to leave. He shouldn't have come. This wasn't his scene anymore. His "group of buddies" a few tables over were laughing about things he was no longer a part of.

"Just let me know if you think you can carve some time into your schedule," Dan told Garrett. He nodded a goodbye to Warren and Ben as the emcee continued talking, then turned, making a beeline for the door. The humid early evening air fanned his face as he stepped out onto the sidewalk. It was still light out, and there were a fair number of people milling around Main Street.

Since Peter Yardley had brought the town into national spotlight, the extra money from tourism had resulted in a beautification project to the city street, and string lights lit storefronts. There was even talk of getting some of the old telephone lines buried and acquiring another much-needed cell tower in town.

Somewhere, an acoustic band was playing at a nearby restaurant. Maybe even at the bandstand in the middle of town.

Didn't matter. He didn't have anyone to go sit on a blanket under the stars with and listen to the soft sounds of summer in Brandywood.

Spending time with Avery today had only made that loneliness stronger. Worse than being a stranger in town was being someone who everyone thought they knew—and didn't really want around. Even if they wouldn't say it out loud.

And now, his first real challenge for the business that was going to *turn everything around* for him was already on the brink of catastrophe. He headed down the sidewalk, toward the parking lot, avoiding looking at the couples holding hands as they strolled down Main.

"Hey man, wait up." Garrett's voice sounded behind him, and Dan slowed to a stop.

He turned as Garrett approached, concern on his face. Warren had also followed but was several steps behind Garrett. "You didn't need to run out—I wasn't trying to make fun of you," Garrett said.

Dan smirked. How the tables had turned, hadn't they? That Garrett would ever be worried about hurting Dan's feelings would have been a ludicrous thought just a few years ago. He shook his head. "Nah, that's not it. I just didn't want to interfere with your happy hour. I'm good."

"You sure?" Garrett crossed his arms, and Dan noted the new tattoo he'd gotten on his arm peeking out from under his shirtsleeve. Some type of white flower, maybe a lily. Warren came closer and stopped beside Garrett.

"Yeah, positive." He released a slow stream of air from his lips, his chest loosening. This was so much worse with Warren around, listening. "I know that wedding is a bigger project than I can handle. I just know the girl. She's been coming to the lodge with her family for years, and I didn't know how to let her down."

Garrett ducked his chin at him, his eyes narrowing a smidge at the corners with some sort of unspoken understanding. "I'll carve out time to help you. I've been there. I would have tried to build the Taj Mahal in three days for Sam, even when I didn't think she'd be with me. But you know what I think?"

Dan raised a brow in response. All the men in his family were determined to give him advice, whether he wanted it or not. The weight of Warren's gaze wore heavily on Dan, and his neck muscles felt taut and rigid.

"Never wait to have the important conversations with people. Putting them off only leads to bigger problems in the long run." Garrett stuffed his hands in his pockets. "So a sitting room and a front porch. Anything else you need done?"

"Whole place could use a tune-up and some paint, but that might be a stretch. I figure some of the bigger projects I planned can wait until I'm done with this thing."

Garrett pulled a notepad from his front shirt pocket and handed it to Dan with a pen. "Make a list of your priorities. We'll see what we can fit in. I'll get Luis to take over on our current project for a few days and then get a crew together."

Dan breathed a sigh of relief. *Thank God.*

"Thanks so much for this." Dan scribbled a few lines, squinting as he wrote. Garrett taking over was a double-edged sword, and acid rose in his throat. Putting his pride down around Garrett was never easy, especially when Garrett really didn't have any reason to bend over backward like he was, except for the fact that he was a better man than Dan. Always had been.

Dan finished writing and gave the notepad back to Garrett. "You'll have to give me a payment schedule. The way Jason and I worked out the loan is that I front some costs and then he distributes funds once I give him the receipts. Which usually then goes to paying the next portion of the work. But in this case, it's going to be a lot all at once." And Dan already owed Jason the interest payment for the month.

"As long as I can pay my workers and some of the material costs, that's all I need right now. We'll figure out the rest later."

Would he have the money to pay the workers? He'd need to start doing some of the paperwork for all of this. Actually, he probably should write up a contract with Avery. She was his client. He needed to act like a business owner, especially if he was involving other people's time and money like this.

"Thank you again, Garrett. I owe you. I mean, I already

owe you—but once again, I'm in your debt." Dan started to turn away, then stopped. "Oh, by the way, I'm having the whole family come over Saturday afternoon for a cookout. I'll send Sam the details."

Garrett left, giving a nod to Warren as though he understood he wanted to talk to his younger brother. Warren stepped forward and crossed his arms.

"A woman named Avery?"

Dan grimaced and shoved his hands in his pockets. "Look, Warren—"

"*The* Avery? As in the girl you were so into and who screwed you over when you were in high school? Who you threw things away for?"

"The one and the same."

Warren's face clouded. "Well, fuck her. Why are you trying to do anything to help her?"

"Because it's not her fault that Ken died and I bought the Serendipity. Her whole wedding shouldn't have to be ruined over stuff that happened between us years ago."

Warren shook his head slowly. "You're a better man than I am. I wouldn't lift a finger to help her."

I'm not a better man than you, not by a long shot. And he wasn't good at faking things either.

"I'm not pretending it isn't a colossal pain in the ass. But I guess that's part of owning a business and doing a bunch of pain-in-the-ass things to make sure the customer is happy. Plus, she's going to pay the full rental fee, which will go a long way to help with some of the recent costs I had with that damned septic system." Dan gave him a half-hearted smile he was certain Warren would see right through. But he didn't want to defend the decision to Warren.

Warren shrugged. "I guess." Warren came closer. "Just be

careful. The last time you were around that woman, she really messed you up. You deserve better than that. Especially after you went through all that crap with Melissa this year."

"Avery's getting married, remember?" Dan smirked. "You sound more like Alice each day."

"Right. But that doesn't mean you can't get hurt. Like I said. Be careful. Okay?"

Dan nodded. "I'll be fine."

Warren gave him a skeptical look. "If you say so. But if you need anything—tell me, will you?"

Leave it to his older brother to see through any façade he thought he'd perfected. Dan watched him go back to Yardley's, his heart heavy.

Warren knew about the situation better than anyone. Dan had thought only of Avery during that week she'd been his.

And he'd gotten himself in trouble as a result.

He'd been careless, and he hadn't been the only one to get hurt. Both Warren and Corbin had been furious Dan had taken the fall for everything that happened with Avery. Warren couldn't stand to hear Dan being compared to their notorious drug-dealing birth father who had abandoned them. And Corbin had been devastated that Dan had taken so much on his shoulders for a girl he barely knew. *And my friendship with Corbin never recovered.*

For the first couple of years that had followed, Dan had truly believed he hated her. That anger had motivated him to become a cop and prove to the world around him he was not only an upstanding citizen, he also wouldn't tolerate crime.

He climbed into his truck, and the slam of the door next to him made the space feel empty. The air was scorching and suffocating, and he started the engine, his gaze swiveling to the empty spot where that St. Christopher medal had swung for so long. He'd put it there to remember never to let a woman—any woman—get the better of him.

But Melissa had found a way, hadn't she?

She'd known how to hit him where it would hurt the most—and how to push his buttons in a way that even he hadn't been able to control. Add that to his reputation for being a bully and the trouble he'd gotten into as a teenager, and there wasn't a person outside his family who had believed Dan when he'd told his side of the breakup story.

And just like that, his career as a cop had been over.

The chief hadn't asked for Dan's resignation, but the implication had been there.

You're an embarrassment.

He turned the air-conditioning to full blast, tugging at the collar of his T-shirt. Sweat had beaded on his forehead and dripped down his temples.

It had all started with Avery. With that damned party he never should have taken her to. Didn't matter that he hadn't touched a drop of alcohol. Or what he'd done to help her afterward.

He'd never confronted her about it, though, because he hadn't had the chance. And now that she was finally here again after twelve years, he'd gone right back to helping her, putting her needs first, pretending that conflict hadn't happened when she'd waved a check in his face.

The last two days had been as confusing as hell, especially when it seemed as if she still needed friendship. But what the hell did he know about her life, her fiancé, or her?

He was doing this for the money, and he needed to stop doubting that. Clearing up the past now wasn't worth either of their time.

Because she's getting married, and then she'll be out of your life forever. Even if the man she's marrying seems like an obvious prick. What man chose rock climbing for a honeymoon? And didn't know his fiancée hated it?

She doesn't need rescuing.

Doesn't want rescuing.

He wouldn't make that mistake again.

CHAPTER TWENTY-THREE

Avery

12 Years Ago

AVERY TOSSED THE PING-PONG BALL, the music in the house so loud that she could hardly think, let alone concentrate on the red Solo cups on the other side of the table. The ball bounced off the rim of a cup, then to her shock, it landed inside it.

The people on her side of the table whooped, and Dan caught Avery in his arms, swinging her around in a hug. She laughed as he set her down, feeling woozy. One of Dan's friends offered her a high-five. "Maybe we should have her on the basketball team instead of you, Danny boy. You all up for another game?"

"Har, har." Dan's arm curled around her shoulder, and she rocked back against him, feeling unsteady. "I think we're going to get some fresh air."

They left to the sounds of protests, and Avery let him guide her out of the house and onto the lawn. "We didn't have to go if you didn't want to."

Dan shrugged. "I'm trying not to drink tonight. Playing beer pong could be a disaster for that if we lose next time."

The night air was cool on her burning cheeks, and she was glad he had his arm around her. It made it easier for her to walk without having to worry about how tipsy she felt. She sucked in a deep breath. "I love the smell of smoke from campfires." Her gaze landed on a bonfire near the side of the lake. "Let's go sit there."

Dan led her toward the bonfire, which had the bonus of being relatively private. A few log benches had been set up around it for seating, but the only other people around were on the far side, by the waterline—a couple that was cuddling.

Avery sat on the ground, using the log as a backrest, and Dan sat beside her. She leaned her head on his arm, watching the flames as they danced in the firepit and licked the inky blackness of the sky with sizzles and pops. "This has by far been my favorite vacation in a long time."

Dan reached for her hand and interlaced his fingers with hers. Her hand felt dwarfed by his—not that she minded. "Do you go on a lot of vacations?"

"Yeah, all the time. My parents love—*loved* traveling. We spent last Christmas in London, then went to Paris for New Year's. And Vail for skiing." Realizing how rich and privileged she sounded, she added, "It helps being an only child."

"That sounds incredible. Where was your favorite place you've been?"

"Probably Florence." Avery grinned, thinking back on it. "And not just because I'm half-Italian and they have the best gelato." She shrugged, feeling clear-headed about this, although the alcohol was making it hard to form her words quite right. "I just remember wandering around the Uffizi—it's an art museum in Florence—thinking about how the Renaissance started there, in that city. All the painters whose work I lived and breathed as a little girl."

He listened intently, which was strange considering she felt like she risked boring him. Most guys her age didn't get that excited about art like she did, especially not the popular jocks who partied. "When I was a little girl, my dad had these art books in his office, and I used to comb through them for hours, trying to imitate what I saw. Being in Florence, there was"—she sighed happily—"a different pulse to life. Like an energy. Just waiting to be captured."

She didn't want to bore him, so she stopped and squeezed his hand. "What about you? Where's your favorite vacation been?"

Dan shifted. "I haven't been anywhere like you've been. But my parents took us twice to the Outer Banks in North Carolina. That was fun."

Now she really felt like an ass. She pulled away and gave him an apologetic look. "I'm sorry, I didn't mean to sound like such a snob—"

Dan cut her off with a soft kiss on the lips, holding her chin in his thumb and forefinger. "I wouldn't have asked if I didn't want to know, Avery. I think it's awesome that you've been to all those places. I'm hoping someday I can travel the world like that. See those places. Get a little farther than the Appalachians."

"I'll go with you." She smiled at him. "We can be travel influencers, and go anywhere we like. Do whatever we want."

"Whoa, lady. What if you don't want to do the same things I want to do?" Dan tipped his chin down. "You've already been to all the good places. Plus, I might be a picky eater. Maybe I won't be into the local foods."

"You know there's a McDonalds everywhere."

"There's not one in Brandywood." Dan gave her a pointed look.

"Fine, then I promise to taste test everything first, to make sure it's not something that'll make you gag."

Dan chuckled, pulling her closer so she was sitting on his lap. "Guess what?"

"What?"

"I'm not picky." He nestled his chin against the top of her head. "And I'm happy to travel anywhere that makes you happy."

She loved being close to him this way. Loved sitting under the stars with him. Loved the smell of whatever cologne he'd put on. She didn't know guys' colognes, but whatever it was, she decided it was her favorite smell because it would forever remind her of him.

"Okay, well, that's a relief. Because I love food. I love trying new things. My dad and I make a game of it. We'll go to a new place and purposely look for something we've never tried before and get it."

"You're pretty fearless when you want to be." His voice was a low rumble in her ear. "I like that about you."

She pulled away and shook her head. *No, I'm not.* Would he like her less if he knew how often she gave in to fear? How she rarely stood up for herself? "Actually, I'm not that good at being fearless. I don't enjoy disappointing people—especially my parents. It's probably my biggest fear."

"I said 'when you want to be.'" Dan traced his thumb over her bare shoulder, and it caught on the spaghetti strap of her top. "I don't know anyone in school that's great at being brave and confident all the time, do you?"

He was right. Most of her friends—even the confident ones, like Erika—occasionally buckled under peer pressure. But as strange as it was, she felt if he could be around her all the time, she'd feel free to be herself. "What about you? What's your biggest fear?"

Dan looked away, toward the fire. An orange glow lit his features, casting the curves of his face into deeper shadow. "You really want to know?"

She studied him, resisting the urge to close her eyes for a minute. Then she nodded. "I want to know you. Everything."

Dan squeezed her hand, still looking at the fire. "I'm afraid people will be right about me."

"How's that?" She rubbed her eyes, feeling them burning from the smoke.

Dan looked back at her, then pushed a strand of hair behind her ear. "My dad—my birth dad—he was a real asshole. A troublemaker and a criminal. He really hurt my mom. But now and then when I do something that might land me in trouble or detention or something, I hear those whispers that I have bad blood. And then I worry—maybe there's a part of me that is rotten. Maybe someday I'll hurt my mom, too, by letting her down, by being like him."

Avery narrowed her gaze at him, then wrapped her arms around his neck. "I don't buy it."

He furrowed his brow. "You don't buy what?"

She felt cross-eyed looking at him this close, so she put her cheek against his. "I don't buy that blood is bad like that. I think we get to choose who we are—and our path forward. Sure, maybe your birth dad was an ass, but did he raise you? No. He has nothing to do with who you are."

Whistles and hollers punctured the silence around the bonfire as the crowd inside the house moved out into the back yard. A kid wearing shot glass necklaces stopped in front of them, then held out two necklaces. "It's tequila fountain time!"

Dan shook his head, refusing the necklace. But Avery took one and put it around her neck, because—why not? This was her first party ever, after all. When would she ever get a chance at a tequila fountain at home?

Plus, Dan was with her. He'd take care of her.

"Avery, maybe you should take it easy."

"I've taken it easy for the last three years of high school. Watched from the sidelines as everyone else had fun. Even the school principal used me as the butt of a joke in a school assembly last year when the faculty was roasting the juniors before we got our rings." Her voice sounded as bitter as she felt when she mimicked, "Avery Moretti here at the assembly? Oh good, good. I wasn't sure if her parents would allow her to come."

She shook her head and stood, feeling wobbly. The noise intensified outside. "I'm done taking it easy. From now on, I want to live life on my own terms, with no one telling me what to do."

"You know, you're still going to need to live with your parents." Dan got up and put a hand on her elbow.

Avery slid her arms around him and held on tightly. She didn't want to think about that—or about leaving here in a few days. Being around Dan made her feel more alive than she'd ever felt. How could she leave it all behind?

CHAPTER TWENTY-FOUR

Dan

12 Years Ago

THE SMELL of wood smoke permeated Dan's clothes, but he was thankful for it. Whoever had used the bathroom before him had thrown up in the bathtub. The smell was so overpowering that Dan flipped the fan on and started the shower to wash the vomit away.

Gross.

He covered his nose with the collar of his shirt, breathing in the smoky scent as he tried not to gag. One of the hardest parts of being the person who always was designated driver or stayed sober during these parties was that his senses were always sharp. Drunk people had a different tolerance for dealing with things they normally wouldn't be able to.

Washing away the rest of the vomit, he cleaned up the

disgusting toilet seat, then peed and washed his hands, eager to get out of the bathroom.

He hurried through the house as he tried to get back to the bonfire where he'd left Avery with Corbin and his brother Curtis. Next time he had to pee, he'd just go into the woods. He was not dealing with that again.

How Adam's parents were cool with him throwing a party like this year after year, he didn't know. There was no way they couldn't know about it. The place was in shambles.

On the way out the back door, he almost slammed headfirst into Garrett Doyle, who was coming into the house. Dan glared at him. "Get out of my way, asshole."

Garrett was one of the few guys nearly as big as Dan who wasn't on the basketball team. But he was well-liked, and his girlfriend, Katie, had been junior prom queen. Garrett didn't move. "Everyone's got a right to the door, dickweed." His words slurred, and Dan shoved him to the side with little effort.

He's totally drunk.

"Like father, like son, eh, Doyle?" Dan threw him a venomous look. He hated Garrett. Everyone assumed Dan and Garrett were similar, since Garrett's dad was the town drunk and Dan's birth father had been a drug dealer. It didn't help that the two of them were always in detention together. But Dan was nothing like Garrett. Garrett actually *was* a troublemaker, and half the time Dan ended up in trouble it was because of him.

Before Garrett could react, Katie came stumbling over and got between them. "Back off, Klein. Garrett's *my* boyfriend. Stop being so in love with him and get your own."

In love with him? So that was how she wanted to play this?

Normally, her words would have pissed him off even further. But he didn't want to deal with either of these jackasses tonight. He flipped Garrett off, then kept going.

He had to get back to Avery.

The grass on the lawn was already wet from dew, and Dan's flip-flops were soaked by the time he reached the bonfire. He found Corbin laughing, one hand smacking a djembe drum that had been passed around the circle. Avery was gone.

He stiffened, whirling around in a circle, his heart beating faster. *Where did she go?*

Dan grabbed Corbin by the shoulder. "Dude, where's Avery?"

Corbin blinked blearily at him. "I don't know. She was just here."

Scanning the logs set up as seats around the bonfire, Dan's chest tightened with sudden pressure. *She's gone. Shit.*

She was drunk. After the tequila, she'd become floppy, and he'd tried to convince her to leave. But he was worried now. She could do something like wander into the lake and drown. *I shouldn't have left her by herself. She doesn't know anyone else. She's drunk.*

His palms grew slick as he thought of the possibilities.

Dan left Corbin and ran toward the water, his heart pounding. As he drew closer, a familiar skunk-like scent drifted over from the shoreline. A strange sense of disappointment washed over him as he spotted Avery sitting with a few people by the shore. One of them was Curtis. A bowl was being passed among them.

She couldn't know how much he hated drugs, even though he'd told her about his birth dad. And he didn't get mad at his friends who experimented with stuff like that. But he didn't want it for Avery. She was too good for it.

Upon reaching her, Dan tucked his arms under her armpits from behind and lifted her. "Let's go."

"Hey, wait . . . these are my new friends . . ." Avery pointed weakly at the people she was with, and Dan met Curtis's eyes. He said nothing, and his gaze was hard.

He must be the supplier.

Poor Corbin.

After all the trouble Corbin and his grandfather had gone through to get Curtis back on his feet, this was how he turned around and thanked him. The guy was still on probation. He'd have to tell Corbin about this, but right now wasn't the time. Corbin was too drunk to do anything about it right now.

Dan dragged Avery away, and she wasn't easy to move. "I wanted to try it," she protested. "He said he had something that could help me do even better at school."

"Yeah, I'm sure he did." He had to get her away from this scene. Much as she'd wanted to come, this wasn't what he wanted Avery to remember when she thought of him. He didn't want to be the guy who'd encouraged her to break every rule her parents had for her. If they found out, they'd hate him for it.

She was stumbling, and he was going to get nowhere fast with her this drunk. Stopping, he slipped his arm under her knees and lifted her into his arms.

"Where are we going?" Avery leaned her head into his shoulder. She reeked of smoke and alcohol and weed.

No way he could take her back to the lodge like this. He doubted she'd even be able to find her way to her room. It had taken little to get her drunk, despite his attempts to stop her. But she'd insisted, saying she wanted to live "for once."

You're an idiot, Dan. You should have taken better care of her.

What if she ended up with alcohol poisoning? That wasn't too far of a stretch, considering how drunk she was.

Once he reached his truck, he set her down by the

passenger door. "Can you stand long enough for me to open the door?"

She didn't answer, her head bobbing.

"I'll take that as a no." Dan held her with one arm, then struggled to open the door. Setting her inside, he closed the heavy door.

This was such a bad idea.

He never should have brought her here. But the lure of having the girl he liked at a party had been too much. And for the first hour, it had been fun. Because Avery was fun. And she could fit in well for someone who never partied. But this wasn't fun. This was frightening and made him feel stupid and like the bad guy everyone assumed he was.

Once inside his truck, he started the engine, then glanced at Avery. She gave him a lopsided smile, then climbed on all fours across the center console and onto his lap. "Hey, you."

Being straddled would do nothing for his ability to focus. She kissed him, her arms weaving around his neck. It didn't take long for that kiss to turn passionate and wild, and she peeled her shirt from her torso.

He shouldn't let this get out of control either.

Dan's breath caught as he glimpsed two perfect breasts beneath the lacy black fabric of her bra. She grabbed his hands, then set them on top of her breasts, and he rubbed his palms against her. "God, I want to touch you so badly."

"Then touch me." She leaned forward and tugged at his lip with her teeth. "I want you to."

The temptation was almost more than he could overcome. Then he kissed her and shook his head. "You're drunk, Avery. I'm not. Trust me when I tell you I want to. But I'm not doing anything else with you when you're this drunk." He reached for her shirt, determined. Even if she got mad at him, he had to be the responsible one. *She's too drunk to consent.*

She'd just gotten the shirt over her head when she straightened suddenly. Then her eyes widened as she covered her mouth.

Dan barely got the door open in time as she leaned out the driver's side door and threw up.

Great.

He held her hair back as she emptied the contents of her stomach, then grabbed a few napkins from the dashboard. "Here," he told her when she'd finished.

"Oh, I do not feel good." She wiped her mouth, fisting the napkins.

"I bet." Dan helped her into her own seat and handed her a water bottle. "You going to be okay while we drive back?"

Avery curled her legs into the seat and rested her head against the window. "I dunno." She closed her eyes.

He didn't know either. And he really didn't know what to do with her. He emptied the melted ice from an empty soda cup in his cupholder and handed it to her. "In case you need to throw up again."

What in the hell am I going to do? I can't take her back to the Serendipity like this.

And even if he could get her to her room, he would feel terrible just leaving her like that. She needed someone to help her through this. He'd gotten her into this mess. He was going to get her out of it, even if he was the one who got in trouble.

He drove off, and after about ten minutes he pulled into his own neighborhood. Much as his parents didn't approve of underage drinking, they at least knew he'd been at a party. And Mom was a nurse. She could help.

Dan parked his truck in the driveway. Avery appeared to have fallen asleep, and he gathered her into his arms, then headed to the front door. At the last minute, he changed his mind. He wouldn't be able to unlock the door with her in his arms, and he didn't want to wake everyone up by ringing the doorbell.

Warren might answer the basement door, though.

He carried Avery around to the side of the house, then down the steps to the basement walkout. He knocked and held his breath. *Please still be awake.* It was one in the morning.

Warren opened the door a minute later, wearing shorts but no shirt. He furrowed his brow at Dan. "What the hell did you do?"

He winced at his brother's reaction. Out of all the people he knew, Warren was the most likely to help him when things got out of hand. And he was older than Dan, so he had more experience with stuff like this.

"Uh . . . this is Avery." Dan pushed past him, then carried Avery in, his arms aching now. He lowered her onto the basement couch, then straightened as Warren closed the door and came over. Avery rolled to her side, her eyes still closed.

"And Avery is? Obviously drunk. How old is she? What the hell are you thinking bringing her here?" Warren was one of the few people Dan could take a dressing-down from. But that was also because he'd been doing it for Dan's whole life.

"She's eighteen—sort of my girlfriend. She and her family are staying at the lodge, and she snuck out to come to Adam's party with me tonight."

Warren's eyes narrowed. "You been having sex with her?"

Dan shrank back. *Like it's any of his business.* "No!"

"You called her your girlfriend. I just wanted to make sure you're clear the lines of consent do not cover—"

"Thanks, I'm good on that. God, how stupid do you think I am?" Mom and Dad had drilled that into their heads well enough.

"I don't know, Dan. You just brought a drunk girl to Mom and Dad's."

Avery rolled over once again, then sat, her hand over her mouth. *Crap.* Dan grabbed a decorative hand-blown glass bowl from the coffee table and dumped the decorations in it to the floor. He held it out for Avery, who promptly threw up.

"Ugh." Warren grimaced. "Let me go get her some water."

"Water?" Dan raised a brow. "Won't that just make her throw up more?"

Warren shook his head. "Trust the person who's in college on this. Water. Lots of it. And Ibuprofen. Not Tylenol, because it's bad to combine that with alcohol. Best way to ward off a hangover. Which, from the looks of it, she may have, regardless. But this will help. Sit tight."

Warren started toward the basement steps, and Dan called out quietly, "Hey, War?"

His older brother glanced back.

"You gonna tell Mom and Dad?"

Warren smirked. "No. But I'm not an idiot. You're the one with a bowl of puke in your hands."

He hated that anyone in his family had to meet Avery like this. She deserved to be shown off. *She deserves a lot better than you.*

An hour later, Dan finished cleaning up the bowl with the outside hose, then trekked back into the house. Avery had roused well enough to take a shower and change into a T-shirt Dan had fetched her. Warren had given up his bedroom for her and had taken the couch.

Dan slipped into the room. The bedside lamp was still on, throwing an orange glow onto Avery's sleeping form. Her wet hair was in disarray, but she looked beautiful. Dan sat on the bed beside her, and the weight on the mattress roused her. She peered at him through slits in her eyes. "Hey."

"You feeling better?"

She nodded, sleepily, then uncurled her hand from where

she'd perched it under her cheek. She held it out to him. "Stay with me?"

His parents would kill him if they knew. But Warren wasn't going to tell them. And in the morning, he'd get up really early, before dawn, and take her back to the lodge. Avery could sneak back in, and maybe the few hours of sleep would help her seem less drunk.

She was asleep again by the time Dan decided to stay beside her in the bed. Leaning over her to turn off the lamp, he stared at her profile, and his heart squeezed in his chest.

He knew nothing about love. He'd never felt a fraction of what he felt for Avery with any of the girls from school.

He knew he could love her, though. She was smart, funny, sweet, and gorgeous.

But what does that mean when we'll be at different schools for the next year? In different states? Could we actually have anything beyond this week?

CHAPTER TWENTY-FIVE

Now

THE ITCHING WAS the first thing Avery had noticed that morning, but Mom had been the one to see the rash first. Sitting in a folding chair in the former dining room, she chewed on a cinnamon roll—which was the softest, pillowiest one she'd ever tasted—while her mom applied pink calamine lotion to her arms.

"Oh my gosh, try this cinnamon roll. It's incredible. Dan's sister made it." Avery tried to nudge her plate toward her mom, but Mom set it farther back on the table.

"Stay still, Avery. I want to make sure I get all the rashes. And you shouldn't be eating that. Between poison ivy, sunburn, and everything else, you're going to be a mess for your wedding day. You're going to show up to your wedding *como un desastre.*"

Like a disaster. "Nice, Mom."

Her stomach clenched. Unless what she needed to do was accept that nature was going to win this round. Her wedding day was heading for failure, and the more she tried to resist it, the more she ended up with raccoon chases, poison ivy, goose attacks, and front porch collapses.

"I don't understand how I could go to bed feeling fine and wake up covered in poison ivy," Avery said, giving up the attempt to reach her plate as Mom blocked it with her body and soaked a cotton pad. She held back the urge to scratch, wishing she could return to her breakfast.

Erika, who had done her the favor of running to the pharmacy in town, stood at the other side of the folding table, concern on her face. Erika referenced her phone. "It says poison ivy can show up even four days after you've come into contact with it. And you were rubbing your arms, remember?"

"How long is this rash going to be here?" Avery's fingers curled into fists, more from the itch than from Erika's news.

Erika bit her lip.

Oh, no. What does that mean? "How long, Erika?"

"Two to three weeks."

Mom kept an even expression as she capped the bottle of calamine. "This is a catastrophe."

Avery tried to keep her breath even. "Two to three weeks. Okay." She would look like this for her scheduled wedding day. The rashes were on the insides of her arms, not completely obvious. But Bryan would notice and see.

Erika tried to give her an encouraging smile. "Yeah, you never know—it could go away so much faster."

Avery absorbed the news with a small nod. "Okay, so what can I do? What remedies are there? Besides this god-awful pink stuff? I swear it makes the itching worse, Mom."

"You can take an oatmeal bath," she said.

"Or cortisone cream. And cold compresses," Erika added,

reading from her phone. "And Claritin. Which I have for this damned ragweed allergy. Almost like fate was preparing us, right?"

Fate has a great sense of humor right now. Or is trying to get its message very, very clear.

Mom put her hand on Avery's wrist. "I'm calling your father. He can call in a prescription to the local pharmacy for prednisone, which should help. He used to do it all the time at his office for this sort of thing. In the meantime, I want you taking it easy today."

A prescription. She hadn't even thought of that. Thank goodness her father was a doctor, too—it saved her the phone call to Bryan, and telling him about how she'd gotten such bad poison ivy was something she didn't want to do yet.

The sound of a drill and boards clattering overshadowed her thoughts for the moment. Dan's brother-in-law had arrived with a construction crew at six in the morning, bringing both noise and chaos. Avery could tell from the frown on Mom's face her patience was running thin—and the noise really wasn't helping.

She'd evaded a big discussion with Mom yesterday, though, by claiming to be exhausted and going to bed early—which had been true. The wine from a few nights ago had given her a headache, one stress had exacerbated.

And somehow, this morning she'd woken up to the usual missed phone calls and texts from Bryan, but she couldn't find it in her to care.

Avery groaned and leaned across the table, grabbing the cinnamon roll once more. "I don't have time to waste pampering myself. I promised Dan I would help get this place—"

"Don't worry about him." Mom couldn't seem to keep the terseness from her voice.

Avery stood and stamped her feet, the itch growing intolerable. Had the calamine only made it worse? "I made a promise to help. Besides, what am I going to do? Sit around here and try to control the urge to scratch myself? This is just a setback."

As she spoke the words, she couldn't help noticing Erika avoiding her gaze.

A setback. One among many.

"Well, I for one will not be playing the role of landscaper and mother of the bride. We need to settle on a new caterer today—which you really should be there for, Avery."

"You know what would be fun?" Avery chewed the cinnamon roll slowly, remembering Erika's suggestion to have a sunrise ceremony and breakfast. Her mother would never let that fly, but maybe something else? Something more casual?

Mom was giving her a blank look, as though waiting for her to continue.

"A local food truck or two. We could scale back the current plans, and instead of doing everything so fancy, we could get great local food, and maybe a country band. Lawn games and Adirondack chairs with fire pits. You know, like all the things we've always loved doing in Brandywood every summer we've come here. Give our guests a real taste of life at the lake, not some fancy black-tie soiree that could be anywhere."

Mom was blinking rapidly, the look on her face unreadable.

Avery took it as her cue to continue speaking. "And then it wouldn't matter so much what everything looks like outside. Because it wouldn't have to be perfect. Just . . . Brandywood."

A smile hinted at the corners of Erika's mouth. "That could be fun."

Mom shot her a scalding look. "Have you both lost your minds? The invitations already say black tie. What on earth are you thinking?"

"Mom, I don't care whether I have oysters Rockefeller or

chicken satay or cocktail wieners in grape jelly and a cheese ball. I'd rather just have a relaxed, fun wedding at a place I love."

"Avery, you may not care about those details now, but that's only because you've been through the wringer this week. When your guests start arriving, you're going to wish you'd taken the time to do things right." Mom crossed the room for a cup of coffee on the TV table Dan had set up with drinks. "And you're not thinking about Bryan. You really think he would be fine with some backcountry, half-assed wedding? He's a professional. His friends are professionals. His mother is a very elegant woman. I'm certain she'd be horrified."

That much was true. Bryan's mother *would* be horrified. But Bryan would likely push back on the idea first. God knows he'd had an opinion about every other detail of this wedding and exercised his veto power liberally.

"I don't have to tell Bryan . . ." Her voice was soft.

Mom peered at her with razor sharp perception, her eyes widening. "This is about *Dan Klein,* isn't it? Avery, it's about time you get your head out of the clouds. You have a man who is successful and knows how to manage your flightiness. You're really going to let that go for some small town loser who can't even run a proper business?"

Avery stiffened and glanced at Erika, who had remained silent. Erika was watching her with interest.

Avery had been too hot-headed and offended to take the time to listen to her friend's concerns. Now she wished she could ask what she thought without Mom present. She didn't need Mom turning on Erika—not when Mom *loved* Bryan.

Then Avery thought about what Mom had just said and frowned. "You forgot about love."

Mom sipped her coffee, tapping her acrylic nails against the side of the paper cup. "What are you talking about?"

Avery cleared her throat. "You said Bryan is successful and knows how to manage me. You mentioned nothing about him loving me."

Mom released a guttural sigh of frustration. "Well, of course he loves you. That's a given. He wouldn't have asked you to marry him if he didn't love you."

"It's not a given," Erika said and grabbed a grape from a fruit bowl. "Not everyone gets married for the right reasons. You never actually know what's going on within the context of a relationship, do you, Mrs. M.?"

Avery's mom blanched. She'd used that exact line to describe her own failed marriage before—and in front of Erika. While Avery appreciated Erika's help, the line Erika was toeing was hazardous. Mom could get nasty when backed into a corner, even with someone like Erika.

"I'm not saying Bryan doesn't love me. But the most important thing we're doing here is getting married, right? Whether it's a black-tie affair or a honky-tonk hoedown shouldn't matter."

"I can't believe we're even having this discussion." Mom bristled, then gave Avery another knowing glance. She pointed at the window. "*Te conozco perfectamente.*" *I know you well.* "This is about that man out there. It wasn't enough that he tried to ruin you when you were so young. You're going to let him ruin the best relationship you've had."

Absent-mindedly, Avery scratched the rash on her forearm, then crossed the room to glance out the window. Sure enough, Dan was out there with Peyton and a few members of the crew. He was digging something up with a shovel, sweat dripping down his face.

Doing back-breaking work to help her dreams come true.

What if Mom was right? What if she'd let Dan get too close —and now he was influencing her thoughts about Bryan?

And what did it mean if she was increasingly more excited about that idea? "You know what, Mom? Erika's right. People never do know what's going on inside a relationship. And I wouldn't be the first woman in our family to change their mind about a fiancé, would I? In fact, I'd say the women in our family seem to do that a lot—including you. We're all cursed, aren't we?"

Mom's lips pressed to a line, and she gave Avery a hard look. She couldn't argue with that, and they both knew it. Mom rolled her eyes. "You better hope there's no family curse. Because if there is, then Dan won't be the one for you either, Avery. You've only been engaged once."

Then Mom came closer. "But if you want to use that excuse to throw yourself at that man, go right ahead. I promise you this: it didn't end well the last time you did it. It won't end well now. Because Dan Klein doesn't care about what's best for you. And he never did."

This conversation was spiraling quickly out of control. Her mom had exposed Avery's innermost impulses and confusion and now was taking advantage of the fact that Avery hadn't fully thought out any of it.

Putting a target on Dan's back like this to her mom would be just about the dumbest thing Avery could do. He was trying to help her. By giving Mom any room to think she could let romantic thoughts of him affect her, she'd just made his life a lot harder. Mom would take her anger out on him.

Avery flinched and turned her back to the window. "You're getting ahead of yourself, Mom. Because I didn't say I was interested in Dan. I'm over him. I have been for a while."

She said it convincingly, her voice calm and settled.

But why does it hurt to say that?

CHAPTER TWENTY-SIX

DAN PARKED his truck in front of his parents' house, sighing as the engine cooled. His body ached, his head hurt, and just about the only thing that might give him relief was a massage, but he hated the thought of a random stranger touching him. He rolled his stiff neck and unlocked the door.

Mom had called earlier that afternoon and left him a voicemail, asking him to stop by, and, frankly, he couldn't have welcomed the break from the Serendipity more. Garrett's crew were moving at lightning speed on the renovation since they'd arrived the day before, which had left him working outside, doing landscaping with Peyton and Erika.

Avery's mother had insisted Avery take a break from the work today, after the poison ivy rash on her arm seemed more inflamed, and he'd had to side with her mother on that one. Much as she'd been a good sport about doing what she could to help, Avery was looking miserable. Her personality had receded since her mother's arrival, too, and she was more quiet, serious.

Or she was avoiding him.

Dan opened the door to the truck and made his way down the sidewalk. Before he could reach the front door, it opened, and his mom came out, a broad smile on her face. She was still in her nursing scrubs, as though she'd just gotten home from work. "I thought I heard you pull up."

She'd cut her graying blonde hair into a bob recently, and somehow it still looked a little odd to see her with such a short haircut. It suited her, but she looked more like he remembered his grandmother had looked. Now and then, he was reminded his parents were getting older. He really should call Mom more often.

Meeting him by the front steps, she pulled him into a hug. "Come on in. I was just making pork chops—feel like staying?"

"If you're asking me if I can say no to your pork chops, you've got the wrong son." He winked, following her into the house.

"Since when don't I like Mom's pork chops?" Warren's voice came from the living room, and Dan lifted his head in surprise.

What the heck is Warren doing here?

Warren stood as Dan shut the door behind him. Dan studied him as he removed his shoes and put them in a basket by the door, like his mom had always asked them to do. "I didn't see your car outside."

"I walked. That's the advantage of living a few streets down from Mom and Dad's."

The hair on the back of Dan's neck stood, and he crossed his arms, feeling strangely ambushed. He looked at Mom. First her out-of-the-blue request to stop by, now Warren's surprise appearance. This felt like an ambush. "What's going on? If this is about Avery, I can handle myself just fine, you know."

Mom gave Dan a puzzled look, then frowned, her gaze darting back and forth between her sons. "Avery?"

Uh . . .

Warren shook his head and then covered his eyes with his fingertips. "You're a moron, Dan."

"Who's Avery? Here, come this way." Mom kept moving into the kitchen, and both Dan and Warren followed.

"Isn't that why you called me?" Dan asked, a sheepish feeling creeping into his chest.

Mom went over to the stove and clicked off the frying pan. She pulled a serving plate from the cupboard and transferred pork chops onto it. "I called you because Garrett mentioned to Sam, who told Laura, who told Jen, you've been sleeping on an air mattress. And being a mom, I couldn't stand the thought of my son on the floor. So, I'm giving you the furniture from the guest room. I know money is tight right now with all you've invested in that place, and we're not using the furniture that often."

Oh.

Dan's gaze went to Warren's face, which held a laughing smirk.

"Anyway," Mom continued. "I wasn't thrilled that I had to hear about this through the grapevine, which meant to me you would never tell me, and it also meant you'd probably try to pull some 'I don't need your help' macho pride thing and say you didn't want the bedroom set. I asked Warren to come over to help you move it all into your truck." She pulled a sheet pan of roasted potatoes from the oven. "I'm not taking no for an answer."

Dan hadn't expected the gesture, and his throat felt oddly scratchy. He swallowed hard, then shifted his weight from one foot onto the other. "Thanks, Mom."

She grinned at him, then took a steaming bowl of green beans to the kitchen table. "You're welcome. You all can eat, then move the set. I had Dad disassemble it last night. If you're lucky, he may even get home from work in time to help you boys move it." She pulled three plates down and set them on the table. "Now, who's this Avery?"

Warren joined Mom in helping to set the table, and Dan picked at a stain on his thumb where a plant he'd pulled had left a sticky residue. "You remember when I was eighteen and went to Adam's party?"

Mom's expression darkened. "Don't think I could forget that one, kiddo." Then her blue eyes widened. "Not that Avery. The same girl?"

"She's the reason he's got Garrett over there doing reno on the Serendipity." Warren folded napkins and set them under the forks.

Not wanting to feel useless, Dan went over to the sink and washed his hands. Drying them, he pulled out three cups. "It's a little more complicated than that. Mr. Harrison told her he'd reserve the Serendipity for her wedding, which is next Saturday. And she just found out he died and the place was sold to me this past Sunday. She's been on an air mattress and sleeping bag since then, too. There're no vacancies in any Brandywood-area hotels." He filled the cups with iced water.

"Oh, that poor girl. That's terrible." Mom pulled her chair out and gestured that they should sit. "Why didn't you tell me, Dan? I could have offered her a room. Until last night, I had that guest bedroom all set up—but if she's interested, she could still take a bunk bed in the kids' room. Warren and Alice's kids are supposed to spend the night here and there, but they can always just sleep with Dad and me. They're kids."

The thought of Avery in his childhood bedroom made him uncomfortable. Dan shook his head. "Her mom and best friend are here too, now, so I don't think there's enough room for everyone. But it's a nice thought."

"Oh, my goodness. Daniel Joseph Klein! You mean to tell

me you have three women sleeping on the floor in the middle of a construction zone? Didn't I raise you better than that? You are getting me on the phone right this minute with Avery's mother, and I'm inviting them over."

Warren's brow furrowed. "Mom, you really think you should interfere like that? You're forgetting that this girl wrecked Dan's life twelve years ago."

"This isn't interfering. This is called being hospitable. I'm not forgetting. But I'm also not forgetting that Dan made the choice to take responsibility for something he didn't do." Mom reached for her purse on the kitchen counter and dug her cell phone out of it. She held it out to Dan. "If this were any other person, would you be objecting to me offering a room, Warren?"

"I can think of an entire list of people I would—"

Mom cut him down with a look. "You know what I mean. If it was another random stranger."

"I would absolutely not let some random stranger into my house, no. Especially not if my kids are there." Warren sat at the dinner table. "And you don't have to solve every problem, Mom. Dan already said no. Let him make that decision without you forcing his hand."

"I'm not trying to force your hand." Mom gave Dan an apologetic look. "Am I being pushy? That wasn't what I intended. I just feel awful thinking about those poor women. And it's been so long since Avery, I didn't think she . . . well, I just didn't think."

It was funny how things worked with Mom and Warren, especially when it was just the three of them like this, which was so rare. Dan could barely remember a time when Dad and Jen hadn't been in the picture, but sometimes a flash of a memory came back like this. Mom holding both their hands as they crossed the street. Or pushing them on swings. Random little pieces of a lifetime he couldn't remember.

In some ways, Warren had always been more of the warrior than Mom. Warren was fiercely protective like that. Always had been. Mom—she'd always been a soft place to land.

Dan reached out and squeezed his mom's hand. She was the best person he knew, really. Someone he aspired to be like.

And he hated how many times he messed up and caused her pain.

After the breakup with Melissa . . .

. . . or fighting with Garrett so publicly . . .

. . . or the accusations that came from being involved with Avery . . .

. . . or every time he got in trouble . . . facing Mom had been the worst part of it. Knowing he was less like her and more like the man who had broken her heart.

Dan tipped a smile at her. "It's fine, Mom. You're right. It's a good idea. And they would only need the room for a night or two, because I'm getting furniture delivered on Saturday."

Mom's face fell. "Oh, so you don't need the guest room furniture?"

"Actually, I do. I rented furniture for the rooms, but not for my room. Didn't feel it was worth the extra fee." He gave her an encouraging smile. The last thing his tired and sore body wanted was to move furniture tonight, but it obviously meant a lot to her. "Let's eat—then we call Avery, okay?"

CHAPTER TWENTY-SEVEN

Avery
12 Years Ago

AVERY HAD NEVER FELT SO sick her entire life. She knelt in
front of the toilet, stuck between wanting to throw up and not
being able to, her head pounding, her mouth dry like cotton,
her skin feeling ill-fitting and too tight.

This is a hangover.

A tap on the door forced her to jerk her head upright, and
she cleared her throat. "One minute."

"Avery? Is everything okay? Dad and I have been waiting
for you to come down for over forty minutes. At this rate, we
won't make the ten o'clock train."

Shit. She'd forgotten that train ride her father wanted to go
on. As if she were still in grade school and got excited about
train rides through the mountains. Mom seemed to think that
now that Avery was a teenager, she was going to make horrible

mistakes. Dad, on the other hand, seemed to think she was stuck in pigtails.

There wasn't any way she could hide this. And a trip on any type of moving object sounded like being in the fourth circle of hell. She breathed out and wiped her mouth with the back of her hand, struggling from her hands and knees onto her feet. She held on to the sink and steadied herself, catching a glimpse of her bloodshot eyes in the mirror.

Avery splashed water on her face, then dried it with the towel. The scent of fabric softener made her stomach lurch, strangely, and she wrinkled her nose.

Sighing, she opened the door. "I think I have food poisoning from that crab cake last night," she told her mom, leaning on the door. "I've been sick all night."

Mom's eyes widened. "What? Why, what happened? Why didn't you wake Dad or me?"

Avery shrugged. "I didn't think it was necessary. So you could hold my hair? I just figured I'd tell you in the morning." She slunk past her mom toward her bed and collapsed on it. Dan's T-shirt was tucked safely under her pillow. She'd spent part of the morning with her face buried in it because it smelled like him.

Her own clothes from last night were in a plastic bag in the false bottom of her suitcase, where she normally stored her dirty laundry for the return trip. She wouldn't be able to wash them until she got home, but they would be safe there.

Mom sat beside her on the bed and placed her cool hand on Avery's forehead, searching her eyes. "You look like you're feeling terrible." She took out her phone. "Why don't I see if Dad can come up and take a look at you?"

"No, he doesn't need to." Avery curled her knees up in the fetal position and pulled a cover over her shoulders.

"Honey, I didn't marry a doctor for nothing. There's an

advantage in knowing he can help take care of your child," Mom said, then stood. "Can I get you water? Maybe some Gatorade?"

A slick of nervous sweat broke out on Avery's forehead. Would her father be able to recognize the difference between a hangover and food poisoning? Avery could swear she smelled the alcohol coming out of her own pores, but she'd taken another shower just now, so hopefully all Mom smelled was her shampoo and body wash. "Don't get Dad. I'm fine. I just need to sleep. I haven't thrown up in a couple of hours now." That much was true.

"Avery, I'm getting your father." Mom started toward the door.

Avery's mind raced. "And then you wonder why I don't want to live with you," she managed. The words sounded horrible, and Avery regretted them for their unnecessary cruelty. Mom was being nice and trying to help her.

But Mom froze in the doorway.

She turned, setting a hand on the door frame, and looked over her shoulder. Hurt painted on her features. "Okay. Have it your way. You want to lie here miserably without help, that's up to you. I'm going to see if I can get your father to take me into town. If you need something from the drugstore, let me know."

The door clicked closed as she left.

Ouch.

It had worked, but why did she feel so terrible?

Then again, she deserved to feel terrible. In the past few days, she'd snuck out of the lodge, gotten drunk, almost gone skinny-dipping, and then spent the night with a guy.

She'd spent the night with Dan.

Not sexually, but by his side.

That part of it all made her heart beat faster, a mixture of exhilaration and wonder. He'd curled his arm around her waist, and she'd loved every second.

She should feel bad for all this—the lying and sneaking out and doing things she would have never dreamed of doing that would make her mom completely furious.

Pushing her fingers through her wet hair, she forced herself to sit and take a sip of water from the bottle on her nightstand. Dan had given it to her before they'd parted and told her to make sure she kept refilling it and drinking more.

She remembered little of what had happened after she'd gotten drunk at the bonfire. The last thing she remembered clearly was, she'd been hitting a drum with Dan's friend, whose name escaped her because he'd introduced himself when she was already drunk. And then she'd been down by the lake with a group of people who were smoking, and Dan had found her. And then she'd woken up at Dan's parents' house. Scattered bits and pieces were fragmented in-between.

Getting drunk had felt like fun at the time, but now she was sure she'd never let another drop of alcohol pass her lips again. The thought of it made her want to hurl.

She pulled her phone out and clicked through to see a text from Dan fifteen minutes ago. It must have come while she was in the shower.

Dan: *Hope you're feeling all right. Miss you. Let me know when you wake up.*

Avery: *I'm awake now. Feeling AWFUL.*

Leaning back against her pillow, she considered asking her mom to bring her a ginger ale from town later but then decided against it. Avery needed to apologize before she asked for any favors from her mom.

Her phone beeped again, and she clicked it on.

Dan: *Up for some company? I just saw your parents leave.*

Avery: *Um, yes, please.*

A moment later, there was a knock on her door. She scrambled from the bed and crossed toward the door. She opened it and found Dan standing there, holding a large brown paper bag with a handle. "Hey, drunk girl." He grinned at her, his eyes dancing with laughter.

"Oh, shut up." She pulled him into the room, feeling better at the sight of him.

"Nice pjs." He set the bags on the dresser and pulled out a single sunflower for her from one bag. "For you."

Her smile widened as she took it, twirling it in her hands as she sat back on the bed. A wave of sickness crashed over her, and she leaned back. "It's beautiful. And did I mention I'm never drinking again?"

"I think I've heard that from all my friends at some point in their partying days. They all end up doing it again, though." He pulled out a bottle of Gatorade next. "Here. Drink up. It'll help. I also have crackers, chicken soup from my favorite restaurant in town—that I had to beg the owner, Bunny, to give me because she wasn't serving lunch foods yet. More meds in case you have a headache. And this . . . "

Dan pulled a leather journal and matching long leather pouch from the bag and sat beside her. "It's a sketchbook and pencils," he said, holding it out, a bit shyly. "Because you said how much you like drawing and stuff."

She raised her eyes to him, shocked. No guy had ever given her anything, let alone out of the blue and for no reason. "Wow, thank you." She took it and hugged it to her heart. "And thank you—for taking care of me last night."

"Well . . . I kind of like you." Dan reached over and tucked a wet strand of her hair behind her ear. "It's the least I could do."

"I kind of like you, too." She scanned his eyes for a split second before dropping a kiss to his lips.

He returned it briefly, then pulled away and stood. "I should get back to work. You never know when someone will need a bike or fishing rod or any of the other really important things I take care of."

She groaned and held her hand out for him. "Do you have to?" She waggled her brows suggestively. "I promise to give you a good tip if you stay."

He coughed out a laugh. "I promise you I *want* to stay. But maybe we can figure out a way to meet up later if you're feeling better?"

She nodded. "I wish we could spend the whole day together. Of course, it'd probably be better if I sleep first, so I'm not a zombie."

He kissed her on the forehead and then left with a wink.

Flopping down on the bed, Avery scooted the sunflower to the side. She didn't know how she'd explain it to her mom, who would zero in on anything in her room like a hawk. She wished she could press it and keep it forever, but it was so thick, she doubted it was possible. She'd figure out what to say. There wasn't any way she was throwing out the first flower ever given to her by someone other than her parents or grandparents. And those had been for ballet recitals.

Running her fingertips over the center, she closed her eyes. She'd never really thought about receiving flowers before, but whenever her friends had received flowers from crushes, they got roses. Which were nice—but . . . generic?

A sunflower felt like something more, in a way. Dan had taken the time to think about what she might like. Or maybe what he thought of her. She didn't really have a favorite flower, but this could be it.

Taking out her new sketchbook, she flipped to the first page and pulled out a pencil. If she couldn't take the flower back with her, at least she could draw it. Keep it forever that way.

She drew until she fell asleep. When she stirred, the housekeeper was knocking on the door to her room.

Avery crawled out of bed, checking the time on her phone. Almost noon. *Wow*.

She politely told the housekeeper she didn't want help today and then closed the door. Going back to the bed, she sat, then pulled the soup out of the bag Dan had brought. It wasn't hot anymore, but somehow it was still warm, and one spoonful made her stomach gurgle. She was starving, and the soup was delicious.

She ate it quietly, thinking about how—for as much smothering as her mom did—the warm, maternal stuff other people talked about didn't seem to come along with it. Dad was the one who got her things like soup and crackers when she was sick. Neither of them really ever took off work, because Dad had his own practice and Mom was his business manager, so they were both gone most of the time. Spending long stretches of her summer vacation alone wasn't unusual.

What would Mom be doing now that her parents were divorcing?

Avery had been so mad that she hadn't asked. *What will Mom do?* There was no way she'd want to work for Dad if they were divorcing.

She finished the soup and Gatorade, both of which made her feel better. Getting dressed, she went back to the hall and gave the housekeeper her trash to take away. At least she wouldn't have to face questions about that. Across the hall, she tapped on Mom's door. She didn't answer.

A knock on her father's door revealed he was still gone, too, so she went back into her own room. For a couple about to get divorced, they certainly spent a lot of time with each other. Unless as soon as Dad dropped Mom into town, he went off somewhere else. Weird.

As she looked out the window, the sight of the oak tree made her smile at the memory of shimmying down it the previous night. A slight scrape on her palm was the only evidence of that clandestine action. Dan brought out a side of her that made her feel alive and seen.

She pulled her hair into a ponytail and grabbed her flip-flops. Even if Dan was going to be working, she'd still rather hang out with him. Maybe she could help him out.

She left her room and headed downstairs. Outside, the world sounded like crickets and cicadas and smelled of freshly mown grass. She headed for the Sports Shack and caught sight of him helping a mom and her daughter with a paddleboard. She stopped several feet away and watched him, her heart fluttering. The brightness of the sunlight made her head hurt more, but she didn't care.

As Dan walked back toward the Sports Shack, he caught sight of her and smiled.

"Hey," she said, smiling at him.

"Avery?" Mom's voice came from nearby.

A strange, paralyzing fear strangled her throat, and Avery held her breath, looking around. Her mom sat near the Adirondack chairs by the boat launch. She watched Avery warily, her brow furrowed.

Mom can't know about Dan.

Avery turned away from him and hurried over to her mom. "Hey, there you are." She slowed as she neared her mother.

"Ya veo que tienes un amigo nuevo." Mom nodded her head toward Dan. *I see you have a new friend.*

"Nope." Avery sat in the chair on the other side of her. "I was just going to ask him if he'd seen you. The housekeeper told me she saw you out here." *All these lies are getting hard to keep track of.* Then she saw her mom's eyes were red-rimmed and puffy, as though she had been crying. "Oh, Mom, are you okay?"

"No, Ave, I'm really not."

It was probably her own fault. She hadn't been the nicest to Mom the last few days, and especially this morning. She bit her lip, playing with a thread on the frayed hem of her jean shorts. "Mom, I'm really sorry. I know I was awful this morning. I really wasn't feeling well—not that it's any excuse. And I know I haven't been the nicest the last few days. I just really don't want to go to Tampa."

Mom sighed and brushed away a tear from her cheek. "Honey, it's not that I'm dying to go to Tampa. But Uncle Leon has a place there that we can stay—for free—because he's between renters. Things are going to change for us now that your dad and I are splitting up. Your dad has agreed to some alimony, but I won't have money for the lifestyle you're used to. And I have to find a job and start all over again. I have no pension of my own, Ave. Just whatever I've put in Social Security, which isn't much because I didn't take a salary while working for your dad."

"I don't understand it, Mom." Avery shook her head, feeling sick all over again. She squinted against the glare of the sun reflected off the lake. "Why now? Doesn't everyone say things get better once your kids are out of the house?"

"This is one of those cases when the only reason we lasted as long as we did is for you, honey. According to your father, anyway. Most people never know what's really going on within the context of a relationship."

Her words confirmed what Avery feared—Dad was the one who was really pushing for divorce. "Then why not wait until I'm out of high school? Why throw a bomb into my life now?"

Mom didn't answer and leaned back against her seat. She

lowered her sunglasses from the top of her head and wiped her cheeks again.

They sat in silence a moment longer before Mom asked, "How are you feeling? I hope you won't be disappointed, but Dad went out on the train ride by himself. I went into town for a bit, but I didn't want to leave you too long in case you decided you needed something."

"I'm better." Avery scooted her hands under her thighs, leaning forward. "I didn't really want to go on that train ride anyway. It's been a long time since it excited me."

A wistful smile twisted Mom's lips. "When you were a little girl, you would get so excited anytime we came up here and you could see the tracks and the trains. They fascinated you. Probably because your dad was. You always were a daddy's girl. Which is probably why you want to go with him."

"It's not just that—"

"Ave, you need to realize this isn't something I'm doing *to* you. It just is what it is. But Miami isn't something I can offer you. You have to come to Tampa with me. Eighteen or not, you're still my daughter. And I'm still in charge of taking care of you. I signed up for this job for life, kiddo. That doesn't change whether you're two, or twelve, or twenty, or thirty-two. You're always going to be my kid. You might not see until you're older how much I love you and want the best for you, but that's okay. I'm just going to keep loving you."

Avery's gaze darted to Dan, whose back was turned as he stacked a croquet mallet back onto the rack. Maybe she'd still been a kid when she'd come here this week—or felt like one anyway. But this week had changed her. And she couldn't go backward.

CHAPTER TWENTY-EIGHT

Now

Despite how horribly the week had started, Avery could hardly believe the transformation as she finished mulching a garden bed. She stood and stretched, her back aching, then pulled off the garden gloves. The sight of the dark, fresh mulch, neatly lined edges, and gorgeous flowers they'd picked up from the nursery made Avery's heart skip. The pinks and yellows of the flowers were spectacular—hopefully, they'd attract butterflies by the time her wedding came.

Erika had finished the garden bed she'd been working on already and was over by the cooler, grabbing a beer. With Mom and Dan's mother, ironically.

Mom and Erika had gone to stay with the Kleins for the last two nights, at Avery's insistence. They had offered a room with two twin-sized bunks, and Avery had wanted them both to be comfortable for a few nights. Poor Erika had been sneezing and blowing her nose all week, and Mom's back couldn't really handle the floor. If anyone was going to stay behind and sleep on the air mattress, it was going to be her.

Dan had even offered to let her have the bed he'd brought back from his parents' house, but she'd declined that, too. Something about soldiering through this made her feel proud. Like she'd faced these obstacles head-on and overcome them.

Mom hadn't been thrilled with the arrangement, but she'd quickly warmed up to Dan's mother—only to discover they'd met during one lake vacation years earlier. It was odd, seeing Dan's mother and Mom acting like fast friends. Few people knew how to get her mom out of her shell, and thinking about it made Avery's eyes grow misty and her chest tight.

Mom had spent so long being bitter and angry, she didn't have many friends left. Even though Mom could be difficult, seeing her lonely hurt. Because Mom had been convinced for so long that people only let her down and hurt her, and in the end she'd made the self-fulfilling prophecy come true by isolating herself and giving in to her insecurities.

But seeing her laughing now with Dan's mom, wearing a large sun hat, garden gloves on—it gave Avery hope.

Three days of having a professional crew on hand had made a world of difference to the property. The drywall had been installed in the sitting room and was ready to be painted, and the front porch was rebuilt. Garrett's crew was every-where. And they were fast, too.

She gave a satisfied smile. And the landscaping work she'd been doing with Erika had come along quickly now that the mothers, Peyton, and Dan had joined them. They'd weeded everything and spread mulch today. Tomorrow, they'd plant some more flowers and be done, with a few days to spare before Bryan arrived.

Truthfully, Avery wasn't sure when the grounds to the

Serendipity had looked this good. Maybe she hadn't really paid attention during previous visits, but nothing stood out in her memory about the gardens being overly impressive before.

Her fingernails hurt from pulling, her arms still itched, and the sunburn on her face had peeled, but it had been worth it all.

Dan came around the corner, a rake in hand, and paused when he saw her. "I was just coming over to help you finish up, but it looks like you don't need me."

She smiled. "I told you I'm just as fast as spreading mulch with my hands as you are with that damn rake."

Dan chuckled. "I swear my legs would go numb if I tried to crouch and kneel as much as you do. I'm not as young as I once was." He set the rake in a nearby wheelbarrow, then gathered up the garden tools around them. "Quitting time." He gave her mother a wary glance and lowered his voice. "Who would have predicted that, huh?"

"It's all your mom's doing." Avery shrugged. "Mom is outspoken and doesn't beat around the bush. If she didn't get along with your mom, she'd let us all know. But your mom seems to have calmed her down." She rolled her neck to stretch it. "Thank you, Dan. For doing all this. I know it must have been expensive and went completely off your plan."

He shrugged, glancing away. "I was going to do it anyway."

Avery drew a sharp breath. That was how it had gone lately every time she thanked him. He'd brush it off like it wasn't a big deal. Like he hadn't gone out of his way for her. Didn't meet her gaze either.

The rest of the time, they got along fine. She'd done her best to put any nagging doubts about this wedding to the side, called Bryan in a timelier manner, and treated Dan more like a casual acquaintance. She'd let herself get carried away with the disasters earlier in the week, the false feeling of closeness to

Dan. It wasn't fair to Bryan—or to Dan. She'd hurt Dan before by believing they had to be meant for each other.

When she'd first met Dan, she was sure he was her soul mate. That she was in love. But he'd been her first everything.

She'd been too inexperienced to know a week of knowing someone did not equal really knowing them at all. Yet she'd never connected as easily before she'd met Dan. Even with Bryan, it had taken months before she'd felt as comfortable with him as she had with Dan after just a few hours.

Was that because he'd already seen me at my worst when we first met? She'd definitely missed his friendship when she left Brandywood all those years ago.

Avery stepped closer to him. "Why do you do that, Dan?"

He raised a brow. "Do what?"

"Act like it's nothing. Like you were just going to do this all anyway so it means nothing that you're doing it now."

He picked up a trowel and tossed it in the wheelbarrow. "It doesn't mean anything, Avery. And anyway, *I* didn't do much. Garrett and his crew saved the day. I was just making things worse. And it fits: Garrett's the hero in the family anyway. I tend to screw up more than him."

Ouch. She helped him in gathering the tools. "And you resent him for it?"

Dan pulled off his gloves, a line of dirt showing at his wrists. "I don't, actually. I mean, I was never high in the family ranking when it was just the three of us Klein kids. There was Warren, the brilliant straight-A student on scholarship, who was quarterback of the football team, and Jen, the golden child. Jen thought she was trying to give me some competition for rebellious screw-up for a while, but she's too likable for that role."

Avery pursed her lips. Her friends who had siblings had complained about similar birth order ranking issues. She usually kept quiet because they couldn't know or understand what it was like not to have any siblings when you wanted them so badly. She thought about what Dan had said, though, then frowned. "Weren't you, like, a really amazing basketball player? I thought you had scholarships waiting or something?"

Dan shifted his weight back onto his back foot. "Yeah, well. I didn't end up playing my senior year. After that, opportunities for basketball dried up. And I just kept dropping in the family totem pole."

Dan hadn't played basketball? It seemed crazy he would have given that up. "How's that?"

"We added two more siblings to the mix. My sisters from my biological dad. A few years back, we all sort of came together, and now we all celebrate holidays and birthdays and everything together. One big, happy family. Garrett's on that side of things. And so is my sister Laura and her husband Mark, who are coming tomorrow with all the hotel amenities you'll need for your guests. They've been running her family cabins for a while now, and they're going to give me a quick lesson on the hospitality industry in the morning." Dan picked up the handles to the wheelbarrow and started toward the shed, which was in the opposite direction from where everyone else stood.

She followed him. "But you realize none of that makes you the family screw-up, right?"

Dan threw her a look over his shoulder, his eyes searching hers for a split-second. "I'm fine with it, Avery. It's a lot easier to do when you've been letting everyone down for decades. You didn't know me well when we were younger. Didn't know I had a reputation for being a bully, and a racist, too."

Avery stumbled. "A racist?"

"Yup." His fingers curled on the handles of the wheelbarrow. "Word on the street was that I hated Latinos." He smirked at her. "Guess they didn't know about the Cuban-Italian girl I hooked up with as a senior."

She stared at him, dumbfounded. *What?* She'd never even remotely detected a trace of racism in him.

"Why would they say something like that?"

"Well, I mean, I was very vocal about hating a lady who was Latina. And her daughters." He ducked his chin at her. "My sisters Sam and Laura. Their mother was Venezuelan. I may have made some less than wonderful remarks when I was young and stupid and angry because I thought they stole my father and left my mom struggling. I regret using names, though —not trying to excuse it."

She cringed. She knew that feeling all too well. Even though she could tolerate Tina's presence better now, she'd hated her for years. And it had taken her a while to separate how she felt about her father and Tina and how she felt about her half-sisters. If she was honest, sometimes she still struggled with it. Their family had replaced hers, and going to their house in Miami was always a reminder of how little she fit in there. Pictures on the wall didn't include Avery; just Tina, her dad, and the girls.

Avery didn't even open the Christmas cards Tina sent anymore. The twins in perfectly matched outfits to Tina and her dad. A beautiful family with no space for her.

She went over to where he stood, and the earthy scent of the mulch and dirt that had filled the wheelbarrow grew stronger. "That doesn't make you a bad person, Dan. It makes you a kid who was left trying to figure out his emotions about a bad person. And I get it—you didn't do any of this for me, but all I was trying to say was that you don't need to go the self-deprecating route to prove it. I'm out here getting sunburned and windblown, but you didn't have to be right here beside me doing it. And I appreciate it."

She started to walk away, and her hand grazed against his.

His fingers curled, then caught hers, ever so slightly. Just a whisper of a touch.

But enough to make her feel like he'd placed a hot iron against her fingertips.

Her breath caught in her throat, her heart slamming against her ribs. Instead of pulling her hand away, the way she should have, her fingers brushed against the soft inside of his palm, tantalizing and shooting sparks up her skin.

She expected him to let go, but he didn't, and their eyes met.

How is it possible? Twelve years later, he still makes my heart race and flutter.

His voice was low, husky. "Don't underestimate how that sun makes you look, Avery. I like the tanned look a lot more than that pencil skirt and bun you showed up with on Sunday."

His words made her heart beat even faster. *Bryan, Avery. You're engaged to Bryan. Let go of his hand.* But she didn't. His thumb trailed against hers, encircling it. "You mean you didn't like the pencil skirt?"

"It's not that I didn't like it. It hugged your curves, and you can't not appreciate that. But this is more you."

God, she'd let this go too far. But instead of stepping away, she quirked a brow at him. "My curves?"

He leveled his chin, his lips twitching. "You've always had a fantastic ass, Avery, one that—"

"Hey, guys, is—" Erika rounded the corner, then stopped, staring at them.

They sprang apart, and Avery felt heat flood her face. *Did Erika see them holding hands?*

Avery straightened, plucking a piece of mulch from her skirt. "Great progress today," she managed to Dan, striding toward Erika. "What's up?"

Erika gave a look back at Dan, then followed her. "Avery . . ."

When they were out of earshot from Dan, Avery shot her a hard look. "Don't say a word."

"It's not any of my business." Erika shrugged. "But figure out which guy you actually want before Bryan shows up for your wedding."

"Nothing happened. We were just talking."

"Right." Erika rolled her eyes. She lowered her voice further as they drew closer to her mom and Dan's mom. "Maybe you didn't see it because you were involved in it, but the way you two were staring at each other—like you just wanted to tear each other's clothes off—I'm pretty sure you have some serious things to think about, Avery. And I'm not saying it's a bad thing. But sort it out now, before you're that bride at the altar pulling a Sandra Bullock like in *While You Were Sleeping*."

Avery let out a slow stream of breath, the reference to their favorite movie making her stomach twist. She could practically visualize it, too. Avery grabbed her by the elbow to stop her from going any further. "It's not like that. I don't want you to think—"

"It doesn't matter what *I* think. It's Bryan you should be worried about." Erika's gaze looked pensive as she looked back in the direction they'd come from. "Because I tell you what—all it's going to take is one look at the way you two interact, and Bryan's going to know there's something between you and Dan."

"And I am worried about Bryan, I am." Avery's shoulders sank. "But there's nothing between Dan and me. Not anymore." She sighed, watching as one member of Garrett's crew took down a shutter on the second floor, near the window she'd once climbed out of to go to a party with Dan. The crew was repainting the exterior tomorrow morning.

"I'm really worried about you." Erika pulled a hair elastic from her wrist, then tugged her hair into a ponytail. And even though Avery hadn't done the best job appreciating Erika, she felt the weight of guilt now. Erika didn't have to be there. Digging in garden beds and popping allergy pills every few minutes. She was there because she cared. Her gaze flitted to her mom.

So is Mom.

They'd rallied, despite the ludicrousness of Avery's request, to make her dream wedding come true. Guilt churned in her gut, and Avery leaned over and pulled Erika into a tight hug. "You don't have to worry. Everything is going to be fine."

She sounded more confident than she felt. *Will it be fine? Do I still have feelings for Dan? And why am I no longer sure about Bryan?*

Avery let Erika go and walked back with her toward her mom.

Mom fanned herself with her straw hat with an oversized wide and floppy brim. "I think we're all ready to quit for the day."

"Yeah, I think that would be a good idea. We've been working hard this week. Time off would be good." Avery gave Erika a concerned look. Her eyes were puffy again. She'd put her best friend through so much this week.

God, have I always been so self-absorbed?

Mrs. Klein popped open a water bottle. "Did Danny tell you the whole family's coming tomorrow to help? I won't be here in the morning—I'll be watching all the kids so the grown-ups can get actual work done—but then we're having a cookout. I'm sure Dan's invited you all."

Dan had mentioned nothing, and Avery felt her mom's eyes on her. "Oh, wow, that's lovely of them. I didn't know."

As though he'd been part of the conversation, Dan approached from the shed. "Yeah, we'll probably take the jet boat out at some point, too. Do some tubing."

"Didn't you invite them?" Mrs. Klein shook her head.

Dan grimaced. "I was gonna, Mom. I just assumed they'd be here anyway."

Mrs. Klein reached over and squeezed Avery's mom's forearm. "Well, I'm inviting you."

"Thanks for selling me out, Mom," Dan said dryly. "And you're all invited, of course."

"That sounds great," Mom said, giving Dan one of her fakest smiles. Thank goodness Dan didn't know Mom well enough to know how she acted when she loathed someone but didn't want it to be too obvious.

A flare of disappointment went up Avery's chest. She wished Mom's admiration for Mrs. Klein would translate into reevaluating her opinion of Dan.

From the smirk on Dan's mouth, it was clear enough he knew he wasn't welcome in their conversation. He nodded, then called out to Peyton, who was walking by carrying a stack of shutters. "Hear that, MacLuckie? Cookout tomorrow."

Peyton gave a crooked smile. "Sounds good. I'm going to be here anyway, right?"

As he walked away, Mom gave Peyton a second glance. "Does he live here?" she asked Dan, as if she hadn't really noticed Peyton's comings and goings.

Dan nodded. "Yeah. Room and board are part of our arrangement."

"Will that affect the number of rooms you have available for guests?" Mom asked with concern.

"No, ma'am." Dan gave her the slightest of salutes, then

addressed the rest of them. "I'm heading out for the evening. See you all tomorrow. Bye, Mom. Good luck with all the minions in the morning."

As he disappeared into the house, Avery grabbed a water bottle from the cooler. *Where is he going?*

It wasn't any of her business. But she couldn't help feeling like he was leaving to avoid being around her. Or maybe her mom. She was being nicer to him now that his own mom was around, but she doubted Mom would ever be anything other than cordial to Dan.

Once Mom made up her mind about someone, good luck changing it. And she would always hate Dan.

Always.

CHAPTER TWENTY-NINE

With the internet now connected, Dan had picked up a TV set from the store that night and set it up in his room at the lodge. He flipped through channels aimlessly, figuring this would be a night in which he spent more time trying to pick something to watch than watch it. Melissa had complained he had the bad habit of falling asleep within five minutes of any movie they picked, and she wasn't wrong.

But he was too agitated to sleep tonight.

Too fucking horny.

That moment in the garden had surprised him.

You still want her.

Was it normal not to get over that first love?

Thinking about Avery would do nothing to help him now. He clicked off the TV, then stood and went into the hallway. Peyton appeared to have turned in for the night—the door to his room was closed. Dan leaned against the door frame, trying to keep out thoughts of Avery.

Or maybe a little fantasizing about her would be enough just to deal with his lust and move on.

As he decided that would be the best course of action, the doorbell rang.

Grumbling as he walked, Dan made his way down the hallway toward the front door. Japanese beetles were swarming the front porch light as he looked through the peephole.

Avery.

He took a moment to gather himself, then opened the door, swallowing back a deep breath. "Hey."

"Hey. I left the key here—the one you gave me when—we went out earlier." She swatted a few beetles away, ducking from their crazy flight. "I hope I didn't wake you."

Nine on a Friday night? She really must think he had no social life. He held the door open, and she passed under his arm.

As he shut it, the soft tick of beetles dive-bombing the door sounded softly against the wood.

She grimaced and combed her fingers through her hair. "I know it's late—I'm so sorry. Your mom took us out to this local farm that had pit beef—why didn't I ever know that was a Maryland thing? It was amazing. I may have even convinced Mom to let me use them for my wedding caterer." She grinned. "It finally feels like everything is coming together for this thing."

She's happy. *About her wedding.* And somehow, that hurt him deep in the gut. He'd done his best to give her space and stay away the last few days, but seeing her now made him want to hold on to the moment a little longer. "Do you want anything? Glass of milk? Beer? Bottle of water? That's about all I have."

She hesitated, then nodded. "A beer might be good."

He went to the kitchen to grab a couple of beers. When he returned, she'd wandered into the sitting room, which smelled of fresh drywall mud. After untwisting the cap, he handed her the bottle. "I was hoping to do some wainscotting, but this'll do for now, don't you think?"

Garrett had even taken the time to add recessed lighting, like Dan had planned.

Avery smiled, taking a swig from her beer. "It's great, Dan." Her footsteps echoed as she took a few steps toward the window. "Feel like sitting out on the old dock? It'd be a shame not to. One last time, anyway."

The way she said it made his throat tighten.

One last time.

Like the first night they'd met, when they rowed across the damned lake, then sat there, spilling their daydreams and hopes to each other.

He nodded mutely, then gestured toward the back door.

As they made their way outside, Dan watched her closely, silhouetted in the moonlight. He never should have let that comment about her fantastic ass slip this afternoon. But *damn.*

He'd been watching her all week. Despite their rocky start, they'd been relating much more civilly. He'd seen traces of her witty sense of humor, her tenacity, and her exuberance—all traits he'd been attracted to all those years ago. It had taken every ounce of strength not to stare at her, to let his eyes drag over her soft skin, her sweet curves. She'd been pretty when she was eighteen, but as a thirty-year-old woman, she was a knockout. *But she isn't yours to look at, you idiot.*

A frog jumped into the water as they made their way onto the dock, slipping beneath the surface with a soft splash. She walked about halfway down, then sat and hung her legs over the side. Resting her weight back on one hand, she looked over the water, her profile to him as he sat beside her, keeping his distance. "I still think you're lucky, you know?" She closed her eyes, tilting her face toward the stars.

"Yeah? Why's that?" The last thing he felt right now was

lucky. The bitter tang of the hops from the beer made him swallow.

"To live here."

Sure. His fingers enclosed around the base of the cold bottle. "You think so, eh?"

"Yeah. Because I was thinking about it earlier this week, when you were saying all that stuff about the gossip in a small town. It's still better than being in a city of hundreds of thousands and not knowing anyone." Avery took a pull from her beer and then set it beside her.

She let her eyes wander over the dark tops of the tree line. "There are times I love it. Being anonymous appeals to the introverted part of my personality. And there's sort of an equanimity to it. The guy at the deli who's an asshole to the customers is equally an asshole to everyone, not just to me. But people still line up because he makes amazing sandwiches."

"Yeah, that probably wouldn't go over so well in a place like Brandywood. The Wongs—that couple who run the Baltimore Deli—they're also some of the nicest people in town. They know everyone by name." Dan ran his hand over the condensation on the smooth part of the bottle, then picked at the label. "Not that we don't have assholes in town. But they're usually the quirky ones people tell stories about. Or who are known for their antics. Ken Harrison was a bit of an asshole, come to think of it."

She drew one knee up and propped her elbow against it, resting her head against her open palm. "Is that why you quit working here?"

Quit? He followed the trail of stars, finding the curl of Scorpio's tail. He'd never really been into science, but astronomy and constellations had fascinated him. And that last night he and Avery had spent together when they were kids, they'd stared up at the stars, and he'd pointed them out to her.

He pulled his mind from the memory. That had also been the night that led to his getting fired from the lodge.

"I didn't quit, Avery. Mr. Harrison fired me. That was right after I was accused of giving you drugs."

Avery looked down, her fingertips kneading the back of her neck. "I didn't know that."

He shouldn't go down this path. Things couldn't be fixed with a simple conversation. Too many years had gone by, and the damage had been undoable. He chose his words carefully, focusing more on what had happened between them rather than the fallout of the accusations that had been leveled his way.

"I waited for a long time for you to call or text me, Avery. But it was radio silence from you. Nothing."

"My mom took my phone. I wasn't allowed to use it or any social media all year. And she started reading my email, too." She scratched at the rash on one of her arms absent-mindedly, then stopped herself. "It was kind of a nightmare until I moved out for college. I was only allowed to go to school, come home, and study."

"Then why not after high school?" *I loved you, Avery.*

Even when he'd been sure he never wanted to see her again, he kept wondering if he would.

She swallowed another sip of beer, then looked away. "Self-preservation, I guess. I figured if you didn't feel about me what I felt for you, then what was the point? Would you have even wanted me to contact you? It's not like I heard from you after then either."

He peeled off the label, then crumpled it into his fist.

No, I still hated you then.

But had he really? Because staring at her, it was hard to imagine hating her. More likely, he'd hated what she'd put him through.

But what had she meant? *I figured if you didn't feel about me what I felt for you, then what was the point?* Dan wondered if that meant Avery had wished he'd made contact. That they'd reconnected. What would their lives have looked like if they had reconnected earlier and not stayed apart? He wanted to tell her he would have reached out if he'd known that. If he'd been aware she'd thought there could be more between them, he would have tried. That he'd loved her. *But there is no point suggesting that now, Klein. That ship has definitely passed.*

He sighed, then lifted his beer in a toast. "Well, here's to mended fences. And your wedding. I never expected meeting again under these circumstances, but hell, if we're going to meet again at this age, at least I'm glad to see you happy."

He sounded a lot more sincere than he felt.

She clinked her beer bottle against his and smiled. "Thanks, Dan."

"I swear to God, woman, if you thank me for one more thing, I'm going to purposely make you suffer for it." He winked at her.

"Yeah? What would that involve? You can't exactly threaten me with much. I've already gone through a ruined wedding venue, attack from a crazy raccoon and a goose, poison ivy and sunburn, and family drama."

"I could toss you off the dock." He shoved her shoulder slightly, then gripped it.

She jumped back, laughing nervously. "You would do something like that."

He rubbed his eyes. "Not anymore. A long time ago, I wouldn't have thought twice about it. But I wouldn't want to go in there after you now, which might be the consequence for me, and that's enough reason to stop myself from doing it. I fall asleep on the couch after nine these days. Eat Cheerios for breakfast."

"Yeah, you're practically in need of a walker." She rolled her eyes. "We're not *that* old."

"Old enough. When was the last time you had sex three times in, like, an hour? When you were eighteen?" Maybe it was the beer emboldening him, but he did like seeing her squirm when he brought that up.

To her credit, she threw her head back and laughed. "True. God, I can't even imagine that anymore. That's nuts."

"Yup." *I was nuts about you.*

She sighed, then finished her beer. "That week I spent with you . . . was the best and worst week of my life. The most fun and the saddest." Avery stood, blocking the light of the moon from his face. "I'm sorry I never got to apologize for things in person, Dan. Since I didn't get to say it to you before, I *am* sorry."

That he could even have somewhat of a conversation about this with her was evidence that he was ready to let it go. He nodded and stood, brushing off his backside. "Like I said, water under the bridge. Ready to go to bed?"

They walked back in silence, then parted at the stairs. Goodnights always felt awkward with her, so he just nodded and then kept going as her footsteps faded up the stairs.

Dan had just climbed onto his bed when he heard a loud, piercing scream from upstairs. The sound of the mattress rustling followed as he rolled off it, scrambling for his shorts. He yanked them on, leaving his shirt behind as he ran out of the room.

Should he go back for his gun?

He didn't bother, taking the stairs two at a time at the sounds of a scuffle upstairs.

"Get it away!" Avery was screaming. "Get it away!"

He burst into her room, but Peyton had apparently beaten him in getting there.

A snake slithered toward the wall.

Avery stood on top of a metal folding chair, the contents of her suitcase scattered all over the room. She had some sort of white lotion smeared over her face, with her hair piled into a messy bun, and she was braless wearing a ribbed tank and a pair of short sleep shorts.

Peyton stepped over the strewn clothes toward the snake. "That little thing got you upset?"

"Little thing?" Avery's voice came out in a shriek. "It's, like, seven feet long!"

Mayyyyybe three. But hey, at least she overestimates lengths.

Peyton reached down and grabbed the snake by the head, then picked up the body with his other hand. "It's just a little rat snake. Not gonna bite you unless you scare it. But it's not venomous. I'll just go put this fellow outside where he belongs. You take care of the lady." Peyton gave Dan a laughing wink, then carried the snake out the door.

Dan tried not to laugh at Avery's overreaction. He'd dealt with enough snakes to know most of the ones in this area weren't venomous. But he imagined San Diego had its fair share of rattlesnakes—hence her reaction.

Stepping over her clothes, he held out a hand to help her down from the chair. "It's fine. Snake's gone. Where did it come from?"

She shook her head, refusing to get down. "I am not sleeping in here. It was in the damned sleeping bag."

Dan crossed back to the bag, then zipped it fully open and shook it. Nothing. "It probably just crawled in one of the days when the doors were left open. It was just a rat snake anyway, Avery. They're harmless."

"And how do you know it's the only one?" She shook her head. "You don't have any idea how much I hate—no, loathe—snakes."

She looked legitimately terrified. *City girl*. He forced back a smile.

"I don't know that it's the only one." He shrugged. "There could be more, I guess. But they probably aren't venomous. There aren't a lot of venomous snakes in Maryland—just the copperhead and the timber rattlesnake, and they're kinda rare."

"*Just* the copperhead and timber rattlesnake?" Her eyes widened. "You're saying while the doors have been wide open and snakes have been, apparently, free to slither into the lodge, just copperheads and timber rattlesnakes could have ventured in?" She gave a whole-body shiver. "That thing brushed against my leg, Dan. That's how I found out it was there."

He stared at her, blinking, trying and failing not to notice the fact that she was bra-less. *Those nipples* . . . "So . . . what then?"

"So I'm not sleeping here." Avery crossed her arms, which helped him focus. Had she seen him staring?

"Okay, well, how about you get down from that chair, at least?"

She shook her head.

Dan gave an exasperated sigh, then approached her with a few quick strides. He lifted her up, then threw her over his shoulder and started out of the bedroom.

"What the hell are you doing?" Avery squeaked, slapping his back with her open palm.

He headed down the hallway and started down the stairs. "Are you going to sleep in there?"

"No."

"Are you going to walk around up there?" he asked. She was still remarkably easy to carry, it turned out.

"Probably not." Her voice sounded like a grunt from the way he was carrying her.

He reached his room, then lowered her to the bed. "Then

you're sleeping in here. With me. Because I can't stay upstairs all night. I'm tired, and I have a long morning ahead of me moving furniture."

Avery's eyes widened, the irises looking especially gray in contrast to the lotion on her face. She seemed to realize what he was looking at and lifted a nervous hand to her face. "I forgot I was putting my night cream on when this all happened." She rubbed it in as she sat on the bed. "I can't stay here, Dan. That would be so wrong on so many levels. If Bryan finds out—"

"Then don't tell him." Dan turned off the light, which was attached to the ceiling fan, and crawled onto the bed. "It's just to sleep. Which we both need. Just lie down and get some."

She shot him a look in the darkness that he didn't have to see her expression to understand, and he guffawed.

"Get some *sleep*. And they say men have their heads in the gutter. I'm not offering you sex, woman." He rolled onto his side, turning his back toward her.

This is fine. It'll be fine.

Avery didn't respond for a few minutes, and he blinked in the darkness. At last, she lay down. "How do you know there aren't any snakes in *here*?"

"I don't. In fact . . ." He brushed his foot against her calf lightly. "Oh no, what's that?"

"Stop it!" Avery jerked her leg away. "*If* I'm going to stay here, there are going to be rules. You're going to stay on your side, got it? No touching. No pretending there are snakes near me."

Dan let out a slow sigh. "Got it." Didn't stop him from thinking about those perky breasts right next to him, though.

Right. Like it's going to help things if she notices you have a hard-on.

He said nothing for a while, and she relaxed after a while,

her body less tense. Then, several minutes later, her breathing deepened, and he guessed she was asleep.

"Goodnight, Avery," Dan whispered. *I wish you had found me sooner. I would have wanted you back, any way I could have you.*

CHAPTER THIRTY

Dan
12 Years Ago

THE BELL DINGED after Dan slammed the giant sledgehammer down on the platform, and he grinned as he looked up at the flashing lights on the carnival game. Avery had convinced him to take his hand at the high striker, which tested a player's strength—supposedly. These games always seemed rigged. But playing sports had its benefits. The game operator handed him the teddy bear, and he turned and gave it to Avery, who hugged it. "I knew you could do it," she said.

Her confidence in him had been half the reason for his success.

Dan's fingers interlaced with hers as they wandered away from the game booths and toward the rides. The air held a mixture of scents: cotton candy and popcorn and fried food and farm animals from the nearby agricultural booths. As a kid,

Dan had loved it when his mom took him to the county fair. The lines to get into the fairgrounds were always packed in the evenings, with nearly everyone from Brandywood and nearby towns paying a visit at some point during the weekly event.

He'd bought them wristbands so they could go on as many as they wanted, and they'd already gone on all of them twice, since there weren't that many at a fair this small. The only thing they hadn't managed was the Ferris wheel, which had a line that looked to be at least a half-hour-long wait. "Do you want to try that line again?"

Avery checked her watch. "I still have two hours before my parents want me in. We may as well."

He bought them cotton candy and a soda to share while they waited in line, then they made their way over toward it. He still didn't know how she'd convinced her parents to let her out alone—she'd asked to grab some dinner and go to the movies with one of the teenage girls who worked at the front desk, and they'd agreed to it, miraculously. It only gave them a few hours alone, but for once she didn't have to sneak in or out of her room.

"Do you ever take those long shutter exposure pictures? I think the ones I've seen of Ferris wheels are my favorites," Avery said, the lights of the wheel glinting against her eyes in the fading light of the day, making them shine.

Dan stole a piece of cotton candy from her. "Nah, I don't have that great of a camera yet. I'm saving up for one. I'm hoping I can use the money I get for graduation to buy one. But someday. And then I'll go all over the place taking pictures of Ferris wheels, just for you."

She leaned back against him, her cheek tilting against his chest as she sighed. "I don't want to leave this summer. Promise to text me every day?"

"I promise." He turned her to face him, then set his hands

in the back pockets of her jean shorts, scooting her closer. He didn't care about the stony looks he attracted from people around them as he dropped a kiss to her lips. She tasted like cotton candy, and he let his mouth linger on hers longer than he'd intended. "I hate that you're leaving," he whispered as they pulled apart.

She only had two days left here, and as the day of her departure rapidly approached, the more he dreaded thinking about the morning he'd get up and go to the Serendipity and she wouldn't be there.

For the first time in his life, he was actually looking forward to the start of the school year, just so he wouldn't have to go daily to a place where he'd be missing her more.

Avery wrapped her arms around his waist and snuggled closer. For the first time since they'd met, they didn't talk much as they waited in line together, just slowly making their way up toward the front. Whatever had drawn them together was stronger than super glue and gravity and all those scientific comparisons Dan didn't really do well enough in school to make.

He couldn't believe how strongly he felt for her in such a brief span of time.

No question about it, he loved her. This had to be love—he was sure of it. And he had said nothing yet, but maybe the Ferris wheel would be the perfect place to confess his feelings.

His palms broke out into a sweat as they climbed on board, and Avery leaned back into his arms as the pod started forward, swaying in the warm summer air. Avery linked her hand with his, then glanced at him. "You seem nervous."

"Eh, I don't love heights."

"Really?" She looked surprised. "They don't bother me."

As they climbed higher, her thumb brushed against the inside of his palm, tickling him and shooting sparks down his arm at the same time. "Do you think we can see the lodge from here?"

"Probably not," he said, then looked over the edge. "But you can see Main Street pretty well. That's Yardley's right there. And St. John's—that's where my family goes to church." He pointed at the church steeple. "And that over there is the high school—"

"Where my jock boyfriend plays varsity basketball?" She seemed to realize her slip-up instantly, stiffening.

Boyfriend?

The thought did something funny to his solar plexus, like she'd hit it and now he couldn't breathe.

But it wasn't in a bad way. In a way that his heart was beating so hard that he figured she might hear it. "That's right," he said after a moment, his fingers tightening on hers.

She smiled, then they kissed again, this time more breathlessly and intensely than before. This would be a perfect time to tell her he loved her—except for the fact that their tongues were busy stroking each other's, and the only thing he really wanted to do was get off this damned Ferris wheel and be alone with her.

She gave a little whimper, and her hand smoothed down from his neck, over the front of his shorts, and rubbed against his hard dick. He groaned in response, trying to discreetly sneak his hand up her shirt.

They composed themselves and caught their breath on the way down. Dan breathed out heavily. As they got off the ride, he caught sight of Adam Sorensen and some of the other basketball players and their girlfriends waiting in line. They clapped as Dan and Avery got off the Ferris wheel.

"Good show, you two!" Adam hollered through cupped hands.

"Get a room!" one of the other players called out.

"Oh, my God." Avery's cheeks burned bright red. "I think we should probably go now."

With the bear he'd won for her tucked under one arm and his other arm around her shoulder, they hurried away from the carnival and toward the parking lot. They climbed into his truck, and both of them sat in the cab's silence for a moment before sneaking a glance at each other as he started the engine.

Dan grinned at her. "Sorry about that."

She laughed and shook her head. "I can't believe that just happened." Then she reached around the back of her head and pulled off a silver necklace she wore. She held it out to him.

"I have something for you."

"Oh, yeah? What is it?" Dan reached out and took it. The medal on it was still warm from her skin, and it looked worn.

"St. Christopher. It belonged to my grandfather. To keep us safe. When we go on all those adventures we've talked about."

He ran his thumb over the figure on the medal. A family heirloom? This was too valuable to give someone she'd just met days ago, wasn't it?

Unless he meant as much to her as she meant to him. A lump formed in the back of his throat.

This was so crazy. Yes, they'd gotten to know each other over the last few days. They'd even spoken about their long-term dreams and where they wanted to end up. But this felt even more permanent, as if Avery sincerely wanted Dan in her life going forward. And he realized he wanted that, too. But he wasn't confident he should receive something so precious. *What if he messed up and lost it?*

He shook his head. "I can't take this, Avery. I'm sure it's really valuable to you."

She closed his fingers over it, leaving her fingers on his. "It is. That's why I want you to have it. And it's not the most valuable thing I want to give you, Dan." She looked away, clearly nervous. "Is there anywhere we can go . . . to be together?"

Dan breathed out, the pulse in his neck throbbing. "Are you sure you're ready?"

Avery met his gaze, then nodded. "I know it's crazy, because we've only known each other for a few days, but I think I love you, Dan. You're the only person I've ever met who makes me feel like I can be myself. I don't have to be anything or anyone around you. I can just be me. And I want to be with you—completely."

Dan nodded, too nervous to speak. He wanted to tell her he loved her, too, but would it just sound like he was saying it because he wanted to have sex with her? He drove in silence, thanking Warren silently.

His older brother had tossed him a box of condoms the morning after the drinking incident. "Just in case," Warren had said with a wry look.

Dan had been worried Mom would find them while doing his laundry, so he'd stuck them in the glove compartment of his truck.

He drove to a field near Gulliver's Pass, where an old sheep pasture had overgrown in the last thirty years, and pulled under the shade of a tall oak. Cops sometimes came this way to look for trespassers, but he and Corbin had spent many long nights with metal detectors combing the fields there without getting stopped.

Turning off the engine, he pulled a blanket out from the back seat. "You sure about this?" he asked.

She nodded and reached for the phantom necklace around her neck. Her fingers brushed her collarbone. "Yes." Then she added, "Are you?"

He closed the space between them in the cab and kissed her. "Of course. Avery, I've never felt like this either. You mean everything to me. Everything." At that, she smiled and blushed, and Dan knew without a doubt he wanted her in his future.

They got out of the truck, and Dan laid the blanket down a few feet away from the passenger side. A hundred thoughts assailed him, but he pushed them away. Whatever he was worried about, he'd figure it out. Or they would together. Then again, when she'd been sexually confident, he'd felt like a bumbling moron.

Avery kicked off her flip-flops, then took his hand and led him to the center of the blanket. Her arms curved around his neck. "I don't know what to do," she admitted, her lips soft against his jawline as she stood on her tiptoes.

He let out a throaty murmur and cupped her face in his hands to keep his fingers from shaking. She looked so beautiful standing there, the moonlight on her skin, her auburn hair cascading over her shoulders in waves. Brushing his lips against hers, he kissed her mouth gently, deepening the pressure as she relaxed into his arms, her lips parting against his.

Kissing her was natural, and he felt steady and sure. He was aware of everything: the pounding of his heart, the sweet melody of the tree frogs and crickets mixed with the occasional hoot of an owl, the woods, and the rustle of the grass around them as he pulled her shirt off gently, then took off his own.

She moistened her lips, reaching back to unclasp her bra, and he helped her, sucking in a breath as the fabric fell away and revealed her breasts, pink nipples hardening to his touch. He laid her down on the blanket, and she pulled away her shorts, then her underwear, and she was naked—it almost did him in.

He swallowed, then pulled down his own shorts. Her gaze went right to his groin, and he fought the impulse to cover himself. He knelt and took out a condom, tearing the packaging open with his teeth, then rolled it on, his hands still feeling unsure.

When he lowered his body to hers, he kissed her to steady himself again. She didn't close her eyes this time, her eyes locked with his. "Will it hurt?" she asked, her voice small but a hot whisper against his ear.

He shook his head. He wanted to remind her he didn't *really* know, but that wasn't what she wanted right now. Corbin had told him the key to making a girl happy was to take your time. *Which is the last thing I want to do.*

But he did. He fought the temptation his body was aching for with her right there, so close, so ready. He kissed her gently, remembering how he'd felt when they'd been making out, and how much he'd wanted her then, and hoped she'd felt the same way.

His tongue dipped into her mouth, their kiss growing more passionate as his hands smoothed over her breasts, her back arching as he cupped them. The more he touched her, the more she seemed to moan in his arms, to tilt her hips toward his until they were both panting, tantalized by being so close to the precipice, so close to the ecstasy of him being inside her.

When he pushed between her legs at last, she was hot and wet, and her body received him with the same trembling enthusiasm. She cried out and wrapped her arms around him. All he could think was that he had to go slower. . . .

"Dan . . . I love you," she whispered as he pushed deeper. Faster. "I love you so much."

I love you, too, Avery. The words lodged in his throat, and he thrust faster, helpless to the rhythm they were creating together. *God, this is fucking incredible.*

"Dan, please . . ."

He slowed, then realized she was asking for release, her nails digging into his back, her body arching against his. He wanted to touch her, wanted to bring her there with him, and he pulled back, his fingers finding the tender spot between her legs, swollen and wet. As he rubbed it, she begged for more, and he found a new rhythm pleasuring her, thrusting deeper and faster until she pushed off his hand, her legs locking around his hips as an earth-shattering cry left her lips.

Her coming did him in, and he let go to his own thrusts until he felt himself on the verge and then gave one last thrust, deep as he throbbed, and came inside her.

Holy fucking . . .

He couldn't even finish the thought as he collapsed on her, exhausted and satiated. They were both shaking, and his lips crept up her neck and sought hers.

No wonder.

This feeling. He got it now. *Life-altering.*

He rolled off her, pulling her into his arms. When her breath had settled, he kissed her temple and asked, "Was it good for you?"

She laughed, running her fingertips along his bare chest. "Are you kidding me? It was amazing. I want to do it again. Immediately."

Dan grinned at her. And then happily, enthusiastically, and only slightly exhaustedly complied.

THE DRIVE back to the lodge was almost impossible for Dan to make. He didn't want to go back. The last few hours had been bliss, and then they'd realized just how far after her curfew they'd gone—two full hours—and Avery had freaked out and texted her dad that she was on her way but had lost track of time.

"I can drop you off before we get to the driveway," Dan said as she checked her phone for the twentieth time. "And watch you walk up. But that way, if your parents are watching, they won't see me dropping you off."

Avery nodded, fidgeting. "Do my lips look swollen to you?"

He shook his head, clearing his throat. *How the hell am I going to function normally around her ever again?*

"My mom saw me watching you a couple of days ago." Avery cleared her throat. "I told her I was going to ask you if you'd seen her, and I think she bought it, but now I'm worried. She won't answer my texts."

"If she had really thought I was the one you were going out with tonight, would she have let you go?" Dan asked.

"No." Her voice was soft.

"Then there's your answer." Dan glided the wheel around a turn. "We'll be there in three minutes. Then you'll be in the clear. Anyway, your dad said it was okay, right?"

"Not exactly. I told him I lost track of time, and he texted back 'okay, be safe.'" Avery drew her knees up to her chest, and Dan smirked. He couldn't remember the last time he'd been able to do something like that while sitting in a car. Shorter people definitely had an advantage with getting comfortable in small spaces.

"But your dad goes easier on you, right?"

She bristled. "My dad can be a jerk when he wants. My mom told me the other day the whole reason they're getting divorced is his fault. So there's that."

Dan breathed out, relief creeping into his gut. Then her dad's affair wasn't a big secret. Avery was handling the news well, given the circumstances. "I'm glad she told you, though. It's always better to know why when it's something like that."

"Well, I mean, it's not like I understand it any better—" Avery stopped short and tilted her head, narrowing her eyes at him. "Wait a second. What are you talking about?"

Shiiiit.

He felt his face flush and was thankful for the darkness in the truck's cab. "Uh, just that you know why your parents are getting a divorce now. Didn't you say your mom gave you the reasons?"

"No, that's not what I said. But it sounds like *you* know something about the reasons." Avery twisted in her seat to face him. "What are you talking about, Dan?"

There's no getting out of this.

If he lied now and she found out later he'd known and then lied about knowing—which, admittedly, was a slim chance, but still. He didn't want to lie to her.

And he also didn't want to be the one to tell her the truth.

"Dan. You better tell me what you know right now." Avery crossed her arms. "If you lie to me now, I swear I will never speak to you again."

He swallowed hard, then said in a low, gravelly voice, "Your dad. I overheard him on the phone with someone the other day. Avery, I think he has a girlfriend."

"What!" Avery's voice rang out in the cab so loud that his ears hurt.

He winced and glanced back at her, but her face was a mask of fury.

"My dad is having an affair, and you found out about it and didn't immediately tell me?" Avery's hands balled into fists. "How dare you? Why would you keep something like that from me?"

He rubbed the back of his neck with his left hand. "I-I didn't know how to tell you. Didn't think it was my place. I wasn't sure who he was talking to anyway, and I didn't want to tell you something that might be wrong."

"Not your *place?* So . . . wait." Avery held her hands out in front of her. "It's your place to sneak me out and fuck me—aka, share the most intensely personal thing on the planet with me— but not tell me something you know I not only want to but need to know. As in my own personal business. What the fuck, Dan?"

He shot her a bewildered look. When she put it that way, it sounded terrible, but he hadn't meant it that way. And she wasn't cutting him even the slightest amount of slack, which was ironic because it seemed like she wasn't even angry with her dad for going out and having an affair. She was only angry with Dan for not telling her.

"I'm the bad guy?" Dan's voice came out louder and angrier and more defensive than he'd intended. They were approaching the lodge, and he pulled over to the side of the road where he'd been intending to drop her off. He parked, then turned to face her. "Your dad is out there with a girlfriend, and you're yelling at me about it?"

"I didn't yell!" Her voice was a shriek at this point.

"Yes, you did. And guess what? I'm not having an affair, Avery. That's your dad. You take it up with him. You're right. It's your personal business. Actually, it's his personal business. It wasn't my place to drop a bomb like that on you. If he wants to go out and fuck other women, that's his deal, and I'm not responsible for that."

"Yeah, but you'll fuck me without saying a word." She was yelling loudly now, her shoulders heaving.

"Yes, I fucked you. And I'd do it again without changing a thing!" This time, he yelled back, aware of how loud they were being. But who was going to hear them all the way over at the Serendipity? They were still far enough away to yell like this with privacy.

Her jaw dropped, then she reached across and slapped him hard against the cheek.

The sound of the slap reverberated in the air, and Avery drew her hand back, which trembled, and stared at it.

Dan flinched, blinking at her without saying a word.

He'd been angry with her before, but her slap had roused a fury in him.

She'd slapped him.

Even his own mother had never done something like that before.

"Get out of my truck." His voice was a low, angry whisper.

She brushed a tear away from her cheek with the back of her hand and turned to go, gathering her purse. As she put her hand on the door handle, a face approached on the other side of the glass, and Avery jumped back with a startled scream.

Mrs. Moretti.

Avery threw the door open and scrambled out of the truck, but her mom caught the door. "You know I heard you two yelling."

Avery covered her face with her hands, her shoulders shaking. "Mom—you don't understand. I—"

"*Cállate.*"

Whatever that meant, Mrs. Moretti said it in such a way that Avery froze in silence. She turned her gaze to Dan, eyes glaring. "You're the kid from the Sports Shack. What's your name?"

His throat was dry, his tongue sticking to the roof of his mouth. His cheek still throbbed from Avery's slap. "Dan, ma'am. Dan Klein."

"Stay the hell away from my daughter, Dan Klein." Then Mrs. Moretti slammed the door, dragging Avery away by the arm.

Dan pounded the steering wheel with his fists, watching for a moment as Avery and Mrs. Moretti made their way toward the driveway. He was angry with Avery, but they'd figure that out later. She was dealing with something bigger now, and she needed him.

Unbuckling, he threw open the door to the truck and followed. "Wait up," he said, trotting to catch up to them.

Mrs. Moretti whirled to face him. "No, listen here." She dropped Avery's arm and came closer. "I don't know what you've been up to, what you've been doing, but I know your type. You see a rich girl coming here on vacation, and you think you can just have your jollies with her, and that she'll be your little slut for the week, right?" She shook her head. "And you may have charmed your way into her pants and taken advantage of her, but *I'll be damned* if you ever touch her again."

Avery raced up to her side. "Mom, no, it wasn't like that—"

"Shut the hell up, Avery."

Dan wedged between them in an instant. "Mrs. Moretti—"

"Don't you dare tell me what to do with my daughter." Mrs. Moretti squared off with him, and for a moment Dan thought she just might punch him in the face.

Avery set a hand on his forearm. "Dan, just get out of here." Then she dropped her hand to her side.

"Avery, I can't—"

"Leave! Just go! You're only making things worse." Tears fell freely onto her cheeks, and the last thing he wanted to do was leave.

But she turned and strode away, leaving him there with her mother.

After a few seconds, Mrs. Moretti turned and followed her.

Dan walked numbly back to his truck, climbed inside, and lowered his forehead to the top of the steering wheel, resting it against the backs of his hands.

How in the hell am I going to fix this?

CHAPTER THIRTY-ONE

Avery
9 Months Ago

AVERY SIGNED the paperwork as the movers unloaded the last of her boxes into Bryan's living room. She'd intended to bring more of her furniture and hired them a few weeks earlier, but she'd ended up selling most of her stuff. Bryan had suggested they put the money toward the wedding since he already had furniture.

The movers left, and Avery closed the door, turning back toward the living room. Bryan would be home soon from work, and she wanted to surprise him with dinner.

Wading past the boxes, she went into the kitchen and opened the cooler she'd packed from her own place. She unpacked what she could into the fridge, even though there wasn't much space, then took out the ingredients to make shrimp alfredo and a salad.

The door opened, and Bryan's keys jingled as he set them in the glass dish he had for them on the entryway console. Avery stepped out of the kitchen with a smile. "Hey, babe."

Bryan stood at the front door, staring at the stacks of boxes. "Wow. I like what you've done with the place." He grimaced at the mess.

She laughed and wiped her hands on her apron. "Don't worry, I'll have it all unpacked by tomorrow. Besides"—she came over and slung her arms around his neck—"I just figured we could pretend the boxes were like the rock formations at Arches National Park and have celebration sex in the great, wild outdoors of the living room tonight."

Bryan returned her kiss with a skeptic look. "I think I'll pass on that one," he said with a chuckle. "We might get buried in a landslide."

She returned to the kitchen to finish dinner, a nervous feeling simmering in her stomach. They were so different in the way they inhabited spaces, which made Avery sometimes worry that she wouldn't be able to live up to his expectations. Moving in together had been his idea. He didn't think it made sense for them both to be paying rent when they were going to be getting married in nine months.

"Hey, I called the owner of the Serendipity today. He's going to reserve the place for our wedding next summer."

Bryan came into the kitchen, his necktie hanging over one shoulder, and unbuttoned his collar. "You sure I can't convince you to jump in that car? I'll whisk you away to Vegas, and we can be married within a few hours."

She enjoyed seeing the more spontaneous side of him occasionally. Grinning, she stirred the alfredo sauce as she squeezed some lemon juice into it. "Nope. The Serendipity is where my dream wedding happens. Nine months will go by so fast, you'll see."

"Tell that to a pregnant woman," Bryan replied wryly. "You should hear the OB doctors talk about it."

They ate dinner, and Bryan went to bed shortly afterward, leaving Avery in the living room to unpack.

Around midnight, Avery arched her back, stretching out the lower part of her spine. She'd been hunched over for hours. It was definitely time to get some rest, and she'd attack the rest of this tomorrow.

Avery got ready for bed quietly, then crept toward Bryan's room—their room now. She tiptoed into the room, then pushed aside the covers, slipping into bed beside him. He was asleep, but she couldn't resist the urge to reach over and cuddle with him. She should have gone to bed earlier with him. This was the first night together in their home, after all.

Bryan roused sleepily, then stiffened. "What are you doing?"

"Just thought you might want to snuggle." She kissed his earlobe playfully. "Or something else."

Bryan checked his cell phone. "Avery . . . it's after midnight. I have to get up in four hours."

"I just—"

"If you're going to come to bed so late, please try not to wake me up. It's rude, and I have to be rested for my job." Bryan lay back down, then rolled over, his back toward her.

She winced, her heart beating harder and painfully. And though she had been inconsiderate, a tear formed in her eye and slipped out onto her cheek. She brushed it away, then turned her back to Bryan. "I'm sorry," she whispered.

Bryan shifted again, then sat up. Flipping the light on, he tried to turn her to face him. She pushed back, not wanting to look at him, but he forced her anyway, and she lay on her back, her head on the pillow. "Come on, babe. Don't cry. I was up waiting for you to come to bed for a really long time. I guess I was just disappointed you didn't come in earlier." He wiped tears from her cheeks, leaned over her, and kissed her.

She didn't feel like kissing him.

But as the kiss continued, she forced herself to relax. He may not have been nice, but he was trying to make up for it. And even though hadn't *really* apologized, he was obviously sorry.

This will be a transition, Avery. It's been a while since you've lived with someone. You'll just have to learn to adjust again.

CHAPTER THIRTY-TWO

Now

BRYAN'S HAND rested against Avery's hip, and she snuggled closer to him sleepily in the dark.

Oh, hello there . . .

It'd been a long time since they'd had middle-of-the-night, half-awake sex, but he was clearly hard, and she pushed herself against him, the tantalizing feeling of his nearness instantly making her wet.

She rubbed her ass against his length, and his hand slipped under the waistband of her shorts. She murmured in response.

Rubbing back and forth, she felt him harden further still, his fingers dipping lower, then lower still, then stalled. "Please . . ."

Then he parted her with his fingers, pushing one deep inside her as she arched back against him. His other hand came up under her shirt, cupping one breast, then stroking and

pinching her nipples as she rocked back against him rhythmically.

"Oh, God . . ." One finger, then two, deep inside her,
pushing in and out. He used the tip of his forefinger to rub
against the tender spot between her legs, making her hotter,
wetter, pulsing against his fingertips. She pushed against him,
the soles of her feet flexing against his legs.

His breath was on her neck. "God . . . you're so fucking
wet."

She froze, drawing in a sharp breath at the voice.

Not Bryan.

She awakened fully and stilled. "Dan!"

The bed. The snake. The . . . oh God, *what the hell did I
just do?*

Scrambling from the bed, she flopped onto the floor, pulling
the sheet with her.

The light flipped on, and Dan was on his feet, staring
at her.

She was still panting, panties still soaked, her body still
craving him.

No, not him. Bryan. Right?

She'd been sure it was Bryan, wasn't she?

"What just happened?" She stared at him, horrified with
herself.

He shook his head, obviously just as addled by sleep as
she'd been. "I don't know. You woke *me* up!"

She covered her face. "Oh my God, oh my God, oh my
God. I thought you were—"

He sucked in a breath, and her gaze snapped up.

Somehow, I just made it worse.

"You thought I was your fiancé?" His face darkened.

"I-I don't know. I mean, I was half-asleep. I just . . . felt you there, and I assumed, and I . . . you didn't seriously think I was waking you up for sex, did you?"

"I was . . ." Dan shook his head. "Don't turn this around on me. I actually *was* asleep. You were up against me. I'm a man, Avery, and we get turned on when there's a beautiful woman within our grasp."

Avery hugged her arms to her chest. *He thinks I'm beautiful? The worst thing? Right now, she wasn't thinking about Bryan. I want to fuck Dan. I want to be dragged back to bed to finish what we started. Stop, Avery.*

Things with Bryan had never been that hot. He didn't like being woken up. She should have known it wasn't Bryan. *When was the last time we had sex?*

After taking a deep breath, she pressed her hands against her burning cheeks, then sat back down on the mattress. "I am so sorry. I'm not trying to blur the lines of consent here. I truly was just . . ."

"No, it's fine. I apologize, Avery. It won't happen again."

She wrapped the sheet over her legs. "You don't have to apologize, Dan. Like you said, I'm the one who woke you."

Being up in the middle of the night had a way of making her tiredness feel heavier and her brain thick and soupy. "I just cheated on my fiancé," she said in a flat voice, staring at her hands. "Oh, *fuck.* I detest cheaters, and now I'm one of them."

Dan shrugged. "Avery, you didn't cheat on your fiancé, okay? Stop beating yourself up over it." He reached over and plucked the pillow from the side where he'd been sleeping. "But it's probably a better idea if I sleep on the floor for the rest of the night." He grabbed a blanket from the foot of the bed and laid it out, then put the pillow down on it. He turned the light back off, leaving them in darkness.

Avery crawled back onto the mattress and lay on her back. *It counts. You just cheated on Bryan. He'd count it for sure.*

The absolute worst part? She was now so horny, but there was no way she could do anything with Dan in the room. *Even though I desperately need the release. When was my last orgasm?*

No, she couldn't think like that.

In eight days, she was marrying the man she loved.

She let out a discontented grunt and squeezed her eyes shut. This was all going to be *interesting* in the morning.

THE SMELL of coffee woke Avery, and she roused, blinking at the streams of light coming in through the window. She whirled around, checking the room for signs of Dan, but he was gone.

His pillow was still on the floor, though.

Shit. Shit. Shittitty shit.

She got to her feet and scanned the room. Her clothes were still upstairs in the bedroom she'd abandoned, where she should have spent the night on the floor, snake or no snake.

Turns out you had a snake in the bed after all.

She gritted her teeth, angry with her inner voice. *Come on! Jokes, right now?*

First thing this morning, she was going to call Bryan and confess. Tell him all about it.

He had a right to know what had happened. The whole truth.

Her engagement ring seemed to sparkle in response.

"I'm a terrible person," she whispered.

She rubbed her eyes, swept her hair back into a ponytail, then left the room, creeping silently up the stairs. She'd almost made it to the room, when Peyton stepped out into the hallway, fully dressed for the day.

"Good morning!" He grinned. "Don't worry. I checked the room. No snakes this morning. You sleep okay after all that excitement? Probably a lot more comfortable in an actual bed than on the floor any—"

Fantastic. Someone else who knows. She stared him down. "You cannot tell anyone about that, Peyton."

His brows drew together. "I wasn't plan—"

"Not a soul."

Peyton drew his thumb and forefinger across his lips like he was zipping them shut. "Got it, Miss Avery."

"You can just call me Avery. I'm not your schoolmarm."

Peyton chuckled and shook his head. "No wonder he likes you so much. You're like a torn shoe and a crooked foot."

"Like a what?"

"You know. A perfect match." Peyton beamed, then continued downstairs, whistling as he went.

A perfect match? Right. What was an apt comparison to two things attracted to but horrible for each other?

She hurried into the room and dressed, grateful that Peyton had checked it for snakes, despite his comments about Dan.

She still had a week of being around Dan before she was supposed to get married. Five days before Bryan was supposed to get into town.

Finding her cell phone among the clothing she'd tossed on the floor when she'd thrown her suitcase at the snake, she checked for notifications. Thankfully, now that she was doing a better job of texting Bryan in the mornings and evenings, he had calmed down. It had helped that Dan had gotten Wi-Fi, and she could contact Bryan more easily now.

Avery closed the door to the room, staring at Bryan's phone number.

Hey babe, it's me. Yeah, you know, the new owner of the Serendipity? Turns out I have unresolved feelings for him. And

I almost fucked him last night. Totally accidentally. I shouldn't have been there, of course, but I ignored my better judgment. But I'm telling you now, so that makes it all better, right?

If the roles were reversed, she wouldn't forgive Bryan for it.

You don't almost "accidentally" fuck someone.

Because deep down, she knew she'd let the whole thing happen. She'd crawled into that bed with him knowing full well how things could end up.

Be honest.

Twelve years ago, she'd done a lot of lying, too. Because of Dan.

He had a way of bringing out both the best and worst in her.

She dialed Erika through a messaging app to circumvent the service issue. Erika picked up on the second ring.

"Hey. You all awake yet?"

Erika sounded groggy. "I am. Dan's nieces and nephews all arrived, like, a half-hour ago, and there are a *lot* of them. It's as if a preschool came over."

"You need to get over here." Avery started folding her clothes and putting them back in the suitcase.

"Why?" Erika's voice was instantly more alert.

"Because I really, really messed up." She shoved the rest of her clothes in without folding them and zipped up the case.

A soft shuffling sound came from the other end of the line, along with Erika's breathing. A minute later, Avery heard a door closing. "You slept with him, didn't you?"

"Not exactly." She cleared her throat, then sat on the folding chair. "I *almost* slept with him. There was a snake in my sleeping bag, and I got scared, so I ended up sharing the bed with him—"

"As one does with a person they're extremely attracted to

and once had a sexual relationship with." Erika groaned. "Continue."

"So, in the middle of the night, I woke up, and he was hard, and I was half-asleep and disoriented and assumed I was with Bryan—"

"Is that really the excuse we're going with here?" The disbelief dripped from her voice.

"Yeah, well, it's true. Haven't you ever—"

"No, I rarely wake up in a bed without realizing I'm with an ex instead of my boyfriend."

"All right, well, that's beside the point. I realized it was him before it got as far as actual sex. But Erika, what the hell am I supposed to do? I started thinking about it and realized that even if I'm not supposed to be with Bryan because of this curse thing—"

"God, please tell me we are *not* back to that again." Erika let out a long sigh. "Avery, do you want to marry Bryan or not? Because that's really what this comes down to. He's a person, you know. Not just a disposable peg in the game of *Curse of the Three Fiancés*."

"I know that." Avery leaned back, her eyes sweeping the room for any sign of another snake.

"Do you, though? Because you want to know what I think? Bryan is a control freak. I think you shouldn't marry him. I think you're wondering if you should marry Dan, which is preposterous. And I think you know that, but you're purposely considering someone who is a terrible choice for you because you naturally gravitate toward men who are terrible choices for you. Then when things blow up in your face, you get to blame it on this family curse rather than take responsibility for the fact that you made a horrible choice in the first place."

Avery felt as though Erika had reached across the phone and punched her in the face. She stared at the phone, the smiling picture of her best friend in the contact profile picture. *She thinks Bryan is a controlling asshole* and *that I shouldn't marry him?* What?

Nausea rose in Avery's stomach, up to her throat.

Then she hung up the phone.

What the fuck?

Her esophagus felt as if she had swallowed a hot lump of coal and it was slowly burning its way down.

Erika had hinted more than once that she thought Bryan was controlling, but she'd never been so mean about it. But if she truly felt that way, why go to so much trouble to help her get the wedding venue ready? Why bother to show up here at all? And if Erika really thought marrying Bryan was such a mistake, why hadn't she flat-out told her that? *And why mention marrying Dan in that spiel, too? I almost went too far with the man, not suggest I thought I should marry him.*

As she stared at her ring again, she blinked hard.

The family curse.

Was she spiraling headlong into inevitable fate?

She'd been fighting all the disasters of the week, thinking she could change the outcome.

But what if . . . what if she was wrong?

Mom hadn't married the two other men she'd been engaged to because she was convinced Dad was her true fated match. And look how well that had turned out for Mom. He'd cheated on her, left her for a younger woman, then started a new family. The "love of Mom's life" had turned her into a resentful person who couldn't get over having a husband who had betrayed her that way.

Once, Mom had confessed to Avery that Tina hadn't been Dad's first affair either. That she'd suspected over the years he'd had multiple, quieter affairs, and that had been the reason she'd started working at Dad's practice. To control things. Eventually, Mom's need to control things had spilled into Avery's life. She couldn't have the perfect husband, so she was determined to have the perfect daughter.

And for a while, it had worked. It was easy enough for Mom to do it with Avery because it was like a Pavlovian response—Avery got her mom's approval and praise whenever she did things Mom wanted her to do. And that felt good. So Avery had, for eighteen years, done everything she could to make Mom happy, frequently choosing Mom's happiness above what she wanted for herself.

Dan had been her first foray into independence away from Mom's control. But had she really struck out and done things that made her happy?

". . . Bryan is a control freak . . . you naturally gravitate toward men who are terrible choices for you . . ."

When was the last time she'd heard from her old friends in San Diego? She and Bryan always went out with his friends these days. Their first date had been to his favorite restaurant, they lived in his place with his furniture, she wore the clothes he liked, didn't do her hobbies anymore. Even her freaking honeymoon was about him.

But if she wasn't supposed to be with Bryan, then . . . *then nothing*. What was she meant to do with this?

Feeling worse than she had when she'd come up there, Avery tucked her phone into the pocket of her sundress and went downstairs. Voices were filtering in from the dining room, and Avery hesitated as she drew closer. Not just Peyton and Dan—there was another man's voice. Had his family already arrived?

The man in the dining room was older—about her mom's age—with a pleasant-looking expression. He stood at the table, filling a paper plate with the breakfast foods Dan had ordered.

And then there was Dan, who leaned against the table, holding a paper cup of coffee. She couldn't meet his eyes.

"Good morning," the man said, stepping toward her and smiling warmly. "So you're Avery." He held out a hand. "It's so nice to finally meet you. I'm Bob, Dan's father. Betty has been telling me so much about you. And your mom and friend Erika —they're such lovely people. It's been wonderful having them with us this week."

Betty and Bob? Could their names be anymore small-town America? Avery averted her gaze from Bob's perceptive blue gaze and swallowed hard. Just what had Dan's mother told him about her? She shook his hand. "Nice to meet you."

Bob laughed and took a bite of his croissant. "Don't worry, you don't have to look so nervous. We know Dan thinks the world of you. You must be someone very special to him."

"All right, Dad." Dan sipped at his coffee, his tone exasperated. "You're making Avery uncomfortable." He met Avery's gaze. "Sleep well?"

He's not seriously teasing me about that incident in front of his father. "Great, thanks."

She made a beeline toward the breakfast table just so she could turn her back to them both.

Her stomach felt like a jumble of knots.

Someone special?

CHAPTER THIRTY-THREE

"Hey, Avery, help me settle a debate here, will you?" Dan's sister Laura leaned into the hallway from the bedroom across the hall.

Avery set down the bottle of Windex, exchanging a glance with Sam. The two of them had been going through the upstairs rooms and wiping down the bathrooms, a job Avery was grateful to have company for. She'd liked Sam instantly—they had a lot in common. They were both artists, both spoke Spanish, both knew what it was like to grow up with a Latina mother—among other things.

Crossing into the other room, Avery was surprised to see Dan in there with Laura and her husband, Mark. She hadn't seen Dan all morning and assumed he was still outside working. Dan stood, leaning against the footboard of the bed, his arms crossed. It amazed Avery how little Dan resembled his other sisters, who were petite brunettes.

Laura set her hands on her hips. "Do you ever take your hair dryer with you on trips?"

"All the time." Avery saw Sam creeping into the door frame, out of the corner of her eye.

"And why is that?" Laura dropped her chin.

"Because the ones in the hotels suck. My hair never dries right with them." The corners of Avery's mouth twitched. She had a feeling she knew where this was going.

"What about those fancy ones mounted right on the wall? Aren't they fantastic?" Laughter shone in Laura's eyes, and Dan shook his head. Clearly, Laura was enjoying this.

"Oh, those are the worst ones."

Dan threw his hands up in exasperation. "Okay. So I know nothing about blow dryers. You win."

Sam poked in her head. "Did Avery agree with you?" she asked Laura.

"Word for word." Laura grinned and then gave Mark a wink. "At least Mark didn't fight me when I debated him on it." She held up a small velvet bag. "I'm telling you, Dan, a few of these with you in the supply closet is more than enough for those people who forget to pack one or need one. Don't waste money on the mounted ones."

Dan's mouth twisted. "I always thought they were handy."

"Yeah, how many times did you use them?" Avery teased, taking a few steps back toward the door.

Shaking his head, Dan straightened. "Next, you're going to all tell me to install the toilet paper with the paper hanging over."

"You're definitely supposed to hang it over," Sam called as they went back into the room they'd been cleaning. She laughed as Dan grumbled.

Avery picked up the Windex again and sprayed down the bathroom mirror as Sam cleaned the toilet. "You guys seem to get along well," Avery said, still smiling at the exchange.

"Yeah, we do." Sam adjusted her rubber gloves as she set

down the toilet bowl cleaner. "I mean, it took a long time, and *a lot* of mistakes were made—on both sides—but I think the dust is all pretty settled now. He's a great brother. And uncle, too. He's spoiled my daughter rotten. Sometimes I beat myself up for the way we all treated one another when we were younger, but what are you going to do?"

Sam shrugged and gave a chagrined smile. "Between the cultural Latina upbringing, being Catholic, and now being a mom, I'm condemned to feel guilty about something at all times."

Avery threw her head back with laughter. "That's for damn sure. I don't know about the mom thing, but the other two are a part of my daily narrative."

"Oh, trust me, mom guilt is by far the worst one. I've called Dan's mom three times to check in on Reese." Sam gave Avery a more curious glance. "But you know, you seem to get along pretty well with Dan, too."

"He's great." The words felt like the most honest thing she'd said about Dan recently. *He is great. And any woman would be lucky to have him.* Avery paused and looked at her own reflection in the mirror for a moment, noticing the hint of color in her cheeks. "I worry he doesn't realize that about himself, though. Especially after his ex."

"Oh, did he tell you about her?" Sam wrinkled her nose as she flushed the toilet. "Yeah, she was awful. She did a lot to tear him down, you know? Was constantly gaslighting him—making him feel like she was the only person who really cared about him. She used to actively sneak onto his phone and delete messages people had sent him. Just to make him feel insecure about his family and friends. She's a piece of work."

Sneak onto his phone ...

Avery stiffened and avoided her own gaze in the mirror, her throat feeling dry.

Bryan would never do anything like that—would he?

She needed to stop comparing her situation with Dan's. They weren't the same at all.

"That's terrible," Avery said, her voice cracking. "How long were they together?"

"Not that long." Sam frowned and wiped down the seat with a paper towel. "A year or so? They moved in together really fast, which surprised us all because Dan is pretty cautious. But apparently, she was pushing for it immediately." Sam put the toilet brush into the cleaning caddy they were taking from room to room and straightened. "You ready to go to the next room?"

"Yeah, I'll be right behind you." Avery smiled, and Sam ducked behind her to leave the bathroom. As Sam left, Avery's smile faded. She swallowed hard, looking at her reflection again.

Maybe Dan and I have more in common than just attraction.

Because the attraction was powerful. Especially after last night. She could picture him clearly, coming into that bedroom, shirt off, the hard, rigid muscles of his torso as he'd thrown her over his shoulder to carry her downstairs.

Her mind kept returning to the night before, and the details seemed less clear each time she thought about it. Had she really believed it was Bryan? Or had she just been happy to ignore reality for the bliss of good sex?

She tried calling Bryan a few times since the morning but didn't get through. Maybe he was working at the hospital today.

But Erika's words kept coming back to her, too.

Bryan was very particular and liked everything just so, but Avery found some of those things about him loveable. Of course, it was frustrating when he got irritated and angry about things not being done his way, but then again, he was usually right about the way he did things. Milk *did* spoil faster when it was kept in the door. Shoes *were* really dirty. The sun *was* really damaging to skin. Wine *should* aerate before it was poured.

She couldn't argue with his logic about most things he was rigid about.

And neither could she complain he wasn't as spontaneous and fun as someone like Dan. She'd known that about Bryan when she'd started dating him, so comparing him to a guy she only spent a handful of days with wasn't fair.

She loved Bryan. Not everything had to be perfect. They were committed and happy. And marriage would take work—but that was marriage, right?

All these talking points, she'd reminded herself of repeatedly. As though she was trying to convince herself to believe them. And deep within, she felt maybe she was being manipulated.

Avery and Sam cleaned the bathrooms over the next hour, finishing around the same time as Laura and Mark placed the last of the supplies in each room. They headed downstairs, ready to take a break for the day.

As Avery got to the bottom of the stairs, a lump formed in her throat.

The Serendipity was transformed. Furniture, including wall decorations, was set up—the whole place looking better than she'd ever seen it.

Would Bryan work tirelessly and get his family to come do all this to give you the wedding of your dreams—especially if it wasn't to him?

She slipped out onto the new front porch. Dan and his dad were assembling Adirondack chairs on the front lawn with Warren and Jason, while Alice and Jen painted them with wood stain. Garrett had taken the front porch swing down and was sanding it. The furniture movers and Garrett's crew were packing up for the day—almost fifteen people in all. People Dan had gathered to help bring this dream to life for her. They were laughing and joking, and Avery watched them, her chest growing tighter.

His family was wonderful.

The sort of family she'd watched with envy when she went on vacations with her parents as a child. And clearly they'd faced their share of challenges, but it only seemed to have brought them closer.

Her family challenges had only fractured them more. Pushed them further apart.

A silver sedan turned into the driveway, then stopped beside the moving truck. A tall, good looking man stepped out, and the Kleins all looked his way.

Dan approached the man, and they shook hands, but Avery was too far away to hear their exchange. She stepped off the front porch steps and onto the lawn.

Jen rose from the grass and came toward Avery, paintbrush in hand. "Hey, you doing okay?" Jen gave her a bright smile.

"Yeah." Avery stretched, then inspected the poison ivy rashes on her arms. They were still there, but the prednisone had helped. "Just ready to take a break. I don't think I've ever done so much manual labor in my life."

Jen scanned the exterior of the Serendipity. "The place looks fantastic. I'm sure it will be beautiful for your wedding."

"It's amazing. Better than I could have hoped for." Avery looked back at the man with Dan. "Who's that?"

"He owns the furniture company," Jen said, then frowned. "Used to be one of Dan's closest friends, actually."

"Oh, I should go thank him, then," Avery said and started toward him.

Jen caught up with her. "Avery, just so you know—"

"Is that Danny Klein's baby sister?" The man smiled broadly at Jen and left Dan's side. He came over to Jen and gave her a warm hug. "I have to tell you, those sugar cookies you make—my staff is practically demanding they become a regular staple at our office parties. And they'll only order birthday cakes from your place. You're a hit, kid."

"Thanks, Corbin." Jen smiled.

"Who's this?" Corbin asked, then held his hand out to Avery. "Corbin White."

Avery shook his hand. "Avery Moretti. I'm so glad to meet you. And I have to thank you for helping get all the furniture together for my wedding."

Corbin's smile froze, and his hand dropped to his side. He glanced over his shoulder, toward Dan, then back at Avery. Then he took a step back. "Glad I could help." His tone was cool as he headed back toward Dan. "We should take a minute to sign off on the paperwork. Want to head inside?"

Avery tried to make eye contact with Dan, but he didn't look at her. He and Corbin disappeared into the lodge, and Avery looked at Jen. "What was that all about?"

Warren seemed to come out of nowhere, beside Jen. "You should probably ask Dan, Avery. Just an old friend of Dan's, but, uh—I think you met him once at a party Dan took you to years ago."

She'd met him? Avery had no memory of meeting him. She thought back hard on the party. *White.* Then she cringed.

Was that the guy who had given her drugs at the party?

Oh, God, no wonder he had acted weird. "Oh." Avery bit her lip. "Um, you know, actually, I should probably just go in there."

Before Jen or Warren could stop her, Avery hurried toward the lodge. She slipped in through the open front door and headed toward the sound of the men's voices.

They were arguing.

". . . you kidding me, man? You know I never would have rented you this stuff if I knew."

"A sale is a sale, Corbin. No point in turning down money over something that happened twelve years ago."

"Yeah, but not to that bitch. No, thank you. You know I have principles."

Avery slunk back. *That bitch?* Did Corbin mean her?

Corbin continued. "And why you still doing her favors, man? She's trouble."

"Corbin, don't be ridiculous. She's just a client. But I can get over what happened twelve years ago, because doing this wedding gives me a nice fat paycheck at the end. That's all you should be looking at, too. Principles be damned."

Avery felt her heart fall.

A nice, fat paycheck.

She'd heard enough. Slipping away, she rushed up the staircase as tears brimmed in her eyelids.

They weren't friends. He wasn't doing this because he cared. She was his customer.

You mean nothing to Dan Klein. You're nothing but a dollar sign.

CHAPTER THIRTY-FOUR

The jet boat sped across the water, country music blaring. With the wind in his face and his hands on the wheel, Dan felt his chest ease. He hadn't been out on the water all summer, despite his nieces and nephews begging him to take out the boat.

He'd almost sold the damn thing just to get more funds for the lodge. Not everyone could fit on the boat these days, and he'd left half of them on the shore, but he glanced back and smiled. Warren and his oldest son, Cameron, were on the inner tube, and he pushed the engine faster, towing them as they hooted and hollered.

Avery and Erika had hopped on for this ride, along with Peyton and Alice and his oldest niece, Sarah. Avery had changed into a bathing suit, and Erika had persuaded her to get on the boat, despite Avery's protests. She had barely looked at him all afternoon and seemed muted. Probably because of what had happened between them last night.

And that sea-green bikini was doing nothing but distracting Dan.

The truth was, he'd avoided her all day, too, half-pissed with her for leaving him with the worst case of lust he'd had in a while.

And that wasn't the worst part of it.

No, the worst part of it was that by crossing things physically with her, it was a lot harder to figure out where his feelings for her ended and lust began.

He didn't want her to have a fiancé.

And last night had only solidified that.

Love her? Maybe not. But he wanted her. And he didn't want to share her with anyone.

But what could he say? Dump your fiancé so we can go fuck and then see where it goes?

He wasn't in a place where he could offer any sort of commitment to any woman. And if he was right about her fiancé, the last thing she needed was another relationship with Dan.

He couldn't possibly be what she needed. He didn't know if he knew how to trust any woman, really. Or himself.

Dan sighed and slowed the boat to a stop. Trying to rid himself of the darker thoughts, he moved to the stern and tugged in the tow line. "Who's next?" he asked, looking around. "Sarah?"

His niece shook her head shyly. "I don't want to."

"Are you sure, honey?" Alice asked, wrapping her arm around her daughter. "All you kept talking about at home was how much you wanted to."

Sarah shook her head again.

"I'm not going in the water," Erika said. "I'm a Miami girl, where the water temperature is perfect. This is frigid."

All eyes fell to Avery, who didn't appear to be having much fun.

"I'll do it," Avery said at last. She stood, taking off her

sunglasses. "I can't remember the last time I did something like this. May as well, right?"

"It's easy," Warren said, climbing onto the boat with Dan's help. Dan pulled Cameron on beside him. Warren shook the water out of his hair. "If Cameron can do it, you've got nothing to worry about."

Avery and Warren switched places. Dan handed her the life vest and tore his gaze from her as she shimmied into it. He pulled the inner tube closer. "Just hold on to the handles here."

"Do I just climb on?" she asked, slipping into the water. She let out a slight squeal. "I forgot how cold this lake can be. You're right, Erika. The water in Miami is much better."

"Told you," Erika said, with a laugh.

"I'd probably suggest lying on it with your stomach against the raft, since this is your first time," Warren said from beside him. "You can bounce real hard on it, and if you're not holding on the way you should and sitting on it, you'll bounce right off."

Once Avery was situated, Dan let the tow line out and climbed back into the boat. Peyton shook his head warily and laughed. "So she'll scream bloody murder at a tiny rat snake but then hops on a tube with no problem."

"Rat snake?" Alice raised her brows, then looked around the interior of the boat as though one was in there with them.

"Last night." Peyton stretched his arm back on one seat. "She found a rat snake in her sleeping bag and screamed like it had bitten her. I woke up thinking someone was getting stabbed or something."

Dan headed back to his seat, tensing at the conversation. Avery had fortunately already floated far enough out that she couldn't hear it, but Peyton had already said too much. *Son of a bitch.* He needed to reevaluate this kid's usefulness.

"And she still slept in the sleeping bag after that?" Alice sounded alarmed. "That would freak me out."

"Not to mention Avery is terrified of snakes. Hates them with the fire of a thousand suns," Erika chimed in.

"Yeah, I mean, I took the snake out and went back to bed. It was fine."

To put an end to their discussion, Dan roared the engine to life. The boat shot forward, followed by Avery's shriek. He checked over his shoulder. She was hanging on with a giant smile on her face.

Dan dropped his sunglasses down from the top of his head and leaned back in his seat. Why was it that her smile affected him so much?

He enjoyed making her happy.

Seems like nothing has changed there either.

He sped around for a while, checking on her at intervals, stopping at last when he noticed Avery had dropped lower from the raft. With her arms outstretched to their full length, her legs were fully in the water.

He climbed to the back and pulled the tow line in when Avery lifted her head sharply. For as happy as she'd looked at first, that expression had been equally replaced with a more serious look. *What the hell happened?*

"Can you come in here for a second?"

Dan gave her a curious look. "Into the water?"

"Yes. Please."

"Everything okay?" Warren asked, standing. Alice joined him, looking down at Avery.

Erika scrambled back with Dan. "Avery! What happened? Are you okay?"

Dan had already jumped in. He swam over toward her, his pulse going faster.

When he reached her, he put one hand on the raft. "Are you hurt?"

Avery shook her head, then gave him a hard stare. "I—uh. I

lost my grip and dropped down . . . and when I pulled myself back up . . ." She leaned closer and then whispered in a low voice, not making eye contact. "I lost my bottoms."

Laughter choked out of the back of Dan's throat.

"Stop it!" Avery shoved his shoulder, looking mortified but cracking a smile. "This is serious."

Despite her protests, Dan threw his head back and laughed harder. *Something like this would happen to Avery.*

"It's not funny." Still, she laughed. "I had to keep my legs down so I wouldn't flash the whole damn lake."

"It's a little funny."

Everyone on the boat was staring at them like they'd gone nuts. "Hey Alice, can you grab me a towel? It appears we've had a wardrobe malfunction out here."

Just like he had, the adults on board guffawed.

"Nice, just announce it to everyone." Avery glared at him, but laughter still shone in her eyes.

"I mean, they're going to find out. Come on, I'll pull the raft over. Then we can just try to cover you up as you climb on board."

Alice handed the towel to Erika, who unfolded the towel and stretched it out so Avery would be shielded from view as she climbed on.

"Will you block me from behind? I don't want your parents seeing my ass from the dock."

Dan chuckled. "Language. There are kids on the boat." Then he nodded. "I'll do my best."

He came up behind her and slipped his hand on her waist. "I'll help push you onto the back, and Erika can wrap the towel around you as soon as you're above the water, okay?"

Erika crouched and shook her head. "You'll do just about anything to get Dan's attention, eh, Ave?"

Even though she said it in a joking manner, Avery stiffened beneath the palms of his hands.

"Hilarious." She didn't look happy.

Together, they helped her climb out. As Avery wrapped the towel around her waist, she cringed. "Sorry, everyone. Maybe a bikini was a terrible choice for tubing."

"Yeah, well, you learn a thing or two when you've spent enough time in Brandywood," Alice said cheerfully, helping her back over the seats. She was the quietest of the Klein clan, and the most laid-back. Which Dan imagined you had to be to have as many children as they had.

Avery gave her a grateful smile, then sat, hugging the towel to her waist.

Dan took the boat back in. Avery couldn't stay out there half-naked.

As he pulled closer to the dock and slowed, Erika came to the front of the boat, peering at the dock. "Avery, isn't that . . ." She froze, setting a hand on the back of Dan's seat.

Dan followed the direction where Erika was looking. A newcomer was on the dock with his parents and Avery's mom— a dark-haired man of medium build with short, spiky hair and a trim beard.

He didn't have to ask who he was. Avery's face gave it away.

A stunned look filled Avery's eyes, then she spoke, her voice almost impossible to hear over the engine.

"Bryan."

CHAPTER THIRTY-FIVE

Avery
12 Years Ago

"Maria, keep your voice down. You're going to wake up other guests," Dad hissed as Mom paced in the bedroom.

"You will not leave this room tonight." Mom gave Avery a hard look. She'd already taken Avery's cell phone and gone through all her text message history with Dan. Her gaze swept the room and landed on the sunflower Avery hadn't ever had the heart to get rid of and had kept in a guest cup from the dining room instead.

Mom plucked it out of the cup. "And I suppose this is from him?"

Avery gave a numb nod and curled her knees up, setting her feet flat on the bed. She hugged her knees, resting her cheek against them. Her world felt like it was crashing, falling apart, ripping at the seams.

Mom broke the sunflower in half and tossed it into the closest trash can.

She'd only half-heard Mom's recriminations. Her answers had been truthful but hollow to her own ears. The text messages had been damning enough. Through them, Mom had learned about her sneaking out and the party and the drinking and the hangover. The make-out sessions.

All of it.

Yet none of it seemed to matter. Because Avery kept staring at Dad, thinking about how he was having an affair.

No wonder he didn't want her in Miami with him. He'd moved on, and his newly single life didn't include time for an eighteen-year-old daughter.

Dad had blown up their family for another woman.

Not that it was easy to muster up a single shred of sympathy for Mom right now. She didn't want to see either of them. Yet here they were, both in her face at midnight.

Dad had been strangely quiet during all this, not saying much about the ruination of "daddy's girl" and how terrible she'd been. But his disappointment was no less clear either.

"Is there anything else you want to tell us? Anything else you're hiding?" Mom crossed her arms.

Avery set her chin between her knees and sucked in a breath. She looked straight at Dad. "Other than the fact that Dad's having an affair with someone he's been calling this week, no."

Mom blanched, then her lips pursed. She turned toward her father. "You've been *calling her* while we're here? You promised, George."

Avery's heart felt squeezed intensely, her breath choked. *Mom knew.*

Dad raised his hands defensively. "Tina just wanted to find

out if I got here safely. That's it. I don't know how Avery knows about it, but I have been discreet."

"Clearly, you haven't been that discreet." Mom set her hands on her hips. "Yes, I know about your father's girlfriend. Now you see why I say no to Miami? I was hoping to tell you in a better way than this, but your father's moving in with her when we get back from vacation."

Oh, God.

Avery had to hold back the bile, feeling sick.

That was why her dad didn't want her? Because he was moving in with his new girlfriend?

Avery struggled for a breath. "Y-You didn't tell me . . ." She closed her eyes, feeling like she couldn't produce any more tears. How it was possible to go from one extreme emotion to the opposite within an hour, she didn't know. But that was what had happened.

She wished she'd never left that field with Dan. Or that they'd run away together from there.

"Avery, I'm sorry—"

"You're telling her you're sorry, George? I'm the one you cheated on. I'm the one you're leaving for your whore. Why are you telling Avery you're sorry?" her mom ranted.

Avery wanted to yell back, but why bother? Her dad didn't want her in his life. He'd just made that clear.

"You could come stay with Tina and me on weekends—"

"She will not be spending time with your *puta*."

"Mom, just stop. Clearly, the choice I thought I had was just my imagination." If only she was finished with high school, she could just move out and try to make it on her own. But she had no idea how to forge forward alone.

"I am sorry, Avery," her dad mumbled.

Her mom swore, then stomped to the closet and pulled out her suitcase. She threw it open to toss her clothes into it.

As she did, Avery stiffened.

Oh, no . . .

Mom had already shifted the false bottom of the suitcase. She found the notebook Dan had given her first, along with the pencil case. She flipped the notebook open and went through the drawings Avery had made the last couple of days, including the one of him. As her gaze narrowed on it, Mom did what she did best: she tore it from the book and ripped it in two.

Avery sank miserably onto the bed as Mom pulled out the bag with the dirty clothes from the party. She took one sniff, then held it out to her father. "You know what this smells like? You were smoking pot, weren't you?"

"No, I—" Avery gritted her teeth. To be honest, she couldn't really remember. She had spotty memories of a pipe being passed around, but she didn't remember smoking it. There was another memory of a small, clear plastic bag being pressed into her hand. But what had she done with it?

And right at that moment, Mom pulled the bag from the pocket of her dirty shorts. A bag with small pills.

Mom gasped and looked at her in horror.

Even Dad took a step forward.

There was absolutely no way out of explaining that. *Oh, God.*

AVERY STARED AT HER HANDS, her fingers shaking, both from fear and from lack of sleep the night before. For as many times as she had been in the dining room of the Serendipity, she'd never paid attention to the various pockmarks in the wood grain of the table. Had the table been covered by a tablecloth? She couldn't remember. She shifted under the weight of the four adult stares in her direction: Mom and Dad, Mr. Harrison, and a police officer.

"Avery, answer the question," Mom snapped.

Avery's gaze shifted to her mom. The room felt claustrophobic and hot, and the pressure on her chest was tight. She wanted more than anything to text Dan, tell him she was sorry, warn him about everything, but Mom had said she would not be getting her phone back for a "long time." And they hadn't let her out of their sight either.

"Avery Lucia! Answer the police officer's question!"

She blinked at the police officer numbly, then cleared the thickness from the back of her throat. "What was the question again?"

Her mother threw her hands up in exasperation.

The officer gave her a gentle look. "I asked if you could tell me more about where you got the drugs from."

"I'm positive it was that boy. The one who works here," Mom said, nodding for emphasis. "He dragged her out in the middle of the night and got her drunk. And she's underage, too, Officer. That has to be illegal."

Avery shook her head. "No, no, it wasn't him. I swear. And he didn't get me drunk, Mom. I did that on my own. He drank nothing but soda. If someone is going to get in trouble for me drinking, it should be me."

The officer shifted his weight, and her gaze fell on his handcuffs. Would she be arrested?

"No one is getting into trouble for that. But I need to know what you can tell me about the drugs." The officer had kind blue eyes, but that was the only feature she really noticed about him. Right now, he seemed to be the only person in the room who wasn't emotional, and it oddly made her trust him.

"I was pretty drunk. I don't remember too much about how

that all went down." Avery bit her lip, a fresh wave of humiliation descending on her. Having to admit her drunkenness in front of Mr. Harrison and the officer was a new level of embarrassment.

"What do you remember?" the officer prodded.

Dad leaned across the table and covered her hand with his. "Sweetheart, cooperate with the police. It's important they find out who's distributing amphetamines in town."

She closed her eyes. By the time she'd even sat at the bonfire, she had already been buzzed. Someone had offered them Jell-O shots coming into the party, and she'd had four. It didn't take long for her to get wasted after that.

Dan's friend extended his hand. "You must be the woman who's got Dan all nervous."

She grinned. "I'm Avery. Like the label company."

He laughed and gave her his name. "I always tell people I'm the only White guy in Brandywood who can actually play basketball."

. . . and then . . . a faint memory of taking money out of her purse. Handing it to someone. For the pills? What even were they?

But what was his name? "C—" Avery shook her head. "I can't remember. His name started with a C or a K, I think. One of Dan's friends. I think his last name is White. But Dan did nothing. Please, he doesn't deserve to be punished for anything."

"That sounds like a lot to go on, Officer." Dad stood. "I don't want to keep putting her through this. She clearly doesn't remember anything else."

Avery narrowed her eyes at him. Her dad was always less strict than her mom, but this time he'd been a little too soft. Maybe because he felt guilty. Because he didn't want her. He probably wanted to have sex with his girlfriend all over the damn house, without Avery interrupting. Then she shuddered at the thought of Dad having sex with anyone.

Mom didn't budge. "I hope you'll pursue this young man to the full extent of the law. I want to press charges."

Dad adjusted his glasses. "I don't know if there are any charges to press—"

"You stay out of it." Mom glared at him.

Avery's cheeks burned, and she held her breath. Normally, Mom wouldn't let this sort of information about Avery be known, but Mom clearly wanted to humiliate her. Tears brimmed in her eyes, and she brushed them away with her fingertips.

"Oh, for goodness sake, Maria." Dad came up behind Avery and pulled out her chair. "Avery, why don't you go outside and sit by the lake for a few minutes. Give your mother and me a chance to talk and finish up here with the police officer and Mr. Harrison."

Avery stood, keeping her gaze low. Her knees felt wobbly.

"No, she can't. I don't trust her to go out there. The minute we let her go, she'll go running off to find that boy. Mark my words. She stays here."

"I'm not going to go find him, Mom," Avery said, though she was tempted just to make that a lie and go anyway. This might be the only chance she'd get to talk to Dan.

"Don't worry, Mrs. Moretti. We'll make sure the boy doesn't go near her," Mr. Harrison said, his aged voice cracking.

"She won't go looking for him anyway, Maria." Dad put a hand on Avery's shoulder. "We can trust her to go outside. Right, sweetheart?"

Avery met her dad's eyes, and for some reason that just made the tears come faster.

I'm going to miss him so much.

She wiped the tears away and nodded. "Yes, Dad."

Avery slipped outside, her shoulders shaking as sobs broke from her. Stopping in front of the lake, she looked over at the Sports Shack, hoping Dan would be there.

He wasn't.

Would she ever see him again?

Grabbing a handful of pebbles, she tossed them into the lake. They splashed softly, ripples radiating out from where they'd broken the surface, then slipped into the murky depths below.

She shivered, feeling cold. She hadn't eaten yet, which probably contributed to her feeling sick. She grabbed a blanket from a nearby basket and wrapped it around her shoulders, then sank down into an Adirondack chair.

"Ave?" Dad's voice came from behind, and she stiffened. He sat in the chair beside her, drawing a deep breath through his nose. "You doing okay?"

Avery nodded, unable to find her voice.

"You all packed? Remember, we have to leave at four to make it to the airport."

She nodded again and twisted a loose thread on the blanket around her finger.

Avery sank back, feeling worse with every passing moment.

All she wanted was to see Dan one last time. Tell him she'd realized how stupid it had been to get mad at him. That she didn't blame him. But her mom was watching her like a hawk. Maybe when she got her cell phone back, she could text him, even if it took a few weeks.

She worked up the courage, then took a letter out of her pocket she'd scribbled in the night, hoping she could give it to Mr. Harrison. He'd be the least likely to oppose, she'd assumed, but now even that looked like an impossibility. Maybe Dad could be moved. He'd always been softer with her. "I know you and Mom are angry with me. And that you don't want me to ever talk to Dan again, but I need to tell him some things. I slapped him, Dad, and I feel horrible about it."

"You slapped him?" Dad raised a brow.

The thought of it made her want to throw up. "He told me he heard you talking to your girlfriend on the phone. And I was mad at him for not telling me sooner. But it wasn't his fault. And I love him, Dad. I need him to know." She held out a letter to her father with shaking hands. "Will you please make sure he gets this? So I can apologize?"

Dad stared at the letter, then took it. He nodded and tucked it in his pocket. "I'm sorry about how this week went," Dad finally said. He clasped his hands, his seat squeaking as he leaned back. "I just wanted us all to have one enjoyable week together."

"Then you shouldn't have started the whole week with a pile of lies. You should have told me you were cheating on Mom. That you didn't w-want me because you have a girlfri—" She couldn't choke out the last few words. She sniffled and swallowed back tears.

"Sweetheart, you need to understand. I had already decided I was going to get a divorce before I pursued anything with Tina. I didn't just dump your mom for her. Mom's just mad I moved on so fast."

"But you told Mom? That you were going to go sleep with someone else because you were planning to divorce her?" Avery's eyes narrowed at her father.

Her father averted his gaze.

Didn't think so.

"Seriously, Dad. You couldn't even wait until you were divorced? You had to date the first bimbo you met?" Her anger poured through her words thickly, her voice quivering. "And now I'm stuck going to Tampa because you'd rather move in with your girlfriend than with me."

Dad ducked his chin and looked chastened by her words. "Your mom made it clear she doesn't want anyone else 'mothering' you. And I respect her request. I love and trust Tina, but it's harder for your mother. The thought of having someone else step into her role for the school year is more than she's emotionally prepared to handle right now."

It was a shitty excuse. If he'd wanted her, he would have fought to have her around. But he didn't. He wanted to be with whoever this "Tina" woman was.

"But why, Dad?" Avery wiped her cheek with her palm. "Why couldn't you and Mom just work out your differences? You've been together for twenty years—couldn't you just figure it out? Why did you have to get a girlfriend and ruin any chance of reconciliation?"

Dad clasped his hands, his shoulders sagging. "Your mom . . . it's tough being her spouse, Avery. She doesn't let me have any friends. Doesn't let me pursue any hobbies. I don't have any room to breathe and be anything other than her husband, twenty-four-seven. And then when she's angry—which is a lot—she withholds physical affection."

"Ew, Dad, I don't want to know that." Her parents' sex life was something she didn't want to think about at all.

"But it's important. And it's part of why I felt the need to move on, Avery. I've been holding on for a long time, waiting for your mom to be a partner to me. You don't know what it's like—"

"Dad." Avery's voice held a warning. She shook her head firmly. "That's not any of my business. And I really don't want to hear anything else. What you did is indefensible. There's nothing you can say to make me think differently. And seriously—as much as I'm mad at Mom right now, bad-mouthing her isn't exactly going to make me like you more."

Dad held up his hands. "I'm not bad-mouthing. Or"—he

adjusted his glasses—"I'm not trying to anyway. It's just that as a parent, you worry maybe you set a poor example. And staying with your mom wasn't healthy for me, Avery. It felt like the best thing at the time for you, but it really wasn't. Your mom is a good person, and she loves you. But I worry about how hard she is on you. I don't want to see her crush your spirit, sweetheart. You're allowed to make mistakes."

Tears blurred Avery's vision. "Then why are you making me go live with her? Why are you being so selfish? If you claim she's so awful now, then why feed me to the wolves?" Her voice shook, and she tore off the blanket, clambering to her feet.

Her dad stared at her, his face pinched, eyes blinking.

He didn't have a response.

He couldn't respond.

Because he's just selfish. He's picking himself over you.

At last, her dad struggled to his feet. He pulled her into his arms, his shoulders shaking with tears. "I'm so sorry, sweetheart. I'm not trying to abandon you. I just can't do it anymore. I'm so tired, honey. And I'm so sorry."

Avery wrenched herself free from him. He'd never seemed more broken.

But no matter how he tried to paint it, he'd given her up.

A disgusted feeling rose inside her, making her want to throw up. She didn't want to go with him. She wanted to be as far from him as possible.

She was going to Tampa—but this time, it was by choice.

CHAPTER THIRTY-SIX

Dan

12 Years Ago

DAN AND CORBIN rode in silence in the back of Mom's car. Mom had been strangely quiet, which Dan hadn't expected. She'd come to the jail, bailed out both him and Corbin, and now was driving them home.

At last Dan, broke the silence with a glance at Corbin. "What are you going to do?"

"I don't know." Corbin sank back against his seat, looking out the window. He sighed, his eyes closing. "I just . . . I couldn't give them Curtis's name, you know? He's my brother. And my pop was just in the hospital last week with his heart. This could kill him."

Mom lifted her chin sharply. "And you don't think it will hurt him just as badly if you're accused of this, Corbin? Tell the police the truth. It's the best for everyone involved."

Corbin flinched. That was the thing he'd told Dan he hated the most. That people whispered about Curtis, "Once a junkie, always a junkie."

And no one knew more than Corbin how much Curtis had dealt with. "Yeah, but no offense, Mrs. K—I can take the heat. Curtis is still on probation."

That Corbin was having this discussion at all in front of Dan's mother just showed how much he trusted her. Which didn't surprise Dan. And Mom loved Corbin, too. She'd never betray his trust.

But his mom was also one of the best people on the planet, and not just because she was his mom. She'd dealt with her own personal hell, with Dan's biological father being one of the bigger drug suppliers in the tri-state area. Not that Dan's father had been in their lives then. Thank God for his stepfather, who had adopted Dan when he was still a toddler.

She dropped Corbin off at his home and then drove Dan back to their house. They pulled in, and Mom shut the engine to the minivan off but didn't get out. "So are you going to tell me anything more? Dad picked up your truck from the lodge, you know. Said he found an open box of condoms in the glove box."

Dan squirmed under the weight of her questioning gaze.

"Dan, just what have you been up to recently? I respect your privacy, and I know you're turning into a grown man, but I've always prided myself on your being responsible. Now I'm picking you up from jail for drug trafficking, you got fired from your job, and you're out having casual sex—I mean, do you even have a girlfriend? I work in a NICU, love. I don't need to remind you to be responsible about that."

"I-I don't know." Dan sighed and rubbed his burning eyes. He hadn't slept all night and then gone into work only to find himself detained for questioning, fired by Mr. Harrison, and then arrested. That phone call to his parents had been the single most humiliating moment of his existence. And Avery hadn't even bothered to send him a message. Was she still mad at him?

Was he still mad at her?

"I met a girl at the lodge. She's a guest. And I think I love her, Mom."

"You think? Or you know?"

Mom had a way of looking at him like she could read his thoughts. Dan opened the sliding door to the minivan to let some air in, feeling himself sweating. "I know. I love her. And I made some mistakes this week. Snuck out and snuck her out. Took her to Adam's party. Her parents found out, then I guess they found some drugs Curtis sold her, and the rest you know about." He felt like an idiot. An embarrassed idiot.

"What drugs?"

"Adderall, I think." Avery had said something when she was drunk about getting something that would help her be better at school. Dan could kick himself for not paying more attention.

Mom ran her fingers through her sandy-blonde hair and looked out the windshield, squinting into the sun. "Dan, it's not that I'm disappointed that you lied and did things I wouldn't approve of. It's that I'm worried you may have lost your head over what can arguably be called a quick fling and put a whole lot at risk as a result. Do you have any idea what this will do to your chances for that basketball scholarship? Or to Corbin if his family is roped back into the court system again?"

Dan held his head in his hands. "I know, Mom. I know."

"You know who your real dad was. Brandywood is a small town. I can do everything in my power to set the record straight for you, and I don't think there's any real case to be made against you, but people talk. Comparisons will be made."

"My real dad is Dad." Dan's gut burned.

"I know that, but—"

"No, Mom. I'm serious. If you don't get that right, then no one else will."

Mom nodded, chastened. "You're right, I'm sorry." She opened the door to the minivan and stepped out. "And this girl? What happens with her now?"

"I don't know." Dan got out of the minivan and stretched. It had been a long time since he fit in the back of that minivan comfortably. "I didn't even get a chance to tell her I love her. And she leaves tomorrow."

"Well, if you love her, tell her." Mom crossed her arms. "Not that I won't ground you for a while. Though I don't know if I can really think up any punishment that's going to be worse than what happens if you can't convince Corbin to tell the police the truth."

Dan sighed. He wished that was something in his power to do. Corbin was many things, including being both fiercely loyal and as stubborn as a mule.

Corbin would never give up his brother to save himself. His life would be ruined—no university would touch him with something like this on his record. Selling any type of amphetamines was a big deal.

"I'll do what I can." Dan hugged his mom. "I wish I never had to say this, but thanks for coming and getting me out of jail. And by any chance, can I borrow the minivan for a few minutes before my grounding starts? I need to run to the lodge for a minute."

Mom rolled her eyes. "I'll drive you. But after that, I mean it, kid. You're grounded."

DAN AVOIDED GOING through the front door of the lodge. The best chance he had of seeing Avery was to go in through the back door. He'd go up to her room from that back staircase and knock—hopefully, she would answer.

He slunk around the side of the lodge, sticking close to the tall row of fountain grass along one garden bed—glad he could hide near it. Mr. Harrison had told him he never wanted to see him on the property again. Dan's mom might be angry to find out he hadn't told her that, but that didn't matter compared to not getting the chance to tell Avery he was sorry.

And that he loved her.

The back door was open—Mr. Harrison never locked it during the day—so Dan hurried in. He was almost to his goal of getting to Avery's room when a door a couple of doors down opened. Avery's dad stepped out, then startled when he saw Dan.

His face quickly turned red. "I ought to punch you square in the jaw," he growled in a low voice.

Dan stepped back, but for once his towering height didn't bother him. Avery's dad was several inches shorter than him. Probably why he didn't punch Dan. He held up his hands. "I just . . . I want to talk to Avery."

"No." Mr. Moretti shook his head firmly. "You have no idea what you did, asshole. What fucking right did you have to listen in on my personal business and then tell my daughter about it?"

"But I love your daughter, and I—"

"Oh, please." Mr. Moretti glared at him. "You think I don't remember what it's like to be a teenage boy? My daughter is beautiful. And talented. And she's going somewhere in life. She doesn't need a deadbeat drug abuser like you to drag her down into the abyss."

What had Avery told him? "I just want to tell her—"

"And I said no." Mr. Moretti stepped closer. "And here's

the thing, bucko. She doesn't want to see you. She told me all about how you took advantage of her while she was drunk. You knew she was too drunk to consent. Didn't you, though?"

Avery had said that? Dan felt a sick feeling grip his throat. "I didn't touch her that—"

"That's not what she says. Luckily for you, going down the long road of litigation is an expensive ordeal I'd rather not fight on two fronts right now, with everything I have going on with my soon-to-be-ex-wife. I'd rather just get you out of her life. But if you insist on trying to contact her, I'll encourage her to file charges against you, understood?"

Dan steadied himself against the wall.

Was it possible Avery had really accused him of that?

His every text to her had gone unanswered. Was she that angry?

Or had he just never really known her?

Mr. Moretti tilted his head as though considering something. Then he added in a low voice, "If it comes to litigation, who do you think people will believe? Surely, not the kid whose biological father is in prison for drug trafficking? Criminals beget little criminal children, don't they?"

Dan's head reeled. *How does he know that?*

Then he remembered. He'd told Avery about his biological father the first day they'd met. She must have told him.

An ache grew from his chest, right at his heart, clawing its way outward until his lungs felt like fire.

"*. . . she's going somewhere in life. She doesn't need a deadbeat drug abuser like you to drag her down into the abyss. She doesn't want to see you. She told me all about how you took advantage of her while she was drunk.*" Dan realized something crucial at that moment. He'd never had a chance.

Avery used everything I've done this week against me. And she may have ruined my best friend's life.

"Criminals beget little criminal children, don't they?"

Maybe. But assholes also beget assholes, it seemed.

He turned and walked away, his jaw clenched.

He might have been wrong about what type of person Avery was, but that didn't mean Corbin should have to suffer the consequences. She'd made an accusation against Corbin that wouldn't go away so easily.

Unless someone else takes the blame.

And who wouldn't buy it? Dan was the one who'd been running around with the girl from out-of-town. He'd even taken her to a party.

His classmates knew he had ADHD. Access to Adderall. A bottle of it was sitting in his medicine cabinet at home.

Dan leveled his chin. Mom would be pissed, but it was the only way to solve this without letting Corbin take the fall for Avery's accusation. Dan would go to the police station again, tell them he'd given Avery the drugs. He'd gotten everyone into this by getting involved with Avery. This was on him.

CHAPTER THIRTY-SEVEN

Now

"Go over this again with me." Bryan opened his suitcase on the luggage rack, combing through it as Avery towel-dried her hair. She'd taken a shower and slipped into a robe while he changed. "You lost your bathing suit bottoms—how?"

"It was just a silly accident," Avery said, crossing the room for her suitcase. She crouched on the floor and unzipped it. "The force of the water just ripped them off."

"But what were you doing tubing in the first place?" He wrinkled his nose, looking around at the room. "Did they paint in here recently? This place is really off-gassing some horrible chemical." He opened the slider, pulling the screen back, then rolled his eyes. "Great. The screen is ripped. So we either end up with mosquito bites or ingest toxins. I'm going to ask for a new room."

"This is the biggest room they have, Bry." The open

window allowed the sounds of the cookout below to filter in from the back lawn. But as soon as Bryan had arrived, he'd gone into "guest" mode, and Dan had been forced to pull away from the cookout and get them into their room. Bryan just assumed she moved into this room with him because he'd arrived, not because she hadn't been well-situated before.

But Bryan wasn't supposed to be here for another five days.

She'd hugged him, telling him what a fantastic surprise it was to see him.

She heard a child squeal with laughter, wishing she could still be down there. Even Mom and Erika had left because Bryan had told them he'd made dinner reservations for them all. "You know, I think we can join the cookout outside if you're hungry. The owner said we were welcome."

"I think I'd rather go into town, thanks." Bryan checked his watch. "You should get dressed. I told everyone to meet us down in the lobby at six."

Avery caught her reflection in the mirror. Her wet hair curled naturally, loose and wavy. She usually straightened it, but she didn't feel like doing it tonight. She liked the way she looked.

Grabbing one of her new sundresses, she went into the bathroom and pulled it on. It was yellow with large paisley swirls and flowers and a flowy skirt. And though it was pretty enough for dinner, she'd worn it earlier in the week because it was comfortable too. She slipped into a pair of sandals she'd bought, then put on some light makeup.

She opened the door and found Bryan sitting on the bed, wearing his typical khakis and black polo shirt. His head was bent over her phone as he scrolled through it. As she drew closer, he lifted his head and raised a brow. "Is that new?"

"Yeah, you like it?" She smiled, giving a small twirl. "And it has pockets."

His expression was of distaste. "It's loud. Not very you. You usually don't like colors like that."

"No, I do. You're the one who told me you prefer neutral tones."

"I never said that." Bryan frowned, examining her phone. "You don't seem to have any problem with your service at all."

"Yeah, you said that. I remember it perfectly. Remember when I wore that red dress to the wedding? And the owner got the Wi-Fi problem fixed, so I should be fine for service when I'm here now."

"No, I didn't say that. You're remembering it wrong. I wouldn't have objected to a red dress. I have no idea what you're talking about. And why are your arms looking so terrible? Your face, too? Don't you care about the photos?"

Her heart fell, her smile faltering. It would have been much nicer if Bryan had thrown out a compliment, but she'd brought on his anger with the sunburn and welts. *He'd probably prefer they're covered up.* "Um, I can go change."

"We don't have time for that." He stood, handing her phone to her. "Let's go."

A hard lump formed in her throat. Giving a quick nod, she tilted her head toward the bathroom. "Just gonna grab a lip gloss."

She hurried to the bathroom, then closed the door, setting her back against it.

The tears that welled in her eyes were unexpected, choking her.

Why am I crying?

Bryan didn't like outfits like this. What had she been expecting?

And right now, given what she'd done last night, she had no room to be angry with him for it.

Brushing back the tears, she checked her reflection again,

then left the bathroom. They went downstairs, where Mom and Erika waited.

As they made their way outside, Erika dropped back to walk beside her. "What's he doing here so early?"

Avery gave her a hard look. "He's here for the wedding."

"You know what I mean." Erika shook her head.

By then they'd reached the rental cars and split up. Mom drove Erika in the car she'd rented, while Bryan took Avery.

Avery settled back against the seat as Bryan pulled out of the driveway. He reached across the console and took her hand, his fingers interlocking with hers. Out of the rearview mirror, the Serendipity vanished from view.

And with it, any joy I felt, too.

BRYAN HAD another surprise in store for Avery. As though the evening couldn't have gotten any worse, Dad and Tina stood outside the front door to The Dutchman, holding hands. Sitting beside them on a bench were Avery's sisters, Vivienne and Madeline, who both seemed absorbed in their cell phones. Neither of them looked up.

Wow, they have phones? Avery remembered fighting her father to get one when she started driving.

Mom stiffened beside her, muttering a Spanish curse word under her breath.

"Dad." Avery hung back with Mom, who'd put an arm on Avery's as though for support. "What are you doing here?"

"Don't you remember? We were planning on getting in town today." As they reached Dad, he released Tina's hand.

Really? The week had flown by so quickly, Avery had stopped paying attention to arrival dates. But Dad was right. He'd said something about arriving at the Serendipity early.

Avery gave her father a hug, then turned to her stepmother. Tina wasn't much older than her—only ten years—which made calling her a stepmother particularly difficult. And for all Dad's efforts, Tina and Avery had never really gotten close.

She leaned forward and offered Avery a kiss on the cheek, her blonde hair looking like she'd just gotten out of an appointment for a blow-out rather than an airplane and car ride. *Does she carry a curling iron in her purse?*

"Tina, you remember my friend Erika," Avery reintroduced them stiffly. Mom offered a cool hello to Dad and then Tina.

"Girls, come over here and say hello to your sister," Dad said sternly. He shook his head as they rolled their eyes, putting their cell phones down. "I swear, these damn phones these kids have these days."

"I'm pretty sure parents still have to buy them for their kids, don't they?" Mom said, the corners of her mouth twitching.

Avery pressed her lips together to hold back her smile. Much as Mom's resentment got old, sometimes she got a good zinger in there. *And she's right.*

Still, these were her sisters, and maybe, someday, when they were older, they could put the family drama behind them the way Dan's family had done. She grinned at them as they gave her reluctant hugs. "You all ready to be junior bridesmaids?"

"Yeah, Mom has our dresses, but she wouldn't even let us try them on at home," Vivienne complained, shooting Tina a look.

"That's because I didn't want you getting them dirty before the big day." Tina's voice was edged with exasperation.

"Can we see your dress, Avery?" Madeline asked brightly.

"Maybe when we get back tonight," Avery said, then shot Bryan a look as the group started into the restaurant. She went to his side. "How did you orchestrate this entire dinner here with my dad?"

"Unlike you, my cell phone service was working just fine this past week." Bryan held the door for her.

His voice dripped with resentment. And Avery couldn't help feeling like, somehow, Bryan was miserable to have come to Brandywood earlier than planned. *So why did he come? He doesn't seem happy to see me.*

"ARE YOU CLENCHING YOUR JAW?" Bryan asked during dessert, reaching over and rubbing her neck gently. "You seem tense."

"No, why would I be tense?" She offered him a smile. "I'm just glad you're here."

Bryan leaned over and kissed her, continuing to knead the knots in her neck as she tried to relax. She *had* been clenching her jaw. But then again, being forced to have dinner with Dad and Tina and Mom was one of the most stressful things she could think of.

As they wrapped up the dinner, Erika gave her an encouraging smile across the table, which made Avery's heart throb painfully. She'd been such a jerk to her friend and owed her a big apology. Even if Erika shouldn't have said that about Bryan, she'd been helping Avery all week.

"You know what we should do?" Erika said, her eyes unusually bright. "We should go out tonight. Just us women. Like a mini-bachelorette party. There are some good bars on Main Street, right, Mr. Moretti?"

"Am I invited?" Mom asked.

No, Mom, you're not invited to crash our girls' night out. But Avery didn't have the heart to say that, especially in front of Tina. "Of course." But would that mean Tina would want to come, too?

Bryan shifted with discomfort beside her. "It's been a long day. We should probably go back to the lodge and rest up. We've got a long week ahead of us."

"No, I think it would be fun," Avery said, reaching over and squeezing his hand. The last thing she wanted to do was go back and have a serious discussion with Bryan. "I'd like to go."

They got the check, and Dad paid for the bill, then they stood. "Why don't you ladies go wait in the car for Avery? I'd like to talk to her and Bryan for a few minutes." He held out keys to Tina. "You can take the girls out, sweetheart."

As they left, Dad came around from the other side of the table. He shifted a dessert plate and then held out his hand to the chairs. "Why don't you and Bryan sit for a moment, Ave?"

Avery glanced at Bryan, but he was staring at the empty dessert plate. Then she sat at a chair beside him.

Dad pulled out a chair and adjusted his tie. "Avery, um . . . before you hear it from anyone else, Bryan called me last night. He wanted to know if I'd ever heard of a man from Brandywood named Daniel Klein."

What?

Avery's heart froze. She stared at Bryan's profile. "What do you mean?"

Bryan turned cool eyes toward her. "I got so frustrated trying to get through to the Serendipity that I started searching online for information on the lodge. And I found a newspaper article about it—in an obituary." Bryan's eyes narrowed. "When were you planning to tell me the owner had died and the place was sold?"

"I . . ." Avery's heart hammered in her chest. Dread clawed up her throat. *Oh God, what did Dad tell Bryan about Dan?*

"So I called your dad. And boy, did he have an interesting story to tell me."

Avery held on to the edge of the table, feeling like she might fall over. "W-What are you talking about, Dad?" She gave him a hard look.

This is why Bryan's here early. He had found out about Dan. And her father had been the one to tell him.

"All I said is that the owner's an ex-boyfriend of yours—"

"Not an ex-boyfriend, Dad. And you had no right to go . . . what, telling on me? To my fiancé?" She shook her head at him. Then looked at Bryan. "I was going to tell you all about Dan, babe. I just thought we should have that conversation in person."

Bryan didn't respond, his face lacking in expression. Avery hated this look. He'd clearly already formed an opinion, and it wouldn't matter what she said. *But why on earth would he go behind my back like this?*

Avery stood. "We're done here. Ready to go, Bry?"

Bryan tapped his fingers against the tabletop, then nodded. "Thanks for dinner, George."

As Avery and Bryan walked out, Avery fumed, her hands shaking. *Dad really did it this time.* "You had absolutely no right to do that, Bryan."

"Were you really going to tell me about the ex?" Bryan's look was cold, exacerbated by the darkness of the evening.

"I—" Avery combed her fingers through her hair. "I didn't want to say anything over the phone. I only found out he was at the lodge when I arrived." She looked around the parking lot. "Look, I'm just going to go out with Erika for a few hours. I mean, I doubt we'll get wild with my mom there, right? And then we can talk."

"I said I didn't want you going out tonight." Bryan's voice was hard.

"I know, but—" Avery came closer to him and took his hands. "Given we don't all live in the same state, there aren't going to be that many chances for me to go out with them before we get married. I'd like to—"

"They don't have your best interests at heart here, Avery. If they did, they would have called me, told me about this situation."

"Oh, come on, Bry—"

He took out his phone, punching into the screen. "We're going back to that fucking lodge. I tried to get us a room somewhere else, but there's no availability anywhere in this fucking town."

What the actual fuck? He's angry with me?

Being angry in return would get her nowhere. She needed to de-escalate this before it got out of hand, especially in public like this.

Avery nodded, trying to take a steady breath. "Okay. Okay. Sweetie, calm down. Let me just tell them tonight's not going to happen."

"We're going, Avery. They can figure it out." Bryan took her hand, then started toward the sidewalk.

Avery glanced back toward the parking lot. She should go back and tell them, at least. But she didn't want to risk angering Bryan any further.

CHAPTER THIRTY-EIGHT

DAN SCRAPED down the grill grates, watching as Peyton made his way back into the lodge. Thank God for that kid. He'd turned into a jack-of-all-trades for the week, taking on any job that Dan asked of him. Right now, that was manning the lodge, something Dan didn't quite have the stomach for.

The thought of Avery spending the night in Bryan's arms had made him so sick that he'd barely eaten at dinner.

He sighed, shaking the coals down, then turned to pick up the trash.

Even though most of his family had gone home, Mom and Dad had stuck around to help him clean up.

Mom came out of the French doors with another trash bag in hand. "We're done with the dishes in there. Anything else you need, honey?"

Dan looked back at her, and her eyes locked with his. Mom's lips pressed together, a sad look coming to her face. Within a few seconds, she'd crossed the space toward him. She folded him into her embrace. "Honey. You look miserable."

No use trying to fool his mother.

Dan hugged her back and sucked in a shallow breath. "I never thought I'd see her again."

"I know." Mom squeezed his forearm as she stepped back. "But you know, she's not married yet. You should tell her how you feel about her before it's too late."

"How I feel about her . . ." Dan rubbed his neck. "I don't know how I feel about her, Mom. And what right do I have to fuck up her wedding plans?"

"You don't." Mom shrugged. "And maybe it's terrible advice. But if you love her, then you owe it to yourself to tell her. There was a time when I drove you over here to do just that—and correct me if I'm wrong—but I don't think you ever did."

"I probably deserve to be alone, Mom. There's too much Redding in me. Too much statistical probability that I'll only hurt and embarrass her in the long run."

Mom tilted her head to the side. She sighed, then crossed to the edge of the patio, shaking her head. "If that's how you feel, then I failed you, Danny."

She'd failed him?

Dan went to her side, stuffing his hands in his pockets. "What are you talking about? You have never failed me."

Mom twisted her wedding ring. "Your father—not Dad— was a complicated man with a lot of flaws, Dan. But he was also a vibrantly passionate, intelligent man. Gosh, and he was fun. I loved him. Wow, did I love him. He wrote me songs on the guitar and just stole my breath away."

Dan stared at her in shock. He'd never heard Mom talk about his birth father that way. "What are you—"

"You have heard one narrative. And that's the narrative you've accepted. The negative one. The one where David Redding was a terrible, horrible drug dealer who left his wife for another woman and abandoned his family. And yes, that's all true. But why in the hell would you assume if you are *anything* like that man, you got the negative traits only? So, let's say you're right. Let's say you inherited half of his traits—which by the way, you seem to forget you're half me, too. But if you're right, I hardly think it's possible you only inherited the undesirable traits. So, clearly I need to do a better job telling you about the good ones. Did you know your birth dad was an amazing basketball player? He was tall, just like you."

"Mom, stop." Dan stared at his feet.

"No, I'm not going to stop. I've done you a disservice by letting you only hear bad things about that man. And if no one else is going to tell you the good things, then it's up to me. One time, he—"

"All right, I get it." Dan held up his hands.

"I seriously doubt that you do." Mom crossed her arms.

"Really, Mom. I get it. You don't have to keep singing his praises." And despite feeling irritated, he couldn't help feeling a smile tickling his lips. *How does she have the ability to make me feel better about things like this?*

Because oddly, she had. In a weird way. He'd never even thought about what she'd said.

"Dan, listen, in all seriousness, I'm worried about you. I know your relationship with Melissa was terribly hard on you, sweetheart. And what she did to you—I still want to slap her when I see her around town."

Dan balked in shock. *His mom wanted to what?*

She pursed her lips. "Yes, I know, I preach forgiveness. But you're my baby boy. Even my forgiveness has its limits." Mom sniffed and went on. "But I think your knee-jerk reaction—quitting the force, buying the Serendipity—may have left you feeling more isolated than you really are. People in town ask me about you constantly. I run into your friends from the force, and they always tell me how much you're missed. And while we're all proud of what you're building here, I don't want your relationship with Melissa to define how you see yourself. You're a heroic, good man."

God, she is the best of the best. How he loved and appreciated his mom. Dan put his arm around her shoulders. "Thanks, Mom, but I'm no hero."

Mom sighed deeply, then set her head against him. "Don't let yourself be a victim, Dan. You're the only one in charge of who you get to be—of your own path. But if you choose to stay on the victim lane, it will end up leaving you angry and alone. So even if it means cutting down jungle vines with a machete, forge a fresh path to who you want to be and what makes you happy."

Dan laughed and kissed the top of her head. "You know, you might make more money as a motivational speaker than a nurse."

"Oh, honey, how do you think I got to be good at motivational speaking? I talk to people in pain all day." Mom touched his cheek as she pulled away. "And I recognize someone who's in pain when I see them."

CHAPTER THIRTY-NINE

"Do you want to talk?" Avery sat on the edge of the bed, watching as Bryan went through his nighttime routine.

He finished his set of push-ups and sat. "About?"

"Anything?" She sat on her hands. She hated when he did this. He'd shut her out for days sometimes, telling her he wasn't ready to talk. His therapist had told him it was a more productive way to handle confrontations, and she really wanted to punch that guy in the face.

Try being the partner who's dying to discuss the disagreement rather than drag it out for so long.

At last, Bryan's eyes narrowed at her. He got onto his back and did crunches. "Did you fuck him?"

She pressed her mouth to a line. "He was the first guy I slept with, Bryan, but it was a long time ago. We haven't talked about every sexual partner you've had either, you know."

"And this past week?"

She couldn't tell him about the night before. *No way.*

Confessing it might make her feel better, but it would destroy their relationship.

Besides, she meant nothing to Dan. She couldn't get what he'd said to Corbin out of her mind.

"I don't think Dan can hardly tolerate me, babe. That's about the extent of what he feels for me. We clashed several times this week."

Bryan didn't respond, his breathy counting the only sound in the room. He finished twenty reps, then lay flat on his back. "We're not getting married here."

"Oh my God, we've been through this. This is where my mom got married. My grandmother got married. *That's* what I think of when I come here, Bryan. I think of them. And the thirty years I've come here on summer vacation. Not some guy I met when I was eighteen and spent a couple of days with."

"A couple of days?" Bryan propped himself up on his elbows. "You slept with him after knowing him for only a couple of days?"

Okay, so maybe that was the wrong thing to say.

"I was eighteen. You never did something stupid at eighteen?"

"So I guess the whole 'we have to get to know each other before we have sex' thing didn't apply back then?" Bryan stood, stretching one arm, then the other.

Avery curled her fingernails into the palms of her hands. "I'd like to think I was a lot more mature by the time we started dating. Would you have preferred I just jump into bed with you after the first date?"

"You apparently did with this guy—so sure, why not?" Bryan stopped the exercise routine and loomed over her.

Fix this, Avery. You owe it to him. You screwed up, now fix this.

She sighed, then stood, taking his hands. "Why are we here, Bryan?"

"I thought we were here to get married."

A bubble of anxiety rose in her chest, making her feel like she was going to pass out. She tried to steady her breath, wanting to be the calm one. *The bad one in the relationship is you. Do better, be better. You can fix this and make it work.*

"Then just relax. There's nothing to worry about. That's why I'm here, too." She stood on her tiptoes and kissed him. "Everything is going to be fine. I'm going to go downstairs and grab a bottle of water. Want something?"

Bryan looked slightly mollified. "Water would be great." He started doing squats as she slipped out of the room.

She went into the kitchen, her hands shaking. The farther she got from Bryan, the more the pressure in her chest released, the more tears welled in her eyes.

"Avery. We're getting a divorce."

She'd been in the damn dining room just a few doors down.

Five words that had shattered her universe.

And she'd run. For the first time in her life, she hadn't listened to them, ignored their calls, slipped out of the role that they'd crafted for her.

She'd taken off running, straight to that boathouse.

And for a few days, she'd lived. *Actually lived. Mistakes and all. Big and small.*

She'd fallen in love.

Because even if she'd been eighteen, even if he'd been the first, even if it seemed impossible that anyone could find the love of their life waiting for them in a boathouse on a chance meeting . . .

. . . she had.

She then thought back to what her dad had said all those years ago. She'd hated every word out of his mouth, had heard abandonment over anything else. How had he phrased it?

"Staying with your mom wasn't healthy for me, Avery. It felt like the best thing at the time for you, but it really wasn't. I'm

not trying to abandon you. I just can't do it anymore. I'm so tired, honey. And I'm so sorry."

Had she simply believed for all this time that staying with Bryan was *the best thing at the time?*

For so long, she'd questioned her choices when they hadn't fit into the nice, neat box that others wanted for her. So she'd been a chameleon, changing herself for what she thought would make her happy for the short term.

Except with Dan.

Dropping the bottle of water on the floor, Avery wiped the tears from her eyes and pushed forward, one foot in front of the other, then went back upstairs.

She pushed open the door to find Bryan in plank pose.

Tilting her head to the side, she asked, "Have you ever deleted any text messages from my friends?"

Bryan lifted his head sharply, then sat. "What?"

"I was just wondering . . ." Avery shut the door behind her. "Because I haven't had many texts from my old friends in a long time. And someone I was talking to recently was telling me she knew someone who did that in a relationship."

Bryan's eyes narrowed, and he didn't respond.

"The crazy thing, Bryan? When this woman was telling me this, all I could think about was you." Avery heard the words coming out of her mouth, astonished with herself for saying it out loud. She came closer. "All I thought about was, Bryan would do something like that. He'd pick up my phone and delete a text from someone he didn't want me to talk to, like Tad. And you know what? That's not okay."

"I've never deleted any messages from Tad." Bryan scrambled to his feet, his face reddening.

"And it's also really not the point." Avery crossed her arms. "Because the thing is, it honestly doesn't matter whether you've done it. The only thing that matters is that I know you would do it, if it occurred to you. That you have no problem with me leaving my friends, and hobbies, and interests, and *life* behind to fit into your world and your vision of what I should be."

Bryan stared at her stonily, his jaw clenched.

Her heart pounded as she reached over and pulled off her engagement ring. She held it out to him. "I'm not the woman you really want, Bryan. If I was, you wouldn't want me to change my clothes, my friends, my life. You'd love me exactly as I am. I can't marry you, Bryan. I can't be with someone who wants me to be . . . someone I'm not. I'm sorry."

She continued to hold out the ring, but Bryan didn't take it. Carefully, she set it on the bed. She'd expected him to say something by now. To have some reaction. But nothing. He continued to simply stare at her.

Feeling oddly uncomfortable, Avery went to the luggage rack and zipped up her suitcase and carry-on. Thank God she'd left her wedding dress in her mom's room.

Bryan was still staring at her, not speaking.

She stopped at the door and furrowed her brow. "Aren't you going to say anything?"

"What the fuck for? Clearly, I flew all the way here for nothing. What sort of bitch leads a man on until the week before their fucking wedding?"

"Bryan, that's not fair. I'm sorry. I don't think I made you happy—"

"You'll never find a man who will treat you better than I did. You'll never have your ridiculous fairy tale wedding. Know your place. You think you deserve to be treated like a fucking princess after pulling this?"

Her fingers curled around the handle of the suitcase, gripping it. "No, that's where you're wrong, Bryan. What I don't deserve is your derision, your scorn, or your highhandedness. I deserve respect, courtesy, and kindness—something you know nothing about."

"Don't think you'll get out of this marriage, Avery. I'm not going anywhere."

"Well, luckily for me"—Avery tossed her long hair back over her shoulder—"I don't need your permission to leave. I have two working feet of my own. And I won't be back."

Then she went out the door.

CHAPTER FORTY

Dan leaned against the boathouse wall. A long time ago, this thing would have been filled to the brim with canoes and paddle boards, kayaks and skiffs. Now all it housed was his jet boat and a single canoe. He chuckled, thinking of the way Avery had lost her bathing suit bottoms earlier, then slid down against the wall with a sigh.

He thought about what his mom had told him earlier this evening, about how he should tell Avery he cared about her, but . . . what good would it do?

He was certain Avery was under the thumb of a narcissistic, controlling asshole, and that was a bigger obstacle than he knew how to confront.

Convincing someone to leave a situation of toxic abuse—even if they knew it was bad for them—was one of the hardest things anyone could do. He knew. He'd been in that situation. Melissa's manipulation and control had worried his family. They'd tried to talk him out of it.

And the more he'd tried to pretend, the worse things had gotten.

Until she'd finally pushed him so far that, in a moment of sanity, he'd broken up with her.

"Klein in name only."

That was what Melissa had hurled at him right before he broke up with her. Funny how that had made him snap.

A soft footstep sounded outside the door, and Dan braced himself, alert, as the door to the boathouse opened, the hinges giving a horrible screech.

He blinked against the darkness, then Avery's soft voice called questioningly, "Dan?"

What the hell is she doing here?

Dan stood, closing the space between them. The moonlight spilling in from the open doorway showed the trails of tears on her cheeks. "What happened?" *The asshole must have hurt her.*

"I was looking for you." She drew a shaky breath. "I just got a feeling I might find you out here."

"Did he—"

"I called it off with Bryan."

Dan took a step back, dumbfounded.

The sounds of the nighttime insects chirping and rustling in the brush were the only noise for a moment.

"Did something happen?" he finally asked. He really didn't feel like getting into a fight tonight, but if Bryan had done anything to her, he couldn't let it go unchecked.

"Yeah." Avery sniffled, then choked out a tearful laugh. "Yeah, something happened. I mean, no, Bryan didn't hurt me or anything, if that's what you're thinking. But it just became crystal clear from spending a few hours with him that we are all wrong for each other."

She took a deep breath and then sighed. "It turns out, once we met, you gave me something I didn't know was missing in my life: the freedom to be myself." She shrugged. "And after you, I lost it again. Until now."

Dan's heart seemed to slow to a stop, and he sucked in a shallow, painful breath.

She wiped her cheek with the back of her hand. "You're the only person I've ever been able to be myself with."

She wiped another tear away, and Dan lifted his hand to her cheek. His thumb brushed her cheek gently, moving over the trail left behind by her tears. "Then why didn't you ever come back, Avery?"

Her voice was almost inaudible. "I didn't think you would want me. I was sure the way we left things . . . I didn't think we could fix it. You never answered my letter."

He tilted his head back, his eyes narrowing. "What letter?"

"The one I asked my dad to give you." She wrapped her arms around her torso, as though feeling ill, some of the missing puzzle pieces falling into place. She cleared her throat. "I asked him to give you a letter where I apologized for slapping you. I asked you to forgive me because I knew I shouldn't have. I shouldn't have gotten so mad. When I never heard back, I just assumed you hadn't forgiven me."

Dan shook his head. She'd gone to her dad because she trusted him more. But she couldn't have known what an ass her Dad had been. What he'd said. "I never got a letter, Avery."

"Yeah, I'm figuring that out." Avery rubbed her eyes. "He promised—"

"Your dad was furious at me for telling you about his affair. I came to see you, and he said you'd told him I took advantage of you while you were drunk. That if I ever tried to see you again, he'd press legal charges."

Avery dropped back, covering her mouth. "What?"

He wrinkled his nose. "Don't worry, I eventually decided there was a good chance that wasn't true. But when I was young and still in high school, it scared the shit out of me. Not to mention the fact that the drug charges blew up my life, and my best friend's."

She set a hand on his forearm, as though dazed.

She doesn't know about any of this.

He could kick his eighteen-year-old self for not shouting her name, demanding to see her, shouting he loved her.

But he'd been scared.

Worse still, he'd believed he just might be the horrible person everyone thought he could be thanks to his birth father's genes.

"What . . . what do you mean about drug charges?" Avery gave him an even look, as though she was ready to hear about something she didn't want to know but needed to find out.

"They accused me and my friend Corbin of selling you drugs. I think Corbin's brother Curtis sold you something while you were too drunk to remember, but you apparently accused Corbin instead of Curtis. Curtis was on probation, and their grandfather was sick in the hospital, so Corbin didn't want to snitch on Curtis.

"So I went to the cops. Told them I gave you the drugs. They were similar to what I had a prescription for, because I have ADHD. I got dropped from the basketball team. My dad's lawyer got the charges dropped since I hadn't confessed to actually selling anything. But I lost my basketball scholarships. Corbin was furious when he found out I didn't tell him I was going to take the blame, and and then I was universally hated by everyone my senior year, especially when we lost in basketball that year."

"Oh, my God. Dan, I had no idea." Her voice was breathless. "That's why Corbin looked at me the way he did today. *That's* why you hated me." She dropped her hand, as if she felt she had no right to touch him now.

"That's why I was angry with you, yeah."

She wandered past him, the fire in her step flattened, her shoulders sinking. She stared at the lake, her breath shallow. "I ruined your life."

What could he say? For years, he'd believed the same thing. He'd pegged so many of the problems on her, believing if he'd just been smarter, if he'd stayed away from her, his life would have been better for it. The anger at her had only pushed him further into the man everyone perceived him to be for so long—an irritable bully who was brash and frequently too hard on the people around him.

That was what made Melissa's accusation when he'd gone to get Milo so believable.

Dan Klein—the asshole.

Not a far stretch for anyone to accept. Which was why no one on the force had tried to encourage him to stay. At least, that was how he'd perceived their reactions.

"I think your knee-jerk reaction—quitting the force, buying the Serendipity—may have left you feeling more isolated than you really are. People in town ask me about you constantly. I run into your friends from the force, and they always tell me how much you're missed."

Then Avery had come back into his life, and he'd realized she hadn't ruined his life after all. She'd just been what he was missing the whole time. He stood, shoulder-to-shoulder with her, his fingers brushing against hers. His throat felt dry, and then he said, "I'm the one who decided to take the blame. But in the end, I think not being with you was what ruined my life, Avery."

Her fingers curled into his and then interlocked, holding his hand. Tears fell onto her cheek, and she didn't wipe them away, sniffling. "What happened with Corbin?"

"We're not close anymore—he was angry and felt guilty, and it made it hard for us to keep up our friendship. He was even upset at me for not telling him whose wedding he was helping facilitate."

"I'm sorry, Dan. I-I had no idea. I'm so sorry."

Dan pulled her closer, pushing his fingertips through the strands of hair at the back of her neck, cradling her head. He kissed her forehead, and she sucked in a deep, shattered breath, tilting her head back against his hand.

"I never stopped wanting you. Even when I was angry," he whispered. His lips trailed down her cheek. "I wanted you the moment you left my truck that night so many years ago. I wanted you when you walked through that goddamn door last week."

His lips found hers in the darkness, soft, tasting like her tears. Her warm breath was on his mouth, and he kissed her gently, the distance between them closing as he lowered his hands down her back, then curved around that perfect ass.

He hoisted her up, her legs wrapping around his waist as their mouths collided, a passion between them unleashed like a lightning storm over the lake in the heat of summer. His tongue lashed against hers as they breathed one breath, the broken pieces between them put together.

Her tears mixed with their kisses, and Dan pulled away from her and set her down. She was vulnerable and hurting right now. As much as he might want her, she probably needed comfort a lot more than she needed sex. Even if they connected physically so strongly.

And that didn't even take into consideration the fact that Bryan was still inside. He couldn't exactly take Avery back to his room while the guy was in the lodge. Would he be leaving now that Avery had broken up with him?

Dan reached for her hand. "You want to take a break from the Serendipity for a bit?"

"That would be amazing."

"Good." He tugged her toward the boathouse. "I have the perfect getaway."

CHAPTER FORTY-ONE

With the engine to the jet boat off, the night seemed perfectly still out in the middle of the lake, the sky awash with more stars than Avery had seen in ages. Without the light pollution of a city nearby, she could make out the Milky Way. The bright light of the moon was the biggest obstacle to seeing the stars, but it helped make other things more visible— like Dan.

She sat back against the seat, sipping on a beer Dan had brought—he'd grabbed a cooler that was already packed from the earlier cookout—and looked back over at Dan, who'd put the anchor down just to keep them from drifting.

If anyone had told her she'd end this night sitting on Dan's boat having just broken off her engagement—well, who was she kidding? It was terrifying. And exhilarating. She still didn't even know if it felt real.

She'd just thrown away her dream wedding.

He wiped his hands on his shorts and then sat beside her. "You doing okay?"

"I think." She sipped the beer again. "I'm trying not to think about what I'm going to do about my wedding." God, this was going to be a disaster. This wasn't canceling wedding plans several months before the event. People were supposed to arrive in the next few days. They had flights. Hotel rooms.

She couldn't cancel most of her wedding vendors at this point—it was too late in the contract.

And she owed Dan money for the Serendipity. She swallowed hard, remembering what she'd overheard him say to Corbin. "Did you only agree to do my wedding for the money?" she asked. Dan gave her a questioning glance, and she said, "I overheard you tell Corbin I was nothing but a big, fat paycheck."

Dan grimaced. "I told him that so he'd calm down and not do something emotional like take the furniture back. His movers were still on the property, and he was fuming that I hadn't been more forthcoming." Then he rubbed his shoulder. "I'm not going to lie. The money was a good incentive. But it was more like a bonus. I already wanted to tell you yes before you gave me a reason to."

She appreciated his honesty and sighed, rubbing her open palm against the bottle. It was such a huge contrast to Bryan, who had a way of changing the topic when she asked him about anything that might involve admitting he'd done something wrong. "I keep thinking about everything I've realized about Bryan this week, and I just . . . how could I miss it? How wasn't it more obvious to me?"

Dan turned his body toward hers, propping his arm up on the seat behind him. "Because you love him." The lights on the boat threw a yellowish glow on his features. "It's hard to get so deep into a relationship and realize the person you're with is horrible for you. And it's possible to love them, even after you realize that. Standing up for yourself and leaving is the hardest part, though, and you've already done that."

A lump formed in the back of her throat. "I just worry—it went too smoothly. I handed him the ring back, and he was insulting about it, yes, but then he said, 'Don't think you'll get out of this marriage, Avery. I'm not going anywhere.'" She ripped the label from the bottle. "And for the first time, I feared him. Like he somehow thinks he can talk me out of breaking up with him."

"He probably does think that." Dan searched her face. "But he was never violent toward you, was he? Did he ever hit you?"

Avery shook her head. "He yelled. He could definitely fly off the handle and take it out on an inanimate object. But he never hurt me."

"I may have to kick him off the property if that's the case. It sounds like he's a ticking time bomb."

"No, I mean—" Avery sighed. *Bryan wouldn't ever physically hurt her.* "Maybe tomorrow morning? I do feel bad for the guy. He flew all this way to get married, and I just dumped him. I don't want to kick him out of the lodge with no place to go."

"Will you at least stay with me tonight? Just so I can keep an eye out? I'd rather not spend the night worrying if he's going to snap."

Avery tried to downplay any fear Dan had sparked in her heart and gave him a coy smile. "Is that how you're planning on getting me back to your bed?"

"Once again, I'm not offering sex." Dan's lips curved up in a grin.

"But it's not off the table, is it?" Avery glided her hand onto his thigh. "Just to be clear."

Dan shifted, his eyes locking with hers. "I don't think it's clear."

She laughed, scooting closer to him, her fingertips trailing up his thigh. "How about now?"

Dan's lips grazed her jawline and made her stomach flutter. "Getting less clear by the second."

Then she smirked, tilting her head to the side. "Are you trying to get me to beg?"

His mouth found its way to her earlobe, his hand sliding behind her, with soft, gentle pressure on her back. "It depends what type of begging we're talking about here."

Shivers ran down her spine.

It had been her first time with Dan all those years ago, which had made it stand out. But they'd grown up away from each other, been with other people since then. She couldn't help wondering what it would be like to be with him now, and her body seemed to be five steps ahead of her. She felt the familiar tug of longing in her core, the need for satisfaction.

She pushed up her long skirt, then straddled him. Setting her arms around his neck, she met his gaze, and the lust she saw there made her center turn to jelly. "This clearer?" She dropped her lips to his, soft at first, but fully and deeply, her lips moving over his with demanding insistence until his lips parted and their tongues collided.

Letting out a moan of satisfaction, Avery ground her hips into his. She wanted to tease him, feel his hardness against her. After last night, she'd been insanely horny, and she didn't want to wait any longer.

She pulled back, then hoisted her dress over her head and tossed it to the side.

Dan let out a low, appreciative breath, his gaze traversing her body, moving to her breasts, then back to her face. Dan slid his hands along her waist, then up, grabbing her breasts over her bra and squeezing her hard. "God, I want you, Avery."

"Then what are you waiting for?" She tugged at his shirt.

He set a hand on her wrist. "I don't have any condoms on the damn boat."

Oh. That.

She bit her lip. "I'm clean—always use them. And on the pill." She searched his gaze. *Does he not want to do this?*

Dan seemed to sense her insecurity, and he smiled, then tugged his shirt over his head.

He's . . . gorgeous.

She'd seen that bare chest and abs that first day back, but she hadn't let herself indulge in really taking a look. Now she did. The long, thick ropy muscles of his chest were taut, just like those rock-hard abs, leading to a perfect V of soft, tawny hair.

She ran her fingertips over the smooth skin of his chest, remembering how when they were younger he'd been so nervous when they had sex. Was he thinking about that now? He kissed her once again, this time more passionately, his arm encircling her waist, pushing her down against him.

His free hand found its way up to her bra clasp and unhooked it in one deft move. He tugged it off, releasing her breasts to the balmy night air. "God, you're so fucking beautiful." Dropping his head between her breasts, he palmed one in his hand, his long fingers gripping her firmly, pinching her nipple, as his mouth descended on the other breast.

Avery let out a groan, arching her back as he drew her nipple into his mouth, sucking, tugging gently with his teeth, making her wetter than before. He moved to the other breast, and she moaned in response, wishing he was out of those damn shorts and between her legs. Her abs clenched, desperate to feel him inside her.

Instead, Dan set her on the seat beside him and stood. He dropped his shorts and then knelt in front of her. "Been dying to taste you, Avery," he growled, then drew her panties down and tugged them off.

He pushed her knees apart, then lowered his mouth between her legs. She groaned loudly, thrilled at the fact that she didn't have to be quiet, even if the sound carried over the water. She couldn't be quiet with this anyway.

Dan glided his tongue over her, then slid his finger inside her.

She moaned even louder. "Oh, yes . . ."

Within a few seconds, she was panting, her own climax building, her brain feeling like liquid.

"I want you to fuck me," she managed.

"Not yet," Dan said, gripping her tightly to him.

Her thighs clenched against his head, and he held on, his tongue and fingers moving rhythmically, each stroke dizzying. "Please . . ."

"I want you to come." He didn't release her, and she cried out, her body shuddering with the force of her release.

He responded by lifting her up and sitting her back down on him, straddling him once again. This time, she reached down and grabbed his length, then lowered herself onto him, crying out with exquisite pleasure as he buried himself inside her deeply.

"Fuck me, please. Harder," she moaned, wrapping her arms around his neck, her mouth seeking his.

As they kissed once again, he thrust harder still, drilling into her with an intensity and need for fulfillment. Her legs drew tight around his waist, and she rocked against him, grabbing the seatback to push herself into his groin, making small circles against him.

The effect was dizzying, her breath so shallow that she felt lightheaded. "Please, Dan."

He thrust harder and harder, until she moaned loudly,

surprised by the intensity of her climax, completely shattered by it. She slumped against him, and he groaned, his release within seconds of her own.

Avery rested her body against his, spent and satiated. She had little certainty about much right now, but she knew one thing: she'd never been happier than when she was in Dan's arms.

CHAPTER FORTY-TWO

DAN ROUSED as Avery climbed out of the bed. *I can't believe she's here with me.* He sat up, and she leaned down and kissed him, tucking her hair behind her ear.

"You don't have to get up. I'm just going to the kitchen to get a bottle of water. I woke up thirsty and then realized I drank no water last night." She straightened, then checked her phone on the nightstand. "It's only four-thirty. Go back to sleep. I'll be right back."

Dan stretched. She turned the flashlight on her phone, then tiptoed out of the room. The door clicked shut behind her. He rolled over onto his side, reaching out and touching the sheets where she'd been sleeping. The warmth of her body remained on the sheets, radiating onto his skin, and he closed his eyes.

They'd gone right to sleep after bringing the boat in, both exhausted from the day. And maybe it wasn't the best plan to have her here with him come morning—especially with her family staying here—but he didn't want to take any chances with Bryan still on the property.

You still love her, don't you?

Darkness enveloped his mind, and he started to drift back to sleep.

Fighting exhaustion, he waited for Avery to return, his body aching with the effort.

Dan sat up in bed, his brain addled with sleep as he blinked, feeling one step behind. Groggily, he made his way to the door and opened it.

He went toward the kitchen and opened the door, expecting to see her there. The clock on the wall startled him. Almost five in the morning. She'd been gone for a half-hour.

More awake now, Dan flipped on the kitchen light. He didn't know what he was looking for—it's not like Avery would hide in the cabinets—but a panicked feeling crept up his chest.

He headed for the stairs. Taking them two at a time, he raced down the hallway, then tried the knob on the door to the room that had been Bryan and Avery's.

The knob turned in his hand, and he pushed open the door. The bed was still made, the room stripped of luggage.

Bryan is gone.

He knocked on the door across the hall. A moment later, it opened, and Erika blinked out at him from a crack. "Dan?"

"Avery's not there, is she?"

Erika pushed the door open farther. "What do you mean?"

"Not sure yet." Dan's heart pounded as he stepped back. "Can you check with her parents? I'm going to have a look outside."

"Dan, what's going on?" Erika hugged her arms to her chest, but Dan was already moving away from her.

He didn't have time for her questions. *They might just be talking somewhere.*

But Bryan's rental car was gone.

Where the hell is Avery?

Something was wrong.

Dan hurried back to his room. He grabbed his cell phone from the nightstand, then called Avery's phone. It rang a few times, then went to voicemail.

"Don't think you'll get out of this marriage, Avery. I'm not going anywhere." Wasn't that what Avery had said Bryan told her?

"He yelled. He could definitely fly off the handle and take it out on an inanimate object. But he never hurt me."

But Dan knew things could escalate when controlling assholes had the rug pulled from underneath them. He'd seen enough domestic abuse situations not to be worried about this.

He slammed his palm into the nightstand with frustration. He should have kicked that prick out of the lodge last night.

Would Avery have gone with him somewhere willingly? She'd seemed pretty damned certain about things being through last night on the boat, enough for Dan to put his hesitations to the side.

By the time Dan went back out to the front porch, Avery's parents and Erika were out there, too. "What's going on, Dan?" Avery's mom asked, her face lined with worry.

"Bryan's gone—and I think Avery's with him."

"Oh, for Pete's sake." Mr. Moretti shook his head and started back toward the door. "They're engaged, Klein. Let it go already."

"Avery broke it off with Bryan last night."

Erika's and Mrs. Moretti's expressions registered shock, and Avery's dad turned slowly. "What?"

"She gave him his ring back. Told him she wouldn't marry him."

"So maybe she changed her mind." Mr. Moretti's eyes were hard.

"Except she got up at four-thirty to go get a glass of water and then vanished."

"Didn't you check their room?" Terror was written across Maria's face as she hugged her robe tightly shut.

"I did."

Mr. Moretti stepped back onto the porch, and a beetle flew past his face, ricocheting off his glasses. "How do you know she left at four-thirty to get water?"

He hesitated. This was going to sound awful, and maybe it was. But there wasn't getting around that now. "Because she spent the night with me."

George's punch came before Dan could duck, connecting with his cheek in an explosion of pain. "You stupid son of a bitch. What have you done?"

Dan reeled back, fury flaring in him, his hands tightening into fists. He took one step toward George, then Erika was between them. "No, Dan. Stop!" Erika set a hand on his chest as Dan squared off with George, their eyes locked with hatred.

"Wait, who's that?" Avery's mom stepped to the end of the porch, peering into the darkness.

Dan turned. Peyton was coming up the driveway, holding something small in his hands. *What the hell is he doing up?*

As he got closer, Peyton looked up at them with surprise. "What're you all doing up so early?"

"I could ask you the same thing."

Peyton stopped at the steps. He appeared to be holding a cell phone—nothing exciting. "I'm a light sleeper. I heard someone up about a half-hour or so ago, then saw Avery and her fiancé getting in the car to go someplace." Peyton held up the phone. "Halfway down the drive, the guy stops and chucks this cell phone out the window into the woods. I've been looking for it ever since. Dang thing finally rang a couple of minutes ago. Helped me find it."

Avery's cell phone. This isn't an accident.

Mrs. Moretti covered her mouth.

If Bryan had thrown Avery's cell phone out the window, it was because he wanted to cut off her ability to communicate. No way she'd gone for a "friendly drive."

Dan fought the urge to hug Peyton.

Thank God for him.

He took the phone from Peyton, then turned to Avery's mom. "Call the police, give them the address here. Tell them Avery's been taken against her will."

Pushing past Mr. Moretti, Dan hurried into the lodge and found his way over to Mr. Harrison's old office. He flipped on the light, then found the gun safe he'd put under the desk.

After opening it, he pulled out his gun and holster, then strapped it to his waist. Returning to his room, he dressed quickly, throwing on his tennis shoes and a T-shirt. He didn't have time for more than that.

The familiar flashing of red and blue was approaching when Dan rejoined the group on the front porch.

Dan rushed past the Morettis and raced toward the car. The cop inside was a buddy of his, Greg Paulson, who rolled down the window as Dan approached. "We need an APB on a possible kidnapping victim, thirty-year-old female traveling with a suspect who is a presumed threat to her life. He may be armed, I don't know. The vehicle was a white Toyota Prius, a rental car, so we may be able to get GPS tracking from the rental place. You can get more details from Maria Moretti." He pointed toward Maria. "She is the abductee's mother."

Clapping his hand on the side of the police car, Dan hurtled away, heading toward his truck.

Erika intercepted him there. "Where are you going?"

"I'm going after her." Dan hopped into the truck, grabbing the keys from the visor. As he turned the engine on, Erika climbed into the passenger seat.

"I'm coming with you."

"No, you can't. This is police business."

"You're not a cop, are you?" Erika lifted a brow. "That's my best friend. If that asshole has taken her, it's my fault for not doing something more, sooner."

He didn't have time to waste arguing with her. He tossed Avery's cell phone at her as he backed down the driveway. "Do you know her passcode?"

"Yup. See, you need me already." Erika punched it in.

He tore onto the street. "Pull up the Find My app. Bryan uses it to track her. Maybe the reverse is true."

He might already be headed in the wrong direction, but fortunately the road in front of the lodge made a giant loop around the lake. Even if Bryan had gone the other way, there was only one way to the highway. Hopefully, he'd be heading that way rather than attempting to go down backroads.

Of course, if he's violent, he might just do that. Would he hurt her? Is he capable of that?

Dan couldn't think about that. He knew how this could end.

"You're right. I got it. Pulling up his location now." Erika's voice bubbled with emotion, and she sucked in a tearful breath. "I had no idea he was this bad."

"Neither did I." Dan's throat hurt from tension. He didn't have water in his truck, but a sip of flat four-day-old warm soda helped ease the feeling that his throat might tear. "But I should have done a better job of protecting her." Dan had let himself fall asleep while Bryan had closed in.

But kidnapping?

Dan hadn't expected that.

He couldn't even think about the chaos that might follow all this. It didn't matter.

Nothing mattered except getting Avery back.

CHAPTER FORTY-THREE

Avery counted her breath, trying to think.

This is Bryan. He won't hurt you, will he? He loves you. He's just mad. You can talk him down from his anger, make him happy again.

She wanted to strangle that voice in her head.

If Bryan didn't want to hurt her, he never would have forced her to come against her will.

She'd run into him in the Serendipity. He was sitting on the bottom step, head in his hands. And even though it wasn't a conversation she wanted to have at four-thirty in the morning, especially after the things he said to her, she felt she owed him something.

So, she'd gone over to him.

"Can we talk for a few minutes?" Bryan asked, his voice low.

"Right now?" Avery crossed her arms, shivering. "I don't want to wake other people up."

Bryan nodded, the sound of his breath the only noise besides the low hum of the air-conditioning coming through the registers. "Outside, then. Maybe we can go for a quick drive. I just need to ask you some things. And I've scheduled my flight for ten in the morning out of Pittsburgh, so I need to be leaving here soon anyway."

A quick drive. Bryan liked to go for drives when he was upset, so that was nothing unusual. But at this hour? But he was right—if he was going to get to Pittsburgh two hours before his flight, he'd need to leave by at least six to drive there.

Seeing her hesitation, Bryan stood, his face pained. The night lights in the hallway cast a blueish tint on his skin, and tears were in his eyes. "Please, Avery. Don't you think I deserve some answers? Some closure? We were going to get married in a week."

So she'd gotten in the car with him, against her better judgment. She had her cell phone with her, after all, which meant if things got heated, she could always ask him to pull over and have him drop her off somewhere. Ask Dan to pick her up.

That was when the thought occurred to her to text Dan and let him know where she was going.

Except as soon as she'd started to type the message, Bryan leaned over and plucked the phone from her hands. She'd been so stunned that she could do nothing but simply watch as he rolled down the window and tossed it outside into the woods while still driving.

And then he'd locked the door and sped up. And she'd yelled, demanding that he take her back. He'd ignored her, hadn't said a word, and kept going, speeding on the back, twisting roads so fast that she had to grip the handle above her door and felt car sick.

The soft sounds of rock music strummed through the speakers on volume ten, like he always set it. She moistened her lips and balled the fabric of her pajama shorts, then snuck a glance at him. Her throat hurt from screaming, her breath came in dry heaves tinged with nausea.

Trying to keep her voice from shaking, she said, "Please, Bryan." Tears filled her eyes, and she dug her nails into her palms. "Please stop this. You said you wanted to talk. We can talk. But take me back."

Bryan cleared his throat, and his eyebrows drew together as though he'd forgotten she was in the car with him. He didn't respond, his eyes darkening before he looked back at the road.

"We can't go back, Avery. We're getting married. Even if I have to drive us all the way to Vegas from here. We love each other. You're just not thinking clearly right now." Bryan came to a stoplight and turned on the turn signal.

Avery's eyes flitted to the lock. Would she have time to open it? Jump out? The back of her neck broke out in a sweat.

"That's not a good idea."

She lifted her eyes. He was giving her a hard stare.

Her stomach dropped. *He knows you want to run.*

"What are you going to do? Run me over?" Her voice broke. "You've already kidnapped me. Because that's what you're doing, you get that? Taking me against my will."

The light changed to green, and Bryan stepped on the gas. "You made me do that."

You made me . . .

Avery let out a slow breath. *Her fault.*

Then there was another voice in her head, one she didn't listen to often.

The one that had led her to Dan last night.

You didn't make him do any of this. People are allowed to change their minds. The words connected with her throat, and she said, "I'm not responsible for your actions, Bryan. You asked me to go for a drive and talk. This is not talking. This is kidnapping." Emotion flared in her chest, tears welling in her eyes. "And I want to go back. Take me back."

"Back to him? To Dan Klein? Because that's the real issue here, isn't it?"

"You think this is about Dan? As though that's why I called off the wedding?" Avery's eyes narrowed, and she hugged her arms to her chest protectively. "I want to go back. But only because being here this week made me realize how much I've been under your thumb. How good of a job you do controlling me. You don't respect me. You may not even love me—just the idea of who you want me to be."

"That's a load of bullshit. If you hadn't found someone else, you wouldn't be doing this. You're a fucking liar, Avery! You lied every time you picked up that phone this week. You think I couldn't tell you were having an affair? And now you're trying to turn around and paint yourself out to be some sort of victim so you can justify your cheating."

"Bryan, please. Just stop the car and let me out. I'm not going to marry you. I really don't care what reason you use to accept that fact. You want to believe I cheated? Fine. You want to think I'm just an asshole who never loved you? Fine. Neither of those are true, but taking me against my will isn't going to work, because I will never marry you." She set a hand on her throat, her voice cracking.

Bryan's face turned purplish, and he yelled, "We *are* getting married! You think I've shelled out a small fortune to purchase you the wedding of your dreams for nothing? Too late, Avery! The money has been spent. I'm getting what I fucking paid for!"

And this is why you don't argue back.

Avery shrank away from him. "Please, Bryan. You're a good man. You save lives every day. You can't do this."

Bryan sniffed, his eyes glued to the road. "Yes, I can. Because if you don't, I swear I'll kill myself. And then that'll be on your head for the rest of your life. Is that what you want?"

Bryan appealed to her with tears in his eyes. "You want me dead? I won't live without you, Avery. You're mine. I love you. I can change. We can work through our problems, but you never even gave me the chance, did you? You never asked me to change anything."

She stared at him, her chest aching as her heart rate slowed.

Play the game one last time, Avery. Maybe it will save you here. It's not the time to be brave and stand up for yourself. It's the time to survive.

"Of course I don't," she whispered. "No . . . I-I love you. I don't want you dead. I just"—she swallowed hard—"I'm . . . sorry."

Sorry. How many times had she used that word to calm him down and get out of fights?

Even if she didn't mean it, even if he didn't buy it, her words seemed to calm him down. He didn't slow, but he didn't threaten anything else either.

She'd never really seen the cruel lines at the corner of Bryan's mouth, had she? How could she have been so oblivious? Or had she simply tried to convince herself that things weren't so bad?

She scooted closer to the passenger side door, the dappled light of early morning filtering in through the windshield, glaring against her eyes like a strobe. She set her hand on the armrest, inching her fingers closer to the lock.

When she saw her chance, she had to move quickly. Bryan might be the driver, but she'd have the advantage of time, wouldn't she? She could unbuckle the seat belt with her left hand, unlock and throw the door open with her right. Then she'd jump out.

Even if he was driving and she had no idea where she was.

The thought of jumping out when he was zooming along at sixty miles an hour on a mountainous road was terrifying. She'd break something for sure. And when he pulled the car over and came after her?

She'd be too hurt to get away from him.

And that would be it.

New plan.

She couldn't dare risk jumping at this speed.

In the passenger door mirror, a truck approached at high speed, the only other car she'd seen for a while. It crossed the double lines and then roared past them, and Bryan muttered a curse under his breath. "Fucking asshole."

But as the truck continued to barrel forward on the road ahead of them, Avery froze.

She recognized the truck.

Dan.

Her heart slammed into her ribs, her knees shaking. She was barefoot still, and her toes dug into the carpet of the car mat.

He'd come after her.

Oh, God. She tried to keep her breath even. What was he going to do?

Up ahead, the truck slammed on its brakes, tires squealing as the tail swung out, the truck skidding to a perpendicular stop to them, blocking the road.

Bryan didn't have time to stop fully, and there was nowhere to go. Avery braced for impact, shielding her face as the Prius screeched, then slammed into the bed of the truck with a sickening crunch.

Time seemed to slow as the air bag inflated. Hand shaking with such force that she couldn't get the button the first few times, Avery unlatched her seat belt, her legs wobbling as she unlocked the door and threw it open.

She ran, her legs barely supporting her, barely noticing the impact of the pavement against her bare feet, loose asphalt digging into the soles of her feet.

Erika came out from the passenger side of the truck and was running toward her. Her friend caught her, arms tight around her, Erika's voice soothing her with words she couldn't understand or process.

Turning her cheek on Erika's soft shirtfront, Avery looked back toward the Prius.

Bryan was facedown on the road, and Dan was zip-tying his wrists together.

Despite his basketball shorts and T-shirt, Dan looked every bit the part of a cop right then. He lifted his chin, his eyes meeting hers with a fierce intensity that made her knees collapse.

"It's over, Avery. You're safe," Erika whispered in her ear, smoothing her hair back.

The squeal of police sirens cut through the air, distant but speeding toward them.

She closed her eyes and hugged Erika tightly. *I'm safe.*

CHAPTER FORTY-FOUR

"Is this really necessary?" Dan asked as the nurse from the emergency department came back into the room.

"You were in a Category Three accident. Sorry, Officer." The nurse shrugged and left him by the bed to go pick up a probe. "Mostly for observation."

"I'm not a cop," Dan gritted out, then shifted as she attached it to his finger. The entire frame seemed to grate as he moved.

The nurse gave him a surprised look. "Really? There are a lot of officers out in that hallway. They usually only do that when it's one of their own."

They're here? Dan sucked in his cheeks. He knew what she was referring to because he'd been a part of that for so long. Coming to stand watch at the hospital whenever someone got injured on the job. Never let the injured officer be alone.

Climbing out of bed, Dan ignored the nurse's protests and pulled back the curtain to the room. At least a half-dozen officers that he could see were out there, some of them his closest friends. Greg Paulson was among them. He lifted his chin up, then turned and gave a slow clap.

Dan promptly pulled the curtain shut and heard laughter break out. He chuckled. "Assholes."

But inside, he felt about ten feet tall. He'd missed that. That sense of comradery he'd known on the force. Knowing people had his back. He'd felt adrift, for want of a better word, since he'd resigned. *Wronged.* But knowing they were out there —*backing me*—felt right.

He settled back into the bed. "I need to find out about the other patient who came here with me—Avery Moretti."

"I'm sorry, Officer, but I can't discuss other patients with you."

Dan grunted. This was ridiculous. What he wanted was to go check on Avery, be with her.

Not sit here for observation.

I'm fine.

His truck was totaled. Bryan had been injured and was likely somewhere in this hospital, under arrest. But that would be another problem for another day. Right now, Dan had more pressing things to worry about.

He was at the bottom of the barrel for funds.

And he doubted Avery was okay, given what had happened. They'd only had a few minutes to talk before the ambulances had arrived and split them up.

Someone approached the curtain and pulled it back. George Moretti. "Can I come in?" he asked, his voice low.

Dan sighed, his cheek seeming to throb in response. He'd forgotten about the bruise on his face until then. "Yeah."

George came in and clasped his hands in front of him, hanging back. "I—uh . . ." He let out a long, slow breath and then stepped closer. "I need to thank you. For what you did for my daughter. Your quick thinking and actions saved her life."

Dan's jaw clenched as he met the man's eyes. He wanted to tell him to go to hell. To get out. Her dad had played a large part in why he'd believed Avery didn't care about him so many years ago, and Dan would never get those years back with her. Avery's parents had been to blame, not her, but that didn't make what had happened much better.

They didn't deserve a daughter who was as wonderful as Avery was. Neither of them. They didn't know how good they'd had it with her, and they had never appreciated her enough.

For a moment, Dan considered telling him all those things.

But you can't do that, Dan.

Somehow, he was sure George Moretti already knew. And if he wanted to have a path forward, he had to forgive George for what he'd done, for Avery's sake.

Because Dan had only been thinking of Avery when he'd gone after her—not George or Maria Moretti.

"I love your daughter, Mr. Moretti. That's why I did it. I have *always* loved her." He put an extra emphasis on the word, his eyes staying locked.

George looked away, a shamefaced expression coming into his features. "I know that now." He rubbed his brow. "I'm a dad. And not a very good one, I guess. I figured you were just—"

"I know what you thought. And I'm sorry I allowed you to think that. But I will never hurt her purposely. And for the record, I don't know who told you about my birth dad years ago—"

"Ken Harrison."

Right. He was the most logical person to have done it. Dan nodded. "Well, he failed to mention that I never even met him. And my mom—she's an amazing woman. I was raised by her. And my stepfather, who is also a fantastic father. That other guy you compared me to"—Dan shrugged—"who knows, maybe we have some things in common. Both good and bad. But I know *you* better than I know him, and that's saying a lot."

"I believe you, Dan. I'm an asshole for bringing that up." George sighed, and his hands dropped to his sides. "More than that, I believe *in* you. And I know you'll take care of Avery if you two decide you want to see where things go from here. I hope you can forgive me." Then he grimaced and pointed at Dan's cheek. "Especially for that. Gotta admit, I think I may have broken my hand doing it."

Dan shrugged. He wasn't good at words, especially not with the awkward father of the woman he'd loved since he was young. "Not my first punch in the face, sadly. Probably won't be my last with my track record. But thanks. I appreciate the apology." He gestured to George's hand. "Better get that looked at while you're here."

"Yes, you're probably right. All right, then. I should get back to Avery and the family. They're all crowded in her room, worried. Probably driving her crazy, too. It's never a great idea to leave the ex-wife with the new wife."

"Is Avery okay? Where is she?"

"Here in the ED. She has bruises on her chest from where the seat belt stopped her and the airbag deployed. A few lacerations on her feet. Nothing else, thank God. She's been asking about you, though. I'll see if I can talk to someone. Put you two closer to each other."

After George left, Dan leaned back into the bed, staring at the glowing red tip of the probe on his finger. He'd forgotten Avery's father was a doctor. That might help them be able to see each other sooner. Then a hint of a smile came to his mouth as he thought of Avery in her room. George's depiction of the situation there was probably quite accurate.

The curtain pushed back suddenly, and his own mom

rushed in, wearing her scrubs, stethoscope around her neck. Worry lined her face as she came to the bedside. "Oh, my God. It's true."

"Mom! What are you doing here?"

"Someone came into the NICU and told me my son was in the ED. I ran down here just as soon as I could." Mom assessed him quickly, touching his bruised cheek. "What happened? Are you okay?"

"I'm fine, Mom. Bruised and sore. A little whiplash." Dan winced as she set cool fingertips to his neck. "Avery broke up with her fiancé, and he ended up kidnapping her. So I went after them."

Mom blanched. "Is Avery okay?"

"Yeah, I think so. I mean, as well as can be expected. They won't let me see her."

"I'll talk to someone." Mom shook her head, her eyes still worried. "Do you know how long I've had nightmares of this exact scenario? Being at work and getting the call that my heroic son was involved in some accident? Because that's what you are, Dan. And if you can't accept that about yourself after this, I'm not going to be happy with you."

Dan chuckled, and Mom kissed his cheek. "I love you, Mom."

"Love you, too, bud. I'll be back. Going to talk to whoever is in charge here." Mom headed for the curtain.

A flurry of activity outside in the hallway caught his attention. He couldn't see much, but then he heard Avery's voice, followed by several other ones. "You weren't going to tell me where he was?" Avery was saying.

"Well, we need you to rest, Miss," a nurse responded as Avery shoved the curtain to Dan's room back. She wore a hospital gown, which her mom held in the back to keep closed, and the sight of her was comical.

He sat up.

Avery's eyes met his, and a range of emotions went through her face, tears and a smile lighting her lips and eyes. "You."

"Yes?" A smile curled at his lips.

"I am done with having anyone ever tell me I can't see you. Understand?"

He choked on his laughter, then got out of the bed. "Yes, ma'am."

"Good." She pulled away from her mom, holding her gown shut. Then she turned and grabbed the curtain. "We're going to need a little privacy."

"Avery!" Maria gasped as his mom's eyes went wide. Erika snickered as the two mothers stepped out together.

"Get your head out of the gutter, Mom. We just need to talk." Then she pulled the curtain closed, shutting them out.

He liked this side of her.

Avery turned and looked at him, her features relaxing. "You okay?"

He set his hands around her waist and pulled her closer. "Now I am. But I realized I forgot to tell you something."

Worry filled her eyes. "What's that?"

"I forgot to tell you I love you, Avery."

She wrapped her arms around his neck. "You love me?"

He nodded. "I've loved you for twelve years, Avery. And I'll love you for always."

His hand slipped to the small of her back. "Damn, are you wearing anything under this gown?"

"We can hear you," Maria hissed from the other side of the curtain.

They both held back laughter. "Not much," she whispered in his ear, then bit his earlobe. "But we'll have time for that later. Because you're not getting rid of me so easily this time, Dan Klein."

Their lips met in a sweet kiss, and he held her tighter. "Glad to hear it, Avery Moretti. Because I will never stop wanting you here with me. You're all I've ever wanted."

She kissed him again and then laughed. "Oh, one more thing. Did I ever tell you about my family curse?"

CHAPTER FORTY-FIVE

After a day in the hospital, a full day of dealing with police and making phone calls to guests, then a week of an impromptu family reunion among those guests on Avery's side who had come to Brandywood anyway, Avery was exhausted.

She sat in her room in the Serendipity, packing her suitcase. Too much had happened this past week. Too much to process. But she had to go back to San Diego, figure out how to un-extricate her life from Bryan's, and where to go from there.

Breaking up with someone she'd moved in with was a lot more complicated than she'd ever given thought to—it was a lot like a divorce. Which just went to confirm in Avery's mind how close she'd come to making the worst mistake of her life, especially now that Bryan was in jail. His future was uncertain, and Avery didn't want to have to keep reliving that horrible morning, but that was how badly she'd erred. And forgiving herself for that wasn't coming as easily as she thought it might.

Things with Dan had been just what she needed this week —he'd been strong and supportive, kind and caring. They'd decided to stay in separate rooms while she was still at the Serendipity, keep their heads on straight, take things slowly. Much as Avery wanted to be with him, she didn't want her family and friends to worry that she'd just jumped into another relationship without thought.

But she was going to miss him.

A tap sounded on the door, and Avery looked up. "Come in."

Mom opened the door. "You finish packing?"

Avery shook her head, setting her hands on her lap. "Not yet. But soon."

"You better hurry. Erika and Royce are getting worried. We're going to have to speed to make those red-eyes from Pittsburgh." Mom came in and closed the door behind her. "You know, Avery, you don't have to go back to San Diego if you don't want to. Erika volunteered to get your things from Bryan's apartment. And you can come to Tampa until you've got your life put back together. And then figure out where you want to go from there. That's the advantage of you owning your own business that you can do from anywhere."

Avery gave her mom a sad smile. Mom would always keep hoping Avery would come back, and she didn't fault her for it. "Thanks, Mom. I know you would help. I just—I need to go close that part of my life, you know? Figure out where I want to be, what I need to do."

Mom sat on the floor beside her. "You . . . you could go to Miami, too, you know. Dad tried hard this week with you before he went home. I know he feels horrible about the way things have been with you. And he feels responsible about what happened with Bryan, since he told him about Dan."

"Well, Mom, he should feel bad about that." Avery laughed sardonically and shrugged. "I'm not trying to be a bitch about it, but he quit being my father a long time ago, and one week won't be enough to make up for years of making me feel like I was less important to him than his new family. But it's okay. I don't want to hold on to that anger and resentment. And neither should you. It hasn't done you any good, has it?"

Tears slid down Mom's cheeks, and she wiped them with the back of her hand. "No, it hasn't. But I'm older than you are, Avery. It's a way of life for me."

"Well, we'll have to work through it together. You and me. It's not fair that we get to be bitter shrews while Dad goes on living the high life with his picture-perfect family. And maybe the thing is, I never had the father I thought I had. And I have to make peace with that. Just like you have to make peace with never having had the husband you wanted."

Mom sniffled and wiped her cheeks. "Will you forgive me, Avery? I only ever wanted the best for you, but I was terrible. I didn't appreciate what a wonderful daughter you've always been."

Avery's throat thickened with tears, and she leaned across the suitcase and pulled her mom into a hug. "Of course I forgive you, Mom." She pulled back and set her hands on Mom's thin shoulders. "I'm not saying it will be easy, but we'll find a way forward. And I haven't always been wonderful either. But I love you, and you're my mom. I want you in my life."

Nodding, Mom kissed her cheek. She stood and headed for the door, then paused. "Those words, 'I love you.' Never hold them back. Say them when you have the chance." Then Mom winked and left the room. "I'll be in the car with Erika and Royce."

Avery zipped up her suitcase and stood. She knew what Mom was talking about—or better yet, who.

All week long, she'd held back from telling Dan she loved him. She'd given him her heart so wholly before, blurted out how much she loved him when they were teenagers. And even though it had taken him twelve years, he'd finally said it, too.

So why can't you say it now?

Avery squeezed her eyes shut.

Because I can't stay. I have to go close the last chapter of my life before I start a new one. And the last time I told him I loved him, I hurt him.

She grabbed her suitcase handle, picked up her carry-on, and made her way to the door. The Serendipity was quiet now, most of the guests having left already. After a week of noise and bustle, it was odd hearing it empty again.

She looked for Dan on the ground floor but didn't see him anywhere. Pausing by the sitting room entrance, she pictured him here that first day she'd seen him again after twelve years. Shirtless, wild beard, sledgehammer nearby.

He'd put everything he wanted to do with this place to the side and given the Serendipity back to her.

And now she was walking out the door again.

"Dan?"

He didn't answer.

She went out to the front porch. He was sitting there, in the darkness, on the front porch swing. She paused when she saw him, her heart thumping hard.

"I'm getting ready to go," she said.

Dan stood and came toward her. "You know you can stay here, right?"

She nodded, her throat tight.

"I have to fix some things, Dan. You know I do. But I will come back. I promise."

Dan pulled her into his arms and gave her a tight embrace.

He kissed her temple. "I love you. Just don't make it twelve years this time, Moretti."

Before she could say anything else, Dan pulled away abruptly, then went into the lodge as though he couldn't bear to watch her leave.

Avery wiped a tear from her eye, then pulled her suitcase down the steps. As the wheels of her suitcase bounced against the gravel, the tears came faster. She reached the front of the car, then stopped.

Where are you going, Avery?

She wanted to be fierce, strong, and independent.

She wanted to be free.

But at Dan's side, she'd always been all those things. He wouldn't hold her back. He'd hold her up.

Avery looked through the windshield at the awaiting gazes of her mom and Erika. Then she gave one shake to her head.

They understood. Smiling, Erika blew a kiss as Avery's mom backed the car down the driveway.

Leaving the luggage in the driveway, Avery turned and raced back up to the lodge. She opened the front door and ran inside.

"Dan!" she called. Tears still made their way down her cheeks. "Dan!"

He didn't answer.

She ran to the sitting room and saw him through the French doors heading out to the dock. Taking off her shoes, she left them by the doors and lifted her skirt, flying across the patio and onto the back lawn. "Dan!"

He stopped, then turned to look back at her.

Breathlessly, Avery ran toward him, feeling more sure-footed with every step. Maybe she'd just had to know she was free to leave. That he'd never stop her from doing what she needed to do for herself. Maybe that was why it hadn't seemed clear until that moment, but now doing anything other than staying felt crazy.

She stopped when she was still a few feet from him, on the dock. "Dan." She tried to catch her breath. "I love you. I can't leave you. Whatever I need to fix, I'll fix it from here. With you. If you'll let me."

He looked around as though they had an audience, but it was just the tree frogs and the crickets, the stars and the waxing moon. He came toward her slowly. Then he lifted her into his arms and kissed her deeply, passionately. "Took you long enough."

IN THE MIDDLE of the night, when Avery awoke, she snuggled closer to Dan.

A tear slipped onto her cheek, and she wiped it away, then trailed her fingers over Dan's jaw, hoping to wake him.

His lips twitched, and she leaned forward and kissed him.

He responded with a murmur, then kissed her back languidly.

"Are you awake?" She curled her fingertips around the back of his neck.

"Are you sure I'm the right man in bed with you?" he grunted back.

She snorted a laugh. "Hilarious. *Dan.*"

Dan's hand smoothed down over her bare hip, then grazed her ass. "Yup. Perfect ass. Must be Avery."

"Har, har. Hopefully, you're not expecting any other visitors."

"Wouldn't you like to know? All those summer flings just line up around the block to find their way back here, obviously." He smacked her lightly, then slid his hand flat, cupping her ass tightly. "You realize I take my sleep seriously, Miss?"

She pulled his lower lip into her mouth, then sank her teeth against it. "So you plan on punishing me?"

He growled, then caught her mouth in a deep, demanding kiss.

She softened under the strength of his kiss, taking him in deeper as his mouth slanted over hers, his tongue as unyielding as his lips. She let out a throaty moan, digging the fingers of one hand into the hair at the nape of his neck, her nails into his chest.

Their shower sex had been amazing, but it had been fast and passionate. Two lovers reunited at a frenzied pace, wanting everything all at once.

This was different. This was what they'd started that night they'd woken up, sleepily groping each other.

Goddamn, Dan knew what he was doing now. Twelve years had made a man out of him in more ways than one.

No fumbling or hesitation. His hands grabbed her wrists, pinning her back onto the bed as his lips dragged down her jawline, nibbling her earlobe, caressing her collarbone, then moving to suck her nipples with long, deep pulls that had her insides turning to liquid.

He curved one arm around her waist, then pulled her back against his chest on their sides spooning, his hard length pushed against her. One hand continued to caress her nipple, pinching it between his thumb and forefinger, and the other dipped down between her legs, parting her folds.

"All I want to do is bury myself inside you, baby." His fingers thrust inside her, and she buckled against him, whimpering, driven by the need to have him own her.

He traced a fingertip to the swollen bud of her arousal, slick and jolting her like electricity. "I'm gonna make you come. Relax into me. Feel how wet you are?"

She responded by reaching back and gripping his length. She matched the thrusts of his fingers with pumps of her own until she was breathing so hard, her heart pounding so loudly, she could hear it in her ears, her brain incapable of coherent thoughts.

"Stay with me, baby. Let's just worry about you right now," Dan ordered, and she realized her grip had turned into one squeeze.

She released him, arching back as he brought her closer to ecstasy. Then she felt the explosion of nerves crackle through her body, her moans turning into a chorus of, "Oh, yes," that sounded far away as he pulled out his fingers.

He pushed his knee between hers, then positioned himself behind her and thrust inside her deeply, right to her core. "I want to feel you coming against me," he said, and she was help-less to do anything but cooperate, clenching around him tightly.

When she'd caught her breath, he rolled onto his back. "Ride me, and we can come together this time."

As she pulled free of him, they both gasped, and she turned, her legs shaking, and straddled him. She lifted her hips, then lowered herself down on his erection, her body welcoming him deeply again.

"God, you're beautiful, Avery. Ride me, baby, hard."

She flexed her feet flat against the bed, her body rocking over him, each movement threatening to undo her all over again. He placed his hands on her hips, helping push her hard against him as he thrust, waves of a second release building inside her, her abs curling reflexively each time he buried himself deep within her.

She placed her hands on his shoulders and found a rhythm with him, grinding against him hard, pushing through the sensitive, electric jolts that promised to free her. At last, her body burst, sizzling white-hot spots dancing in her vision as she embraced the release.

"Come on, baby. Come hard for me. You're so fucking gorgeous."

Then he gave another hard thrust and joined her, the force of his release making her double over as she felt him throb deep within her, his groan loud in her ear. Then they collapsed on the bed, spent, shaking . . . *together*.

CHAPTER FORTY-SIX

One Year Later

AVERY'S HAND wrapped tightly around the leash, and she laughed at Mom's horrified expression. "He's going to drool all over your dress," Mom said, trying unsuccessfully to get Milo to sit.

"Mom, I live with his drool on my clothes daily. Why should my wedding dress be any different?" Avery crouched and hugged him, posing with Milo as Dan's sister Sam snapped a picture.

Getting Milo had been the best present Avery could have given Dan—and it had been easier than she'd expected. She'd taken a closer look at her catering contract, then gone to Melissa and agreed not to sue her for breach of contract on her wedding catering in exchange for the dog. All in clear legal terms that Melissa could never use to contest Milo's ownership. She'd even let Melissa keep the catering deposit.

After Avery had moved to Brandywood, Corbin had reached out to Dan and apologized for the rift between them. Their friendship had grown again, and he was even one of Dan's groomsmen today.

Avery had never imagined the Serendipity would go from the vacation home of her heart to her actual home, but after months of doing the renovations Dan had dreamed up, they'd reopened. Her graphic design business had been easy enough to move, and Dan had started working as a cop again, which he'd missed more than he'd let on.

Hugging Milo one last time, she wrinkled her nose as the dog licked her chin. "Ready to walk down the aisle, bud?"

"You still worried about that curse?" Erika asked as she lined up in front of the French doors that would lead her out to the back lawn.

Avery shrugged. "I guess I broke it after all. Two fiancés are better than three or four, right, Mom?"

Mom rolled her eyes as she took Avery's arm. "I never said I made great choices with men. Maybe that was the problem all along."

As her bridesmaids—Dan's sisters and Erika—filed out the door in front of her, the soft strains of the string quartet on the lawn reached her ears. Then just as she reached the French doors, her dad stepped forward, taking Milo's leash and her other arm.

Both her parents would walk her down, but neither would give her up. They still had a lot of work to do to get to a place where the past would be easy to think of without hurt. But they were both trying. And right now, they were walking with her toward her future.

And that future was Dan.

It always had been.

The guests rose and tears brimmed in her eyes as she saw

Dan standing at the end of the aisle. He covered his mouth with a fist as though clearing his throat, then that giant man she loved so much teared up.

Milo took off, and Dad's arm lurched forward as he dragged Avery and her parents, running, down the aisle. The guests laughed, and Dan caught Milo before handing him off to Warren.

Then Dan pulled her in his arms and kissed her, dipping her back.

The guests burst into raucous applause, cheering. Jason, who was officiating, shook his head. "I don't know that I've ever seen a bride sprint down the aisle before," Jason said when the cheers died down. Then he gave Dan a mock stern look. "And you're supposed to wait to kiss the bride."

Avery wiped the tears from Dan's eyes and laughed, still clinging to him. Dan shrugged. "I've been waiting thirteen years. I think that's long enough."

Then they faced each other, the shimmering waters of the lake behind them, and Avery sighed, looking at the surrounding guests.

The home they'd built was right there on the lawn with them.

They'd just needed the courage to find it.

EPILOGUE

25 Years Ago

"Avery!"

Avery looked up from where she was digging her toes into the sand on the beach by the lake. The water of the lake was too cold, and she didn't like it. Mommy was splashing around with Daddy, trying to get her to go in still. She waved her arms at Avery.

"Come on, Avery! Get in the water. It gets warmer once you're in it for a while," Mommy called.

Avery shook her head. "No!" She drew her lips to a firm line.

Mommy sighed and turned away, back toward Daddy, who floated on a raft.

Avery traced her fingertips along the sand, then dug her nails into the grit. She didn't understand why anyone would go in. *Too cold.*

A shadow blocked the sun, and she hugged her knees into her chest. She smiled. It was that boy she'd met two days ago. They'd played all day together, then his parents had invited Mommy and Daddy over for a cookout.

"Danny!" She scrambled to her feet and hugged him.

He scratched his ear. "You want to play?"

She nodded, and he reached out, tapping her on the shoulder. "Tag, you're it!"

Shrieking, she chased him across the sand, over the grassy picnic area, and then back onto the sand. When she was close to catching him, he jumped—straight into the water.

She jumped after him, smacking him hard on the back. "Got you."

They both climbed out, shivering and laughing, then dried out on the blanket Avery's parents had laid out in the sun.

"Danny! Time to go canoeing, sweetheart."

Danny's mom was calling from the top of the beach area near the parking lot.

He squinted in the sun. "Want to play tomorrow?"

Avery sat up. "I can't. I'm going home tomorrow."

He wrinkled his nose, then sat and faced her. "I wish you didn't have to go home."

"Me, too." Avery sighed. She'd waited for lake week for forever. It went by so fast.

He smiled, turning to look back to where his mom waited. Then he held her gaze and whispered, "We could be married. Then you'd never have to leave."

Avery giggled. "Kids can't get married."

"Then when we grow up." He shrugged. "Deal?"

She brushed the wet sand from the blanket. "Okay. I'll marry you."

Danny snuck another look at his mom, then leaned toward

her and quickly planted a kiss on her cheek. Running away, he called, "See you next summer. Don't forget our deal."

Avery rubbed her hand on her cheek, feeling embarrassed. Then she dropped back onto the blanket and blinked happily into the sun.

We could be married. Then you'd never have to leave.

Avery decided then and there she *would* marry Danny one day, and just like the books Mommy read to her, she would have her happily ever after at the Serendipity. It was where she felt happiest, and Danny was the first boy to ask her . . . *and kiss her.* A deal was a deal.

THANKS SO MUCH FOR READING! If you enjoyed this book, please consider leaving a rating or review. I'd really appreciate it so much and ratings help me to continue bringing you new books. To keep up with all my current releases and grab bonus material (bonus scenes for all series are coming soon) sign up for my newsletter!

And don't miss the next book in the *Brandywood Small Town Romance Series,* Until Forever Ends, available now!

NEWSLETTER AND NEXT BOOK

Want to keep up with me and hear what's going on in my world? Join my newsletter on my website! I have freebies and giveaways, exclusive content and, of course, you get to hear all about upcoming book news, my life, and my small army of children.

I hope you enjoyed Dan and Avery's story. Thank you so much for reading; my readers really are what make this possible and I am so grateful for you! If you enjoyed this book, I'd love it if you took the time to leave a rating or review at your favorite book retailer. It truly goes a long way.

And if you'd like to stick around and see more of the world of Brandywood, you can! The next Brandywood story (about Lindsay Yardley and Travis Wagner and the infamous Yard-ley/Wagner feud) continues in Until Forever Ends!

ACKNOWLEDGMENTS

This story idea started with the women in my own family, who just didn't seem to be able to marry the first men they got engaged to (including me!). It's been a pleasure to bring this story to life and especially to see Dan's story arc change from the first book until now.

I couldn't do this, though, without the help of a top-notch team of editors who help bring everything I write to a shine. My amazing editor Marion Archer was the reason this story was able to really come to life as I handed her a manuscript that couldn't quite decide what it wanted to be. Without her guidance and direction, I would have been lost!

Many thanks also to Julie Simms, Amanda Coleman, and Julie Deaton, C.S. Lakin, and the WordSlayers team for helping me shore up the rest of these edits with diligence and care.

HUGE thanks to Anne Jones, who helped set my head straight when I was feeling really stressed about the direction of this book; you've been a wonderful friend and "critiquer" of my work for so long—thank you, thank you, thank you.

Lisa Boyle for your critique and being a sounding board whenever I had my (millions) of questions and vents.

And to my wonderful family who is always cheering me on. I love you!

ABOUT THE AUTHOR

Annabelle McCormack spins you tales of epic historical adventure, heartfelt romance, and complex family dynamics with strong female protagonists to make things interesting. She is a graduate of the Johns Hopkins University's M.A. in Writing Program. She lives in Maryland with her very-patient-with-her-antics husband, where she is increasingly losing the battle to her army of five homeschooled small children.

Visit her at www.annabellemccormack.com or http://instagram.com/annabellemccormack to follow her daily adventures.